Robert Louis Stevenson (1850–94), was born and educated in Edinburgh. He was a sickly child, and most of his adult years were to be spent travelling in search of a climate which would do least damage to his lungs. Following the family tradition in civil engineering, he went to Edinburgh University in 1867. More interested in literature and the bohemian life, he changed to law and qualified as an advocate in 1875. Thereafter he gave himself to his creative ambitions, with frequent visits to London and to France, where he met Fanny Osbourne, a married American woman who was to become his future wife.

Stevenson began with essays, short stories and travel writing, most notably *Travels with a Donkey in the Cevennes* (1879). He went to California to marry Fanny in 1880. The journey nearly killed him, but he wrote of his experiences in *Across the Plains* (1892), *The Amateur Emigrant* (1895) and *The Silverado Squatters* (1883). He is, perhaps, best remembered for his first novel *Treasure Island* (1883), and his early reputation was made with this and other examples of adventure fiction, not least *Dr Jekyll and Mr Hyde* which appeared as a paperback thriller in 1886. The great Scottish novels followed, with *Kidnapped* (1886), *The Master of Ballantrae* (1889), and *Weir of Hermiston* (1896), which was left unfinished at his death. *Catriona* (1893), was always planned as the immediate sequel to *Kidnapped*, but had been delayed in the writing.

Stevenson spent seven years in the South Seas, settling for the last five on the island of Upolu in Samoa, where he died suddenly from a cerebral stroke at the age of forty-four.

ROBERT LOUIS STEVENSON

Shorter Scottish Fiction

Introduced by
RODERICK WATSON

CANONGATE
CLASSICS
60

This edition first published as a Canongate Classic in 1995 by Canongate Books Ltd, 14 High Street, Edinburgh EH1 1TE. Introduction copyright © Roderick Watson 1995.

The publishers gratefully acknowledge general subsidy from the Scottish Arts Council towards the Canongate Classics series and a specific grant towards the publication of this title.

Set in 10pt Plantin by Palimpsest Book Production Limited, Polmont, Stirlingshire. Printed and bound in Finland by WSOY.

Canongate Classics
Series Editor: Roderick Watson
Editorial Board: Tom Crawford, John Pick, Cairns Craig

British Library Cataloguing in Publication Data
A catalogue record for this volume
is available on request from the
British Library.

ISBN 086241 555 1

Contents

Introduction

From his earliest years, Stevenson's engagement with the world of the imagination, was a strange marriage of moral and supernatural forces. His young nurse Alison Cunningham ('my second Mother, my first Wife') had thrilled him with stories of the sufferings of the Covenanters in the 'killing times' of Scotland's past and, as in the works of James Hogg, these tales were soon spiced with accounts of witchcraft and possession. Indeed the omnipresence of the devil and his works had long been a potent factor in the Scottish understanding of what the spiritual life might be, so that the righteous had always felt besieged by potent forces from without themselves.

—Or indeed, from within, for surely the arch tempter is no more than a projection of all that we fear and all that we desire in the depths of our own hearts? This division, and this ambiguity, was to rule Stevenson's imagination for the rest of his life. It leads us into strange territory in which history, geography, folklore, the scientific, the moral, the physical and the spiritual, all meet and mingle with the symbolic freedom of somehow materialised dreams. (This is indeed the hidden narrative realm of that fervent young 'mother-wife': divided and yet also deeply intimate, puzzling, dangerous, attractive and thrilling.) These are the roots from which Stevenson's best fiction stems, and it is these roots which allow us to claim a deeply Scottish genesis for stories such as 'Jekyll and Hyde' and 'Markheim', even although they are, in fact, physically located in London.

So it was very much under 'Cummie's' spell that Stevenson planned 'A Covenanting Story-Book' in his teens, listing in his notebooks possible titles such as 'Satan's power exemplified: the story of Baillie Grierson and Mrs Elspeth Montcleith'; 'Strange Adventures of the Reverend Mr Solway'; 'the Devil of Crammond'; or indeed 'The Story of Thrawn Janet'. The only one of these early stories to survive is 'The Plague Cellar' which dates from 1864 or perhaps 1866. Never published (and indeed Stevenson forbade its publication when it turned up among his family's papers) 'The Plague Cellar' shows how strongly the growing boy's imagination was marked by Covenanting tales of blood and righteousness. Indeed, the budding author planned a novel about the Covenanters, but finding the task beyond his 16 years he produced a little pamphlet instead, *The Pentland Rising* (1866), which marked the bicentenary of the insurrection and the battle of Rullion's Green.

Published at his father's expense Stevenson's 'first book' was full of passionate indignation at the fate of the 'martyrs' who were executed in Edinburgh and Glasgow, but 'The Plague Cellar' is a more ambiguous piece of work altogether, even although it contains references to actual historical figures such as John Neilson of Corsack (whose tortured ghost appears to Ravenswood) and James Sharp the minister in favour of episcopacy who condemned the Covenanters at their trial. Clearly the work of an apprentice writer, 'The Plague Cellar' still displays what would become Stevenson's characteristically vivid use of setting, weather and physical contrast (snow and fire) and, whether intended or not, it is markedly ambivalent about the faith it seems to sympathise with. Thus the power of the scriptures is represented by painted Dutch tiles, but these Biblical scenes of miracles are distorted by the flames of the fireside until they seem like visions from some inferno. Then again, Ravenswood enters the plague cellar intent on knowledge, power and vengeance for his defeated cause – but what he finds there is only madness, emptiness and mystery. To enter that cellar has been death for generations, and even those who boarded it up had to die: it is indeed the symbolic repository for the unconscious drives that attract us so strongly, but which we cannot bear to face.

The same deeply Scottish combination of religiosity and terror (righteousness and blood) marks 'Thrawn Janet', early planned, but not written for nearly 20 years when it was published in *Cornhill Magazine* for October 1881. Stevenson tells us that the story was written in the summer of that year, during a visit to his parents' house at Kinnaird, above Pitlochry. It was followed in the same months by a first draft of 'The Merry Men', and in these two stories we can see how the author's imagination was moving from its folk-roots in tales of supernatural wonder towards a more complex account of what was beginning to dawn on him, in more existential terms, as the terror of being.

In 'Thrawn Janet', the local community is convinced from the start that old Janet M'Clour is a witch. The voice of reason, in the shape of the reverend Soulis, a keen young minister fresh from his college learning, thinks it knows better. But in the end it is the broad Scots voice of the community which is proved correct in all its prejudices, for Soulis is overwhelmed by his encounter with the 'black man' who has inhabited Janet's dead body, and he is left a sadder and a wiser soul. (The black man was a common Scottish manifestation of the devil.) The story ends on a note of self satisfaction, for the folk voice which narrates it has been proven right, concluding that ever since then 'the deil has never fashed us in Ba'weary.' But Soulis is fashed, for he is a grim and haunted creature, walking the roads and 'groaning aloud in the instancy of his unspoken prayers'. In a strange transformation of roles and sex, the minister himself has become the very figure of terror and speculation among the parish folk that Thrawn Janet used to be. He has sained the community all right, but at the cost of his old self and all his former assurance.

Fettes, who tells the story of 'The Body Snatcher' has also been ruined by what he saw. As class assistant to the notorious 'Anatomist' Robert Knox (given only as 'Mr K—' in the story) he too has aligned himself with the forces of science and medical progress, except that we soon see him to be a weak-willed and dissipated young man. In the cause of self-advancement, Fettes is too easily persuaded by Wolfe Macfarlane, his immediate superior, to go along with the murderous practices of Burke and Hare, and indeed to turn a blind eye to Macfarlane's own murder of the importunate Mr Gray, who seems to have some strange hold over that young 'man of the world'. 'Wolfe' is well named, for he divides humankind between 'lambs' who believe in 'Hell, God, devil, right, wrong, sin, crime, and all the old gallery of curiosities', and 'lions' like himself (and the aspirant Fettes) who laugh at such stuff as fit only to 'frighten boys'. This Nietzschean contempt for the rules of the superstitious herd is terribly overturned when what the pair thought to be hidden and dismembered comes back to confront them – resurrected indeed – when they open yet another 'plague-cellar' door into what lies beyond the grave, or beneath the conscious, rational mind. The experience ruins Fettes, turning him into a melancholy alcoholic for the rest of his life, but on the other hand, with a fine sense of how hypocrisy can flourish in polite society, Stevenson allows Wolfe Macfarlane a long and successful career as a prosperous London doctor.

Prosperity, respectability, thrift, godliness, and all the douce values of bourgeois Edinburgh are affectionately mocked in 'The Misadventures of John Nicholson'. In this retelling of the fable of the prodigal son – in the well-rounded shape of amiably fatuous John Nicholson – Stevenson exorcised the demons of his own past in comic form. John is a disappointment to his godly father, just as Stevenson was to his, but John's failings have less to do with the young Stevenson's bohemian habits, and more to do with an absurd concatenation of circumstances which conspire with his own nature – mild, plump and disorganised – to make him look like a desperate criminal on the run on no less than three separate occasions in his life.

If the corrosive relations between sons and fathers were later to lie at the tragic heart of *Weir of Hermiston*, here they are played out in a lighter and more generous vein. As for the terrible polarities of a Calvinist God, Stevenson confesses that John's case can only be 'perplexing for the moralist' adding, with his tongue firmly in his cheek, that his hero 'was a mere whip-top for calamity; on whose unmerited misadventures not even the humourist can look without pity, and not even the philosopher

without alarm.' Pity and alarm are far from our minds,
however, as we laugh at John's complacent ineptitude.
And Stevenson sends-up all the conventions of disgrace
and romance by having his hero saved in the end by a
sickly and artistic younger brother, and by his youthful
sweetheart Flora Mackenzie, somehow transformed from
his memories of a creature 'slender, and timid, and of
changing colour, and dewy-eyed', to an 'undecorative',
plain-talking, large-featured, practical woman more than
able to take 'Fatty Nicholson' in hand. As a Christmas
story published in *Cassell's Christmas Annual* for 1887, the
tale is happily concluded on Christmas day with a flourish
worthy of Dickens, and it is marked, too, by the most
detailed and affectionate account which Stevenson was
ever to give of the social and architectural topography
of the city of Edinburgh in the days of his own youthful
misadventures.

'The Pavilion on the Links' and 'The Merry Men' might
be considered together, as tales of adventure and romance
on Scotland's wilder shores. Both stories bring a young
protagonist into contact with his future wife, and in each
case the young lady's father is a compromised, or indeed
a mad individual who must die in the course of the tale.
Yet this love interest (with its oddly primal undertones) has
little to do with where the real power of these stories is to
be found. 'The Pavilion on the Links' is much the lesser
of the two, for the mysteries beneath its telling turn out
to depend on a rather far-fetched plot about wronged
Italian revolutionaries seeking revenge on a defaulting
banker. Some of the scenes are prophetic of the fort
in *Treasure Island* (still to be written at this time), with
the tense little group besieged in their pavilion at night,
white faces in the lamplight, guns at the ready and the
sound of the surf outside. But the symbolic force of the
story comes from how Stevenson has imagined a setting
in which the absurdity of an Italianate summer pavilion
confronts the emptiness of beach and sea on a remote
Scottish shoreline, presided over only by seagulls and the
sea, and by ever menacing quicksands. It is against this
backdrop that the love plot must be worked through,

with the protagonist Frank Cassilis and his erstwhile friend Northmour in bitter rivalry for the affections of the banker's daughter. Frank seems curiously boyish for a 30 year old, even one who has hitherto renounced society and women, and the changing dynamics between himself and his violent friend Northmour seem stronger in this dream-like isolation than the ostensible love-interest or the ramifications of the revenge plot. —Here, too, I think, are prescient echoes of Long John Silver and Jim Hawkins, of David Balfour and Alan Breck, of the Master of Ballantrae and Henry Durie.

'The Merry Men' takes a not dissimilar setting, but in placing it in the past – sometime after the 1745 rising – Stevenson seems to bring it much closer to the deep, rich and ambiguous Calvinist roots which nourish the other stories in this collection. Once again the 'other' is given its due in a story of great symbolic complexity. The other may indeed be the devil, or more likely he is just a 'black man' mistaken for the devil, in the fevered mind of old Gordon Darnaway, who lives on his remote little island off the west coast of Scotland.

As a once pious Calvinist, Darnaway is demented by guilt and a sense of his own religious bad faith, for he has found God's hand at work in the tempests which have wrecked ships on his shore, and he has become greedy for their treasure or just, perhaps, for the sight of what he takes to be divine justice at work. The tide-ripped reefs where ships meet their doom are known as 'the merry men' and the island's name is Aros, or 'Aros Jay, I have heard the natives call it, and they say it means the *House of God*'. This is the place where the Holy Spirit foundered as the great galleon *Espirito Santo* went down, and it's where the *Christiania* or perhaps the *Christiana* ran aground, which old Darnaway can only read on splintered wood as *Christ-Anna*.

Narrated by Gordon Darnaway's nephew, 'The Merry Men' has a much more complex vision of duality than 'Thrawn Janet', 'The Body Snatcher' or 'The Pavilion on the Links', for the whole landscape has been re-imagined by Stevenson's art to make it a theatre for his vision of the horror of the sea, and ultimately of existence itself. Old Darnaway's conscience may conjure up fears of the devil as a black man, or he may dread the shape of a fish lurking like a 'bogle' below his boat, but these are only the shadows of his own guilt, coloured by his Cameronian past. In Stevenson's text it is the actual physical world of the sea and the sea coast which moves us most as a place of terror and personified energy, where white waves are 'the skipper's daughters' and 'the merry men' spout and dance on the deep with a roar like mirth or 'portentous joviality'.

Young Charlie realises that 'God's ocean' is also a 'charnel ocean', a place of constant change like life itself, where indeed we all perch, like his uncle, drunk with glee 'out here in the roaring blackness, on the edge of a cliff . . . head spinning like the Roost . . . foot tottering on the edge of death . . . ear watching for the signs of shipwreck'. For in the last analysis the sea is only a mirror of ourselves, and in calmer moments its 'sea-runes' reflect no more than our own preoccupations. We may choose to interpret the drama around us in Manichaean terms, seeing it as old Darnaway does, as a struggle between God and the devil. But Stevenson's eye and his fine descriptive powers, give us only one world, and it is *this* world, as mad and senseless as the storms of Aros Jay, with none other than God Himself 'riding on the tempest'. This imagery of sea and storm with humankind perched, terrified or exalted, on the edge of a cliff is the most unforgettable aspect of Stevenson's tale. It will return, although subdued, in our next story.

From the terror of being to the terror of personal identity, 'Markheim' takes us a step closer to Dr Jekyll. Written in late 1884, three years after 'The Merry Men', and intended as a Christmas story to 'curdle the blood' (as was *Jekyll and Hyde* scarcely more than a year later) this story was not published until 1886. The circumstances of Markheim's plan to rob the old dealer, not to mention his extremely disturbed state of mind at the time, are very reminiscent of Raskolnikov's visit to Ilyona Ivanovna, the old money lender whom he murders in *Crime and Punishment*, and his subsequent meeting with Svidrigaylov, the debauched 'other' who seems to know his inmost heart so well. It's more than possible that Stevenson had already read the Russian novel in a French translation, and we know from his letters that he had certainly read *Le Crime et le Châtiment* by the spring of 1886. Questions of influence or attribution are less significant however, than the imagery which 'Markheim' shares with 'The Merry Men', and these links show that Stevenson has his own way of looking at questions of the stable and unstable self.

The angel, daemon, devil or double who appears at the end of 'Markheim' is characteristic of Stevenson's tendency to give material form to the 'other self', just as the old Covenanters never doubted the literal presence of the devil in the world all about us. Even if 'the visitor' is only a projection of Markheim's disturbed conscience, Stevenson still took the literary decision to externalise that presence as if it were a real person 'who bore a likeness to himself'. Yet despite the fact that Markheim's visitor seems to have supernatural powers (he foresees the return of the maid) he seems resolutely tied, with 'his strange air of the commonplace' to the material world. In his eyes petty failings and grand crimes 'differ not by the thickness of a nail', for death ends all, and 'when life is done my interest falls.'

This is a very materialistic devil, who favours death-bed repentances because they encourage others to sin and hope for forgiveness, when (in his eyes at least) nothing but what happens in this world is truly real. Here Stevenson's roots in the dualistic tendencies of Scottish Calvinism seem to have led him to propose that the world belongs to the devil. (Technically this is akin to the Cathar heresy, but we shouldn't forget that the visitor may turn out to be the devil anyway.) Indeed, the visitor goes on to argue very like a perversely inverted Calvinist, when he suggests that 'the bad man is dear to me, not the bad act . . . ' Only Markheim's surrender at the end can refute this reversed theology, whereupon the visitor's features 'brightened and softened with a tender triumph', and we begin to wonder if the daemon was not an angel after all.

Yet, as was the case with Dostoevsky's writing, the devil

may still have the best tunes in a Stevenson story, for the imagery of Markheim's disturbance is so much more memorable than the tale's moral denouement manages to be. The images and symbols of disturbance start with the amorphousness of the fog in the streets outside, and go on to the little mirror, that 'hand-conscience' which Markheim cannot bear to look into, even before his sense of self is still further destablised by the murder he commits:

> In many rich mirrors, some of home design, some from Venice or Amsterdam, he saw his face repeated and repeated, as it were an army of spies; his own eyes met and detected him . . .

In later passages, Markheim fears the 'besieging army' of people in the street, just as he fears other mens' 'observing eyes', as if 'the solid walls might become transparent and reveal his doing like those of bees in a glass hive; the stout planks might yield under his foot like quicksands and detain him in their clutch ' Such a 'wilful illegality of nature' seems possible in his morbid and excited state, and indeed the same disturbance animates the inanimate world itself, from the dead dealer, that 'bundle of old clothes, and pool of blood' which begins to find 'eloquent voices', to the 'many tongues' of the striking clocks in that 'dumb chamber'.

Vision and speech are at the heart of individual identity and social intercourse, but they are little comfort to Markheim, for everywhere he turns he can find only visions of himself as a spy, or of others' overlooking, while the inanimate world rings with voices of accusation. Of course these fears, like the 'visitor' he meets, are only 'a shadow of himself', rather as the black man was for old Darnaway. Yet 'Markheim', like 'The Merry Men', suggests a greater than merely personal disturbance at the heart of being, for an imagery of the sea, that symbol of universal unrest in the latter story, invades 'Markheim' too. In the first instance this is clearly part of the protagonist's own hyper-excited state:

> . . . the whole room was filled with noiseless bustle and

kept heaving like a sea . . . the faces of the portraits and the china gods changing and wavering like images in water.

Identity crumbles at such moments, as when the murderer is terrorised by a knock at the shop door and feels himself to be 'sunk beneath seas of silence; and his name, which would once have caught his notice above the howling of a storm, had become an empty sound.' Yet this is no more than he has felt about life all along, and as Markheim tries to make conversation with the dealer in the opening pages it is difficult not to recognise a more universal insight in his remarks:

'It is very pleasant to stand here talking; and life is so short and insecure that I would not hurry away from any pleasure – no not even from so mild a one as this. We should rather cling, cling to what little we can get, like a man at a cliff's edge. Every second is a cliff, if you think upon it – a cliff a mile high – high enough, if we fall, to dash us out of every feature of humanity.'

—Every second is a cliff, indeed, and the dealer's shop is full of clocks whose eloquent voices remind him that time 'which had closed for the victim, had become instant and momentous for the slayer'. He shuns mirrors after such a fall because humanity has indeed been dashed from his own features, and his life passes 'soberly before him . . . ugly and strenuous like a dream, random as chance-medley – a scene of defeat.' By comparison, death seems like 'a quiet haven for his bark' and he welcomes it 'with something like a smile'.

Fog and the terrors of unstable identity reappear in Stevenson's most famous story of doubleness and disso- lution, compounded by a sense, too, of the protagonist's loneliness in a maze of respectable streets and squares and noisome wynds and hidden entrances. Set in London as it undoubtedly is, our last tale could not be more clearly marked than it is by the Calvinist forces and the narrow Edinburgh vennels of Stevenson's upbringing.

'Conceived, written, re-written, re-re-written, and printed

inside ten weeks', *Strange Case of Dr Jekyll and Mr Hyde* was produced in 'white-hot haste' in the early winter of 1885. Pressed for money and ideas with equal urgency, Stevenson seems to have made the imaginative breakthrough by means of a screaming nightmare from which his wife awoke him. He wrote the dream down straight away, as a 'fine bogey tale' in which the identity of Hyde served simply as a disguise behind which Jekyll could sally forth to commit crimes. This draft was destroyed, however, when Stevenson, prompted by his wife, began to realise that his subject had a much richer symbolic dimension to offer. Despite the ill health which tied him 'between bed and parlour' in his house at Bournemouth, the 'chronic sickist' immediately poured all his energies into a second version of the story.

The rewritten tale gave him what he had long been moving towards, namely, 'a body, a vehicle for that strong sense of man's double being, which must at times come in upon and overwhelm the mind of every thinking creature'. This fascination was already present in 'Thrawn Janet', 'The Merry Men' and 'Markheim', nor should we forget the play about the secret life of the notorious Deacon Brodie which Stevenson and W.E. Henley had drafted together in the late 1870s. With *Dr Jekyll and Mr Hyde*, however, the author's interest in man's double being become completely explicit, and it was to be further developed in the tension between Alan Breck and David Balfour in *Kidnapped* (published six months later), and again in the deadly enmity between the two Durie brothers in *The Master of Ballantrae*, which appeared in 1889.

Intended as a paper-bound 'shilling shocker' for the Christmas market, the little book was held back by Longman's for a month because the bookstalls were already replete with seasonal issues. So it was January 1886 before the *Strange Case* was first heard of in the streets of London and New York – where it had been published by Scribner's four days earlier. After a slow start – its cheap paper covers did not commend it – the work came to the attention of critics in the quality press, who declared themselves to be 'strongly impressed' by its 'very original genius' and a 'faultlessly ingenious construction'. Other readers responded to what they took to be the tale's moral force, and before long it was being cited as a parable from pulpits throughout the country – a more than ironic fate, surely, since it was Dr Jekyll's mistaken notion of Godliness which led to his dangerous experiments in the first place. Within six months over 40,000 copies were sold in Great Britain alone, while the story was parodied in *Punch* and quickly adapted for the stage on both sides of the Atlantic.

What Stevenson called his 'Gothic gnome' has led a hardy life ever since, and to this day many people know it mainly from its cruder versions on film, while 'Jekyll and Hyde' has passed into common speech, even among those who have never heard of its author. The end result of such success is that few of us can experience the text as its first readers must have done, and we may never be able to recapture the original thrill of horror and discovery when Jekyll's dual identity is finally revealed. Yet it is a story of considerable power and subtlety, and one that touches the very core of its author's insight: 'the gnome is interesting', he wrote, 'and he came out of a deep mine, where he guards the fountain of tears'.

Nineteenth-century European literature is haunted by images of duality, especially in the form of the *Doppelganger*, or man's second shadow self. This late Romantic theme is particularly striking in Dostoevsky's psychological novella *The Double* (1846), while it also features in the relationship between Raskolnikov and Svidrigaylov in *Crime and Punishment* (1866), and in the German tales of E.T.A. Hoffman, especially *The Devil's Elixirs* (1813–16). Most powerful of all these forerunners was James Hogg's *Confessions of a Justified Sinner* (1824), for although he owes a debt to Hoffman, Hogg moved beyond supernatural and psychological romance to place his vision of duality firmly within the darker prospects of Scottish Calvinism.

Of course *Dr Jekyll and Mr Hyde* is set in the squares and alleyways of London, and there is no doubt that it also tells us something about Victorian society and its anonymous cities where respectability and depravity rub shoulders without acknowledging one another, but the story's roots are deeply Scottish. Stevenson knew the pressures of godliness at first hand, after all, for had he not, like Hogg himself, been weaned on tales of the Covenanters? And then again, as a Bohemian student he had pursued a Villonesque career in the narrow streets of old Edinburgh, to the entire horror of his proper, professional and God-fearing parents. 'Men have before hired bravos to transact their *crimes*,' wrote Henry Jekyll, 'while their own person and reputation sat under shelter. I was the first that ever did so for his *pleasures*' (my italics). The puritan Scottish connection could not be more clear.

It is not duality, however, so much as a misconceived notion of unity which drives Dr Jekyll to his frightful experiments. At the age of fifty, after a life of 'effort, virtue and control', he is still not satisfied with the 'incoherency' of his nature, not to mention a certain 'impatient gaiety of disposition'. The desire 'to carry my head high and wear a more than commonly grave countenance before the public' finally prompts his recourse to 'transcendental medicine', by which he attempts to filter out his psyche as if it were some sort of chemical suspension of 'just' and 'unjust' ingredients. The experiment succeeds after a fashion, for Mr Hyde, 'so much smaller, slighter and younger than Henry Jekyll,' is certainly 'more express and single, than the imperfect and divided countenance, I had been hitherto accustomed to call mine'. But the good Doctor himself remains mixed, as all people must be, and it is his weaknesses as 'an ordinary secret sinner' which draw him back to Mr Hyde, as if that personality were some addictive drug, all the more potent for its terrible purity. —'I was the first that could thus plod in the public eye with a load of genial respectability, and in a moment, like a schoolboy, strip off these lendings and spring headlong into a sea of liberty.' This passage reintroduces the sea as an existential symbol, spiked with erotic overtones in this case, even as it echoes another line about the dissolution of responsibility, 'civilisation' and identity, as when King Lear throws his garments to another storm, crying 'Off, off you lendings'.

It's worth reflecting for a moment that chemistry was

the most potent of the sciences in the 1880s, and that Stevenson's fascination with the physical aspects of Jekyll's potion is more profound in its implications than the foaming and fizzing special effects which have featured in so many film versions might at first suggest. First of all, his tale takes on the possibility that the roots of behaviour might be physically or chemically determined, rather than a matter of education or the presence (or absence) or moral strength. Then again, what Jekyll discovers is that we are made of malleable stuff, that our sense of self, and even our very flesh, can melt and change with terrible speed. In late Victorian times, sexual disease, alcohol abuse and drug addiction – from genteel doses of laudanum to the stupor of opium – were as vivid a nightmare for many citizens as ever AIDS, crack or heroin might be today. The outwardly visible and physical dangers of 'pleasure' added more than a frisson to the power of moralising from the pulpit; and there was always a sense – made more vivid by popular (mis)interpretations of Darwin's theory of natural selection – that we do cling to a cliff, barely balanced between our ideals and our appetites, only just above a fall which would indeed 'dash us out of every feature of humanity'. At such times one drink, one step, might make all the difference.

Yet Jekyll's old pleasures were hardly extreme. At worst they had been undignified – 'I would scarce use a harder term'. But in the hands of Edward Hyde, they quickly become 'monstrous'; nor does the Doctor accept responsibility for his *alter ego's* actions, for 'it was Hyde, after all, and Hyde alone, that was guilty'. In the same fashion he confuses being beyond detection and the law with being beyond fate itself – sure evidence that he has confused morality with respectability from the very start. In this context it is very important that even old Utterson, through whose investigations the tale unfolds, can be seen as a better balanced man, for despite his dry and dusty lawyer's nature and a positively Caledonian dedication to austerity, the old fellow keeps in touch with the *bon viveur* Enfield, admits to a love of good wine, and is generally tolerant of the failings of his fellow men. (He does mortify his pleasures a little, mind you, by choosing to drink gin when alone, saving his finer vintages for company.)

In the early stages of the mystery, Utterson, Enfield, and Lanyon are convinced that Hyde is somehow blackmailing Jekyll for some misdemeanours in his past. They think none the worse of their old friend, but seek to help him as best they can. The whole story is told through the overlapping reports of other people, a remarkable device which serves to create a social web of concern around Jekyll's trials, while he alone insists on setting himself apart, in pursuit of a tragically mistaken notion of singleness and consistency in his own life.

Stevenson's narrative, on the other hand, introduces hints of duality from the very start, with Utterson's joking reference to Cain and Abel; or that sinister courtyard, the back door to Jekyll's laboratory, situated in the midst of a cheerful street of little shops; or Jekyll's own house, which shows a wealthy and comfortable front in a square of much decayed grandeur; or Hyde's lair in a dreadful Soho slum, which turns out to be comfortably appointed and tastefully furnished. Even in moments of action Stevenson shows his extraordinary gift for unsettling contrasts, as when Utterson and the butler burst into Jekyll's laboratory, the source of so many strange groans and cries and desperate footsteps, only to find a cheerful fire with a kettle singing on the hearth, books and paper neatly laid by the chair, and all the things laid out for tea – 'the quietest room, you would have said . . . that night in London'. And then of course, in the middle of it all, they find the twitching body of Edward Hyde, with a phial of poison still in his hand.

In his darkest hour, Henry Jekyll longs for what he has lost and imagines himself once more restored, resting safely in 'all men's respect, wealthy, beloved – the cloth laying for me in the dining room at home'. It is a poignant vision, but a revealing bourgeois and materialistic one. This is a man who feels that his own nature is like a bundle of 'incongruous faggots', bound together by someone else's hand, but capable of being split up and more fittingly rearranged. On behalf of this narrow concept of consistency, and on the principle, perhaps, that tidiness is next to Godliness, he was ready to shake 'the very fortress of identity', admitting that 'I for my part, from the nature of my life, advanced infallibly in one direction and one direction only.'

Jekyll pursues this exclusive definition of the whole spirit only to discover – and he cannot conceal his distaste – that 'man will be ultimately known for a mere polity of multifarious, incongruous and independent denizens'. In the last analysis, the old Calvinist constructions of duality are not enough to catch the multiplicity and the incoherent, inchoate nature of being. It is Jekyll's tragedy, and our warning, that in the attempt to deny human nature and to refine himself into a unique and unmixed subject, he releases only the pure and single-minded self of Edward Hyde with a mindless 'love of life', which is as terrible in its indifference as the 'joviality' which young Charles Darnaway heard in the voices of the merry men. The final twist to the tale comes when we realise that it was an unpredictable (and unrecoverable) *im*purity in one of the drugs in Jekyll's potion that actually released the terrible singleness of Mr Hyde in the first place.

Old Utterson recognises a much better model of human assimilation, coherence, and release, as he sits by the fire with a very different elixir – no dualistic 'transcendental medicine' for him – but a bottle of vintage wine made fine by humble craft, and time, and a thousand untraceable steepings:

> In the bottle the acids were long ago resolved; the imperial dye had softened with time, as the colour grows richer in stained windows; and the glow of hot autumn afternoons on hillside vineyards, was ready to be set free and to disperse the fogs of London.

Roderick Watson

The Plague-Cellar

THE WIND howled chilly and with a mournful cadence through the funnel-like closes, up the winding high street and round the castle rock, raising wavelets on the dull Nor' Loch and shaking from the creaking trees such withered leaves as autumn had not taken long before. The filmy clouds that drifted across the crescent moon, now hid her in their dark embrace, now let a glimmering beam fall with a ghastly pallor on the quaint old town. It was freezing pretty hard; and all the streets were slippery; and the more sheltered corners of the Loch had curdled into watery ice, in spite of the gale. There was good promise of snow, before the dawn.

Therefore it was with little satisfaction that Master Ephraim Martext, outed Minister of the Gospel, drew his door shut after him, and strode down the close. There, he was sheltered; but, next moment, as he entered the Grassmarket, the wind nearly bowled him off his feet, by twitching his cloaking round his sturdy shanks. Master Ephraim drew his refractory garment tighter round his frame, and leant against the blast. At the same moment the moon cleared a cloud, only indeed to pass beneath another; but there was time for one pale and uncertain beam to fall upon that scaffold, which had been stained the day before with the blood of five of the Pentland insurgents.

Master Ephraim's brow darkened. 'An evil night,' he muttered: 'Oh Lord! how long wilt thou delay the day of thy vengeance!'

A few minutes' walk, and he entered the indicated wynd, and stopped at the door. Drawing for the key which had been enclosed in the letter, he inserted it into the lock. With a groan the bolt fell back: with a shriek, the door revolved upon its hinges. Carefully the divine closed it after him; and, then, he turned to examine the scene. A wide lobby, and a princely staircase lay exposed to his eyes, the one paved with large flags, the other bordered with carved oak balustrades, and both begrimed with dirt, draped with cobwebs, and carpetted (*sic.*) with dust. For a small space round the door, the air and the entry of persons had cleared away the dust; but Martext could see the prints of ascending feet, faithfully preserved in the covering of the stairs. The whole scene was exhibited (*sic.*) by the yellow radiance of an oil preserved from strong draughts in a stable lantern, and set upon the first landing. A chill smote on the minister's heart. The wind was rough, and the frost nipped his face and hands shrewdly; but he wished himself out again. 'Poor lad!' he thought. 'It would be a shame to leave him. Who have a better right to my assistance and ministration than those who have fought for my church. Nevertheless this is an eerie place, and the air is wondrous unwholesome.'

Then, he gathered courage and hurried up four flights of steps, to where an open door let a beam of flickering red light fall out upon the topmost landing. He entered. The room was long, low, uncarpetted (*sic.*), unfurnished. At one end there lay a heap of discoloured, bemired, and blood-stained cloaks, with a brace of pistols, a drawn sabre, and a Bible with a black bullet hole right through the middle of it. Close by, a great wood fire smouldered with a dull red glow, and leapt occasionally into flickering tongues of flame, in a fire-place lined with blue Dutch picture tiles; and even as the flames leapt up, Moses would strike the rock with his uplifted rod, and the fire would curl round the Hebrew boys and their divine companion in the furnace heated seven times, and the imps that circled St Anthony would toss their deformed arms about and wax and wane changing from squat little Pucks, to colossal Apollyons; and then the flames sank back; and the pictures became stiff tiles again. In front of the fire stood a tall thin sallow man, of some seven and twenty years of age. His face was worn and haggard; his brow was tied up in a bloodstained napkin; and his eye gleamed with a cold, fierce, feverish light. His clothes were torn, disordered, and muddy. Very strange did he look beside the solid, sensible face and black and seemly garments of the worthy divine.

I shall pass over the first greetings which were like most other first greetings. When he was standing before the fire warming his frost-pained fingers, Master Ephraim began: 'Well, Master Ravenswood, and what made you summon me hither? It is a bitter night and a tempestuous: besides it is no great recommendation to the Council to be found with a bluidy rebel and sacrilegious murderer – for so they call you, Master Ravenswood.'

'Do you grudge coming?' inquired Ravenswood, in a surly tone. 'There is yet time to go.'

'Nay, nay, you mistake me,' returned Martext, warmly. 'It would not be seemly for an uncle to desert a nephew, nor a minister, one of the defenders of his faith: I only meant to hurry you; for my absence must not be noticed.'

'I have more need of you than you think, perhaps. Sometimes, I think I shall go mad, sitting up here alone in the old empty house. Last night man Corsack sat opposite me for an hour with his living eyes glaring strangely from his dead face; and he spoke – he said – Bah! Mister Martext, I wish you to pray with me.'

It was an age of superstition: Martext was interested in what he heard. 'What did he say – what did he say, Ravenswood?' he asked, in a hoarse whisper.

'It is strange,' said the other. 'To tell you what he said, I got poor Donald to take the letter to you; and now, when you are here, I dare not speak. I will constrain myself. Listen: you know well enough that my family were among the first to be stricken down by the plague of 1661. My sister, Janet, went into the secret closet on the stair. How she found the spring, Heaven only knows; for when we found her lying, plague stricken, upon the steps without she was only able to say that she had entered the cellar. That night she died. My father determined to penetrate the mystery. With his own hand, he burst the panel in and entered; and, two hours after, an old servant found him lying with the plague mark on him, on the landing at the top of a narrow flight of stairs. Both of them died that evening. Everyone, too, who passed the fatal door, were

stricken like those who entered. In alarm, my mother sent
for workmen to board the entrance up. The carpenters met
the same fate as all the others.'

'I have heard all this before, my young friend,' said
Master Ephraim, observing that the narrator paused; 'nor
is it altogether without parallel. The Lord had permitted,
in his wisdom, that there should be several of these noctious
(*sic.*) receptacles of Death. In part of this city, there are
more than one, whereof the neighbours live in wholesome
dread. But what is all this, Master Ravenswood, to the
words of Nielson's ghost?'

'He said words which I may not mention; but he told
me to essay the entrance of the Plague Cellar.'

'God forbid!'

'I have had other augery,' returned Ravenswood, in
sepulchral tones, his eyes gleaming with a still wilder fire;
'and besides, it is in a glorious cause. He told me, sir, as
plainly as a living man could speak that he who entered
the Plague Cellar should save our Church from it's (*sic.*)
present wretched state.'

Any unbiased spectator could have seen that the words
of Ravenswood took their birth from fever. The baleful
fire in his eyes, the shaking of his emaciated hands, the
volubility and wildness of his words all tended to prove the
same fact. But in matters of superstition, men gave up their
prerogative of common sense in the year 1667. Besides, who
is so deaf as he that will not hear. Master Martext wished to
believe in the possible renovation of his oppressed Church,
and the physical impossibility of the matter did not stick
much in his throat.

'A glorious aim, as you say, kinsman,' he replied – 'a
glorious aim. What is the other augery?'

'It is more certain still. You see here my Bible pierced by
the bullet of an erastian dragoon. After the vision, I opened
it to seek for some divine command. Spared by a miracle
from the course of the ball, I found the command: Seek
and ye shall find!'

For a long time, the preacher sat brooding over the
strange revelations of his companion. At last, he raised
his head. 'And will you dare?' he asked.

'Dare!' was the only answer: but it was made in a tone so firm and so enthusiastic, that all doubt was stilled in Master Ephraim's mind.

'The Lord God of Isaac and of Israel guide and assist you! I myself will wait on the landing above to catch what you may say, if you are too suddenly smitten. I suppose I also must die; but essay, my son, to close the door when you come out, lest when I pass, I should be rendered incapable of spreading the secret.' The minister's heavy face was idealized by his noble determination.

Both rose without a word. Ravenswood went first, his eyes scintillating, his cheeks glowing with a hectic flush. As they passed down the stair, Ravenswood said something so incoherent, that Martext supposed he had not heard distinctly: he was too much excited to think of asking into it's (*sic.*) meaning.

At last the minister paused on the landing, whence he could see distinctly a portion of wainscot where some boards less time stained than the others led him to believe that the cellar door existed.

Ravenswood continued his descent to a corner of the stair where a large axe was propped against a wall. Three vigorous strokes on the crunching boards, burst in the patched-up entrance. Martext was so pleased that he could not see into the space that lay beyond: he heard Ravenswood give a strange, wild, falsetto laugh which rang hideously through the echoing stair: the sound smote him to the heart: he felt very cold. Ravenswood descended the stair, picked up the lantern, and plunged into the mysterious passage.

For a space all was terribly still. The light, which fell across the stair from the ragged entrance, grew fainter and fainter. Martext, in an agony of fear and excitement, craned forward over the shaking balustrade, the dim light falling with strange effect, on his wrought and eager visage.

Suddenly, that hateful laugh burst forth again louder, wilder, higher, more utterly appalling than before. 'Ha-ah!' he yelled. 'See! the plague-spots! for the Church! Glory!' And again, the demon laugh echoed strangely out into the stair.

Next instant, a bright light arose in the passage: something highly inflamable, had been lit. The figure of Ravenswood appeared at the entrance, standing out against the light behind. The wild words, the fiendish laugh, the sudden conflagration had all terrified the divine; yet he did not forget his duty to his church.

'Speak,' he articulated. 'Speak! What have you heard?'

'Ha! Ha! I know you!' replied the madman. 'You are Sharpe – Sharpe the apostate! Do you think I will tell *you!* Glory! Glory! Ah! apostate, murderer! Where is the pardon! Five men died yesterday! Give me the King's letter of mercy! Give it me!'

And he rushed up towards the other. Martext was rooted to the ground with horror: with eyes protruded, he stood waiting for the madman. Then with a long drawn breath, he turned and fled. Up the stair they ran, the dust rising in clouds, the empty vault of the stair echoing to the maniac's howls. Master Ephraim plunged desperately into an open door: the room was pitch dark; he flattened himself against the wall. His pursuer almost touched him, as he passed, feeling in every corner. The moment that the way was clear, Martext dashed forth and ran down the stairs again. He did not know what he was doing: his only object was to escape from the touch of his miserable nephew.

The combustibles in the Plague Cellar had been exceedingly dry surely; for, when Master Ephraim reached that part of the stair in his downward flight, great tongues of flame leapt across the whole path, and curled round the balustrade; while the whole entrance was obscured by pitchy smoke. At no other time would the minister have dared to pass such a barrier. But now, goaded by despair, he plunged through the fire, leapt the remainder of the steps, and fell, half dead with terror, against the massive door.

Recovering his presence of mind and remembering that every minute he might be overtaken and seized, he strove to withdraw the bolt of the lock. What seemed a century elapsed. At last the lock opened. He looked back: Ravenswood, terrified by the flames, was halting irresolutely on the farther side. With a cry of wild joy,

Martext rushed out and pulled the great door to behind him, with a loud crash.

The wind blew bitingly up the close: the snow fell thickly around. Through the great fan light over the door shone the red and flickering glow of the conflagration within. The divine fell on his knees on the powdered pavement and thanked God for his escape.

We are glad that we can supplement the above (drawn from the rev. gentleman's own account) with the following particulars from contemporaneous documents.

We find (in Dr Zophar Cant's 'Special Judgements and Providences') that, that vessel of God, Ephraim Martext, did linger long in a sore fever, raving much and saying that he was plague stricken in his delerium.

Farther, we read in a personal narrative, that the mansion of the Ravenswoods was reduced on that night to four black and tottering walls. So the mystery of the Plague Cellar was never solved.

Thrawn Janet

THE REVEREND Murdoch Soulis was long minister of the moorland parish of Balweary, in the vale of Dule. A severe, bleak-faced old man, dreadful to his hearers, he dwelt in the last years of his life, without relative or servant or any human company, in the small and lonely manse under the Hanging Shaw. In spite of the iron composure of his features, his eye was wild, scared, and uncertain; and when he dwelt, in private admonition, on the future of the impenitent, it seemed as if his eye pierced through the storms of time to the terrors of eternity. Many young persons, coming to prepare themselves against the season of the Holy Communion, were dreadfully affected by his talk. He had a sermon on 1st Peter, v. and 8th, 'The devil as a roaring lion,' on the Sunday after every seventeenth of August, and he was accustomed to surpass himself upon that text both by the appalling nature of the matter and the terror of his bearing in the pulpit. The children were frightened into fits, and the old looked more than usually oracular, and were, all that day, full of those hints that Hamlet deprecated. The manse itself, where it stood by the water of Dule among some thick trees, with the Shaw overhanging it on the one side, and on the other many cold, moorish hill-tops rising toward the sky, had begun, at a very early period of Mr Soulis's ministry, to be avoided in the dusk hours by all who valued themselves upon their prudence; and guidmen sitting at the clachan alehouse shook their heads together at the thought of passing late by that uncanny neighbourhood. There was one spot, to be more particular, which was regarded with especial awe. The manse stood between the highroad and the water of Dule, with a gable to each; its back was towards the kirktown of Balweary, nearly half a mile away; in front of it, a bare

9

garden, hedged with thorn, occupied that land between the river and the road. The house was two stories high, with two large rooms on each. It opened not directly on the garden, but on a causewayed path, or passage, giving on the road on the one hand, and closed on the other by the tall willows and elders that bordered on the stream. And it was this strip of causeway that enjoyed among the young parishioners of Balweary so infamous a reputation. The minister walked there often after dark, sometimes groaning aloud in the instancy of his unspoken prayers; and when he was from home, and the manse door was locked, the more daring schoolboys ventured, with beating hearts, to 'follow my leader' across that legendary spot.

This atmosphere of terror, surrounding as it did, a man of God of spotless character and orthodoxy, was a common cause of wonder and subject of inquiry among the few strangers who were led by chance or business to that unknown, outlying country. But many even of the people of the parish were ignorant of the strange events which had marked the first year of Mr Soulis's ministrations; and among those who were better informed, some were naturally reticent, and others shy of that particular topic. Now and again, only, one of the older folk would warm into courage over his third tumbler, and recount the cause of the minister's strange looks and solitary life.

Fifty years syne, when Mr Soulis cam' first into Ba'weary, he was still a young man – a callant, the folk said – fu' o' book-learnin' an' grand at the exposition, but, as was natural in sae young a man, wi' nae leevin' experience in religion. The younger sort were greatly taken wi' his gifts and his gab; but auld, concerned, serious men and women were moved even to prayer for the young man, whom they took to be a self-deceiver, and the parish that was like to be sae ill-supplied. It was before the days o' the moderates – weary fa' them; but ill things are like guid – they baith come bit by bit, a pickle at a time; and there were folk even then that said the Lord had left the college professors to their ain devices, an' the lads that went to study wi' them wad hae done mair an' better sittin' in a peat-bog, like their forbears of the persecution, wi' a Bible under their oxter an' a speerit o' prayer in their heart. There was nae doubt onyway, but that Mr Soulis had been ower lang at the college. He was careful and troubled for mony things besides the ae thing needful. He had a feck o' books wi' him – mair than had ever been seen before in a' that presbytery; and a sair wark the carrier had wi' them, for they were a' like to have smoored in the De'il's Hag between this and Kilmackerlie. They were books o' divinity, to be sure, or so they ca'd them; but the serious were o' opinion there was little service for sae mony, when the hail o' God's Word would gang in the neuk o' a plaid. Then he wad sit half the day and half the nicht forbye, which was scant decent – writin', nae less; an' first they were feared he wad read his sermons; an' syne it proved he was writin' a book himsel', which was surely no' fittin' for ane o' his years an' sma' experience.

Onyway it behoved him to get an auld, decent wife to keep the manse for him an' see to his bit denners; an' he was recommended to an auld limmer – Janet M'Clour, they ca'd her an' sae far left to himsel' as to be ower persuaded. There was mony advised him to the contrar, for Janet was mair than suspeckit by the best folk in Ba'weary. Lang or that, she had had a wean to a dragoon; she hadna come forrit for maybe thretty year; and bairns had seen her mumblin' to hersel' up on Key's Loan in the gloamin', whilk was an unco time an' place for a God-fearin' woman. Howsoever, it was the laird himsel' that had first tauld the minister o' Janet; an' in thae days he wad hae gane a far gate to pleesure the laird. When folk tauld him that Janet was sib to the de'il, it was a' superstition by his way o' it; an' when they cast up the Bible to him an' the witch of Endor, he wad threep it doun their thrapples that thir days were a' gane by, an' the de'il was mercifully restrained.

Weel, when it got about the clachan that Janet M'Clour was to be servant at the manse, the folk were fair mad wi' her an' him thegither; an' some o' the guidwives had nae better to dae than get round her door-cheeks and chairge her wi' a' that was ken't again' her, frae the sodger's bairn to John Tamson's twa kye. She was nae great speaker; folk usually let her gang her ain gate, an' she let them gang theirs, wi' neither Fair-guid-een nor Fair-guid-day; but when she buckled to, she had a tongue to deave the miller. Up she got, an' there wasna an auld story in Ba'weary but she gart somebody lowp for it that day; they couldna say ae thing but she could say twa to it; till, at the hinder end, the guidwives up an' claught haud of her, an' clawed the coats aff her back, and pu'd her doun the clachan to the water o' Dule, to see if she were a witch or no, soom or droun. The carline skirled till ye could hear her at the Hangin' Shaw, an' she focht like ten; there was mony a guidwife bure the mark o' her neist day an' mony a lang day after; an' just in the hettest o' the collieshangie, wha suld come up (for his sins) but the new minister!

'Women,' said he (an' he had a grand voice), 'I charge you in the Lord's name to let her go.'

Janet ran to him – she was fair wud wi' terror – an' clang to him, an' prayed him, for Christ's sake, save her frae the cummers; an' they, for their pairt, tauld him a' that was ken't, an' maybe mair.

'Woman,' says he to Janet, 'is this true?'

'As the Lord sees me,' says she, 'as the Lord made me, no' a word o't. Forbye the bairn,' says she, 'I've been a decent woman a' my days.'

'Will you,' says Mr Soulis, 'in the name of God, and before me, His unworthy minister, renounce the devil and his works?'

Weel, it wad appear that when he askit that, she gave a girn that fairly frichit them that saw her, an' they could hear her teeth play dirl thegither in her chafts; but there was naething for it but the ae way or the ither; an' Janet lifted up her hand an' renounced the de'il before them a'.

'And now,' says Mr Soulis to the guidwives, 'home with ye, one and all, and pray to God for His forgiveness.'

An' he gied Janet his arm, though she had little on her but a sark, and took her up the clachan to her ain door like a leddy o' the land; an' her screighin' an' laughin' as was a scandal to be heard.

There were mony grave folk lang ower their prayers that nicht; but when the morn cam' there was sic a fear fell

upon a' Ba'weary that the bairns hid theirsels, an' even
the men-folk stood an' keekit frae their doors. For there
was Janet comin' doun the clachan – her or her likeness,
nane could tell – wi' her neck thrawn, an' her heid on ae
side, like a body that has been hangit, an' a girn on her face
like an unstreakit corp. By an' by they got used wi' it, an'
even speered at her to ken what was wrang; but frae that
day forth she couldna speak like a Christian woman, but
slavered an' played click wi' her teeth like a pair o' shears;
an' frae that day forth the name o' God cam' never on her
lips. Whiles she wad try to say it, but it michtna be. Them
that kenned best said least; but they never gied that Thing
the name o' Janet M'Clour; for the auld Janet, by their
way o't, was in muckle hell that day. But the minister was
neither to haud nor to bind; he preached about naething
but the folk's cruelty that had gi'en her a stroke of the
palsy; he skelpit the bairns that meddled her; an' he had
her up to the manse that same nicht, an' dwalled there a'
his lane wi' her under the Hangin' Shaw.

Weel, time gaed by: and the idler sort commenced to
think mair lichtly o' that black business. The minister was
weel thocht o'; he was aye late at the writing, folk wad see
his can'le doon by the Dule water after twal' at e'en; and he
seemed pleased wi' himsel' an' upsitten as at first, though a'
body could see that he was dwining. As for Janet she cam'
an' she gaed; if she didna speak muckle afore, it was reason
she should speak less then; she meddled naebody; but she
was an eldritch thing to see, an' nane wad hae mistrysted
wi' her for Ba'weary glebe.

About the end o' July there cam' a spell o' weather, the
like o't never was in that country-side; it was lown an' het
an' heartless; the herds couldna win up the Black Hill, the
bairns were ower weariet to play; an' yet it was gousty too,
wi' claps o' het wund that rumm'led in the glens, and bits
o' shouers that slockened naething. We aye thocht it büt
to thun'er on the morn; but the morn cam', an' the morn's
morning, an' it was aye the same uncanny weather, sair on
folks and bestial. O' a' that were the waur, nane suffered
like Mr Soulis; he could neither sleep nor eat, he tauld his
elders; an' when he wasna writin' at his weary book, he

wad be stravaguin' ower a' the country-side like a man possessed, when a' body else was blithe to keep caller ben the house.

Abune Hangin' Shaw, in the bield o' the Black Hill, there's a bit enclosed grund wi' an iron yett; an' it seems, in the auld days, that was the kirkyaird o' Ba'weary, an' consecrated by the Papists before the blessed licht shone upon the kingdom. It was a great howff, o' Mr Soulis's onyway; there he wad sit an' consider his sermons; an' indeed it's a bieldy bit. Weel, as he cam' ower the wast end o' the Black Hill, ae day, he saw first twa, an' syne fower, an' syne seeven corbie craws fleein' round an' round abune the auld kirkyaird. They flew laigh an' heavy, an' squawked to ither as they gaed; an' it was clear to Mr Soulis that something had put them frae their ordinar. He wasna easy fleyed, an' gaed straucht up to the wa's; an' what suld he find there but a man, or the appearance o' a man, sittin' in the inside upon a grave. He was of a great stature, an' black as hell, and his e'en were singular to see. Mr Soulis had heard tell o' black men, mony's the time; but there was something unco about this black man that daunted him. Het as he was, he took a kind o' cauld grue in the marrow o' his banes; but up he spak for a' that; an' says he: 'My friend, are you a stranger in this place?' The black man answered never a word; he got upon his feet, an' begoud on to hirsle to the wa' on the far side; but he aye lookit at the minister; an' the minister stood an' lookit back; till a' in a meenit the black man was ower the wa' an' rinnin' for the bield o' the trees. Mr Soulis, he hardly kenned why, ran after him; but he was fair forjeskit wi' his walk an' the het, unhalesome weather; an' rin as he likit, he got nae mair than a glisk o' the black man amang the birks, till he won doun to the foot o' the hillside, an' there he saw him ance mair, gaun, hap-step-an'-lawp, ower Dule water to the manse.

Mr Soulis wasna weel pleased that this fearsome gangrel suld mak'sae free wi' Ba'weary manse; an' he ran the harder, an', wet shoon, ower the burn, an' up the walk; but the de'il a black man was there to see. He stepped out upon the road, but there was naebody there; he gaed a' ower the gairden, but na, nae black man. At the hinder end, an' a bit feared as was but natural, he lifted the hasp an' into the manse; and there was Janet M'Clour before his e'en, wi' her thrawn craig, an' nane sae pleased to see him. An' he aye minded sinsyne, when first he set his e'en upon her, he had the same cauld and deidly grue.

'Janet', says he, 'have you seen a black man?'

'A black man!' quo' she. 'Save us a'! Ye're no wise, minister. There's nae a black man in a' Ba'weary.'

But she didna speak plain, ye maun understand; but yam-yammered, like a powney wi' the bit in its moo.

'Weel,' says he, 'Janet, if there was nae black man, I have spoken with the Accuser of the Brethren.'

An' he sat doun like ane wi' a fever, an' his teeth chittered in his heid.

'Hoots,' says she, 'think shame to yoursel', minister'; an' gied him a drap brandy that she keept aye by her.

Syne Mr Soulis gaed into his study amang a' his books. It's a lang, laigh, mirk chalmer, perishin' cauld in winter, an' no' very dry even in the top o' the simmer, for the manse stands near the burn. Sae doun he sat, and thocht of a' that had come an' gane since he was in Ba'weary, an' his hame, an' the days when he was a bairn an' ran daffin' on the braes, an' that black man aye ran in his heid like the owercome of a sang. Aye the mair he thocht, the mair he thocht o' the black man. He tried the prayer, an' the words wouldna come to him; an' he tried, they say, to write at his book, but he couldna mak' nae mair o' that. There was while he thocht the black man was at his oxter, an' the swat stood upon him cauld as well-water; and there was ither whiles, when he cam' to himsel' like a christened bairn an' minded naething.

The upshot was that he gaed to the window an' stood glowrin' at Dule water. The trees are unco thick, an' the water lies deep an' black under the manse; an' there was Janet washin' the cla'es wi' her coats kilted. She had her back to the minister, an' he, for his pairt, hardly kenned what he was lookin' at. Syne she turned round, an' shawed her face; Mr Soulis had the same cauld grue as twice that day afore, an' it was borne in upon him what folk said, that Janet was deid lang syne, an' this was a bogle in her clay-cauld flesh. He drew back a pickle and he scanned her narrowly. She was tramp-trampin' in the cla'es croonin' to hersel'; and eh! Gude guide us, but it was a fearsome face. Whiles she sang louder, but there was nae man born o' woman that could tell the words o' her sang; an' whiles she lookit side-lang doun, but there was naething there for her to look at. There gaed a scunner through the flesh upon his banes; an' that was Heeven's advertisement. But Mr Soulis just blamed himsel', he said, to think sae ill o' a puir, auld afflicted wife that hadna a freend forbye himsel'; an' he put up a bit prayer for him an' her, an' drank a little caller water – for his heart rose again' the meat – an' gaed up to his naked bed in the gloamin'.

That was a nicht that has never been forgotten in Ba'weary, the nicht o' the seeventeenth o' August, seeventeen hun'er an' twal'. It had been het afore, as I hae said, but that nicht it was hetter than ever. The sun gaed doun amang unco-lookin' clouds; it fell as mirk as the pit; no' a star, no' a breath o'wund; ye couldna see your han' afore your face, an' even the auld folk cuist the covers frae their beds an' lay pechin' for their breath. Wi' a that he had upon his mind, it was gey an' unlikely Mr Soulis wad get muckle sleep. He lay an' he tummled; the gude, caller bed that he got into brunt his very banes; whiles he slept, an' whiles he waukened; whiles he heard the time o' nicht, an' whiles a tyke yowlin' up the muir, as if somebody was deid; whiles he thocht he heard bogles claverin' in his lug, an' whiles he saw spunkies in the room. He behoved, he judged, to be sick; an' sick he was – little he jaloosed the sickness.

At the hinder end, he got a clearness in his mind, sat up in his sark on the bed-side, an' fell thinkin' ance mair o' the black man an' Janet. He couldna weel tell how – maybe it was the cauld to his feet – but it cam' in upon him wi' a spate that there was some connection between thir twa, an' that either or baith o' them were bogles. An' just at that moment, in Janet's room, which was neist to his, there cam'a stramp o' feet as if men were wars'lin', an' then a loud bang; an' then a wund gaed reishling round the fower quarters o' the house; an' then a' was ance mair as seelent as the grave.

Mr Soulis was feared for neither man nor de'il. He got his tinder-box, an' lit a can'le, an' made three steps o't ower to Janet's door. It was on the hasp, an' he pushed it open, an' keeked bauldly in. It was a big room, as big as the minister's ain, an' plenished wi' grand, auld solid gear, for he had naething else. There was a fower-posted bed wi' auld tapestry; an' a braw cabinet o' aik, that was fu' o' the minister's divinity books, an' put there to be out o' the gate; an' a wheen duds o' Janet's lying here an' there about the floor. But nae Janet could Mr Soulis see; nor ony sign o' a contention. In he gaed (an' there's few that wad hae followed him) an' lookit a' round, an' listened. But there was naething to be heard, neither inside the manse nor in a' Ba'weary parish, an' naething to be seen but the muckle shadows turnin' round the can'le. An' then, a' at aince, the minister's heart played dunt an' stood stock-still; an' a cauld wund blew amang the hairs o' his heid. Whaten a weary sicht was that for the puir man's e'en! For there was Janet hangin' frae a nail beside the auld aik cabinet: her heid aye lay on her shouther, her e'en were steekit, the tongue projected frae her mouth, an' her heels were twa feet clear abune the floor.

'God forgive us all!' thocht Mr Soulis, 'poor Janet's dead.'

He cam' a step nearer to the corp; an' then his heart fair whammled in his inside. For by what cantrip it wad ill beseem a man to judge, she was hangin' frae a single nail an' by a single wursted thread for darnin' hose.

It's a awfu' thing to be your lane at nicht wi' siccan prodigies o' darkness; but Mr Soulis was strong in the Lord. He turned an' gaed his ways oot o' that room, an' lockit the door ahint him; an' step by step, doun the stairs, as heavy as leed; and set doun the can'le on the table at the stairfoot. He couldna pray, he couldna think, he was dreepin' wi' caul' swat, an' naething could he hear but the dunt-dunt-duntin' o' his ain heart. He micht maybe hae stood there an hour, or maybe twa, he minded sae little; when a' o' a sudden, he heard a laigh, uncanny steer up-stairs; a foot gaed to an' fro in the chalmer whaur the corp was hangin'; syne the door was opened, though he minded weel that he had lockit it; an' syne there was a step upon the landin', an' it seemed to him as if the corp was lookin' ower the rail and doun upon him whaur he stood.

He took up the can'le again (for he couldna want the licht), an' as saftly as ever he could, gaed straucht out o' the manse an' to the far end o' the causeway. It was aye pit-mirk; the flame o' the can'le, when he set it on the grund, brunt steedy and clear as in a room; naething moved, but the Dule water seepin' and sabbin' doun the glen, an' you unhaly footstep that cam' ploddin' doun the stairs inside the manse. He kenned the foot ower weel, for it was Janet's; an' at ilka step that cam' a wee thing nearer, the cauld got deeper in his vitals. He commended his soul to Him that made an' keepit him; 'and, O Lord,' said he, 'give me strength this night to war against the powers of evil.'

By this time the foot was comin' through the passage for the door; he could hear a hand skirt alang the wa', as if the fearsome thing was feelin' for its way. The saughs tossed an' maned thegither, a long sigh cam' ower the hills, the flame o' the can'le was blawn aboot; an' there stood the corp of Thrawn Janet, wi' her grogram goun an' her black mutch, wi' the heid aye upon the shouther, an' the girn still upon the face o't – leevin', ye wad hae said – deid, as Mr Soulis weel kenned – upon the threshold o' the manse.

It's a strange thing that the soul of man should be that thirled into his perishable body; but the minister saw that, an' his heart didna break.

She didna stand there lang; she began to move again an' cam' slowly towards Mr Soulis whaur he stood under the saughs. A' the life o' his body, a' the strength o' his speerit, were glowerin' frae his e'en. It seemed she was gaun to speak, but wanted words, an' made a sign wi' the left hand. There cam' a clap o' wund, like a cat's fuff; oot gaed the can'le, the saughs skreighed like folk; an' Mr Soulis kenned that, live or die, this was the end o't.

'Witch, beldame, devil!' he cried, 'I charge you, by the power of God, begone – if you be dead, to the grave – if you be damned, to hell.'

An' at that moment the Lord's ain hand out o' the Heevens struck the Horror whaur it stood; the auld, deid, desecrated corp o' the witch-wife, sae lang keepit frae the grave and hirsled round by de'ils, lowed up like a brunstane spunk an' fell in ashes to the grund; the thunder followed, peal on dirlin' peal, the rairin' rain upon the back o' that; and Mr Soulis lowped through the garden hedge, an' ran, wi' skelloch upon skelloch, for the clachan.

That same mornin', John Christie saw the Black Man pass the Muckle Cairn as it was chappin' six; before eicht, he gaed by the change-house at Knockdow; an' no' lang after, Sandy M'Lellan saw him gaun linkin' doun the braes frae Kilmackerlie. There's little doubt but it was him that dwalled sae lang in Janet's body; but he was awa' at last; an' sinsyne the de'il has never fashed us in Ba'weary.

But it was a sair dispensation for the minister; lang, lang he lay ravin' in his bed; an' frae that hour to this, he was the man ye ken the day.

The Body Snatcher

EVERY NIGHT in the year, four of us sat in the small parlour of the George at Debenham – the undertaker, and the landlord, and Fettes, and myself. Sometimes there would be more; but blow high, blow low, come rain or snow or frost, we four would be each planted in his own particular arm-chair. Fettes was an old drunken Scotsman, a man of education obviously, and a man of some property, since he lived in idleness. He had come to Debenham years ago, while still young, and by a mere continuance of living had grown to be an adopted townsman. His blue camlet cloak was a local antiquity, like the church-spire. His place in the parlour at the George, his absence from church, his old, crapulous, disreputable vices, were all things of course in Debenham. He had some vague Radical opinions and some fleeting infidelities, which he would now and again set forth and emphasise with tottering slaps upon the table. He drank rum – five glasses regularly every evening; and for the greater portion of his nightly visit to the George sat, with his glass in his right hand, in a state of melancholy alcoholic saturation. We called him the Doctor, for he was supposed to have some special knowledge of medicine, and had been known, upon a pinch, to set a fracture or reduce a dislocation; but, beyond these slight particulars, we had no knowledge of his character and antecedents.

One dark winter night – it had struck nine some time before the landlord joined us – there was a sick man in the George, a great neighbouring proprietor suddenly struck down with apoplexy on his way to Parliament; and the great man's still greater London doctor had been telegraphed to his bedside. It was the first time that such a thing had happened in Debenham, for the railway was but newly open, and we were all proportionately moved by the occurrence.

'He's come,' said the landlord, after he had filled and lighted his pipe.

'He?' said I. 'Who? – not the doctor?'

'Himself,' replied our host.

'What is his name?'

'Dr Macfarlane,' said the landlord.

Fettes was far through his third tumbler, stupidly fuddled, now nodding over, now staring mazily around him; but at the last word he seemed to awaken, and repeated the name 'Macfarlane' twice, quietly enough the first time, but with sudden emotion at the second.

'Yes,' said the landlord, 'that's his name, Doctor Wolfe Macfarlane.'

Fettes became instantly sober; his eyes awoke, his voice became clear, loud, and steady, his language forcible and earnest. We were all startled by the transformation, as if a man had risen from the dead.

'I beg your pardon,' he said, 'I am afraid I have not been paying much attention to your talk. Who is this Wolfe Macfarlane?' And then, when he had heard the landlord out, 'It cannot be, it cannot be,' he added; 'and yet I would like well to see him face to face.'

'Do you know him, Doctor?' asked the undertaker, with a gasp.

'God forbid!' was the reply. 'And yet the name is a strange one; it were too much to fancy two. Tell me, landlord, is he old?'

'Well,' said the host, 'he's not a young man, to be sure, and his hair is white; but he looks younger than you.'

'He is older, though; years older. But,' with a slap upon the table, 'it's the rum you see in my face – rum and sin. This man, perhaps, may have an easy conscience and a good digestion. Conscience! Hear me speak. You would think I was some good, old, decent Christian, would you not? But no, not I; I never canted. Voltaire might have canted if he'd stood in my shoes; but the brains' – with a rattling fillip on his bald head – 'the brains were clear and active, and I saw and made no deductions.'

'If you know this doctor,' I ventured to remark, after a

somewhat awful pause, 'I should gather that you do not share the landlord's good opinion.'

Fettes paid no regard to me.

'Yes,' he said, with sudden decision, 'I must see him face to face.'

There was another pause, and then a door was closed rather sharply on the first floor, and a step was heard upon the stair.

'That's the doctor,' cried the landlord. 'Look sharp, and you can catch him.'

It was but two steps from the small parlour to the door of the old George Inn; the wide oak staircase landed almost in the street; there was room for a Turkey rug and nothing more between the threshold and the last round of the descent; but this little space was every evening brilliantly lit up, not only by the light upon the stair and the great signal-lamp below the sign, but by the warm radiance of the bar-room window. The George thus brightly advertised itself to passers-by in the cold street. Fettes walked steadily to the spot, and we, who were hanging behind, beheld the two men meet, as one of them had phrased it, face to face. Dr Macfarlane was alert and vigorous. His white hair set off his pale and placid, although energetic, countenance. He was richly dressed in the finest of broadcloth and the whitest of linen, with a great gold watchchain, and studs and spectacles of the same precious material. He wore a broad-folded tie, white and speckled with lilac, and he carried on his arm a comfortable driving-coat of fur. There was no doubt but he became his years, breathing, as he did, of wealth and consideration; and it was a surprising contrast to see our parlour sot – bald, dirty, pimpled, and robed in his old camlet cloak – confront him at the bottom of the stairs.

'Macfarlane!' he said somewhat loudly, more like a herald than a friend.

The great doctor pulled up short on the fourth step, as though the familiarity of the address surprised and somewhat shocked his dignity.

'Toddy Macfarlane!' repeated Fettes.

The London man almost staggered. He stared for the

swiftest of seconds at the man before him, glanced behind him with a sort of scare, and then in a startled whisper, 'Fettes!' he said, 'you!'

'Ay,' said the other, 'me! Did you think I was dead too? We are not so easy shut of our acquaintance.'

'Hush, hush!' exclaimed the doctor. 'Hush, hush! this meeting is so unexpected – I can see you are unmanned. I hardly knew you, I confess, at first; but I am overjoyed – overjoyed to have this opportunity. For the present it must be how-d'ye-do and goodbye in one, for my fly is waiting, and I must not fail the train; but you shall – let me see – yes – you shall give me your address, and you can count on early news of me. We must do something for you, Fettes. I fear you are out at elbows; but we must see to that for auld lang syne, as once we sang at suppers.'

'Money!' cried Fettes; 'money from you! The money that I had from you is lying where I cast it in the rain.'

Dr Macfarlane had talked himself into some measure of superiority and confidence, but the uncommon energy of this refusal cast him back into his first confusion.

A horrible, ugly look came and went across his almost venerable countenance. 'My dear fellow,' he said, 'be it as you please; my last thought is to offend you. I would intrude on none. I will leave you my address, however—'

'I do not wish it – I do not wish to know the roof that shelters you,' interrupted the other. 'I heard your name; I feared it might be you; I wished to know if, after all, there were a God; I know now that there is none. Begone!'

He still stood in the middle of the rug, between the stair and the doorway; and the great London physician, in order to escape, would be forced to step to one side. It was plain that he hesitated before the thought of this humiliation. White as he was, there was a dangerous glitter in his spectacles; but while he still paused uncertain, he became aware that the driver of his fly was peering in from the street at this unusual scene and caught a glimpse at the same time of our little body from the parlour, huddled by the corner of the bar. The presence of so many witnesses decided him at once to flee. He crouched together, brushing on the wainscot, and made a dart like a serpent, striking for the door. But his tribulation was not yet entirely at an end, for even as he was passing Fettes clutched him by the arm and these words came in a whisper, and yet painfully distinct, 'Have you seen it again?'

The great rich London doctor cried out aloud with a sharp, throttling cry; he dashed his questioner across the open space, and, with his hands over his head, fled out of the door like a detected thief. Before it had occurred to one of us to make a movement, the fly was already rattling toward the station. The scene was over like a dream, but the dream had left proofs and traces of its passage. Next day the servant found the fine gold spectacles broken on the threshold, and that very night we were all standing breathless by the bar-room window, and Fettes at our side, sober, pale, and resolute in look.

'God protect us, Mr Fettes!' said the landlord, coming first into possession of his customary senses. 'What in the universe is all this? These are strange things you have been saying.'

Fettes turned toward us; he looked us each in succession in the face. 'See if you can hold your tongues,' said he. 'That man Macfarlane is not safe to cross; those that have done so already have repented it too late.'

And then, without so much as finishing his third glass, far less waiting for the other two, he bade us good-bye and went forth, under the lamp of the hotel, into the black night.

We three turned to our places in the parlour, with the big red fire and four clear candles; and as we recapitulated what had passed the first chill of our surprise soon changed into a glow of curiosity. We sat late; it was the latest session I have known in the old George. Each man, before we parted, had his theory that he was bound to prove; and none of us had any nearer business in this world than to track out the past of our condemned companion, and surprise the secret that he shared with the great London doctor. It is no great boast, but I believe I was a better hand at worming out a story than either of my fellows at the George; and perhaps there is now no other man alive who could narrate to you the following foul and unnatural events.

In his young days Fettes studied medicine in the schools of Edinburgh. He had talent of a kind, the talent that picks up swiftly what it hears and readily retails it for its own. He worked little at home; but he was civil, attentive, and intelligent in the presence of his masters. They soon picked him out as a lad who listened closely and remembered well; nay, strange as it seemed to me when I first heard it, he was in those days well favoured, and pleased by his exterior. There was, at that period, a certain extramural teacher of anatomy, whom I shall here designate by the letter K. His name was subsequently too well known. The man who bore it skulked through the streets of Edinburgh in disguise, while the mob that applauded at the execution of Burke called loudly for the blood of his employer. But Mr K— was then at the top of his vogue; he enjoyed a popularity due partly to his own talent and address, partly to the incapacity of his rival, the university professor. The students, at least, swore by his name, and Fettes believed himself, and was believed by others, to have laid the foundations of success when he had acquired the favour of this meteorically famous man. Mr K— was a *bon vivant* as well as an accomplished teacher; he liked a sly allusion no less than a careful preparation. In both capacities Fettes enjoyed and deserved his notice, and by the second year of his attendance he held the half-regular position of second demonstrator or sub-assistant in his class.

In this capacity, the charge of the theatre and lecture room devolved in particular upon his shoulders. He had to answer for the cleanliness of the premises and the conduct of the other students, and it was a part of his duty to supply, receive, and divide the various subjects. It was with a view to this last – at that time very delicate – affair that he was lodged by Mr K— in the same wynd, and at last in the same building, with the dissecting-rooms. Here, after a night of turbulent pleasures, his hand still tottering, his sight still misty and confused, he would be called out of bed in the black hours before the winter dawn by the unclean and desperate interlopers who supplied the table. He would open the door to these men, since infamous throughout the land. He would help them with their tragic burthen, pay them their sordid price, and remain alone, when they were gone, with the unfriendly relics of humanity. From such a scene he would return to snatch another hour or two of slumber, to repair the abuses of the night, and refresh himself for the labours of the day.

Few lads could have been more insensible to the impressions of a life thus passed among the ensigns of mortality. His mind was closed against all general considerations. He was incapable of interest in the fate and fortunes of another, the slave of his own desires and low ambitions. Cold, light, and selfish in the last resort, he had that modicum of prudence, miscalled morality, which keeps a man from inconvenient drunkenness or punishable theft. He coveted, besides, a measure of consideration from his masters and his fellow-pupils, and he had no desire to fail conspicuously in the external parts of life. Thus he made it his pleasure to gain some distinction in his studies, and day after day rendered unimpeachable eye-service to his employer, Mr K—. For his day of work he indemnified himself by nights of roaring, blackguardly enjoyment; and when that balance had been struck, the organ that he called his conscience declared itself content

The supply of subjects was a continual trouble to him as well as to his master. In that large and busy class, the raw material of the anatomists kept perpetually running out; and the business thus rendered necessary was not only unpleasant in itself, but threatened dangerous consequences to all who were concerned. It was the policy of Mr K— to ask no questions in his dealings with the trade. 'They bring the body, and we pay the price,' he used to say, dwelling on the alliteration – '*quid pro quo.*' And, again, and somewhat profanely, 'Ask no questions,' he would tell his assistants, 'for conscience' sake.' There was no understanding that the subjects were provided by the crime of murder. Had that idea been broached to him in words, he would have recoiled in horror; but the lightness of his speech upon so grave a matter was, in itself, an offence against good manners, and a temptation to the men with whom he dealt. Fettes, for instance, had often remarked to himself upon the singular freshness of the bodies. He had been struck again and again by the hangdog, abominable looks of the ruffians who came to him before the dawn; and, putting things together clearly in his private thoughts, he perhaps attributed a meaning too immoral and too categorical to the unguarded counsels of his master. He understood his duty, in short, to have three branches: to take what was brought, to pay the price, and to avert the eye from any evidence of crime.

One November morning this policy of silence was put sharply to the test. He had been awake all night with a racking toothache – pacing his room like a caged beast or throwing himself in fury on his bed – and had fallen at last into that profound, uneasy slumber that so often follows on a night of pain, when he was awakened by the third or fourth angry repetition of the concerted signal. There was a thin, bright moonshine: it was bitter cold, windy, and frosty; the town had not yet awakened, but an indefinable stir already preluded the noise and business of the day. The ghouls had come later than usual, and they seemed more than usually eager to be gone. Fettes, sick with sleep, lighted them upstairs. He heard their grumbling Irish voices through a dream; and as they stripped the sack from their sad merchandise he leaned dozing, with his shoulder propped against the wall; he had to shake himself to find the men their money. As he did so his eyes lighted on the dead face. He started; he took two steps nearer, with the candle raised.

'God Almighty!' he cried. 'That is Jane Galbraith!'

The men answered nothing, but they shuffled nearer the door.

'I know her, I tell you,' he continued. 'She was alive and hearty yesterday. It's impossible she can be dead; it's impossible you should have got this body fairly.'

'Sure, sir, you're mistaken entirely,' said one of the men.

But the other looked at Fettes darkly in the eyes, and demanded the money on the spot.

It was impossible to misconceive the threat or to exaggerate the danger. The lad's heart failed him. He stammered some excuses, counted out the sum, and saw his hateful visitors depart. No sooner were they gone than he hastened to confirm his doubts. By a dozen unquestionable marks he identified the girl he had jested with the day before. He saw, with horror, marks upon her body that might well betoken violence. A panic seized him, and he took refuge in his room. There he reflected at length over the discovery that he had made; considered soberly the bearing of Mr K—'s instructions and the danger to himself of interference in so serious a business, and at last, in sore perplexity, determined to wait for the advice of his immediate superior, the class assistant.

This was a young doctor, Wolfe Macfarlane, a high favourite among all the reckless students, clever, dissipated, and unscrupulous to the last degree. He had travelled and studied abroad. His manners were agreeable and a little forward. He was an authority on the stage, skilful on the ice or the links with skate or golf-club; he dressed with nice audacity, and, to put the finishing touch upon his glory, he kept a gig and a strong trotting-horse. With Fettes he was on terms of intimacy; indeed, their relative positions called for some community of life; and when subjects were scarce the pair would drive far into the country in Macfarlane's gig, visit and desecrate some lonely graveyard, and return before dawn with their booty to the door of the dissecting room.

On that particular morning Macfarlane arrived somewhat earlier than his wont. Fettes heard him, and met him on the stairs, told him his story, and showed him the cause of his alarm. Macfarlane examined the marks on her body.

'Yes,' he said with a nod, 'it looks fishy.'

'Well, what should I do?' asked Fettes.

'Do?' repeated the other. 'Do you want to do anything? Least said soonest mended, I should say.'

'Someone else might recognise her,' objected Fettes. 'She was as well known as the Castle Rock.'

'We'll hope not,' said Macfarlane, 'and if anybody does – well, you didn't, don't you see, and there's an end. The fact is, this has been going on too long. Stir up the mud, and you'll get K— into the most unholy trouble; you'll be in a shocking box yourself. So will I, if you come to that. I should like to know how any one of us would look, or what the devil we should have to say for ourselves, in any Christian witness-box. For me, you know there's one thing certain – that, practically speaking, all our subjects have been murdered.'

'Macfarlane!' cried Fettes.

'Come now!' sneered the other. 'As if you hadn't suspected it yourself!'

'Suspecting is one thing—'

'And proof another. Yes, I know; and I'm as sorry as you are this should have come here,' tapping the body with his cane. 'The next best thing for me is not to recognise it; and,' he added coolly, 'I don't. You may, if you please. I don't dictate, but I think a man of the world would do as I do; and I may add, I fancy that is what K— would look for at our hands. The question is, Why did he choose us two for his assistants? And I answer, because he didn't want old wives.'

This was the tone of all others to affect the mind of a lad like Fettes. He agreed to imitate Macfarlane. The body of the unfortunate girl was duly dissected, and no one remarked or appeared to recognise her.

One afternoon, when his day's work was over, Fettes dropped into a popular tavern and found Macfarlane sitting with a stranger. This was a small man, very pale and dark, with coal-black eyes. The cut of his features gave a promise of intellect and refinement which was but feebly realised in his manners, for he proved, upon a nearer acquaintance, coarse, vulgar, and stupid. He exercised, however, a very remarkable control over Macfarlane; issued orders like the Great Bashaw; became inflamed at the least discussion or delay, and commented rudely on the servility with which he was obeyed. This most offensive person took a fancy to Fettes on the spot, plied him with drinks, and honoured him with unusual confidences on his past career. If a tenth part of what he confessed were true, he was a very loathsome rogue; and the lad's vanity was tickled by the attention of so experienced a man.

'I'm a pretty bad fellow myself,' the stranger remarked,

'but Macfarlane is the boy – Toddy Macfarlane I call him. Toddy, order your friend another glass.' Or it might be, 'Toddy, you jump up and shut the door.' 'Toddy hates me,' he said again. 'Oh, yes, Toddy, you do!'

'Don't you call me that confounded name,' growled Macfarlane.

'Hear him! Did you ever see the lads play knife? He would like to do that all over my body,' remarked the stranger.

'We medicals have a better way than that,' said Fettes. 'When we dislike a dead friend of ours, we dissect him.'

Macfarlane looked up sharply, as though this jest was scarcely to his mind.

The afternoon passed. Gray, for that was the stranger's name, invited Fettes to join them at dinner, ordered a feast so sumptuous that the tavern was thrown in commotion, and when all was done commanded Macfarlane to settle the bill. It was late before they separated; the man Gray was incapably drunk. Macfarlane, sobered by his fury, chewed the cud of the money he had been forced to squander and the slights he had been obliged to swallow. Fettes, with various liquors singing in his head, returned home with devious footsteps and a mind entirely in abeyance. Next day Macfarlane was absent from the class, and Fettes smiled to himself as he imagined him still squiring the intolerable Gray from tavern to tavern. As soon as the hour of liberty had struck he posted from place to place in quest of his last night's companions. He could find them, however, nowhere; so returned early to his rooms, went early to bed, and slept the sleep of the just.

At four in the morning he was awakened by the well-known signal. Descending to the door, he was filled with astonishment to find Macfarlane with his gig, and in the gig one of those long and ghastly packages with which he was so well acquainted.

'What?' he cried. 'Have you been out alone? How did you manage?'

But Macfarlane silenced him roughly, bidding him turn to business. When they had got the body upstairs and laid it on the table, Macfarlane made at first as if he were going away. Then he paused and seemed to hesitate; and then, 'You had better look at the face,' said he, in tones of some constraint. 'You had better,' he repeated, as Fettes only stared at him in wonder.

'But where, and how, and when did you come by it?' cried the other.

'Look at the face,' was the only answer.

Fettes was staggered; strange doubts assailed him. He looked from the young doctor to the body, and then back again. At last, with a start, he did as he was bidden. He had almost expected the sight that met his eyes, and yet the shock was cruel. To see, fixed in the rigidity of death and naked on that coarse layer of sack-cloth, the man whom he had left well-clad and full of meat and sin upon the threshold of a tavern, awoke, even in the thoughtless Fettes, some of the terrors of the conscience. It was a *cras tibi* which re-echoed in his soul, that two whom he had known should have come to lie upon these icy tables. Yet these were only secondary thoughts. His first concern regarded Wolfe. Unprepared for a challenge so momentous, he knew not how to look his comrade in the face. He durst not meet his eye, and he had neither words nor voice at his command.

It was Macfarlane himself who made the first advance. He came up quietly behind and laid his hand gently but firmly on the other's shoulder.

'Richardson,' said he, 'may have the head.'

Now Richardson was a student who had long been anxious for that portion of the human subject to dissect. There was no answer, and the murderer resumed: 'Talking of business, you must pay me; your accounts, you see, must tally.'

Fettes found a voice, the ghost of his own: 'Pay you!' he cried. 'Pay you for that?'

'Why, yes, of course you must. By all means and on every possible account, you must,' returned the other. 'I dare not give it for nothing, you dare not take it for nothing; it would compromise us both. This is another case like Jane Galbraith's. The more things are wrong the more we must act as if all were right. Where does old K— keep his money?'

'There,' answered Fettes hoarsely, pointing to a cupboard in the corner.

'Give me the key, then,' said the other, calmly, holding out his hand.

There was an instant's hesitation, and the die was cast. Macfarlane could not suppress a nervous twitch, the infinitesimal mark of an immense relief, as he felt the key between his fingers. He opened the cupboard, brought out pen and ink and a paper-book that stood in one compartment, and separated from the funds in a drawer a sum suitable to the occasion.

'Now, look here,' he said, 'there is the payment made – first proof of your good faith: first step to your security. You have now to clinch it by a second. Enter the payment in your book, and then you for your part may defy the devil.'

The next few seconds were for Fettes an agony of thought; but in balancing his terrors it was the most immediate that triumphed. Any future difficulty seemed almost welcome if he could avoid a present quarrel with Macfarlane. He set down the candle which he had been carrying all the time, and with a steady hand entered the date, the nature, and the amount of the transaction.

'And now,' said Macfarlane, 'it's only fair that you should pocket the lucre. I've had my share already. By-the-by, when a man of the world falls into a bit of luck, has a few shillings extra in his pocket – I'm ashamed to speak of it, but there's a rule of conduct in the case. No treating, no purchase of expensive class-books, no squaring of old debts; borrow, don't lend.'

'Macfarlane,' began Fettes, still somewhat hoarsely, 'I have put my neck in a halter to oblige you.'

'To oblige me?' cried Wolfe. 'Oh, come! You did, as near as I can see the matter, what you downright had to do in self-defence. Suppose I got into trouble, where would you be? This second little matter flows clearly from the first. Mr Gray is the continuation of Miss Galbraith. You can't begin and then stop. If you begin, you must keep on beginning; that's the truth. No rest for the wicked.'

A horrible sense of blackness and the treachery of fate seized hold upon the soul of the unhappy student.

'My God!' he cried, 'but what have I done? and when did I begin? To be made a class assistant – in the name of reason, where's the harm in that? Service wanted the position; Service might have got it. Would *he* have been where *I* am now?'

'My dear fellow,' said Macfarlane, 'what a boy you are! What harm *has* come to you? What harm *can* come to you if you hold your tongue? Why, man, do you know what this life is? There are two squads of us – the lions and the lambs. If you're a lamb, you'll come to lie upon these tables like Gray or Jane Galbraith; if you're a lion, you'll live and drive a horse like me, like K—, like all the world with any wit or courage. You're staggered at the first. But look at K—! My dear fellow, you're clever, you have pluck. I like you, and K— likes you. You were born to lead the hunt; and I tell you, on my honour and my experience of life, three days from now you'll laugh at all these scarecrows like a high-school boy at a farce.'

And with that Macfarlane took his departure and drove off up the wynd in his gig to get under cover before daylight. Fettes was thus left alone with his regrets. He saw the miserable peril in which he stood involved. He saw, with inexpressible dismay, that there was no limit to his weakness, and that, from concession to concession, he had fallen from the arbiter of Macfarlane's destiny to his paid and helpless accomplice. He would have given the world to have been a little braver at the time, but it did not occur to him that he might still be brave. The secret of Jane Galbraith and the cursed entry in the day-book closed his mouth.

Hours passed; the class began to arrive; the members of the unhappy Gray were dealt out to one and to another, and received without remark. Richardson was made happy with the head; and before the hour of freedom rang Fettes trembled with exultation to perceive how far they had already gone toward safety.

For two days he continued to watch, with increasing joy, the dreadful process of disguise.

On the third day Macfarlane made his appearance. He had been ill, he said; but he made up for lost time by the energy with which he directed the students. To Richardson in particular he extended the most valuable assistance and advice, and that student, encouraged by the praise of the demonstrator, burned high with ambitious hopes, and saw the medal already in his grasp.

Before the week was out Macfarlane's prophecy had been fulfilled. Fettes had outlived his terrors and had forgotten his baseness. He began to plume himself upon his courage, and had so arranged the story in his mind that he could look back on these events with an unhealthy pride. Of his accomplice he saw but little. They met, of course, in the business of the class; they received their orders together from Mr K—. At times they had a word or two in private, and Macfarlane was from first to last particularly kind and jovial. But it was plain that he avoided any reference to their common secret; and even when Fettes whispered to him that he had cast in his lot with the lions and foresworn the lambs, he only signed to him smilingly to hold his peace.

At length an occasion arose which threw the pair once more into a closer union. Mr K— was again short of subjects; pupils were eager, and it was a part of this teacher's pretensions to be always well supplied. At the same time there came the news of a burial in the rustic graveyard of Glencorse. Time has little changed the place in question. It stood then, as now, upon a cross-road, out of call of human habitations, and buried fathom deep in the foliage of six cedar trees. The cries of the sheep upon the neighbouring hills, the streamlets upon either hand, one loudly singing among pebbles, the other dripping furtively from pond to pond, the stir of the wind in mountainous old flowering chestnuts, and once in seven days the voice of the bell and the old tunes of the precentor, were the only sounds that disturbed the silence around the rural church. The Resurrection Man – to use a by-name of the period – was not to be deterred by any of the sanctities of customary piety. It was part of his trade to despise and desecrate the scrolls and trumpets of old tombs, the paths worn by the feet of worshippers and mourners, and the offerings and the inscriptions of bereaved affection. To rustic neighbourhoods, where love is more than commonly tenacious, and where some bonds of blood or fellowship unite the entire society of a parish, the body-snatcher, far from being repelled by natural respect, was attracted by the ease and safety of the task. To bodies that had been laid in earth, in joyful expectation of a far different awakening, there came that hasty, lamp-lit, terror-haunted resurrection of the spade and mattock. The coffin was forced, the cerements torn, and the melancholy relics, clad in sackcloth, after being rattled for hours on moonless by-ways, were at length exposed to uttermost indignities before a class of gaping boys.

Somewhat as two vultures may swoop upon a dying lamb, Fettes and Macfarlane were to be let loose upon a grave in that green and quiet resting-place. The wife of a farmer, a woman who had lived for sixty years, and been known for nothing but good butter and a godly conversation, was to be rooted from her grave at midnight and carried, dead and naked, to that far-away city that she had always honoured with her Sunday best; the place beside her family was to be empty till the crack of doom; her innocent and almost venerable members to be exposed to that last curiosity of the anatomist.

Late one afternoon the pair set forth, well wrapped in cloaks and furnished with a formidable bottle. It rained without remission – a cold, dense, lashing rain. Now and again there blew a puff of wind, but these sheets of falling water kept it down. Bottle and all, it was a sad and silent drive as far as Penicuik, where they were to spend the evening. They stopped once, to hide their implements in a thick bush not far from the churchyard, and once again at the Fisher's Tryst, to have a toast before the kitchen fire and vary their nips of whisky with a glass of ale. When they reached their journey's end the gig was housed, the horse was fed and comforted, and the two young doctors in a private room sat down to the best dinner and the best wine the house afforded. The lights, the fire, the beating rain upon the window, the cold, incongruous work that lay before them, added zest to their enjoyment of the meal. With every glass their cordiality increased. Soon Macfarlane handed a little pile of gold to his companion.

'A compliment,' he said. 'Between friends these little d—d accommodations ought to fly like pipe-lights.'

Fettes pocketed the money, and applauded the sentiment to the echo. 'You are a philosopher,' he cried. 'I was an ass till I knew you. You and K— between you, by the Lord Harry! but you'll make a man of me.'

'Of course we shall,' applauded Macfarlane. 'A man? I tell you, it required a man to back me up the other morning. There are some big, brawling, forty-year-old cowards who would have turned sick at the look of the d—d thing; but not you – you kept your head. I watched you.'

'Well, and why not?' Fettes thus vaunted himself. 'It was no affair of mine. There was nothing to gain on the one side but disturbance, and on the other I could count on your gratitude, don't you see?' And he slapped his pocket till the gold pieces rang.

Macfarlane somehow felt a certain touch of alarm at these unpleasant words. He may have regretted that he had taught his young companion so successfully, but he had no time to interfere, for the other noisily continued in this boastful strain:

'The great thing is not to be afraid. Now, between you and me, I don't want to hang – that's practical; but for all cant, Macfarlane, I was born with a contempt. Hell, God, Devil, right, wrong, sin, crime, and all the old gallery of curiosities – they may frighten boys, but men of the world, like you and me, despise them. Here's to the memory of Gray!'

It was by this time growing somewhat late. The gig, according to order, was brought round to the door with both lamps brightly shining, and the young men had to pay their bill and take the road. They announced that they were bound for Peebles, and drove in that direction till they were clear of the last houses of the town; then, extinguishing the lamps, returned upon their course, and followed a by-road toward Glencorse. There was no sound but that of their own passage, and the incessant, strident pouring of the rain. It was pitch dark; here and there a white gate or a white stone in the wall guided them for a short space across the night; but for the most part it was at a foot pace, and almost groping, that they picked their way through that resonant blackness to their solemn and isolated destination. In the sunken woods that traverse the neighbourhood of the burying-ground the last glimmer failed them, and it became necessary to kindle a match and reillumine one of the lanterns of the gig. Thus, under the dripping trees, and environed by huge and moving shadows, they reached the scene of their unhallowed labours.

They were both experienced in such affairs, and powerful with the spade; and they had scarce been twenty minutes at their task before they were rewarded by a dull rattle on the coffin lid. At the same moment Macfarlane, having hurt his hand upon a stone, flung it carelessly above his head. The grave, in which they now stood almost to the shoulders, was close to the edge of the plateau of the graveyard; and the gig lamp had been propped, the better to illuminate their labours, against a tree, and on the immediate verge of the steep bank descending to the stream. Chance had taken a sure aim with the stone. Then came a clang of broken glass; night fell upon them; sounds alternatively dull and ringing announced the bounding of the lantern down the bank, and its occasional collision with the trees. A stone or two, which it had dislodged in its descent, rattled behind it into the profundities of the glen; and then silence, like night, resumed its sway; and they might bend their hearing to its utmost pitch, but naught was to be heard except the rain, now marching to the wind, now steadily falling over miles of open country.

They were so nearly at an end of their abhorred task that they judged it wisest to complete it in the dark. The coffin was exhumed and broken open; the body inserted in the dripping sack and carried between them to the gig; one mounted to keep it in its place, and the other, taking the horse by the mouth, groped along by wall and bush until they reached the wider road by the Fisher's Tryst. Here was a faint, diffused radiancy, which they hailed like daylight; by that they pushed the horse to a good pace and began to rattle along merrily in the direction of the town.

They had both been wetted to the skin during their operations, and now, as the gig jumped among the deep ruts, the thing that stood propped between them fell now upon one and now upon the other. At every repetition of the horrid contact each instinctively repelled it with greater haste; and the process, natural although it was, began to tell upon the nerves of the companions. Macfarlane made some ill-favoured jest about the farmer's wife, but it came hollowly from his lips, and was allowed to drop in silence. Still their unnatural burthen bumped from side to side; and now the head would be laid, as if in confidence, upon their shoulders, and now the drenching sackcloth would flap icily about their faces. A creeping chill began to possess the soul of Fettes. He peered at the bundle, and it seemed somehow larger than at first. All over the countryside, and from every degree of distance, the farm dogs accompanied their passage with tragic ululations; and it grew and grew upon his mind that some unnatural miracle had been accomplished, that some nameless change had befallen the dead body, and that it was in fear of their unholy burden that the dogs were howling.

'For God's sake,' said he, making a great effort to arrive at speech, 'for God's sake, let's have a light!'

Seemingly, Macfarlane was affected in the same direction; for though he made no reply, he stopped the horse, passed the reins to his companion, got down, and proceeded to kindle the remaining lamp. They had by that time got no farther than the cross-road down to Auchendinny. The rain still poured as though the deluge were returning, and it was no easy matter to make a light in such a world of wet and darkness. When at last the flickering blue flame had been transferred to the wick and began to expand and clarify, and shed a wide circle of misty brightness round the gig, it became possible for the two young men to see each other and the thing they had along with them. The rain had moulded the rough sacking to the outlines of the body underneath; the head was distinct from the trunk, the shoulders plainly modelled; something at once spectral and human riveted their eyes upon the ghastly comrade of their drive.

For some time Macfarlane stood motionless, holding up the lamp. A nameless dread was swathed, like a wet sheet, about the body, and tightened the white skin upon the face of Fettes; a fear that was meaningless, a horror of what could not be, kept mounting to his brain. Another beat of the watch, and he had spoken. But his comrade forestalled him.

'That is not a woman,' said Macfarlane, in a hushed voice.

'It was a woman when we put her in,' whispered Fettes.

'Hold that lamp,' said the other. 'I must see her face.'

And as Fettes took the lamp his companion untied the fastenings of the sack and drew down the cover from the head. The light fell very clear upon the dark, well-moulded features and smooth-shaven cheeks of a too familiar countenance, often beheld in dreams of both of these young men. A wild yell rang up into the night; each leaped from his own side into the roadway; the lamp fell, broke, and was extinguished; and the horse, terrified by this unusual commotion, bounded and went off toward Edinburgh at a gallop, bearing along with it, sole occupant of the gig, the body of the dead and long-dissected Gray.

The Misadventures of John Nicholson

In which John sows the wind

JOHN VAREY Nicholson was stupid; yet, stupider men than he are now sprawling in Parliament, and lauding themselves as the authors of their own distinction. He was of a fat habit, even from boyhood, and inclined to a cheerful and cursory reading of the face of life; and possibly this attitude of mind was the original cause of his misfortunes. Beyond this hint philosophy is silent on his career, and superstition steps in with the more ready explanation that he was detested of the gods.

His father – that iron gentleman – had long ago enthroned himself on the heights of the Disruption Principles. What these are (and in spite of their grim name they are quite innocent) no array of terms would render thinkable to the merely English intelligence; but to the Scot they often prove unctuously nourishing, and Mr Nicholson found in them the milk of lions. About the period when the Churches convene at Edinburgh in their annual assemblies, he was to be seen descending the Mound in the company of divers red-headed clergymen: these voluble, he only contributing oracular nods, brief negatives, and the austere spectacle of his stretched upper lip. The names of Candlish and Begg were frequent in these interviews, and occasionally the talk ran on the Residuary Establishment and the doings of one Lee. A stranger to the tight little theological kingdom of Scotland might have listened and gathered literally nothing. And Mr Nicholson (who was not a dull man) knew this, and raged at it. He knew there was a vast world outside, to whom Disruption Principles were as the chatter of tree-top apes; the paper brought him chill whiffs from it; he had met Englishmen who had asked lightly if he did not belong to the Church of Scotland, and then had failed to be much interested by his elucidation of that nice point; it was an evil, wild, rebellious world, lying sunk in *dozened ness*, for nothing short of a Scot's word will paint this Scotsman's feelings. And when he entered his own house in Randolph Crescent (south side), and shut the door behind him, his heart swelled with security. Here, at least, was a citadel unassailable by right-hand defections or left-hand extremes. Here was a family where prayers came at the same hour, where the Sabbath literature was unimpeachably selected, where the guest who should have leaned to any false opinion was instantly set down, and over which there reigned all week, and grew denser on Sundays, a silence that was agreeable to his ear, and gloom that he found comfortable.

Mrs Nicholson had died about thirty, and left him with three children: a daughter two years and a son about eight years younger than John; and John himself, the unfortunate protagonist of the present history. The daughter, Maria, was a good girl – dutiful, pious, dull, but so easily startled that to speak to her was quite a perilous enterprise. 'I don't think I care to talk about that, if you please,' she would say, and strike the boldest speechless by her unmistakable pain; this upon all topics – dress, pleasure, morality, politics, in which the formula was changed to 'my papa thinks otherwise,' and even religion, unless it was approached with a particular whining tone of voice. Alexander, the younger brother, was sickly, clever, fond of books and drawing, and full of satirical remarks. In the midst of these, imagine that natural, clumsy, unintelligent, and mirthful animal, John; mighty well-behaved in comparison with other lads, although not up to the mark of the house in Randolph Crescent; full of a sort of blundering affection, full of caresses which were never very warmly received; full of sudden and loud laughter which rang out in that still house like curses. Mr Nicholson himself had a great fund of humour, of the Scots order – intellectual, turning on the observation of men; his own character, for instance – if he could have seen it in another – would have been a rare feast to him; but his son's empty guffaws over a broken plate, and empty, almost light-hearted remarks, struck him with pain as the indices of a weak mind.

Outside the family John had early attached himself (much as a dog may follow a marquess) to the steps of Alan Houston, a lad about a year older than himself, idle, a trifle wild, the heir to a good estate which was still in the hands of a rigorous trustee, and so royally content with himself that he took John's devotion as a thing of course. The intimacy was gall to Mr Nicholson; it took his son from the house, and he was a jealous parent; it kept him from the office, and he was a martinet; lastly, Mr Nicholson was ambitious for his family (in which, and the Disruption Principles, he entirely lived), that he hated to see a son of his play second fiddle to an idler. After some hesitation, he ordered that the friendship should cease – an unfair command, though seemingly inspired by the spirit of prophecy; and John, saying nothing, continued to disobey the order under the rose.

John was nearly nineteen when he was one day dismissed rather earlier than usual from his father's office, where he was studying the practice of the law. It was Saturday; and except that he had a matter of four hundred pounds in his pocket which it was his duty to hand over to the British Linen Company's Bank, he had the whole afternoon at his disposal. He went by Princes Street, enjoying the mild sunshine, and the little thrill of easterly wind that tossed the flags along that terrace of palaces, and tumbled the green trees in the garden. The band was playing down in the valley under the castle; and when it came to the turn of the pipers, he heard their wild sounds with a stirring of the blood. Something distantly martial awoke in him; and he thought of Miss Mackenzie, whom he was to meet that day at dinner in his father's house.

Now, it is undeniable that he should have gone directly to the bank, but right in the way stood the billiard-room of the hotel where Alan was almost certain to be found; and the temptation proved too strong. He entered the billiard-room, and was instantly greeted by his friend, cue in hand.

'Nicholson,' said he, 'I want you to lend me a pound or two till Monday.'

'You've come to the right shop, haven't you?' returned John. 'I have twopence.'

'Nonsense,' said Alan. 'You can get some. Go and borrow at your tailor's; they all do it. Or I'll tell you what: pop your watch.'

'Oh, yes, I daresay,' said John. 'And how about my father?'

'How is he to know? He doesn't wind it up for you at night, does he?' inquired Alan, at which John guffawed. 'No, seriously: I am in a fix,' continued the tempter. 'I have lost some money to a man here. I'll give it you to-night, and you can get the heirloom out again on Monday. Come; it's a small service, after all. I would do a good deal more for you.'

Whereupon John went forth, and pawned his gold watch under the assumed name of John Froggs, 85 Pleasance. But the nervousness that assailed him at the door of that inglorious haunt – a pawnshop – and the effort necessary to invent the pseudonym (which somehow seemed to him a necessary part of the procedure), had taken more time that he imagined; and when he returned to the billiard-room with the spoils, the bank had already closed its doors.

This was a shrewd knock. 'A piece of business had been neglected.' He heard these words in his father's trenchant voice, and trembled, and then dodged the thought. After all, who was to know? He must carry four hundred pounds about with him till Monday, when the neglect could be surreptitiously repaired; and meanwhile, he was free to pass the afternoon on the encircling divan of the billiard-room, smoking his pipe, sipping a pint of ale, and enjoying to the mast-head the modest pleasures of admiration.

None can admire like a young man. Of all youth's passions and pleasures, this is the most common and least alloyed; and every flash of Alan's black eyes; every aspect of his curly head; every graceful reach, and easy, stand-off attitude of waiting, everything about him down even to his shirt-sleeves and wrist-links, were seen by John through a luxurious glory. He valued himself by the possession of that royal friend, hugged himself upon the thought, and swam in warm azure; his own defects, like vanquished difficulties, becoming things on which to plume himself. Only when he thought of Miss Mackenzie there fell upon his mind a shadow of regret; that young lady was worthy of better things than plain John Nicholson, still known among schoolmates by the derisive name of 'Fatty'; and he felt that if he could chalk a cue or stand at ease, with such a careless grace as Alan, he could approach the object of his sentiments with a less crushing sense of inferiority.

Before they parted, Alan made a proposal that was startling in the extreme. He would be at Collette's that night about twelve, he said. Why should not John come there and get the money? To go to Collette's was to see life, indeed; it was wrong; it was against the laws; it partook, in a very dingy manner, of adventure. Were it known, it was the sort of exploit that disconsidered a young man for good with the more serious classes, but gave him a standing with the riotous. And yet Collette's was not a hell; it could not come, without vaulting hyperbole, under the rubric of a gilded saloon; and, if it was a sin to go there, the sin was merely local and municipal. Collette's (whose name I do not know how to spell, for I was never in epistolary communication with that hospitable outlaw) was simply an unlicensed publican, who gave suppers after eleven at night, the Edinburgh hour of closing. If you belonged to a club, you could get a much better supper at the same hour, and lose not a jot in public esteem. But if you lacked that qualification, and were an-hungered, or inclined towards conviviality at unlawful hours, Collette's was your only port. You were very ill-supplied. The company was not recruited from the Senate or the Church, though the Bar was very well represented on the only occasion on which I flew in the face of my country's laws, and, taking my reputation in my hand, penetrated into that grim supper-house. And Collette's frequenters, thrillingly conscious of wrong-doing and 'that two-handed engine (the policeman) at the door,' were perhaps inclined to somewhat feverish excess. But the place was in no sense a very bad one; and it is somewhat strange to me, at this distance of time, how it had acquired its dangerous repute.

In precisely the same spirit as a man may debate a project to ascend the Matterhorn or to cross Africa, John considered Alan's proposal, and, greatly daring, accepted it. As he walked home, the thoughts of this excursion out of the safe places of life into the wild and arduous, stirred and struggled in his imagination with the image of Flora Mackenzie – incongruous and yet kindred thoughts, for did not each imply unusual tightening of the pegs of resolution? Did not each woo him forth and warn him back again into himself?

Between these two considerations, at least, he was more than usually moved; and when he got to Randolph Crescent, he quite forgot the four hundred pounds in the inner pocket of his greatcoat, hung up the coat, with its rich freight, upon his particular pin of the hat-stand; and in the very action sealed his doom.

TWO

In which John reaps the whirlwind

About half-past ten it was John's brave good fortune to offer his arm to Miss Mackenzie, and escort her home. The night was chill and starry; all the way east-ward the trees of the different gardens rustled and looked black. Up the stone gully of Leith Walk, when they came to cross it, the breeze made a rush and set the flames of the street-lamps quavering; and when at last they had mounted to the Royal Terrace, where Captain Mackenzie lived, a great salt fresh-ness came in their faces from the sea. These phases of the walk remained written on John's memory, each emphasised by the touch of that light hand on his arm; and behind all these aspects of the nocturnal city he saw, in his mind's eye, a picture of the lighted drawing-room at home where he had sat talking with Flora; and his father, from the other end, had looked on with a kind and ironical smile. John had read the significance of that smile, which might have escaped a stranger. Mr Nicholson had remarked his son's entanglement with satisfaction, tinged by humour; and his smile, if it still was a thought contemptuous, had implied consent.

At the captain's door the girl held out her hand, with a certain emphasis; and John took it and kept it a little longer, and said, 'Good-night, Flora, dear,' and was instantly thrown into much fear by his presumption. But she only laughed, ran up the steps, and rang the bell; and while she was waiting for the door to open, kept close in the porch, and talked to him from that point as out of a fortification. She had a knitted shawl over her head; her blue Highland eyes took the light from the neighbouring street-lamp and sparkled; and when the door opened and closed upon her, John felt cruelly alone.

He proceeded slowly back along the terrace in a tender glow; and when he came to Greenside Church, he halted in a doubtful mind. Over the crown of the Calton Hill, to his left, lay the way to Collette's, where Alan would soon be looking for his arrival, and where he would now have no more consented to go than he would have wilfully wallowed in a bog; the touch of the girl's hand on his sleeve, and the kindly light in his father's eyes, both loudly forbidding. But right before him was the way home, which pointed only to bed, a place of little ease for one whose fancy was strung to the lyrical pitch, and whose not very ardent heart was just then tumultuously moved. The hill-top, the cool air of the night, the company of the great monuments, the sight of the city under his feet, with its hills and valleys and crossing files of lamps, drew him by all he had of the poetic, and he turned that way; and by that quite innocent reflection, ripened the crop of his venial errors for the sickle of destiny.

On a seat on the hill above Greenside he sat for perhaps half an hour, looking down upon the lamps of Edinburgh, and up at the lamps of heaven. Wonderful were the resolves he formed; beautiful and kindly were the vistas of future life that sped before him. He uttered to himself the name of Flora in so many touching and dramatic keys, that he

became at length fairly melted with tenderness, and could
have sung aloud. At that juncture the sound of a certain
creasing in his greatcoat caught his ear. He put his hand
into his pocket, pulled for the envelope that held the
money, and sat stupefied. The Calton Hill, about this
period, had an ill name of nights; and to be sitting there
with four hundred pounds that did not belong to him was
hardly wise. He looked up. There was a man in a very bad
hat a little on one side of him, apparently looking at the
scenery; from a little on the other a second night-walker was
drawing very quietly near. Up jumped John. The envelope
fell from his hands; he stooped to get it, and at the same
moment both men ran in and closed with him.

A little after, he got to his feet very sore and shaken,
the poorer by a purse which contained exactly one penny
postage-stamp, by a cambric handkerchief, and by the
all-important envelope.

Here was a young man on whom, at the highest point
of loverly exaltation, there had fallen a blow too sharp to
be supported alone; and not many hundred yards away
his greatest friend was sitting at supper – ay, and even
expecting him. Was it not in the nature of man that he
should run there? He went in quest of sympathy – in quest
of that droll article that we all suppose ourselves to want
when in a strait, and have agreed to call advice; and he
went, besides, with vague but rather splendid expectations
of relief. Alan was rich, or would be so when he came of
age. By a stroke of the pen he might remedy this misfortune,
and avert that dreaded interview with Mr Nicholson, from
which John now shrunk in imagination as the hand draws
back from fire.

Close under the Calton Hill there runs a certain narrow
avenue, part street, part by-road. The head of it faces the
doors of the prison; its tail descends into the sunless slums
of the Low Calton. On one hand it is overhung by the crags
of the hill, on the other by an old grave-yard. Between
these two the road-way runs in a trench, sparsely lighted
at night, sparsely frequented by day, and bordered, when
it has cleared the place of tombs, by dingy and ambiguous
houses. One of these was the house of Collette; and at

his door our ill-starred John was presently beating for
admittance. In an evil hour he satisfied the jealous inquiries
of the contraband hotelkeeper; in an evil hour he penetrated
into the somewhat unsavoury interior. Alan, to be sure, was
there, seated in a room lighted by noisy gas-jets, beside a
dirty table-cloth, engaged on a coarse meal, and in the
company of several tipsy members of the junior bar. But
Alan was not sober; he had lost a thousand pounds upon
a horse-race, had received the news at dinner-time, and
was now, in default of any possible means of extrication,
drowning the memory of his predicament. He to help John!
The thing was impossible; he couldn't help himself.

'If you have a beast of a father,' said he, 'I can tell you
I have a brute of a trustee.'

'I'm not going to hear my father called a beast,' said
John, with a beating heart, feeling that he risked the last
sound rivet of the chain that bound him for life.

But Alan was quite good-natured.

'All right, old fellow,' said he. 'Mos' respec'able man
your father.' And he introduced his friend to his companions as 'old Nicholson the what-d'ye-call-um's son.'

John sat in dumb agony. Collette's foul walls and macu-
late table-linen, and even down to Collette's villainous
casters, seemed like objects in a nightmare. And just
then there came a knock and a scurrying; the police, so
lamentably absent from the Calton Hill, appeared upon
the scene; and the party, taken *flagrante delicto*, with their
glasses at their elbow, were seized, marched up to the police
office, and all duly summoned to appear as witnesses in the
consequent case against that arch-shebeener, Collette.

It was a sorrowful and a mightily sobered company that
came forth again. The vague terror of public opinion
weighed generally on them all; but there were private and
particular horrors on the minds of individuals. Alan stood
in dread of his trustee, already sorely tried. One of the group
was the son of a country minister, another of a judge; John,
the unhappiest of all, had David Nicholson to father, the
idea of facing whom on such a scandalous subject was
physically sickening. They stood a while consulting under
the buttresses of Saint Giles; thence they adjourned to the

lodgings of one of the number in North Castle Street, where (for that matter) they might have had quite as good a supper, and far better drink, than in the dangerous paradise from which they had been routed. There, over an almost tearful glass, they debated their position. Each explained he had the world to lose if the affair went on, and he appeared as a witness. It was remarkable what bright prospects were just then in the very act of opening before each of that little company of youths, and what pious consideration for the feelings of their families began now to well from them. Each, moreover, was in an odd state of destitution. Not one could bear his share of the fine; not one but evinced a wonderful twinkle of hope that each of the others (in succession) was the very man who could step in to make good the deficit. One took a high hand; he could not pay his share; if it went to a trial, he should bolt; he had always felt the English Bar to be his true sphere. Another branched out into touching details about his family, to which no one listened. John, in the midst of this disorderly competition of poverty and meanness, sat stunned, contemplating the mountain bulk of his misfortunes.

At last, upon a pledge that each should apply to his family with a common frankness, this convention of unhappy young asses broke up, went down the common stair, and in the grey of the spring morning, with the streets lying dead empty all about them, the lamps burning on into the daylight in indiminished lustre, and the birds beginning to sound premonitory notes from the groves of the town gardens, went each his own way with bowed head and echoing footfall.

The rooks were awake in Randolph Crescent; but the windows looked down, discreetly blinded, on the return of the prodigal. John's pass-key was a recent privilege; this was the first time it had been used; and, oh! with what a sickening sense of his unworthiness he now inserted it into the well-oiled lock and entered that citadel of the proprieties! All slept; the gas in the hall had been left faintly burning to light his return; a dreadful stillness reigned, broken by the deep ticking of the eight-day clock. He put the gas out, and sat in a chair in the hall, waiting and counting the minutes, longing for any human countenance. But when at last he heard the alarm-clock spring its rattle in the lower story, and the servants begin to be about, he instantly lost heart, and fled to his own room, where he threw himself upon the bed.

THREE

In which John enjoys the harvest home

Shortly after breakfast, at which he assisted with a highly tragical countenance, John sought his father where he sat, presumably in religious meditation, on the Sabbath mornings. The old gentleman looked up with that sour, inquisitive expression that came so near to smiling and was so different in effect.

'This is a time when I do not like to be disturbed,' he said.

'I know that,' returned John; 'but I have – I want – I've made a dreadful mess of it,' he broke out, and turned to the window.

Mr Nicholson sat silent for an appreciable time, while his unhappy son surveyed the poles in the back green, and a certain yellow cat that was perched upon the wall. Despair sat upon John as he gazed; and he raged to think of the dreadful series of his misdeeds, and the essential innocence that lay behind them.

'Well,' said his father, with an obvious effort, but in very quiet tones, 'what is it?'

'Maclean gave me four hundred pounds to put in the bank, sir,' began John; 'and I'm sorry to say that I've been robbed of it!'

'Robbed of it?' cried Mr Nicholson, with a strong rising inflection. 'Robbed? Be careful what you say, John!'

'I can't say anything else, sir; I was just robbed of it,' said John in desperation, sullenly.

'And where and when did this extraordinary event take place?' inquired the father.

'On the Calton Hill about twelve last night.'

'The Calton Hill?' repeated Mr Nicholson. 'And what were you doing there at such a time of the night?'

'Nothing, sir,' says John.

Mr Nicholson drew in his breath.

'And how came the money in your hands at twelve last night?' he asked, sharply.

'I neglected that piece of business,' said John, anticipating comment; and then in his own dialect: 'I clean forgot all about it.'

'Well,' said his father, 'it's a most extraordinary story. Have you communicated with the police?'

'I have,' answered poor John, the blood leaping to his face. 'They think they know the men that did it. I daresay the money will be recovered, if that was all,' said he, with a desperate indifference, which his father set down to levity; but which sprang from the consciousness of worse behind.

'Your mother's watch, too?' asked Mr Nicholson.

'Oh, the watch is all right!' cried John. 'At least, I mean I was coming to the watch – the fact is, I am ashamed to say, I – I had pawned the watch before. Here is the ticket; they didn't find that; the watch can be redeemed; they don't sell pledges.' The lad panted out these phrases, one after another, like minute-guns; but at the last word, which rang in that stately chamber like an oath, his heart failed him utterly; and the dreaded silence settled on father and son.

It was broken by Mr Nicholson picking up the pawn-ticket: 'John Froggs, 85 Pleasance,' he read; and then turning upon John, with a brief flash of passion and disgust, 'Who is John Froggs?' he cried.

'Nobody,' said John. 'It was just a name.'

'An *alias*,' his father commented.

'Oh! I think scarcely quite that,' said the culprit; 'it's a form, they all do it, the man seemed to understand, we had a great deal of fun over the name—'

He paused at that, for he saw his father wince at the picture like a man physically struck; and again there was silence.

'I do not think,' said Mr Nicholson, at last, 'that I am an ungenerous father. I have never grudged you money within reason, for any avowable purpose; you had just to come to me and speak. And now I find that you have forgotten all decency and all natural feeling, and actually pawned – pawned – your mother's watch. You must have had some temptation; I will do you the justice to suppose it was a strong one. What did you want with this money?'

'I would rather not tell you, sir,' said John. 'It will only make you angry.'

'I will not be fenced with,' cried his father. 'There must be an end of disingenuous answers. What did you want with this money?'

'To lend it to Houston, sir,' says John.

'I thought I had forbidden you to speak to that young man?' asked his father.

'Yes, sir,' said John; 'but I only met him.'

'Where?' came the deadly question.

And 'in a billiard-room' was the damning answer. Thus, had John's single departure from the truth brought instant punishment. For no other purpose but to see Alan would he have entered a billiard-room; but he had desired to palliate the fact of his disobedience, and now it appeared that he frequented these disreputable haunts upon his own account.

Once more Mr Nicholson digested the vile tidings in silence; and when John stole a glance at his father's countenance, he was abashed to see the marks of suffering.

'Well,' said the old gentleman, at last, 'I cannot pretend not to be simply bowed down. I rose this morning what the world calls a happy man – happy, at least, in a son of whom I thought I could be reasonably proud—'

But it was beyond human nature to endure this longer, and John interrupted almost with a scream. 'Oh, wheest!' he cried, 'that's not all, that's not the worst of it – it's nothing! How could I tell you were proud of me? Oh! I wish, I wish that I had known; but you always said I was such a disgrace! And the dreadful thing is this: we were all taken up last night, and we have to pay Collette's fine among the six, or we'll be had up for evidence – shebeening it is. They made me swear to tell you; but for my part,' he cried, bursting into tears, 'I just wish that I was dead!' And he fell on his knees before a chair and hid his face.

Whether his father spoke, or whether he remained long in the room or at once departed, are points lost to history. A horrid turmoil of mind and body; bursting sobs; broken, vanishing thoughts, now of indignation, now of remorse; broken elementary whiffs of consciousness, of the smell of the horse-hair on the chair bottom, of the jangling of church bells that now began to make day horrible throughout the confines of the city, of the hard floor that bruised his knees, of the taste of tears that found their way into his mouth: for a period of time, the duration of which I cannot guess, while I refuse to dwell longer on its agony, these were the whole of God's world for John Nicholson.

When at last, as by the touching of a spring, he returned again to clearness of consciousness and even a measure of composure, the bells had but just done ringing, and the Sabbath silence was still marred by the patter of belated feet. By the clock above the fire, as well as by these more speaking signs, the service had not long begun; and the unhappy sinner, if his father had really gone to church, might count on near two hours of only comparative unhappiness. With his father, the superlative degree returned infallibly. He knew it by every shrinking fibre in his body, he knew it by the sudden dizzy whirling of his brain, at the mere thought of that calamity. An hour and a half, perhaps an hour and three quarters, if the doctor was long-winded, and then would begin again that active agony from which, even in the dull ache of the present, he shrunk as from the bite of fire. He saw, in a vision, the family pew, the somnolent cushions, the Bibles, the Psalm-books, Maria with her smelling-salts, his father sitting spectacled and critical; and at once he was struck with indignation, not unjustly. It was inhuman to go off to church, and leave a sinner in suspense, unpunished, unforgiven. And at the very touch of criticism, the paternal sanctity was lessened; yet the paternal terror only grew; and the two strands of feeling pushed him in the same direction.

And suddenly there came upon him a mad fear lest

his father should have locked him in. The notion had no ground in sense; it was probably no more than a reminiscence of similar calamities in childhood, for his father's room had always been the chamber of inquisition and the scene of punishment; but it stuck so rigorously in his mind that he must instantly approach the door and prove its untruth. As he went, he struck upon a drawer left open in the business table. It was the money-drawer, a measure of his father's disarray: the money-drawer – perhaps a pointing providence! Who is to decide, when even divines differ between a providence and a temptation? or who, sitting calmly under his own vine, is to pass a judgment on the doings of a poor, hunted dog, slavishly afraid, slavishly rebellious, like John Nicholson on that particular Sunday? His hand was in the drawer, almost before his mind had conceived the hope; and rising to his new situation, he wrote, sitting in his father's chair and using his father's blotting-pad, his pitiful apology and farewell:

'My Dear Father, – I have taken the money, but I will pay it back as soon as I am able. You will never hear of me again. I did not mean any harm by anything, so I hope you will try and forgive me. I wish you would say good-bye to Alexander and Maria, but not if you don't want to. I could not wait to see you, really. Please try to forgive me. Your affectionate son.

John Nicholson.'

The coins abstracted and the missive written, he could not be gone too soon from the scene of these transgressions; and remembering how his father had once returned from church, on some slight illness, in the middle of the second psalm, he durst not even make a packet of a change of clothes. Attired as he was, he slipped from the paternal doors, and found himself in the cool spring air, the thin spring sunshine, and the great Sabbath quiet of the city, which was now only pointed by the cawing of the rooks. There was not a soul in Randolph Crescent, nor a soul in Queensferry Street; in this out-door privacy and the sense of escape, John took heart again; and with a pathetic sense of leave-taking, he even ventured up the lane and stood a while, a strange peri at the gates of a quaint paradise, by the west end of St George's Church. They were singing within; and by a strange chance, the tune was 'St George's, Edinburgh,' which bears the name, and was first sung in the choir of that church. 'Who is this King of Glory?' went the voices from within; and to John this was like the end of all Christian observances, for he was now to be a wild man like Ishmael, and his life was to be cast in homeless places and with godless people.

It was thus, with no rising sense of the adventurous, but in mere desolation and despair, that he turned his back on his native city, and set out on foot for California, with a more immediate eye to Glasgow.

FOUR

The second sowing

It is no part of mine to narrate the adventures of John Nicholson, which were many, but simply his more momentous misadventures, which were more than he desired, and, by human standards, more than he deserved; how he reached California, how he was rooked, and robbed, and beaten, and starved; how he was at last taken up by charitable folk, restored to some degree of self-complacency, and installed as a clerk in a bank in San Francisco, it would take too long to tell; nor in these episodes were there any marks of the peculiar Nicholsonic destiny, for they were just such matters as befell some thousands of other young adventurers in the same days and places. But once posted in the bank, he fell for a time into a high degree of good fortune, which, as it was only a longer way about to fresh disaster, it behoves me to explain.

It was his luck to meet a young man in what is technically called a 'dive,' and thanks to his monthly wages, to extricate this new acquaintance from a position of present disgrace and possible danger in the future. This young man was the nephew of one of the Nob Hill magnates, who run the San Francisco Stock Exchange, much as more humble adventurers, in the corner of some public park at home, may be seen to perform the simple artifice of pea and thimble: for their own profit, that is to say, and the discouragement of public gambling. It was thus in his power – and, as he was of grateful temper, it was among the things that he desired – to put John in the way of growing rich; and thus, without thought or industry, or so much as even understanding the game at which he played, but by simply buying and selling what he was told to buy and sell, that plaything of fortune was presently at the head of between eleven and twelve thousand pounds, or, as he reckoned it, of upward of sixty thousand dollars.

How he had come to deserve this wealth, any more than how he had formerly earned disgrace at home, was a problem beyond the reach of his philosophy. It was true that he had been industrious at the bank, but no more so than the cashier, who had seven small children and was visibly sinking in decline. Nor was the step which had determined his advance – a visit to a dive with a month's wages in his pocket – an act of such transcendent virtue, or even wisdom, as to seem to merit the favour of the gods. From some sense of this, and of the dizzy see-saw – heaven-high, hell-deep – on which men sit clutching; or perhaps fearing that the sources of his fortune might be insidiously traced to some root in the field of petty cash; he stuck to his work, said not a word of his new circumstances, and kept his account with a bank in a different quarter of the town. The concealment, innocent as it seems, was the first step in the second tragi-comedy of John's existence.

Meanwhile, he had never written home. Whether from diffidence or shame, or a touch of anger, or mere procrastination, or because (as we have seen) he had no skill in literary arts, or because (as I am sometimes tempted to suppose) there is a law in human nature that prevents young men – not otherwise beasts – from the performance of this simple act of piety – months and years had gone by, and John had never written. The habit of not writing, indeed, was already fixed before he had begun to come into his fortune; and it was only the difficulty of breaking this long silence that withheld him from an instant restitution of the money he had stolen or (as he preferred to call it) borrowed. In vain he sat before paper, attending on inspiration; that heavenly nymph, beyond suggesting the words, 'my dear father,' remained obstinately silent; and presently John would crumple up the sheet and decide, as soon as he had 'a good chance,' to carry the money home in person. And this delay, which is indefensible, was his second step into the snares of fortune.

Ten years had passed, and John was drawing near to thirty. He had kept the promise of his boyhood, and was now of a lusty frame, verging toward corpulence; good features, good eyes, a genial manner, a ready laugh, a long pair of sandy whiskers, a dash of an American accent, a close familiarty with the great American joke, and a certain likeness to a R-y-l P-rs-n-ge, who shall remain nameless for me, made up the man's externals as he could be viewed in society. Inwardly, in spite of his gross body and highly masculine whiskers, he was more like a maiden lady than a man of twenty-nine.

It chanced one day, as he was strolling down Market Street on the eve of his fortnight's holiday, that his eye was caught by certain railway bills, and in very idleness of mind he calculated that he might be home for Christmas if he started on the morrow. The fancy thrilled him with desire, and in one moment he decided he would go.

There was much to be done: his portmanteau to be packed, a credit to be got from the bank where he was a wealthy customer, and certain offices to be transacted for that other bank in which he was an humble clerk; and it chanced, in conformity with human nature, that out of all this business it was the last that came to be neglected. Night found him, not only equipped with money of his own, but once more (as on that former occasion) saddled with a considerable sum of other people's.

Now it chanced there lived in the same boarding-house a fellow-clerk of his, an honest fellow, with what is called a weakness for drink – though it might, in this case, have been called a strength, for the victim had been drunk for weeks together without the briefest intermission. To this unfortunate John entrusted a letter with an inclosure of bonds, addressed to the bank manager. Even as he did so he thought he perceived a certain haziness of eye and speech in his trustee; but he was too hopeful to be stayed, silenced the voice of warning in his bosom, and with one and the same gesture committed the money to the clerk, and himself into the hands of destiny.

I dwell, even at the risk of tedium, on John's minutest errors, his case being so perplexing to the moralist; but we have done with them now, the roll is closed, the reader has the worst of our poor hero, and I leave him to judge for himself whether he or John has been the less deserving. Henceforth we have to follow the spectacle of a man who was a mere whip-top for calamity; on whose unmerited misadventures not even the humourist can look without pity, and not even the philosopher without alarm.

That same night the clerk entered upon a bout of drunkenness so consistent as to surprise even his intimate acquaintance. He was speedily ejected from the boarding-house; deposited his portmanteau with a perfect stranger, who did not even catch his name; wandered he knew not where, and was at last hove-to, all standing, in a hospital at Sacramento. There, under the impenetrable *alias* of the number of his bed, the crapulous being lay for some more days unconscious of all things, and of one thing in particular: that the police were after him. Two months had come and gone before the convalescent in the Sacramento hospital was identified with Kirkman, the absconding San Francisco clerk; even then, there must elapse nearly a fortnight more till the perfect stranger could be hunted up, the portmanteau recovered, and John's letter carried at length to its destination, the seal still unbroken, the enclosure still intact.

Meanwhile, John had gone upon his holidays without a word, which was irregular; and there had disappeared with him a certain sum of money, which was out of all bounds of palliation. But he was known to be careless, and believed to be honest; the manager besides had a regard for him; and little was said, although something was no doubt thought, until the fortnight was finally at an end, and the time had come for John to reappear. Then, indeed, the affair began to look black; and when inquiries were made, and the penniless clerk was found to have amassed thousands of dollars, and kept them secretly in a rival establishment, the stoutest of his friends abandoned him, the books were overhauled for traces of ancient and artful fraud, and though none were found, there still prevailed a general impression of loss. The telegraph was set in motion; and the correspondent of the bank in Edinburgh, for which place it was understood that John had armed himself with extensive credits, was warned to communicate with the police.

Now this correspondent was a friend of Mr Nicholson's; he was well acquainted with the tale of John's calamitous disappearance from Edinburgh; and putting one thing with another, hasted with the first word of this scandal, not to the police, but to his friend. The old gentleman had long regarded his son as one dead; John's place had been taken, the memory of his faults had already fallen to be one of those old aches, which awaken again indeed upon occasion, but which we can always vanquish by an effort of the will; and to have the long lost resuscitated in a fresh disgrace was doubly bitter.

'MacEwen,' said the old man, 'this must be hushed up, if possible. If I give you a check for this sum, about which they are certain, could you take it on yourself to let the matter rest?'

'I will,' said MacEwen. 'I will take the risk of it.'

'You understand,' resumed Mr Nicholson, speaking precisely, but with ashen lips, 'I do this for my family, not for that unhappy young man. If it should turn out that these suspicions are correct, and he has embezzled large sums, he must lie in his bed as he has made it.' And then looking up at MacEwen with a nod, and one of his strange smiles: 'Good-bye,' said he; and MacEwen, perceiving the case to be too grave for consolation, took himself off and blessed God on his way home that he was childless.

FIVE

The prodigal's return

By a little after noon on the eve of Christmas, John had left his portmanteau in the cloak-room, and stepped forth into Princes Street with a wonderful expansion of the soul, such as men enjoy in the completion of long-nourished schemes. He was at home again, incognito and rich; presently he could enter his father's house by means of the pass-key, which he had piously preserved through all his wanderings; he would throw down the borrowed money; there would be a reconciliation, the details of which he frequently arranged; and he saw himself, during the next month, made welcome in many stately houses at many frigid dinner-parties, taking his share in the conversation with the freedom of the man and the traveller, and laying down the law upon finance with the authority of the successful investor. But this programme was not to be begun before evening – not till just before dinner, indeed, at which meal the reassembled family were to sit roseate, and the best wine (the modern fatted calf) should flow for the prodigal's return.

Meanwhile he walked familiar streets, merry reminiscences crowding round him, sadness also, both with the same surprising pathos. The keen frosty air; the low, rosy, wintery sun; the castle, hailing him like an old acquaintance; the names of friends on door-plates; the sight of friends whom he seemed to recognise, and whom he eagerly avoided, in the streets; the pleasant chant of the north country accent; the dome of St George's reminding him of his last penitential moments in the lane, and of the King of Glory whose name had echoed ever since in the saddest corner of his memory; and the gutters where he had learned to slide, and the shop where he had bought his skates, and the stones on which he had trod, and the railings on which he had rattled his clachan as he went to school; and all those thousand and one nameless particulars, which the eye sees without noting, which the memory keeps indeed yet without knowing, and which, taken one with another, build up for us the aspect of the place that we call home: and all these besieged him, as he went, with both delight and sadness.

His first visit was Houston, who had a house on Regent's Terrace, kept for him in old days by an aunt. The door was opened (to his surprise) upon the chain, and a voice asked him from within what he wanted.

'I want Mr Houston – Mr Alan Houston,' said he.

'And who are ye?' said the voice.

'This is most extraordinary,' thought John; and then aloud he told his name.

'No, young Mr John?' cried the voice, with a sudden increase of Scottish accent, testifying to a friendlier feeling.

'The very same,' said John.

And the old butler removed his defences, remarking only, 'I thocht ye were that man.' But his master was not there; he was staying, it appeared, at the house in Murrayfield; and though the butler would have been glad enough to have taken his place and given all the news of the family, John, struck with a little chill, was eager to be gone. Only, the door was scarce closed again, before he regretted that he had not asked about 'that man.'

He was to pay no more visits till he had seen his father and made all well at home; Alan had been the only possible exception, and John had not time to go as far as Murrayfield. But here he was on Regent's Terrace; there was nothing to prevent him going round the end of the hill, and looking from without on the Mackenzies' house. As he went, he reflected that Flora must now be a woman of near his own age, and it was within the bounds of possibility that she was married; but this dishonourable doubt he damned down.

There was the house, sure enough; but the door was of another colour, and what was this – two door plates? He drew nearer; the top one bore, with dignified simplicity the words, 'Mr Proudfoot'; the lower one was more explicit, and informed the passer-by that here was likewise the abode of 'Mr J. A. Dunlop Proudfoot, Advocate.' The Proudfoots must be rich, for no advocate could look to have much business in so remote a quarter; and John hated them for their wealth and for their name, and for the sake of the house they desecrated with their presence. He remembered a Proudfoot he had seen at school, not known: a little, whey-faced urchin, the despicable member of some lower class. Could it be this abortion that had climbed to be an advocate, and now lived in the birthplace of Flora and the home of John's tenderest memories? The chill that had first seized upon him when he heard of Houston's absence deepened and struck inward. For a moment, as he stood under the doors of that estranged house, and looked east and west along the solitary pavement of the Royal Terrace, where not a cat was stirring, the sense of solitude and desolation took him by the throat, and he wished himself in San Francisco.

And then the figure he made, with his decent portliness, his whiskers, the money in his purse, the excellent cigar that he now lighted, recurred to his mind in consolatory comparison with that of a certain maddened lad who, on a certain spring Sunday ten years before, and in the hour of church-time silence, had stolen from that city by the Glasgow road. In the face of these changes, it were impious to doubt fortune's kindness. All would be well yet; the Mackenzies would be found, Flora, younger and lovelier and kinder than before; Alan would be found, and would have so nicely discriminated his behaviour as to have grown, on the one hand, into a valued friend of Mr Nicholson's, and to have remained, upon the other, of that exact shade of joviality which John desired in his companions. And so, once more, John fell to work discounting the delightful future; his first appearance in the family pew; his first visit to his uncle Greig, who thought himself so great a financier, and on whose purblind Edinburgh eyes John was to let in the dazzling daylight of the West; and the details in general of that unrivalled transformation scene, in which he was to display to all Edinburgh a portly and successful gentleman in the shoes of the derided fugitive.

The time began to draw near when his father would have returned from the office, and it would be the prodigal's cue to enter. He strolled westward by Albany Street, facing the sunset embers, pleased, he knew not why, to move in that cold air and indigo twilight, starred with street-lamps. But there was one more disenchantment waiting him by the way.

At the corner of Pitt Street he paused to light a fresh cigar; the vesta threw, as he did so, a strong light upon his features, and a man of about his own age stopped at sight of it.

'I think your name must be Nicholson,' said the stranger.

It was too late to avoid recognition; and besides, as John was now actually on the way home, it hardly mattered, and he gave way to the impulse of his nature.

'Great Scott!' he cried, 'Beatson!' and shook his hands with warmth. It scarce seemed he was repaid in kind.

'So you're home again?' said Beatson. 'Where have you been all this long time?'

'In the States,' said John – 'California. I've made my pile though; and it suddenly struck me it would be a noble scheme to come home for Christmas.'

'I see,' said Beatson. 'Well, I hope we'll see something of you now you're here.'

'Oh, I guess so,' said John, a little frozen.

'Well, ta-ta,' concluded Beatson, and he shook hands again and went.

This was a cruel first experience. It was idle to blink facts: here was John home again, and Beatson – Old Beatson – did not care a rush. He recalled Old Beatson in the past – that merry and affectionate lad – and their joint adventures and mishaps, the window they had broken with a catapult in India Place, the escalade of the Castle rock, and many another inestimable bond of friendship; and his hurt surprise grew deeper. Well, after all, it was only on a man's own family that he could count; blood was thicker than water, he remembered; and the net result of this encounter was to bring him to the doorstep of his father's house, with tenderer and softer feelings.

The night had come; the fanlight over the door shone bright; the two windows of the dining-room where the cloth was being laid, and the three windows of the drawing-room where Maria would be waiting dinner, glowed softlier through yellow blinds. It was like a vision of the past. All this time of his absence, life had gone forward with an equal foot, and the fires and the gas had been lighted, and the meals spread, at the accustomed hours. At the accustomed hour, too, the bell had sounded thrice to call the family worship. And at the thought a pang of regret for his demerit seized him; he remembered the things that were good and that he had neglected and the things that were evil and that he had loved; and it was with a prayer upon his lips that he mounted the steps and thrust the key into the key-hole.

He stepped into the lighted hall, shut the door softly behind him, and stood there fixed in wonder. No surprise of strangeness could equal the surprise of that complete familiarity. There was the bust of Chalmers near the stair railings, there was the clothes-brush in the accustomed place; and there, on the hat-stand, hung hats and coats that must surely be the same as he remembered. Ten years dropped from his life, as a pin may slip between the fingers; and the ocean and the mountains, and the mines, and crowded marts and mingled races of San Francisco, and his own fortune and his own disgrace, became, for that one moment, the figures of a dream that was over.

He took off his hat, and moved mechanically towards the stand; and there he found a small change that was a great one to him. The pin that had been his from boyhood, where he had flung his balmoral hat when he loitered home from the academy, and his first hat when he came briskly back from college or the office – his pin was occupied.

'They might have at least respected my pin!' he thought, and he was moved as by a slight, and began at once to recollect that he was here an interloper, in a strange house, which he had entered almost by a burglary, and where at any moment he might be scandalously challenged.

He moved at once, his hat still in his hand, to the door of his father's room, opened it, and entered. Mr Nicholson sat in the same place and posture as on that last Sunday morning; only he was older, and greyer, and sterner; and as he now glanced up and caught the eye of his son, a strange commotion and a dark flush sprang into his face.

'Father,' said John, steadily, and even cheerfully, for this was a moment against which he was long ago prepared, 'father, here I am, and here is the money that I took from you. I have come back to ask your forgiveness, and to stay Christmas with you and the children.'

'Keep your money,' said the father, 'and go!'

'Father!' cried John; 'For God's sake don't receive me this way. I've come for—'

'Understand me,' interrupted Mr Nicholson; 'you are no son of mine; and in the sight of God, I wash my hands of you. One last thing will I tell you; one warning I will give you; all is discovered, and you are being hunted for your crimes; if you are still at large it is thanks to me; but I have done all that I mean to do; and from this time forth I would not raise one finger – not one finger – to save you from the gallows! And now,' with a low voice of absolute authority, and a single weighty gesture of the finger, 'and now – go!'

SIX

The house at Murrayfield

How John passed the evening, in what windy confusion of mind, in what squalls of anger and lulls of sick collapse, in what pacing of streets and plunging into public-houses, it would profit little to relate. His misery, if it were not progressive, yet tended in no way to diminish; for in proportion as grief and indignation abated, fear began to take their place. At first, his father's menacing words lay by in some safe drawer of memory, biding their hour. At first, John was all thwarted affection and blighted hope; next bludgeoned vanity raised its head again, with twenty mortal gashes: and the father was disowned even as he had disowned the son. What was this regular course of life, that John should have admired it? what were these clockwork virtues, from which love was absent? Kindness was the test, kindness the aim and soul; and judged by such a standard, the discarded prodigal – now rapidly drowning his sorrows and his reason in successive drams – was a creature of a lovelier morality than his self-righteous father. Yes, he was the better man; he felt it, glowed with the consciousness, and entering a public-house at the corner of Howard Place (whither he had somehow wandered) he pledged his own virtues in a glass – perhaps the fourth since his dismissal. Of that he knew nothing, keeping no account of what he did or where he went; and in the general crashing hurry of his nerves, unconscious of the approach of intoxication. Indeed, it is a question whether he were really growing intoxicated, or whether at first the spirits did not even sober him. For it was even as he drained this last glass that his father's ambiguous and menacing words – popping from their hiding-place in memory – startled him like a hand laid upon his shoulder. 'Crimes, hunted, the gallows.' They were ugly words; in the ears of an innocent man, perhaps all the uglier; for if some judicial error were in act against him, who should set a limit to its grossness or to how far it might be pushed? Not John, indeed; he was no believer in the powers of innocence, his cursed experience pointing in quite other ways; and his fears, once awakened, grew with every hour and hunted him about the city streets.

It was perhaps nearly nine at night; he had eaten nothing since lunch, he had drunk a good deal, and he was exhausted by emotion, when the thought of Houston came into his head. He turned, not merely to the man as a friend, but to his house as a place of refuge. The danger that threatened him was still so vague that he knew neither what to fear nor where he might expect it; but this much at least seemed undeniable, that a private house was safer than a public inn. Moved by these counsels, he turned at once to the Caledonian Station, passed (not without alarm) into the bright lights of the approach, redeemed his portmanteau from the cloak-room, and was soon whirling in a cab along the Glasgow road. The change of movement and position, the sight of the lamps twinkling to the rear, and the smell of damp and mould and rotten straw which clung about the vehicle, wrought in him strange alternations of lucidity and mortal giddiness.

'I have been drinking,' he discovered; 'I must go straight to bed, and sleep.' And he thanked Heaven for the drowsiness that came upon his mind in waves.

From one of these spells he was wakened by the stoppage of the cab; and, getting down, found himself in quite a country road, the last lamp of the suburb shining some way below, and the high walls of a garden rising before him in the dark. The Lodge (as the place was named), stood, indeed, very solitary. To the south it adjoined another house, but standing in so large a garden as to be well out of cry; on all other sides, open fields stretched upward to the woods of Corstorphine Hill, or backward to the dells of Ravelston, or downward toward the valley of the Leith. The effect of seclusion was aided by the great height of the garden walls, which were, indeed, conventual, and, as John had tested in former days, defied the climbing schoolboy. The lamp of the cab threw a gleam upon the door and the not brilliant handle of the bell.

'Shall I ring for ye?' said the cabman, who had descended from his perch and was slapping his chest, for the night was bitter.

'I wish you would,' said John, putting his hand to his brow in one of his accesses of giddiness.

The man pulled at the handle, and the clanking of the bell replied from farther in the garden; twice and thrice he did it, with sufficient intervals; in the great, frosty silence of the night, the sounds fell sharp and small.

'Does he expect ye?' asked the driver, with that manner of familiar interest that well became his port-wine face; and when John had told him no, 'Well, then,' said the cabman, 'if ye'll tak' my advice of it, we'll just gang back. And that's disinterested, mind ye, for my stables are in the Glesgie road.'

'The servants must hear,' said John.

'Hout!' said the driver. 'He keeps no servants here, man.

They're a' in the town house; I drive him often; it's just a kind of hermitage, this.'

'Give me the bell,' said John; and he plucked at it like a man desperate.

The clamour had not yet subsided before they heard steps upon the gravel, and a voice of singular nervous irritability cried to them through the door, 'Who are you, and what do you want?'

'Alan,' said John, 'it's me – it's Fatty – John, you know. I'm just come home, and I've come to stay with you.'

There was no reply for a moment, and then the door was opened.

'Get the portmanteau down,' said John to the driver.

'Do nothing of the kind,' said Alan; and then to John, 'Come in here a moment. I want to speak to you.'

John entered the garden, and the door was closed behind him. A candle stood on the gravel walk, winking a little in the draughts; it threw inconstant sparkles on the clumped holly, struck the light and darkness to and fro like a veil on Alan's features, and set his shadow hovering behind him. All beyond was inscrutable; and John's dizzy brain rocked with the shadow. Yet even so, it struck him that Alan was pale, and his voice, when he spoke, unnatural.

'What brings you here to-night?' he began. 'I don't want, God knows, to seem unfriendly; but I cannot take you in, Nicholson; I cannot do it.'

'Alan,' said John, 'you've just got to! You don't know the mess I'm in; the governor's turned me out, and I daren't show my face in an inn, because they're down on me for murder or something!'

'For what?' cried Alan, starting.

'Murder, I believe,' says John.

'Murder!' repeated Alan, and passed his hand over his eyes. 'What was that you were saying?' he asked again.

'That they were down on me,' said John. 'I'm accused of murder, by what I can make out; and I've really had a dreadful day of it, Alan, and I can't sleep on the road-side on a night like this – at least, not with a portmanteau,' he pleaded.

'Hush,' said Alan, with his head on one side; and then, 'did you hear nothing?' he asked.

'No,' said John, thrilling, he knew not why, with communicated terror. 'No, I heard nothing; why?' And then, as there was no answer, he reverted to his pleading: 'But I say, Alan, you've just got to take me in. I'll go right away to bed if you have anything to do. I seem to have been drinking; I was that knocked over. I wouldn't turn you away, Alan, if you were down on your luck.'

'No?' returned Alan. 'Neither will I you, then. Come and let's get your portmanteau.'

The cabman was paid, and drove off down the long, lamp-lit hill, and the two friends stood on the side-walk beside the portmanteau till the last rumble of the wheels had died in silence. It seemed to John as though Alan attached importance to this departure of the cab; and John, who was in no state to criticise, shared profoundly in the feeling.

When the stillness was once more perfect, Alan shouldered the portmanteau, carried it in, and shut and locked the garden door; and then, once more, abstraction seemed to fall upon him, and he stood with his hand on the key, until the cold began to nibble at John's fingers.

'Why are we standing here?' asked John.

'Eh?' said Alan blankly.

'Why, man, you don't seem yourself,' said the other.

'No, I'm not myself,' said Alan; and he sat down on the portmanteau and put his face in his hands.

John stood beside him swaying a little, and looking about him at the swaying shadows, the flitting sparkles, and the steady stars overhead, until the windless cold began to touch him through his clothes on the bare skin. Even in his bemused intelligence, wonder began to awake.

'I say, let's come on to the house,' he said at last.

'Yes, let's come on to the house,' repeated Alan.

And he rose at once, re-shouldered the portmanteau, and taking the candle in his other hand, moved forward to the Lodge. This was a long, low building, smothered in creepers; and now, except for some chinks of light between the dining-room shutters, it was plunged in darkness and silence.

In the hall Alan lighted another candle, gave it to John, and opened the door of a bedroom.

'Here,' said he; 'go to bed. Don't mind me, John. You'll be sorry for me when you know.'

'Wait a bit,' returned John; 'I've got so cold with all that standing about. Let's go into the dining-room a minute. Just one glass to warm me, Alan.'

On the table in the hall stood a glass, and a bottle with a whisky label on a tray. It was plain that the bottle had just been opened, for the cork and corkscrew lay beside it.

'Take that,' said Alan, passing John the whisky, and then with a certain roughness pushed his friend into the bedroom, and closed the door behind him.

John stood amazed; then he shook the bottle, and, to his further wonder, found it partly empty. Three or four glasses were gone. Alan must have uncorked a bottle of whisky and drank three or four glasses one after the other, without sitting down, for there was no chair, and that in his own cold lobby on this freezing night! It fully explained his eccentricities, John reflected sagely, as he mixed himself a grog. Poor Alan! He was drunk; and what a dreadful thing was drink, and what a slave to it poor Alan was, to drink in this unsociable, uncomfortable fashion! The man who would drink alone, except for health's sake – as John was now doing – was a man utterly lost. He took the grog out, and felt hazier, but warmer. It was hard work opening the portmanteau and finding his night things; and before he was undressed, the cold had struck home to him once more. 'Well,' said he; 'just a drop more. There's no sense in getting ill with all this other trouble.' And presently dreamless slumber buried him.

When John awoke it was day. The low winter sun was already in the heavens, but his watch had stopped, and it was impossible to tell the hour exactly. Ten, he guessed it, and made haste to dress, dismal reflections crowding on his mind. But it was less from terror than from regret that he now suffered; and with his regret there were mingled cutting pangs of penitence. There had fallen upon him a blow, cruel, indeed, but yet only the punishment of old misdoing; and he had rebelled and plunged into fresh sin. The rod had been used to chasten, and he had bit the chastening fingers. His father was right; John had justified him; John was no guest for decent people's houses, and no fit associate for decent people's children. And had a broader hint been needed, there was the case of his old friend. John was no drunkard, though he could at times exceed; and the picture of Houston drinking neat spirits at his hall-table struck him with something like disgust. He hung from meeting his old friend. He could have wished he had not come to him; and yet, even now, where else was he to turn?

These musings occupied him while he dressed and accompanied him into the lobby of the house. The door stood open on the garden; doubtless, Alan had stepped forth; and John did as he supposed his friend had done. The ground was hard as iron, the frost still rigorous as he brushed among the hollies, icicles jingled and glittered in their fall; and wherever he went, a volley of eager sparrows followed him. Here were Christmas weather and Christmas morning duly met, to the delight of children. This was the day of reunited families, the day to which he had so long looked forward, thinking to awake in his own bed in Randolph Crescent, reconciled with all men and repeating the foot-prints of his youth; and here he was alone, pacing the alleys of a wintry garden and filled with penitential thoughts.

And that reminded him: why was he left alone? and where was Alan? The thought of the festal morning and the due salutations reawakened his desire for his friend, and he began to call for him by name. As the sound of his voice died away, he was aware of the greatness of the silence that environed him. But for the twittering of the sparrows and the crunching of his own feet upon the frozen snow, the whole windless world of air hung over him entranced, and the stillness weighed upon his mind with a horror of solitude.

Still calling at intervals, but now with a moderated voice, he made the hasty circuit of the garden, and finding neither

man nor trace of man in all its evergreen coverts, turned
at last to the house. About the house the silence seemed
to deepen strangely. The door, indeed, stood open as
before; but the windows were still shuttered, the chimneys
breathed no stain into the bright air, there sounded abroad
none of the low stir (perhaps audible rather to the ear of
the spirit than to the ear of the flesh) by which a house
announces and betrays its human lodgers. And yet Alan
must be there – Alan locked in drunken slumbers, forgetful
of the return of day, of the holy season, and of the friend
whom he had so coldly received and was now so churlishly
neglecting. John's disgust redoubled at the thought; but
hunger was beginning to grow stronger than repulsion,
and as a step to breakfast, if nothing else, he must find
and arouse the sleeper.

He made the circuit of the bedroom quarters. All, until
he came to Alan's chamber, were locked from without,
and bore the marks of a prolonged disuse. But Alan's was
a room in commission, filled with clothes, knick-knacks,
letters, books, and the conveniences of a solitary man. The
fire had been lighted; but it had long ago burned out, and
the ashes were stone cold. The bed had been made, but it
had not been slept in.

Worse and worse, then; Alan must have fallen where
he sat, and now sprawled brutishly, no doubt, upon the
dining-room floor.

The dining-room was a very long apartment, and was
reached through a passage; so that John, upon his entrance,
brought but little light with him, and must move toward
the windows with spread arms, groping and knocking on
the furniture. Suddenly he tripped and fell his length over
a prostrate body. It was what he had looked for, yet it
shocked him; and he marvelled that so rough an impact
should not have kicked a groan out of the drunkard. Men
had killed themselves ere now in such excesses, a dreary
and degraded end had made John shudder. What if Alan
were dead? There would be a Christmas Day!

By this, John had his hand upon the shutters, and flinging
them back, beheld once again the blessed face of the day.
Even by that light the room had a discomfortable air. The

chairs were scattered, and one had been overthrown; the table-cloth, laid as if for dinner, was twitched upon one side, and some of the dishes had fallen to the floor. Behind the table lay the drunkard, still unaroused, only one foot visible to John.

But now that light was in the room, the worst seemed over; it was a disgusting business, but not more than disgusting; and it was with no great apprehension that John proceeded to make the circuit of the table: his last comparatively tranquil moment for that day. No sooner had he turned the corner, no sooner had his eye alighted on the body, than he gave a smothered, breathless cry, and fled out of the room and out of the house.

It was not Alan who lay there, but a man well up in years, of stern countenance and iron-grey locks; and it was no drunkard, for the body lay in a black pool of blood, and the open eyes stared upon the ceiling.

To and fro walked John before the door. The extreme sharpness of the air acted on his nerves like an astringent, and braced them swiftly. Presently, he not relaxing in his disordered walk, the images began to come clearer and stay longer in his fancy; and next the power of thought came back to him, and the horror and danger of his situation rooted him to the ground.

He grasped his forehead, and staring on one spot of gravel, pieced together what he knew and what he suspected. Alan had murdered some one: possibly 'that man' against whom the butler chained the door in Regent's Terrace; possibly another; some one at least: a human soul, whom it was death to slay and whose blood lay spilled upon the floor. This was the reason of the whisky drinking in the passage, of his unwillingness to welcome John, of his strange behaviour and bewildered words; this was why he had started at and harped upon the name of murder; this was why he had stood and hearkened, or sat and covered his eyes, in the black night. And now he was gone, now he had basely fled; and to all his perplexities and dangers John stood heir.

'Let me think – let me think,' he said, aloud, impatiently, even pleadingly, as if to some merciless interrupter. In the turmoil of his wits, a thousand hints and hopes and threats and terrors dinning continuously in his ears, he was like one plunged in the hubbub of a crowd. How was he to remember – he, who had not a thought to spare – that he was himself the author, as well as the theatre, of so much confusion? But in hours of trial the junto of man's nature is dissolved, and anarchy succeeds.

It was plain he must stay no longer where he was, for here was a new Judicial Error in the very making. It was not so plain where he must go, for the old Judicial Error, vague as a cloud, appeared to fill the habitable world; whatever it might be, it watched for him, full-grown in Edinburgh; it must have had its birth in San Francisco; it stood guard no doubt, like a dragon, at the bank where he should cash his credit; and though there were doubtless many other places, who should say in which of them it was not ambushed? No, he could not tell where he was to go; he must not lose time on these insolubilities. Let him go back to the beginning. It was plain he must stay no longer where he was. It was plain, too, that he must not flee as he was, for he could not carry his portmanteau, and to flee and leave it, was to plunge deeper in the mire. He must go, leave the house unguarded, find a cab, and return – return after an absence? Had he courage for that?

And just then he spied a stain about a hand's breadth on his trouser-leg, and reached his finger down to touch it. The finger was stained red; it was blood; he stared upon it with disgust, and awe, and terror, and in the sharpness of the new sensation, fell instantly to act.

He cleansed his finger in the snow, returned into the house, drew near with hushed footsteps to the dining-room door, and shut and locked it. Then he breathed a little freer, for here at least was an oaken barrier between himself and what he feared. Next, he hastened to his room, tore off the spotted trousers which seemed in his eyes a link to bind him to the gallows, flung them in a corner, donned another pair, breathlessly crammed his night things into his portmanteau, locked it, swung it with an effort from the ground, and with a rush of relief, came forth again under the open heavens.

The portmanteau, being of Occidental build, was no feather-weight; it had distressed the powerful Alan; and as for John, he was crushed under its bulk, and the sweat broke upon him thickly. Twice he must set it down to rest before he reached the gate; and when he had come so far, he must do as Alan did, and take his seat upon one corner. Here, then, he sat a while and panted; but now his thoughts were sensibly lightened; now, with the trunk standing just inside the door, some part of his dissociation from the house of crime had been effected, and the cabman need not pass the garden wall. It was wonderful how that relieved him; for the house, in his eyes, was a place to strike the most cursory beholder with suspicion, as though the very windows had cried murder.

But there was to be no remission of the strokes of fate. As he thus sat, taking breath in the shadow of the wall and hopped about by sparrows, it chanced that his eye roved to the fastening of the door; and what he saw plucked him to his feet. The thing locked with a spring; once the door was closed, the bolt shut of itself; and without a key, there was no means of entering from without.

He saw himself obliged to one of two distasteful and perilous alternatives; either to shut the door altogether and set his portmanteau out upon the way-side, a wonder to all beholders; or to leave the door ajar, so that any thievish tramp or holiday school-boy might stray in and stumble on the grisly secret. To the last, as the least desperate, his mind inclined; but he must first insure himself that he was unobserved. He peered out, and down the long road: it lay dead empty. He went to the corner of the by-road that comes by way of Dean; there also not a passenger was stirring. Plainly it was, now or never, the high tide of his affairs; and he drew the door as close as he durst, slipped a pebble in the chink, and made off down hill to find a cab.

Half-way down a gate opened, and a troop of Christmas children sallied forth in the most cheerful humour, followed more soberly by a smiling mother.

'And this is Christmas Day!' thought John; and could have laughed aloud in tragic bitterness of heart.

SEVEN

A tragi-comedy in a cab

In front of Donaldson's Hospital, John counted it good fortune to perceive a cab a great way off, and by much shouting and waving of his arm to catch the notice of the driver. He counted it good fortune, for the time was long to him till he should have done for ever with the Lodge; and the farther he must go to find a cab, the greater the chance that the inevitable discovery had taken place, and that he should return to find the garden full of angry neighbours. Yet when the vehicle drew up he was sensibly chagrined to recognise the port-wine cabman of the night before. 'Here,' he could not but reflect, 'here is another link in the Judicial Error.'

The driver, on the other hand, was pleased to drop again upon so liberal a fare; and as he was a man – the reader must already have perceived – of easy, not to say familiar manners, he dropped at once into a vein of friendly talk, commenting on the weather, on the sacred season, which struck him chiefly in the light of a day of liberal gratuities, on the chance which had reunited him to a pleasing customer, and on the fact that John had been (as he was pleased to call it) visibly 'on the ran-dan' the night before.

'And ye look dreidful bad the-day, sir, I must say that,' he continued. 'There's nothing like a dram for ye – if ye'll take my advice of it; and bein' as it's Christmas, I'm no' saying,' he added, with a fatherly smile, 'but what I would join ye mysel'.'

John had listened with a sick heart.

'I'll give you a dram when we've got through,' said he, affecting a sprightliness which sat on him most unhandsomely, 'and not a drop till then. Business first, and pleasure afterward.'

With this promise the jarvey was prevailed upon to

clamber to his place and drive, with hideous deliberation, to the door of the Lodge. There were no signs as yet of any public emotion; only, two men stood not far off in talk, and their presence, seen from afar, set John's pulses buzzing. He might have spared himself his fright, for the pair were lost in some dispute of a theological complexion, and with lengthened upper lip and enumerating fingers, pursued the matter of their difference, and paid no heed to John.

But the cabman proved a thorn in the flesh. Nothing would keep him on his perch; he must clamber down, comment upon the pebble in the door (which he regarded as an ingenious but unsafe device), help John with the portmanteau, and enliven matters with a flow of speech, especially of questions, which I thus condense:–

'He'll no' be here himsel', will he? No? Well, he's an eccentric man – a fair oddity – if ye ken the expression. Great trouble with his tenants, they tell me. I've driven the fam'ly for years. I drove a cab at his father's waddin'. What'll your name be? – I should ken your face. Baigrey, ye say? There were Baigreys about Gilmerton; ye'll be one of that lot? Then this'll be a friend's portmantie, like? Why? Because the name upon it's Nucholson! Oh, if ye're in a hurry, that's another job. Waverley Brig'? Are ye for away?'

So the friendly toper prated and questioned and kept John's heart in a flutter. But to this also, as to other evils under the sun, there came a period; and the victim of circumstances began at last to rumble towards the railway terminus at Waverley Bridge. During the transit, he sat with raised glasses in the frosty chill and mouldy fetor of his chariot, and glanced out sidelong on the holiday face of things, the shuttered shops, and the crowds along the pavement, much as the rider in the Tyburn cart may have observed the concourse gathering to his execution.

At the station his spirits rose again; another stage of his escape was fortunately ended – he began to spy blue water. He called a railway porter, and bade him carry the portmanteau to the cloak-room: not that he had any notion of delay; flight, instant flight was his design, no matter whither; but he had determined to dismiss the cabman ere he named, or even chose his destination, thus possibly balking the Judicial Error of another link. This was his cunning aim, and now with one foot on the road-way, and one still on the coach-step, he made haste to put the thing in practice, and plunged his hand into his trousers pocket.

There was nothing there!

Oh, yes; this time he was to blame. He should have remembered, and when he deserted his blood-stained pantaloons, he should not have deserted along with them his purse. Make the most of his error, and then compare it with the punishment! Conceive his new position, for I lack words to picture it; conceive him condemned to return to that house, from the very thought of which his soul revolted, and once more to expose himself to capture on the very scene of the misdeed: conceive him linked to the mouldy cab and the familiar cabman. John cursed the cabman silently, and then it occurred to him that he must stop the incarceration of his portmanteau; that, at least, he must keep close at hand, and he turned to recall the porter. But his reflections, brief as they had appeared, must have occupied him longer than he supposed, and there was the man already returning with the receipt.

Well, that was settled; he had lost his portmanteau also; for the sixpence with which he had paid the Murrayfield Toll was one that had strayed alone into his waistcoat pocket, and unless he once more successfully achieved the adventure of the house of crime, his portmanteau lay in the cloak-room in eternal pawn, for lack of a penny fee. And then he remembered the porter, who stood suggestively attentive, words of gratitude hanging on his lips.

John hunted right and left; he found a coin – prayed God that it was a sovereign – drew it out, beheld a halfpenny, and offered it to the porter.

The man's jaw dropped.

'It's only a halfpenny!' he said, startled out of railway decency.

'I know that,' said John, piteously.

And here the porter recovered the dignity of man.

'Thank you, sir,' and would have returned the base

gratuity. But John, too, would none of it; and as they struggled, who must join in but the cabman?

'Hoots, Mr Baigrey,' said he, 'you surely forget what day it is!'

'I tell you I have no change!' cried John.

'Well,' said the driver, 'and what then? I would rather give a man a shillin' on a day like this than put him off with a derision like a baw-bee. I'm surprised at the like of you, Mr Baigrey!'

'My name is not Baigrey!' broke out John, in mere childish temper and distress.

'Ye told me it was yoursel',' said the cabman.

'I know I did; and what the devil right had you to ask?' cried the unhappy one.

'Oh, very well,' said the driver. 'I know my place, if you know yours – if you know yours!' he repeated, as one who should imply grave doubt; and muttered inarticulate thunders, in which the grand old name of gentleman was taken seemingly in vain.

Oh, to have been able to discharge this monster, whom John now perceived, with tardy clear-sightedness, to have begun betimes the festivities of Christmas! But far from any such ray of consolation visiting the lost, he stood bare of help and helpers, his portmanteau sequestered in one place, his money deserted in another and guarded by a corpse; himself, so sedulous of privacy, the cynosure of all men's eyes about the station; and, as if these were not enough mischances, he was now fallen in ill-blood with the beast to whom his poverty had linked him! In ill-blood, as he reflected dismally, with the witness who perhaps might hang or save him. There was no time to be lost; he durst not linger any longer in that public spot; and whether he had recourse to dignity or conciliation, the remedy must be applied at once. Some happily surviving element of manhood moved him to the former.

'Let us have no more of this,' said he, his foot once more upon the step. 'Go back to where we came from.'

He had avoided the name of any destination, for there was now quite a little band of railway folk about the cab, and he still kept an eye upon the Court of Justice, and laboured to avoid concentric evidence. But here again the fatal jarvey out-manoeuvred him.

'Back to the Ludge?' cried he, in shrill tones of protest.

'Drive on at once!' roared John, and slammed the door behind him, so that the crazy chariot rocked and jingled.

Forth trundled the cab into the Christmas streets, the fare within plunged in the blackness of despair that neighboured on unconsciousness, the driver on the box digesting his rebuke and his customer's duplicity. I would not be thought to put the pair in competition; John's case was out of all parallel. But the cabman, too, is worth the sympathy of the judicious; for he was a fellow of genuine kindliness and a high sense of personal dignity incensed by drink; and his advances had been cruelly and publicly rebuffed. As he drove, therefore, he counted his wrongs, and thirsted for sympathy and drink. Now, it chanced he had a friend, a publican, in Queensferry Street, from whom, in view of the sacredness of the occasion, he thought he might extract a dram. Queensferry Street lies something off the direct road to Murrayfield. But then there is the hilly cross-road that passes by the valley of the Leith and the Dean Cemetery; and Queensferry Street is on the way to that. What was to hinder the cabman, since his horse was dumb, from choosing the cross-road, and calling on his friend in passing? So it was decided; and the charioteer, already somewhat mollified, turned aside his horse to the right.

John, meanwhile, sat collapsed, his chin sunk upon his chest, his mind in abeyance. The smell of the cab was still faintly present to his senses, and a certain leaden chill about his feet; all else had disappeared in one vast oppression of calamity and physical faintness. It was drawing on to noon – two-and-twenty hours since he had broken bread; in the interval, he had suffered tortures of sorrow and alarm, and been partly tipsy; and though it was impossible to say he slept, yet when the cab stopped and the cabman thrust his head into the window, his attention had to be recalled from depths of vacancy.

'If you'll no' *stand* me a dram,' said the driver, with a well-merited severity of tone and manner, 'I daresay ye'll have no objection to my taking one mysel'?'

'Yes – no – do what you like,' returned John; and then, as he watched his tormenter mount the stairs and enter the whisky-shop, there floated into his mind a sense as of something long ago familiar. At that he started fully awake, and stared at the shop-fronts. Yes, he knew them; but when? and how? Long since, he thought; and then, casting his eye through the front glass, which had been recently occluded by the figure of the jarvey, he beheld the tree-tops of the rookery in Randolph Crescent. He was close to home – home, where he had thought, at that hour, to be sitting in the well-remembered drawing-room in friendly converse; and, instead—!

It was his first impulse to drop into the bottom of the cab; his next, to cover his face with his hands. So he sat, while the cabman toasted the publican, and the publican toasted the cab-man, and both reviewed the affairs of the nation; so he still sat, when his master condescended to return, and drive off at last down-hill, along the curve of Lynedoch Place; but even so sitting, as he passed the end of his father's street, he took one glance from between shielding fingers, and beheld a doctor's carriage at the door.

'Well, just so,' thought he; 'I'll have killed my father! and this is Christmas Day!'

If Mr Nicholson died, it was down this same road he must journey to the grave; and down this road, on the same errand, his wife had preceded him years before; and many other leading citizens, with the proper trappings and attendance of the end. And now, in that frosty, ill-smelling, straw-carpeted, and ragged-cushioned cab, with his breath congealing on the glasses, where else was John himself advancing to?

The thought stirred his imagination, which began to manufacture many thousand pictures, bright and fleeting, like the shapes in a kaleidoscope; and now he saw himself, ruddy and comforted, sliding in the gutter; and, again, a little woe-begone, bored urchin tricked forth in crape and weepers, descending this same hill at the foot's-pace of mourning coaches, his mother's body just preceding him; and yet again, his fancy, running far in front, showed him the house at Murrayfield – now standing solitary in the low sunshine, with the sparrows hopping on the threshold and the dead man within staring at the roof – and now, with a sudden change, thronged about with white-faced, hand-uplifting neighbours, and doctor bursting through their midst and fixing his stethoscope as he went, the policeman shaking a sagacious head beside the body. It was to this he feared that he was driving; in the midst of this he saw himself arrive, heard himself stammer faint explanations, and felt the hand of the constable upon his shoulder. Heavens! how he wished he had played the manlier part; how he despised himself that he had fled that fatal neighbourhood when all was quiet, and should now be tamely travelling back when it was thronging with avengers!

Any strong degree of passion lends, even to the dullest, the forces of the imagination. And so now as he dwelt on what was probably awaiting him at the end of this distressful drive – John, who saw things little, remembered them less, and could not have described them at all, beheld in his mind's eye the garden of the Lodge, detailed as in a map; he went to and fro in it, feeding his terrors; he saw the hollies, the snowy borders, the paths where he had sought Alan, the high, conventual walls, the shut door – what! was the door shut? Ay, truly, he had shut it – shut in his money, his escape, his future life – shut it with these hands, and no one could now open it! He heard the snap of the spring-lock like something bursting in his brain, and sat astonied.

And then he woke again, terror jarring through his vitals. This was no time to be idle; he must be up and doing, he must think. Once at the end of this ridiculous cruise, once at the Lodge door, there would be nothing for it but to turn the cab and trundle back again. Why, then, go so far? why add another feature of suspicion to a case already so suggestive? why not turn at once? It was easy to say, turn; but whither? He had nowhere now to go to; he could never – he saw it in letters of blood – he could never pay that cab; he was saddled with that cab for ever. Oh, that cab! his soul yearned to be rid of it. He forgot all other cares. He must first quit himself and this ill-smelling vehicle and of the human beast that guided it – first do that; do that at least; do that at once.

And just then the cab suddenly stopped, and there was his persecutor rapping on the front glass. John let it down, and beheld the port-wine countenance inflamed with intellectual triumph.

'I ken wha ye are!' cried the husky voice. 'I mind ye now. Ye're a Nucholson. I drove ye to Hermiston to a Christmas party, and ye came back on the box, and I let ye drive.'

It is a fact. John knew the man; they had been even friends. His enemy, he now remembered, was a fellow of great good-nature – endless good-nature – with a boy; why not with a man? Why not appeal to his better side? He grasped at the new hope.

'Great Scott! and so you did,' he cried, as if in a transport of delight, his voice sounding false in his own ears. 'Well, if that's so, I've something to say to you. I'll just get out, I guess. Where are we, anyway?'

The driver had fluttered his ticket in the eyes of the branch toll-keeper, and they were now brought to on the highest and most solitary part of the by-road. On the left, a row of fieldside trees beshaded it; on the right, it was bordered by naked fallows, undulating down-hill to the Queensferry Road; in front, Corstorphine Hill raised its snow-bedabbled, darkling woods against the sky. John looked all about him, drinking the clear air like wine; then his eyes returned to the cabman's face as he sat, not ungleefully, awaiting John's communication, with the air of one looking to be tipped.

The features of that face were hard to read, drink had so swollen them, drink had so painted them, in tints that varied from brick red to mulberry. The small grey eyes blinked, the lips moved, with greed; greed was the ruling passion; and though there was some good-nature, some genuine kindliness, a true human touch, in the old toper, his greed was now so set afire by hope, that all other traits of character lay dormant. He sat there a monument of gluttonous desire.

John's heart slowly fell. He had opened his lips, but he stood there and uttered naught. He sounded the well of his courage, and it was dry. He groped in his treasury of words, and it was vacant. A devil of dumbness had him by the throat; the devil of terror babbled in his ears; and suddenly, without a word uttered, with no conscious purpose formed in his will, John whipped about, tumbled over the road-side wall, and began running for his life across the fallows.

He had not gone far, he was not past the midst of the first field, when his whole brain thundered within him, 'Fool! You have your watch!' The shock stopped him, and he faced once more towards the cab. The driver was leaning over the wall, brandishing his whip, his face empurpled, roaring like a bull. And John saw (or thought) that he had lost the chance. No watch would pacify the man's resentment now; he would cry for vengeance also. John would be under the eye of the police; his tale would be unfolded, his secret plumbed, his destiny would close on him at last, and for ever.

He uttered a deep sigh; and just as the cabman, taking heart of grace, was beginning at last to scale the wall, his defaulting customer fell again to running, and disappeared into the farther fields.

EIGHT

Singular instance of the utility of pass-keys

Where he ran at first, John never very clearly knew; nor yet how long a time elapsed ere he found himself in the by-road near the lodge of Ravelston, propped against the wall, his lungs heaving like bellows, his legs leaden-heavy, his mind possessed by one sole desire – to lie down and be unseen. He remembered the thick coverts round the quarry-hole pond, an untrodden corner of the world where he might surely find concealment till the night should fall. Thither he passed down the lane; and when he came there, behold! he had forgotten the frost, and the pond was alive with young people skating, and the pond-side coverts were thick with lookers-on. He looked on a while himself. There was one tall, graceful maiden, skating hand in hand with a youth, on whom she bestowed her bright eyes perhaps too patently; and it was strange with what anger John beheld her. He could have broken forth in curses; he could have stood there, like a mortified tramp, and shaken his fist and vented his gall upon her by the hour – or so he thought; and the next moment his heart bled for the girl. 'Poor creature, it's little she knows!' he sighed. 'Let her enjoy herself while she can!' But was it possible, when Flora used to smile at him on the Braid ponds, she could have looked so fulsome to a sick-hearted bystander?

The thought of one quarry, in his frozen wits, suggested another; and he plodded off towards Craig Leith. A wind had sprung up out of the north-west; it was cruel keen, it dried him like a fire, and racked his finger-joints. It brought clouds, too; pale, swift, hurrying clouds, that blotted heaven and shed gloom upon the earth. He scrambled up among the hazelled rubbish heaps that surround the caldron of the quarry, and lay flat upon the stones. The wind searched close along the earth, the stones were cutting and icy, the bare hazels wailed about him; and so the air of the afternoon began to be vocal with those strange and dismal harpings that herald snow. Pain and misery turned in John's limbs to a harrowing impatience and blind desire of change; now he would roll in his harsh lair, and when the flints abraded him, was almost pleased; now he would crawl to the edge of the huge pit and look dizzily down. He saw the spiral of the descending roadway, the steep crags, the clinging bushes, the peppering of snow-wreaths, and far down in the bottom the diminished crane. Here, no doubt, was a way to end it. But it somehow did not take his fancy.

And suddenly he was aware that he was hungry; ay, even through the tortures of the cold, even through the frosts of despair, a gross, desperate longing after food, no matter what, no matter how, began to wake and spur him. Suppose he pawned his watch? But no, on Christmas Day – this was Christmas Day! – the pawn-shop would be closed. Suppose he went to the public-house close by at Blackhall, and offered the watch, which was worth ten pounds, in payment for a meal of bread and cheese? The incongruity was too remarkable; the good folks would either put him to the door, or only let him in to send for the police. He turned his pockets out one after another; some San Franscisco tram-car checks, one cigar, no lights, the pass-key to his father's house, a pocket-handkerchief with just a touch of scent: no, money could be raised on none of these. There was nothing for it but to starve; and after all, what mattered it? That also was a door of exit.

He crept close among the bushes, the wind playing round him like a lash; his clothes seemed thin as paper, his joints burned, his skin curdled on his bones. He had a vision of a high-lying cattle-drive in California, and the bed of a dried stream with one muddy pool, by which the vaqueros had encamped: splendid sun over all, the big bonfire blazing, the strips of cow browning and smoking on a skewer of wood; how warm it was, how savoury the steam of scorching meat! And then again he remembered his manifold calamities, and burrowed and wallowed in the sense of his disgrace and shame. And next he was entering Frank's restaurant in Montgomery Street, San Francisco; he had ordered a pan-stew and venison chops, of which he was immoderately fond, and as he sat waiting, Munroe, the good attendant, brought him a whisky punch; he saw the strawberries float on the delectable cup, he heard the ice chink about the straws. And then he woke again to his detested fate, and found himself sitting, humped together in a windy combe of quarry refuse – darkness thick about him, thin flakes of snow flying here and there like rags of paper, and the strong shuddering of his body clashing his teeth like a hiccough.

We have seen John in nothing but the stormiest condition; we have seen him reckless, desperate, tried beyond his moderate powers; of his daily self, cheerful, regular, not unthrifty, we have seen nothing; and it may thus be a surprise to the reader, to learn that he was studiously careful of his health. This favourite pre-occupation now awoke. If he were to sit here and die of cold, there would be mighty little gained; better the police cell and the chances of a jury trial, than the miserable certainty of death at a dike-side before the next winter's dawn, or death a little later in the gas-lighted wards of an infirmary.

He rose on aching legs, and stumbled here and there among the rubbish-heaps, still circumvented by the yawning crater of the quarry; or perhaps he only thought so, for the darkness was already dense, the snow was growing thicker, and he moved like a blind man, and with a blind man's terrors. At last he climbed a fence, thinking to drop into the road, and found himself staggering, instead, among the iron furrows of a ploughland, endless, it seemed, as a whole county. And next he was in a wood, beating among young trees; and then he was aware of a house with many lighted windows, Christmas carriages waiting at the doors, and Christmas drivers (for Christmas has a double edge) becoming swiftly hooded with snow. From this glimpse of human cheerfulness, he fled like Cain; wandered in the night, unpiloted, careless of whither he went; fell and lay, and then rose again and wandered farther; and at last, like a transformation scene, behold him in the lighted jaws of the city, staring at a lamp which had already donned the tilted night-cap of the snow. It came thickly now, a 'Feeding Storm'; and while he yet stood blinking at the lamp, his feet were buried. He remembered something like it in the past, a street-lamp crowned and caked upon the windward side with snow, the wind uttering its mournful hoot, himself looking on, even as now; but the cold had struck too sharply on his wits, and memory failed him as to the date and sequel of the reminiscence.

His next conscious moment was on the Dean Bridge; but whether he was John Nicholson of a bank in a California street, or some former John, a clerk in his father's office, he had now clean forgotten. Another blank, and he was thrusting his pass-key into the door-lock of his father's house.

Hours must have passed. Whether crouched on the cold stones or wandering in the fields among the snow, was more than he could tell; but hours had passed. The finger of the hall clock was close on twelve; a narrow peep of gas in the hall-lamp shed shadows; and the door of the back room – his father's room – was open and emitted a warm light.

At so late an hour, all this was strange; the lights should have been out, the doors locked, the good folk safe in bed. He marvelled at the irregularity, leaning on the hall table; and marvelled to himself there; and thawed and grew once more hungry, in the warmer air of the house.

The clock uttered its premonitory catch; in five minutes Christmas Day would be among the days of the past – Christmas! – what a Christmas! Well, there was no use waiting; he had come into that house, he scarce knew how; if they were to thrust him forth again, it had best be done at once; and he moved to the door of the back room and entered.

Oh, well, then he was insane, as he had long believed.

There, in his father's room, at midnight, the fire was roaring and the gas blazing; the papers, the sacred papers – to lay a hand on which was criminal – had all been taken off and piled along the floor; a cloth was spread, and a supper laid, upon the business table; and in his father's chair a woman, habited like a nun, sat eating. As he appeared in the doorway, the nun rose, gave a low cry, and stood staring. She was a large woman, strong, calm, a little masculine, her features marked with courage and good sense; and as John blinked at her, a faint resemblance dodged about his memory, as when a tune haunts us, and yet will not be recalled.

'Why, it's John!' cried the nun.

'I daresay I'm mad,' said John, unconsciously following King Lear; 'but, upon my word, I do believe you're Flora.'

'Of course I am,' replied she.

And yet it is not Flora at all, thought John; Flora was slender, and timid, and of changing colour, and dewy-eyed; and had Flora such an Edinburgh accent? But he said none of these things, which was perhaps as well. What he said was, 'Then why are you a nun?'

'Such nonsense!' said Flora. 'I'm a sick-nurse; and I am here nursing your sister, with whom, between you and me, there is precious little the matter. But that is not the question. The point is: How do you come here? and are you not ashamed to show yourself?'

'Flora,' said John, sepulchrally, 'I haven't eaten anything for three days. Or, at least, I don't know what day it is; but I guess I'm starving.'

'You unhappy man!' she cried. 'Here, sit down and eat my supper; and I'll just run upstairs and see my patient, not but what I doubt she's fast asleep; for Maria is a *malade imaginaire*.'

With this specimen of the French, not of Stratford-atte-Bowe, but of a finishing establishment in Moray Place, she left John alone in his father's sanctum. He fell at once upon the food; and it is to be supposed that Flora had found her patient wakeful, and been detained with some details of nursing, for he had time to make a full end of all there was to eat, and not only to empty the teapot, but to fill it again from a kettle that was fitfully singing on his father's fire. Then he sat torpid, and pleased, and bewildered; his misfortunes were then half forgotten; his mind considering, not without regret, this unsentimental return to his old love.

He was thus engaged, when that bustling woman noiselessly re-entered.

'Have you eaten?' said she. 'Then tell me all about it.'

It was a long and (as the reader knows) a pitiful story; but Flora heard it with compressed lips. She was lost in none of those questionings of human destiny that have, from time to time, arrested the flight of my own pen; for women, such as she, are no philosophers, and behold the concrete only. And women, such as she, are very hard on the imperfect man.

'Very well,' said she, when he had done; 'then down upon your knees at once, and beg God's forgiveness.'

And the great baby plumped upon his knees, and did as he was bid; and none the worse for that! But while he was heartily enough requesting forgiveness on general principles, the rational side of him distinguished, and wondered if, perhaps, the apology were not due upon the other part. And when he rose again from that becoming exercise, he first eyed the face of his old love doubtfully, and then, taking heart, uttered his protest.

'I must say, Flora,' said he, 'in all this business, I can see very little fault of mine.'

'If you had written home,' replied the lady, 'there would have been none of it. If you had even gone to Murrayfield reasonably sober, you would never have slept there, and the worst would not have happened. Besides, the whole thing began years ago. You got into trouble, and when your father, honest man, was disappointed, you took the pet, or got afraid, and ran away from punishment. Well, you've had your own way of it, John, and I don't suppose you like it.'

'I sometimes fancy I'm not much better than a fool,' sighed John.

'My dear John,' said she, 'not much!'

He looked at her, and his eye fell. A certain anger rose within him; here was a Flora he disowned; she was hard; she was of a set colour; a settled, mature, undecorative manner; plain of speech, plain of habit – he had come near saying, plain of face. And this changeling called herself by the same name as the many-coloured, clinging maid of yore; she of the frequent laughter, and the many sighs, and the kind, stolen glances. And to make all worse, she took the upper hand with him, which (as John knew well) was not the true relation of the sexes. He steeled his heart against this sick-nurse.

'And how do you come to be here?' he asked.

She told him how she had nursed her father in his long illness, and when he died, and she was left alone, had taken to nurse others, partly from habit, partly to be of some service in the world; partly, it might be, for amusement. 'There's no accounting for taste,' said she. And she told him how she went largely to the houses of old friends, as the need arose; and how she was thus doubly welcome, as an old friend first, and then as an experienced nurse, to whom doctors would confide the gravest cases.

'And, indeed, it's a mere farce my being here for poor Maria,' she continued; 'but your father takes her ailments to heart, and I cannot always be refusing him. We are great friends, your father and I; he was very kind to me long ago – ten years ago.'

A strange stir came in John's heart. All this while had he been thinking only of himself? All this while, why had he not written to Flora? In penitential tenderness, he took her hand, and, to his awe and trouble, it remained in his, compliant. A voice told him this was Flora, after all – told him so quietly, yet with a thrill of singing.

'And you never married?' said he.

'No, John, I never married,' she replied.

The hall clock striking two recalled them to the sense of time.

'And, now,' said she, 'you have been fed and warmed, and I have heard your story, and now it's high time to call your brother.'

'Oh!' cried John, chap-fallen; 'do you think that absolutely necessary?'

'*I* can't keep you here; I'm a stranger,' said she. 'Do you want to run away again? I thought you had enough of that.'

He bowed his head under the reproof. She despised him, he reflected, as he sat once more alone; a monstrous thing for a woman to despise a man; and strangest of all, she seemed to like him. Would his brother despise him, too? And would his brother like him?

And presently the brother appeared, under Flora's escort; and, standing afar off beside the door-way, eyed the hero of this tale.

'So this is you?' he said, at length.

'Yes, Alick, it's me – it's John,' replied the elder brother, feebly.

'And how did you get in here?' inquired the younger.

'Oh, I had my pass-key,' says John.

'The deuce you had!' said Alexander. 'Ah, you lived in a better world! There are no pass-keys going now.'

'Well, father was always averse to them,' sighed John.

And the conversation then broke down, and the brothers looked askance at one another in silence.

'Well, and what the devil are we to do?' said Alexander. 'I suppose if the authorities got wind of you, you would be taken up?'

'It depends on whether they've found the body or

not,' returned John. 'And then there's that cabman, to be sure!'

'Oh, bother the body!' said Alexander. 'I mean about the other thing. That's serious.'

'Is that what my father spoke about?' asked John. 'I don't even know what it is.'

'About your robbing your bank in California, of course,' replied Alexander.

It was plain from Flora's face, that this was the first she had heard of it; it was plainer still, from John's, that he was innocent.

'I!' he exclaimed. 'I rob my bank! My God! Flora, this is too much; even you must allow that.'

'Meaning you didn't?' asked Alexander.

'I never robbed a soul in all my days,' cried John: 'except my father, if you call that robbery; and I brought him back the money in this room, and he wouldn't even take it!'

'Look here, John,' said his brother; 'let us have no misunderstanding upon this. McEwen saw my father; he told him a bank you had worked for in San Francisco was wiring over the habitable globe to have you collared – that it was supposed you had nailed thousands; and it was dead certain you had nailed three hundred. So MacEwen said, and I wish you would be careful how you answer. I may tell you also, that your father paid the three hundred on the spot.'

'Three hundred?' repeated John. 'Three hundred pounds you mean? That's fifteen hundred dollars. Why, then, it's Kirkman!' he broke out. 'Thank Heaven! I can explain all that. I gave them to Kirkman to pay for me the night before I left – fifteen hundred dollars, and a letter to the manager. What do they suppose I would steal fifteen hundred dollars for? I'm rich; I struck it rich in stocks. It's the silliest stuff I ever heard of. All that's needful is to cable to the manager: Kirkman has the fifteen hundred – find Kirkman. He was a fellow-clerk of mine, and a hard case; but to do him justice, I didn't think he was as hard as this.'

'And what do you say to that, Alick?' asked Flora.

'I say the cablegram shall go to-night!' cried Alexander, with energy. 'Answer prepaid, too. If this can be cleared away – and upon my word I do believe it can – we shall all be able to hold up our heads again. Here, you John, you stick down the address of your bank manager. You, Flora, you can pack John into my bed, for which I have no further use to-night. As for me, I am off to the post office, and thence to the High Street about the dead body. The police ought to know, you see, and they ought to know through John; and I can tell them some rigmarole about my brother being a man of highly nervous organisation, and the rest of it. And then, I'll tell you what, John – did you notice the name upon the cab?'

John gave the name of the driver, which, as I have not been able to commend the vehicle, I here suppress.

'Well,' resumed Alexander, 'I'll call round at their place before I come back, and pay your shot for you. In that way, before breakfast-time, you'll be as good as new.'

John murmured inarticulate thanks. To see his brother thus energetic in his service moved him beyond expression; if he could not utter what he felt, he showed it legibly in his face; and Alexander read it there, and liked it the better in that dumb delivery.

'But there's one thing,' said the latter, 'cablegrams are dear; and I daresay you remember enough of the governor to guess the state of my finances.'

'The trouble is,' said John, 'that all my stamps are in that beastly house.'

'All your what?' asked Alexander.

'Stamps – money,' explained John. 'It's an American expression; I'm afraid I contracted one or two.'

'I have some,' said Flora. 'I have a pound-note upstairs.'

'My dear Flora,' returned Alexander, 'a pound note won't see us very far; and besides, this is my father's business, and I shall be very much surprised if it isn't my father who pays for it.'

'I would not apply to him yet; I do not think that can be wise,' objected Flora.

'You have a very imperfect idea of my resources, and none at all of my effrontery,' replied Alexander. 'Please observe.'

He put John from his way, chose a stout knife among

the supper things, and with surprising quickness broke into his father's drawer.

'There's nothing easier when you come to try,' he observed, pocketing the money.

'I wish you had not done that,' said Flora. 'You will never hear the last of it.

'Oh, I don't know,' returned the young man; 'the governor is human after all. And now, John, let me see your famous pass-key. Get into bed, and don't move for anyone till I come back. They won't mind you not answering when they knock; I generally don't myself.'

NINE

In which Mr Nicholson concedes the principle of an allowance

In spite of the horrors of the day and the tea-drinking of the night, John slept the sleep of infancy. He was awakened by the maid, as it might have been ten years ago, tapping at the door. The winter sunrise was painting the east; and as the window was to the back of the house, it shone into the room with many strange colours of refracted light. Without, the houses were all cleanly roofed with snow; the garden walls were coped with it a foot in height; the greens lay glittering. Yet strange as snow had grown to John during his years upon the Bay of San Francisco, it was what he saw within that most affected him. For it was to his own room that Alexander had been promoted; there was the old paper with the device of flowers, in which a cunning fancy might yet detect the face of Skinny Jim, of the Academy, John's former dominie; there was the old chest of drawers; there were the chairs – one, two, three – three as before. Only the carpet was new, and the litter of Alexander's clothes and books and drawing materials, and a pencil-drawing on the wall, which (in John's eyes) appeared a marvel of proficiency.

He was thus lying, and looking, and dreaming, hanging,

as it were, between two epochs of his life, when Alexander
came to the door, and made his presence known in a
loud whisper. John let him in, and jumped back into the
warm bed.

'Well, John,' said Alexander, 'the cablegram is sent in
your name, and twenty words of answer paid. I have
been to the cab-office and paid your cab, even saw the
old gentleman himself, and properly apologised. He was
mighty placable, and indicated his belief you had been
drinking. Then I knocked up old MacEwen out of bed,
and explained affairs to him as he sat and shivered in a
dressing-gown. And before that I had been to the High
Street, where they have heard nothing of your dead body,
so that I incline to the idea that you dreamed it.'

'Catch me!' said John.

'Well, the police never do know anything,' assented
Alexander; 'and at any rate, they have dispatched a man
to inquire and to recover your trousers and your money,
so that really your bill is now fairly clean; and I see but
one lion in your path – the governor.'

'I'll be turned out again, you'll see,' said John, dismally.

'I don't imagine so,' returned the other; 'not if you do
what Flora and I have arranged; and your business now is
to dress, and lose no time about it. Is your watch right?
Well, you have a quarter of an hour. By five minutes
before the half-hour you must be at table, in your old
seat, under Uncle Duthie's picture. Flora will be there
to keep you countenance; and we shall see what we shall
see.'

'Wouldn't it be wiser for me to stay in bed?' said
John.

'If you mean to manage your own concerns, you can
do precisely what you like,' replied Alexander; 'but if you
are not in your place five minutes before the half-hour I
wash my hands of you, for one.'

And thereupon he departed. He had spoken warmly,
but the truth is, his heart was somewhat troubled. And
as he hung over the banisters, watching for his father to
appear, he had hard ado to keep himself braced for the
encounter that must follow.

'If he takes it well, I shall be lucky,' he reflected. 'If he takes it ill, why it'll be a herring across John's tracks, and perhaps all for the best. He's a confounded muff, this brother of mine, but he seems a decent soul.'

At that stage a door opened below with a certain emphasis, and Mr Nicholson was seen solemnly to descend the stairs, and pass into his own apartment. Alexander followed, quaking inwardly, but with a steady face. He knocked, was bidden to enter, and found his father standing in front of the forced drawer, to which he pointed as he spoke.

'This is a most extraordinary thing,' said he; 'I have been robbed!'

'I was afraid you would notice it,' observed his son; 'it made such a beastly hash of the table.'

'You were afraid I would notice it?' repeated Mr Nicholson. 'And, pray, what may that mean?'

'That I was a thief, sir,' returned Alexander. 'I took all the money in case the servants should get hold of it; and here is the change, and a note of my expenditure. You were gone to bed, you see, and I did not feel at liberty to knock you up; but I think when you have heard the circumstances, you will do me justice. The fact is, I have reason to believe there has been some dreadful error about my brother John; the sooner it can be cleared up the better for all parties; it was a piece of business, sir – and so I took it, and decided, on my own responsibility, to send a telegram to San Francisco. Thanks to my quickness we may hear to-night. There appears to be no doubt, sir, that John has been abominably used.'

'When did this take place?' asked the father.

'Last night, sir, after you were asleep,' was the reply.

'It's most extraordinary,' said Mr Nicholson. 'Do you mean to say you have been out all night?'

'All night, as you say, sir. I have been to the telegraph and the police-office, and Mr MacEwen's. Oh, I had my hands full,' said Alexander.

'Very irregular,' said the father. 'You think of no one but yourself.'

'I do not see that I have much to gain in bringing back my elder brother,' returned Alexander, shrewdly.

The answer pleased the old man; he smiled. 'Well, well, I will go into this after breakfast,' said he.

'I'm sorry about the table,' said the son.

'The table is a small matter; I think nothing of that,' said the father.

'It's another example,' continued the son, 'of the awkwardness of a man having no money of his own. If I had a proper allowance, like other fellows of my own age, this would have been quite unnecessary.'

'A proper allowance!' repeated his father, in tones of blighting sarcasm, for the expression was not new to him. 'I have never grudged you money for any proper purpose.'

'No doubt, no doubt,' said Alexander, 'but then you see you ar'n't always on the spot to have the thing explained to you. Last night for instance—'

'You could have wakened me last night,' interrupted his father.

'Was it not some similar affair that first got John into a mess?' asked the son, skilfully evading the point.

But the father was not less adroit. 'And pray, sir, how did you come and go out of the house?' he asked.

'I forgot to lock the door, it seems,' replied Alexander.

'I have had cause to complain of that too often,' said Mr Nicholson. 'But still I do not understand. Did you keep the servants up?'

'I propose to go into all that at length after breakfast,' returned Alexander. 'There is the half-hour going? We must not keep Miss Mackenzie waiting.'

And greatly daring, he opened the door.

Even Alexander, who it must have been perceived, was on terms of comparative freedom with his parent; even Alexander had never before dared to cut short an interview in this high-handed fashion. But the truth is the very mass of his son's delinquencies daunted the old gentleman. He was like the man with the cart of apples – this was beyond him! That Alexander should have spoiled his table, taken his money, stayed out all night, and then coolly acknowledged all, was something undreamed of in the Nicholsonian philosophy, and transcended comment. The return of the change, which the old gentleman still carried in his hand, had been a feature of imposing impudence; it had dealt him a staggering blow. Then there was the reference to John's original flight – a subject which he always kept resolutely curtained in his own mind; for he was a man who loved to have made no mistakes, and when he feared he might have made one kept the papers sealed. In view of all these surprises and reminders, and of his son's composed and masterful demeanour, there began to creep on Mr Nicholson a sickly misgiving. He seemed beyond his depth; if he did or said anything, he might come to regret it. The young man, besides, as he had pointed out himself, was playing a generous part. And if wrong had been done – and done to one who was, after, and in spite of, all, a Nicholson – it should certainly be righted.

All things considered, monstrous as it was to be cut short in his inquiries, the old gentleman submitted, pocketed the change, and followed his son into the dining-room. During these few steps he once more mentally revolted, and once more, and this time finally, laid down his arms: a still, small voice in his bosom having informed him authentically of a piece of news; that he was afraid of Alexander. The strange thing was that he was pleased to be afraid of him. He was proud of his son; he might be proud of him; the boy had character and grit, and knew what he was doing.

These were his reflections as he turned the corner of the dining-room door. Miss Mackenzie was in the place of honour, conjuring with a teapot and a cozy; and, behold! there was another person present, a large, portly, whiskered man of a very comfortable and respectable air, who now rose from his seat and came forward, holding out his hand.

'Good-morning, father,' said he.

Of the contention of feeling that ran high in Mr Nicholson's starched bosom, no outward sign was visible; nor did he delay long to make a choice of conduct. Yet in that interval he had reviewed a great field of possibilities both past and future; whether it was possible he had not been perfectly wise in his treatment of John; whether it was possible that John was innocent; whether, if he turned John out a second time, as his outraged authority suggested, it was possible to avoid a scandal; and whether, if he went to that extremity, it was possible that Alexander might rebel.

'Hum,' said Mr Nicholson, and put his hand, limp and dead, into John's.

And then, in an embarrassed silence, all took their places; and even the paper – from which it was the old gentleman's habit to suck mortification daily, as he marked the decline of our institutions – even the paper lay furled by his side.

But presently Flora came to the rescue. She slid into the silence with a technicality, asking if John still took his old inordinate amount of sugar. Thence it was but a step to the burning question of the day; and in tones a little shaken, she commented on the interval since she had last made tea for the prodigal, and congratulated him on his return. And then addressing Mr Nicholson, she congratulated him also in a manner that defied his ill-humour; and from that launched into the tale of John's misadventures not without some suitable suppressions.

Gradually Alexander joined; between them, whether he would or no, they forced a word or two from John; and these fell so tremulously, and spoke so eloquently of a mind oppressed with dread, that Mr Nicholson relented. At length even he contributed a question: and before the meal was at an end all four were talking even freely.

Prayers followed, with the servants gaping at this new-comer whom no one had admitted; and after prayers there came that moment on the clock which was the signal for Mr Nicholson's departure.

'John,' said he, 'of course you will stay here. Be very careful not to excite Maria, if Miss Mackenzie thinks it desirable that you should see her. – Alexander, I wish to speak with you alone.' And then, when they were both in the back-room: 'You need not come to the office to-day,' said he; 'you can stay and amuse your brother, and I

think it would be respectful to call on Uncle Greig.
And by-the-by' (this spoken with a certain – dare we
say? – bashfulness), 'I agree to concede the principle of
an allowance; and I will consult with Dr Durie, who is
quite a man of the world and has sons of his own, as
to the amount. And, my fine fellow, you may consider
yourself in luck!' he added, with a smile.

'Thank you,' said Alexander.

Before noon a detective had restored to John his money,
and brought news, sad enough in truth, but perhaps the
least sad possible. Alan had been found in his own house
in Regent's Terrace, under care of the terrified butler.
He was quite mad, and instead of going to prison, had
gone to Morningside Asylum. The murdered man, it
appeared, was an evicted tenant who had for nearly a
year pursued his late landlord with threats and insults;
and beyond this, the cause and details of the tragedy
were lost.

When Mr Nicholson returned for dinner they were able
to put a dispatch into his hands: 'John V. Nicholson,
Randolph Crescent, Edinburgh. – Kirkman has disappeared; police looking for him. All understood. Keep
mind quite easy. – Austin.' Having had this explained
to him, the old gentleman took down the cellar key and
departed for two bottles of 1820 port. Uncle Greig dined
there that day, and Cousin Robina, and, by an odd chance,
Mr MacEwen; and the presence of these strangers relieved
what might have been otherwise a somewhat strained
relation. Ere they departed, the family was welded once
more into a fair semblance of unity.

In the end of April John led Flora – or, let us say, as more
descriptive, Flora led John – to the altar, if altar that may be
called which was indeed the drawing-room mantel-piece in
Mr Nicholson's house, with the Reverend Dr Durie posted
on the hearth-rug in the guise of Hymen's priest.

The last I saw of them, on a recent visit to the
north, was at a dinner-party in the house of my old
friend Gellatly Macbride; and after we had, in classic
phrase, 'rejoined the ladies,' I had an opportunity to

overhear Flora conversing with another married woman on the much canvassed matter of a husband's tobacco.

'Oh, yes!' said she; 'I only allow Mr Nicholson four cigars a day. Three he smokes at fixed times – after a meal, you know, my dear; and the fourth he can take when he likes with any friend.'

'Bravo!' thought I to myself; 'this is the wife for my friend John!'

The Pavilion on the Links

*Tells how I camped in Graden Sea-Wood,
and beheld a light in the Pavilion*

I WAS a great solitary when I was young. I made it my
pride to keep aloof and suffice for my own entertainment;
and I may say that I had neither friends nor acquaintances
until I met that friend who became my wife and the mother
of my children. With one man only was I on private terms;
this was R. Northmour, Esquire, of Graden Easter, in
Scotland. We had met at college; and though there was
not much liking between us nor even much intimacy, we
were so nearly of a humour that we could associate with
ease to both. Misanthropes, we believed ourselves to be;
but I have thought since that we were only sulky fellows.
It was scarcely a companionship, but a coexistence in
unsociability. Northmour's exceptional violence of temper
made it no easy affair for him to keep the peace with anyone
but me; and as he respected my silent ways, and let me
come and go as I pleased, I could tolerate his presence
without concern. I think we called each other friends.

When Northmour took his degree and I decided to
leave the university without one, he invited me on a
long visit to Graden Easter; and it was thus that I first
became acquainted with the scene of my adventures.
The mansion-house of Graden stood in a bleak stretch
of country some three miles from the shore of the German
Ocean. It was as large as a barrack; and as it had been
built of a soft stone, liable to consume in the eager air
of the seaside, it was damp and draughty within and half
ruinous without. It was impossible for two young men to

lodge with comfort in such a dwelling. But there stood in the northern part of the estate, in a wilderness of links and blowing sand-hills, and between a plantation and the sea, a small Pavilion or Belvidere, of modern design, which was exactly suited to our wants; and in this heritage, speaking little, reading much and rarely associating except at meals, Northmour and I spent four tempestuous winter months. I might have stayed longer; but one March night there sprang up between us a dispute, which rendered my departure necessary. Northmour spoke hotly I remember, and I suppose I must have made some tart rejoinder. He leaped from his chair and grappled me; I had to fight, without exaggeration, for my life; and it was only with a great effort that I mastered him, for he was near as strong in body as myself, and seemed filled with the devil. The next morning, we met on our usual terms; but I judged it more delicate to withdraw; nor did he attempt to dissuade me.

It was nine years before I revisited the neighbourhood. I travelled at that time with a tilt cart, a tent, and a cooking-stove, tramping all day beside the waggon, and at night, whenever it was possible, gipsying in a cove of the hills, or by the side of a wood. I believe I visited in this manner most of the wild and desolate regions both in England and Scotland; and, as I had neither friends nor relations, I was troubled with no correspondence, and had nothing in the nature of headquarters, unless it was the office of my solicitors, from whom I drew my income twice a year. It was a life in which I delighted; and I fully thought to have grown old upon the march, and at last died in a ditch.

It was my whole business to find desolate corners, where I could camp without the fear of interruption; and hence, being in another part of the same shire, I bethought me suddenly of the Pavilion on the Links. No thoroughfare passed within three miles of it. The nearest town, and that was but a fisher village, was at a distance of six or seven. For ten miles of length, and from a depth varying from three miles to half a mile, this belt of barren country lay along the sea. The beach, which was the natural approach, was full of quicksands. Indeed I may say there is hardly a better place of concealment in the United Kingdom. I determined to pass a week in the Sea-Wood of Graden Easter, and, making a long stage, reached it about sundown on a wild September day.

The country, I have said, was mixed sand-hill and links; *links* being a Scottish name for sand which has ceased drifting and become more or less solidly covered with turf. The Pavilion stood on an even space; a little behind it, the wood began in a hedge of elders huddled together by the wind; in front, a few tumbled sand-hills stood between it and the sea. An outcropping of rock had formed a bastion for the sand, so that there was here a promontory in the coast-line between two shallow bays; and just beyond the tides, the rock again cropped out and formed an islet of small dimensions but strikingly designed. The quicksands were of great extent at low water, and had an infamous reputation in the country. Close in shore, between the islet and the promontory, it was said they would swallow a man in four minutes and a half; but there may have been little ground for this precision. The district was alive with rabbits, and haunted by gulls which made a continual piping about the pavilion. On summer days the outlook was bright and even gladsome; but at sundown in September, with a high wind, and a heavy surf rolling in close along the links, the place told of nothing but dead mariners and sea disaster. A ship beating to windward on the horizon, and a huge truncheon of wreck half buried in the sands at my feet, completed the innuendo of the scene.

The pavilion – it had been built by the last proprietor, Northmour's uncle, a silly and prodigal virtuoso – presented little signs of age. It was two storeys in height, Italian in design, surrounded by a patch of garden in which nothing had prospered but a few coarse flowers; and looked, with its shuttered windows, not like a house that had been deserted, but like one that had never been tenanted by man. Northmour was plainly from home; whether, as usual, sulking in the cabin of his yacht, or in one of his fitful and extravagant appearances in the world of society, I had, of course, no means of guessing. The place had an air of solitude that daunted even a solitary like myself; the wind cried in the chimneys with a strange and wailing note; and it was with a sense of escape, as if I were going indoors, that I turned away and, driving my cart before me, entered the skirts of the wood.

The Sea-Wood of Graden had been planted to shelter the cultivated fields behind, and check the encroachments of the blowing sand. As you advanced into it from coastward, elders were succeeded by other hardy shrubs; but the timber was all stunted and bushy; it led a life of conflict; the trees were accustomed to swing there all night long in fierce winter tempests; and even in early spring, the leaves were already flying, and autumn was beginning, in this exposed plantation. Inland the ground rose into a little hill, which, along with the islet, served as a sailing mark for seamen. When the hill was open of the islet to the north, vessels must bear well to the eastward to clear Graden Ness and the Graden Bullers. In the lower ground a streamlet ran among the trees, and, being dammed with leaves and clay of its own carrying, spread out every here and there, and lay in stagnant pools. One or two ruined cottages were dotted about the wood; and, according to Northmour, these were ecclesiastical foundations, and in their time had sheltered pious hermits.

I found a den, or small hollow, where there was a spring of pure water; and there, clearing away the brambles, I pitched the tent and made a fire to cook my supper. My horse I picketed farther in the wood where there was a patch of sward. The banks of the den not only concealed the light of my fire, but sheltered me from the wind, which was cold as well as high.

The life I was leading made me both hardy and frugal. I never drank but water, and rarely ate anything more costly than oatmeal; and I required so little sleep, that, although I rose with the peep of day, I would often lie long awake in the dark or starry watches of the night. Thus in Graden Sea-Wood, although I fell thankfully asleep by eight in the evening I was awake again before eleven with a full possession of my faculties, and no sense of drowsiness or fatigue. I rose and sat by the fire, watching the trees and clouds tumultuously tossing and fleeing overhead, and hearkening to the wind and the rollers along the shore; till at length, growing weary of inaction, I quitted the den, and strolled towards the borders of the wood. A young moon, buried in mist, gave a faint illumination to my steps; and the light grew brighter as I walked forth into the links. At the same moment, the wind, smelling salt of the open ocean and carrying particles of sand, struck me with its full force, so that I had to bow my head.

When I raised it again to look about me, I was aware of a light in the pavilion. It was not stationary; but passed from one window to another, as though some one were reviewing the different apartments with a lamp or candle. I watched it for some seconds in great surprise. When I had arrived in the afternoon the house had been plainly deserted; now it was as plainly occupied. It was my first idea that a gang of thieves might have broken in and be now ransacking Northmour's cupboards, which were many and not ill supplied. But what should bring thieves to Graden Easter? And, again, all the shutters had been thrown open, and it would have been more in the character of such gentry to close them. I dismissed the notion, and fell back upon another. Northmour himself must have arrived, and was now airing and inspecting the pavilion.

I have said that there was no real affection between this man and me; but, had I loved him like a brother, I was then so much more in love with solitude that I should none the less have shunned his company. As it was, I turned and ran for it; and it was with genuine satisfaction that I found myself safely back beside the fire. I had escaped an acquaintance; I should have one more night in comfort. In the morning, I might either slip away before Northmour was abroad, or pay him as short a visit as I chose.

But when morning came, I thought the situation so diverting that I forgot my shyness. Northmour was at my mercy; I arranged a good practical jest, though I knew well that my neighbour was not the man to jest with in security; and, chuckling beforehand over its success, took my place among the elders at the edge of the wood, whence I could command the door of the pavilion. The shutters were all once more closed, which I remember thinking odd; and the house, with its white walls and green venetians, looked spruce and habitable in the morning light. Hour after hour passed, and still no sign of Northmour. I knew him for a sluggard in the morning; but, as it drew on towards noon, I lost my patience. To say the truth, I had promised myself to break my fast in the pavilion, and hunger began to prick me sharply. It was a pity to let the opportunity go by without some cause for mirth; but the grosser appetite prevailed, and I relinquished my jest with regret, and sallied from the wood.

The appearance of the house affected me, as I drew near, with disquietude. It seemed unchanged since last evening; and I had expected it, I scarce knew why, to wear some external signs of habitation. But no: the windows were all closely shuttered, the chimneys breathed no smoke, and the front door itself was closely padlocked. Northmour, therefore, had entered by the back; this was the natural and, indeed, the necessary conclusion; and you may judge of my surprise when, on turning the house, I found the back door similarly secured.

My mind at once reverted to the original theory of thieves; and I blamed myself sharply for my last night's inaction. I examined all the windows on the lower storey, but none of them had been tampered with; I tried the padlocks, but they were both secure. It thus became a problem how the thieves, if thieves they were, had managed to enter the house. They must have got, I reasoned, upon the roof of the outhouse where Northmour used to keep his photographic battery; and from thence, either by the window of the study of that of my old bedroom, completed their burglarious entry.

I followed what I supposed was their example; and, getting on the roof, tried the shutters of each room. Both were secure; but I was not to be beaten; and with a little force, one of them flew open, grazing, as it did so, the back of my hand. I remember, I put the wound to my mouth, and stood for perhaps half a minute licking it like a dog, and mechanically gazing behind me over the waste links and the sea; and, in that space of time, my eye made note of a large schooner yacht some miles to the north-east. Then I threw up the window and climbed in.

I went over the house, and nothing can express my mystification. There was no sign of disorder, but, on the contrary, the rooms were unusually clean and pleasant. I found fires laid, ready for lighting; three bedrooms prepared with a luxury quite foreign to Northmour's habits, and with water in the ewers and the beds turned down; a table set for three in the dining-room; and an ample supply of cold meats, game, and vegetables on the pantry shelves. There were guests expected, that was plain; but why guests, when Northmour hated society? And, above all, why was the house thus stealthily prepared at dead of night? and why were the shutters closed and the doors padlocked?

I effaced all traces of my visit, and came forth from the window feeling sobered and concerned.

The schooner yacht was still in the same place; and it flashed for a moment through my mind that this might be the *Red Earl* bringing the owner of the pavilion and his guests. But the vessel's head was set the other way.

TWO

Tells of the nocturnal landing from the yacht

I returned to the den to cook myself a meal, of which I stood in great need, as well as to care for my horse, whom I had somewhat neglected in the morning. From time to time I went down to the edge of the wood; but there was no change in the pavilion, and not a human creature was seen all day upon the links. The schooner in the offing was the one touch of life within my range of vision. She, apparently with no set object, stood off and on or lay to, hour after hour; but as the evening deepened, she drew steadily nearer. I became more convinced that she carried Northmour and his friends, and that they would probably come ashore after dark; not only because that was of a piece with the secrecy of the preparations, but because the tide would not have flowed sufficiently before eleven to cover Graden Floe and the other sea quags that fortified the shore against invaders.

All day the wind had been going down, and the sea along with it; but there was a return towards sunset of the heavy weather of the day before. The night set in pitch dark. The wind came off the sea in squalls, like the firing of a battery of cannon; now and then there was a flaw of rain, and the surf rolled heavier with the rising tide. I was down at my observatory among the elders, when a light was run up to the masthead of the schooner, and showed she was closer in than when I had last seen her by the dying daylight. I concluded that this must be a signal to Northmour's associates on shore; and, stepping forth into the links, looked around me for something in response.

A small footpath ran along the margin of the wood, and formed the most direct communication between the pavilion and the mansion-house; and, as I cast my eyes to that side, I saw a spark of light, not a quarter of a mile away, and rapidly approaching. From its uneven course it appeared to be the light of a lantern carried by a person who followed the windings of the path, and was often staggered and taken aback by the more violent squalls. I concealed myself once more among the elders, and waited eagerly for the newcomer's advance. It proved to be a woman; and, as she passed within half a rod of my ambush, I was able to recognise the features. The deaf and silent old dame, who had nursed Northmour in his childhood, was his associate in this underhand affair.

I followed her at a little distance, taking advantage of the innumerable heights and hollows, concealed by the darkness, and favoured not only by the nurse's deafness, but by the uproar of the wind and surf. She entered the pavilion, and, going at once to the upper storey, opened and set a light in one of the windows that looked towards the sea. Immediately afterwards the light at the schooner's masthead was run down and extinguished. Its purpose had been attained, and those on board were sure that they were expected. The old woman resumed her preparations; although the other shutters remained closed, I could see a glimmer going to and fro about the house; and a gush of sparks from one chimney after another soon told me that the fires were being kindled.

Northmour and his guests, I was now persuaded, would come ashore as soon as there was water on the floe. It was a wild night for boat service; and I felt some alarm mingle with my curiosity as I reflected on the danger of the landing. My old acquaintance, it was true, was the most eccentric of men; but the present eccentricity was both disquieting and lugubrious to consider. A variety of feelings thus led me towards the beach, where I lay flat on my face in a hollow within six feet of the track that led to the pavilion. Thence, I should have the satisfaction of recognising the arrivals, and, if they should prove to be acquaintances, greeting them as soon as they had landed.

Some time before eleven, while the tide was still dangerously low, a boat's lantern appeared close in shore; and, my attention being thus awakened, I could perceive another still far to seaward, violently tossed, and sometimes hidden by the billows. The weather, which was getting dirtier as the night went on, and the perilous situation of the yacht upon a lee shore, had probably driven them to attempt a landing at the earliest possible moment.

A little afterwards, four yachtsmen carrying a very heavy chest, and guided by a fifth with a lantern, passed close in front of me as I lay, and were admitted to the pavilion by the nurse. They returned to the beach, and passed me a second time with another chest, larger but apparently not so heavy as the first. A third time they made the transit; and on this occasion one of the yachtsmen carried a leather portmanteau, and the others a lady's trunk and carriage bag. My curiosity was sharply excited. If a woman were among the guests of Northmour, it would show a change in his habits and an apostasy from his pet theories of life, well calculated to fill me with surprise. When he and I dwelt there together, the pavilion had been a temple of misogyny. And now, one of the detested sex was to be installed under its roof. I remembered one or two particulars, a few notes of daintiness and almost of coquetry which had struck me the day before as I surveyed the preparations in the house; their purpose was now clear, and I thought myself dull not to have perceived it from the first.

While I was thus reflecting, a second lantern drew near me from the beach. It was carried by a yachtsman whom I had not yet seen, and who was conducting two other persons to the pavilion. These two persons were unquestionably the guests for whom the house was made ready; and, straining eye and ear, I set myself to watch them as they passed. One was an unusually tall man, in a travelling hat slouched over his eyes, and a highland cape closely buttoned and turned up so as to conceal his face. You could make out no more of him than that he was, as I have said, unusually tall, and walked feebly with a heavy stoop. By his side, and either clinging to him or giving him support – I could not make out which – was a young, tall, and slender figure of a woman. She was extremely pale; but in the light of a lantern her face was so marred by strong and changing shadows, that she might equally well have been as ugly as sin or as beautiful as I afterwards found her to be.

When they were just abreast of me, the girl made some remark which was drowned by the noise of the wind.

'Hush!' said her companion; and there was something in the tone with which the word was uttered that thrilled and rather shook my spirits. It seemed to breathe from a bosom labouring under the deadliest terror; I have never heard another syllable so expressive; and I still hear it again when I am feverish at night, and my mind runs upon old times. The man turned towards the girl as he spoke; I had a glimpse of much red beard and a nose which seemed to have been broken in youth; and his light eyes seemed shining in his face with some strong and unpleasant emotion.

But these two passed on and were admitted in their turn to the pavilion.

One by one, or in groups, the seamen returned to the beach. The wind brought me the sound of a rough voice crying, 'Shove off!' Then, after a pause, another lantern drew near. It was Northmour alone.

My wife and I, a man and a woman, have often agreed to wonder how a person could be, at the same time, so handsome and so repulsive as Northmour. He had the appearance of a finished gentleman; his face bore every mark of intelligence and courage; but you had only to look at him, even in his most amiable moment, to see that he had the temper of a slaver captain. I never knew a character that was both explosive and revengeful to the same degree; he combined the vivacity of the south with the sustained and deadly hatreds of the north; and both traits were plainly written on his face, which was a sort of danger signal. In person he was tall, strong, and active; his hair and complexion very dark; his features handsomely designed, but spoiled by a menacing expression.

At that moment he was somewhat paler than by nature; he wore a heavy frown; and his lips worked, and he looked sharply round him as he walked, like a man besieged with apprehensions. And yet I thought he had a look of triumph underlying all, as though he had already done much, and was near the end of an achievement.

Partly from a scruple of delicacy – which I dare say came too late – partly from the pleasure of startling an acquaintance, I desired to make my presence known to him without delay.

I got suddenly to my feet, and stepped forward.

'Northmour!' said I.

I have never had so shocking a surprise in all my days. He leaped on me without a word; something shone in his hand, and he struck for my heart with a dagger. At the same moment I knocked him head over heels. Whether it was my quickness or his uncertainty, I know not; but the blade only grazed my shoulder, while the hilt and his fist struck me violently on the mouth.

I fled, but not far. I had often and often observed the capabilities of the sand-hills for protracted ambush or stealthy advances and retreats; and, not ten yards from the scene of the scuffle, plumped down again upon the grass. The lantern had fallen and gone out. But what was my astonishment to see Northmour slip at a bound into the pavilion, and hear him bar the door behind him with a clang of iron!

He had not pursued me. He had run away. Northmour, whom I knew for the most implacable and daring of men, had run away! I could scarcely believe my reason; and yet in this strange business, where all was incredible, there was nothing to make a work about in an incredibility more or less. For why was the pavilion secretly prepared? Why had Northmour landed with his guests at dead of night, in half a gale of wind, and with the floe scarce covered? Why had he sought to kill me? Had he not recognised my voice? I wondered. And, above all, how had he come to have a dagger ready in his hand? A dagger, or even a sharp knife, seemed out of keeping with the age in which we lived; and a gentleman landing from his yacht on the shore of his own estate, even although it was at night and with some mysterious circumstances, does not usually, as a matter of fact, walk thus prepared for deadly onslaught. The more I reflected, the further I felt at sea. I recapitulated the elements of mystery, counting them on my fingers; the pavilion secretly prepared for guests; the guests landed at the risk of their lives and to the imminent peril of the yacht; the guests, or at least one of them, in undisguised and seemingly causeless terror; Northmour with a naked weapon; Northmour stabbing his most intimate acquaintance at a word; last, and not least strange, Northmour fleeing from the man whom he had sought to murder, and barricading himself, like a hunted creature, behind the door of the pavilion. Here were at least six separate causes for extreme surprise; each part and parcel with the others, and forming all together one consistent story. I felt almost ashamed to believe my own senses.

As I thus stood, transfixed with wonder, I began to grow painfully conscious of the injuries I had received in the scuffle; skulked round among the sand-hills; and, by a devious path, regained the shelter of the wood. On the way, the old nurse passed again within several yards of me, still carrying her lantern on the return journey to the mansion-house of Graden. This made a seventh suspicious feature in the case. Northmour and his guests, it appeared, were to cook and do the cleaning for themselves, while the old woman continued to inhabit the big empty barrack among the policies. There must surely be cause for secrecy when so many inconveniences were confronted to preserve it.

So thinking, I made my way to the den. For greater security, I trod out the embers of the fire, and lit my lantern to examine the wound upon my shoulder. It was a trifling hurt, although it bled somewhat freely, and I dressed it as well as I could (for its position made it difficult to reach) with some rag and cold water from the spring. While I was thus busied, I mentally declared war against Northmour and his mystery. I am not an angry man by nature, and I believe there was more curiosity than resentment in my heart. But war I certainly declared; and, by way of preparation, I got out my revolver, and, having drawn the charges, cleaned and reloaded it with scrupulous care. Next I became preoccupied about my horse. It might break loose, or fall to neighing, and so betray my camp in the Sea-Wood. I determined to rid myself of its neighbourhood; and long before dawn I was leading it over the links in the direction of the fisher village.

THREE

Tells how I became acquainted with my wife

For two days I skulked round the pavilion, profiting by the uneven surface of the links. I became an adept in the necessary tactics. These low hillocks and shallow dells, running one into another, became a kind of cloak of darkness for my enthralling, but perhaps dishonourable, pursuit. Yet, in spite of this advantage, I could learn but little of Northmour or his guests.

Fresh provisions were brought under cover of darkness

by the old woman from the mansion-house. Northmour, and the young lady, sometimes together, but more often singly, would walk for an hour or two at a time on the beach beside the quicksand. I could not but conclude that this promenade was chosen with an eye to secrecy; for the spot was open only to the seaward. But it suited me not less excellently; the highest and most accidented of the sand-hills immediately adjoined; and from these, lying flat in a hollow, I could overlook Northmour or the young lady as they walked.

The tall man seemed to have disappeared. Not only did he never cross the threshold, but he never so much as showed face at a window; or, at least, not so far as I could see; for I dared not creep forward beyond a certain distance in the day, since the upper floor commanded the bottoms of the links; and at night, when I could venture farther, the lower windows were barricaded as if to stand a siege. Sometimes I thought the tall man must be confined to bed, for I remembered the feebleness of his gait; and sometimes I thought he must have gone clear away, and that Northmour and the young lady remained alone together in the pavilion. The idea, even then, displeased me.

Whether or not this pair were man and wife, I had seen abundant reason to doubt the friendliness of their relation. Although I could hear nothing of what they said, and rarely so much as glean a decided expression on the face of either, there was a distance, almost a stiffness, in their bearing which showed them to be either unfamiliar or at enmity. The girl walked faster when she was with Northmour than when she was alone; and I conceived that any inclination between a man and a woman would rather delay than accelerate the step. Moreover, she kept a good yard free of him, and trailed her umbrella, as if it were a barrier, on the side between them. Northmour kept sidling closer; and, as the girl retired from his advance, their course lay at a sort of diagonal across the beach, and would have landed them in the surf had it been long enough continued. But, when this was imminent, the girl would unostentatiously change sides and put Northmour between her and the sea. I watched these manoeuvres, for my part, with high enjoyment and approval, and chuckled to myself at every move.

On the morning of the third day, she walked alone for some time, and I perceived, to my great concern, that she was more than once in tears. You will see that my heart was already interested more than I supposed. She had a firm yet airy motion of the body, and carried her head with unimaginable grace; every step was a thing to look at, and she seemed in my eyes to breathe sweetness and distinction.

The day was so agreeable, being calm and sunshiny, with a tranquil sea, and yet with a healthful piquancy and vigour in the air, that, contrary to custom, she was tempted forth a second time to walk. On this occasion she was accompanied by Northmour, and they had been but a short while on the beach, when I saw him take forcible possession of her hand. She struggled, and uttered a cry that was almost a scream. I sprang to my feet, unmindful of my strange position; but, ere I had taken a step, I saw Northmour bareheaded and bowing very low, as if to apologise; and dropped again at once into my ambush. A few words were interchanged; and then, with another bow, he left the beach to return to the pavilion. He passed not far from me, and I could see him, flushed and lowering, and cutting savagely with his cane among the grass. It was not without satisfaction that I recognised my own handiwork in a great cut under his right eye, and a considerable discolouration round the socket.

For some time the girl remained where he had left her, looking out past the islet and over the bright sea. Then with a start, as one who throws off preoccupation and puts energy again upon its mettle, she broke into a rapid and decisive walk. She had forgotten where she was. And I beheld her walk straight into the borders of the quicksand where it is most abrupt and dangerous. Two or three steps farther and her life would have been in serious jeopardy, when I slid down the face of the sand-hill, which is there precipitous, and, running half-way forward, called her to stop.

She did so, and turned round. There was not a tremor of fear in her behaviour, and she marched directly up to me like a queen. I was barefoot, and clad like a common sailor, save for an Egyptian scarf round my waist; and she probably took me at first for some one from the fisher village, straying after bait. As for her, when I thus saw her face to face, her eyes set steadily and imperiously upon mine, I was filled with admiration and astonishment, and thought her even more beautiful than I had looked to find her. Nor could I think enough of one who, acting with so much boldness, yet preserved a maidenly air that was both quaint and engaging; for my wife kept an old-fashioned precision of manner through all her admirable life – an excellent thing in woman, since it sets another value on her sweet familiarities.

'What does this mean?' she asked.

'You were walking,' I told her, 'directly into Graden Floe.'

'You do not belong to these parts,' she said again. 'You speak like an educated man.'

'I believe I have right to that name,' said I, 'although in this disguise.'

But her woman's eye had already detected the sash.

'Oh!' she said; 'your sash betrays you.'

'You have said the word *betray*,' I resumed. 'May I ask you not to betray me? I was obliged to disclose myself in your interest; but if Northmour learned my presence it might be worse than disagreeable for me.'

'Do you know,' she asked, 'to whom you are speaking?'

'Not to Mr Northmour's wife?' I asked, by way of answer.

She shook her head. All this while she was studying my face with an embarrassing intentness. Then she broke out—

'You have an honest face. Be honest like your face, sir, and tell me what you want and what you are afraid of. Do you think I could hurt you? I believe you have far more power to injure me! And yet you do not look unkind. What do you mean – you, a gentleman – by skulking like a spy about this desolate place? Tell me,' she said, 'who is it you hate?'

'I hate no one,' I answered; 'and I fear no one face to face. My name is Cassilis – Frank Cassilis. I lead the life of a vagabond for my own good pleasure. I am one of Northmour's oldest friends; and three nights ago, when I addressed him on these links, he stabbed me in the shoulder with a knife.'

'It was you!' she said.

'Why he did so,' I continued, disregarding the interruption, 'is more than I can guess, and more than I care to know. I have not many friends, nor am I very susceptible to friendship; but no man shall drive me from a place by terror. I had camped in Graden Sea-Wood ere he came; I camp in it still. If you think I mean harm to you or yours, madam, the remedy is in your hand. Tell him that my camp is in the Hemlock Den, and to-night he can stab me in safety while I sleep.'

With this I doffed my cap to her, and scrambled up once more among the sand-hills. I do not know why but I felt a prodigious sense of injustice, and felt like a hero and a martyr; while, as a matter of fact, I had not a word to say in my defence, nor so much as one plausible reason to offer for my conduct. I had stayed at Graden out of a curiosity natural enough, but undignified; and though there was another motive growing in along with the first, it was not one which, at that period, I could have properly explained to the lady of my heart.

Certainly, that night, I thought of no one else; and, though her whole conduct and position seemed suspicious, I could not find it in my heart to entertain a doubt of her integrity. I could have staked my life that she was clear of blame, and, though all was dark at present, that the explanation of the mystery would show her part in these events to be both right and needful. It was true, let me cudgel my imagination as I pleased, that I could invent no theory of her relations to Northmour; but I felt none the less sure of my conclusion because it was founded on instinct in place of reason, and as I may say, went to sleep that night with the thought of her under my pillow.

Next day she came out about the same hour alone, and, as soon as the sand-hills concealed her from the pavilion, drew nearer to the edge, and called me by name in guarded tones. I was astonished to observe that she was deadly pale, and seemingly under the influence of strong emotion.

'Mr Cassilis!' she cried; 'Mr Cassilis!'

I appeared at once, and leaped down upon the beach. A remarkable air of relief overspread her countenance as soon as she saw me.

'Oh!' she cried, with a hoarse sound, like one whose bosom has been lightened of a weight. And then, 'Thank God you are still safe!' she added; 'I knew, if you were, you would be here.' (Was not this strange? So swiftly and wisely does Nature prepare our hearts for these great lifelong intimacies, that both my wife and I had been given a presentiment on this the second day of our acquaintance. I had even then hoped that she would seek me; she had felt sure that she would find me.) 'Do not,' she went on swiftly, 'do not stay in this place. Promise me that you will sleep no longer in that wood. You do not know how I suffer; all last night I could not sleep for thinking of your peril.'

'Peril?' I repeated. 'Peril from whom? From Northmour?'

'Not so,' she said. 'Did you think I would tell him after what you said?'

'Not from Northmour?' I repeated. 'Then how? From whom? I see none to be afraid of.'

'You must not ask me,' was her reply, 'for I am not free to tell you. Only believe me, and go hence – believe me, and go away quickly, quickly, for your life!'

An appeal to his alarm is never a good plan to rid oneself of a spirited young man. My obstinacy was but increased by what she said, and I made it a point of honour to remain. And her solicitude for my safety still more confirmed me in the resolve.

'You must not think me inquisitive, madam,' I replied; 'but, if Graden is so dangerous a place, you yourself perhaps remain here at some risk.'

She only looked at me reproachfully.

'You and your father –' I resumed; but she interrupted me almost with a gasp.

'My father! How do you know that?' she cried.

'I saw you together when you landed,' was my answer; and I do not know why, but it seemed satisfactory to both of us, as indeed it was the truth. 'But,' I continued, 'you need have no fear from me. I see you have some reason to be secret, and, you may believe me, your secret is as safe with me as if I were in Graden Floe. I have scarce spoken to anyone for years; my horse is my only companion and even he, poor beast, is not beside me. You see, then, you may count on me for silence. So tell me the truth, my dear young lady, are you not in danger?'

'Mr Northmour says you are an honourable man,' she returned, 'and I believe it when I see you. I will tell you so much; you are right; we are in dreadful, dreadful danger, and you share it by remaining where you are.'

'Ah!' said I; 'you have heard of me from Northmour? And he gives me a good character?'

'I asked him about you last night,' was her reply. 'I pretended,' she hesitated, 'pretended to have met you long ago, and spoke to you of him. It was not true; but I could not help myself without betraying you, and you had put me in a difficulty. He praised you highly.'

'And – you may permit me one question – does this danger come from Northmour?' I asked.

'From Mr Northmour?' she cried. 'Oh no; he stays with us to share it.'

'While you propose that I should run away?' I said. 'You do not rate me very high.'

'Why should you stay?' she asked. 'You are no friend of ours.'

I know not what came over me, for I had not been conscious of a similar weakness since I was a child, but I was so mortified by this retort that my eyes pricked and filled wth tears, as I continued to gaze upon her face.

'No, no,' she said, in a changed voice; 'I did not mean the words unkindly.'

'It was I who offended,' I said; and I held out my hand with a look of appeal that somehow touched her, for she

gave me hers at once, and even eagerly. I held it for awhile
in mine, and gazed into her eyes. It was she who first tore
her hand away and, forgetting all about her request and
the promise she had sought to extort, ran at the top of
her speed, and without turning, till she was out of sight.
And then I knew that I loved her, and thought in my glad
heart that she – she herself – was not indifferent to my
suit. Many a time she has denied it in after days, but it
was with a smiling and not a serious denial. For my part,
I am sure our hands would not have lain so closely in
each other if she had not begun to melt to me already.
And, when all is said, it is no great contention, since by
her own avowal, she began to love me on the morrow.

And yet on the morrow very little took place. She came
and called me down as on the day before, upbraided me
for lingering at Graden, and, when she found I was still
obdurate, began to ask me more particularly as to my
arrival. I told her by what series of accidents I had
come to witness their disembarkation, and how I had
determined to remain, partly from the interest which
had been wakened in me by Northmour's guests, and
partly because of his own murderous attack. As to the
former, I fear I was disingenuous and led her to regard
herself as having been an attraction to me from the first
moment I saw her on the links. It relieves my heart to
make this confession even now, when my wife is with
God, and already knows all things, and the honesty of
my purpose even in this; for while she lived, although it
often pricked my conscience, I had never the hardihood
to undeceive her. Even a little secret, in such a married
life as ours, is like the rose-leaf which kept the Princess
from her sleep.

From this the talk branched into other subjects, and I
told her much about my lonely and wandering existence;
she, for her part, giving ear, and saying little. Although
we spoke very naturally, and latterly on topics that might
seem indifferent, we were both sweetly agitated. Too soon
it was time for her to go; and we separated, as if by
mutual consent, without shaking hands, for both knew
that, between us, it was no idle ceremony.

The next, and that was the fourth day of our acquaintance, we met in the same spot, but early in the morning, with much familiarity and yet much timidity on either side. When she had once more spoken about my danger – and that, I understood, was her excuse for coming – I, who had prepared a great deal of talk during the night, began to tell her how highly I valued her kind interest, and how no one had ever cared to hear about my life, nor had I ever cared to relate it, before yesterday. Suddenly she interrupted me, saying with vehemence –

'And yet, if you knew who I was, you would not so much as speak to me!'

I told her such a thought was madness, and little as we had met, I counted her already a dear friend; but my protestations seemed only to make her more desperate.

'My father is in hiding!' she cried.

'My dear,' I said, forgetting for the first time to add 'young lady', 'what do I care? If he were in hiding twenty times over, would it make one thought of change in you?'

'Ah, but the cause!' she cried, 'the cause! It is –' she faltered for a second 'it is disgraceful to us!'

FOUR

Tells in what a startling manner I learned that
I was not alone in Graden Sea-Wood

This was my wife's story, as I drew it from her among tears and sobs. Her name was Clara Huddlestone: it sounded very beautiful in my ears; but not so beautiful as that other name of Clara Cassilis, which she wore during the longer and, I thank God, the happier portion of her life. Her father, Bernard Huddlestone, had been a private banker in a very large way of business. Many years before, his affairs becoming disordered, he had been led to try dangerous, and at last criminal, expedients to retrieve himself from ruin. All was in vain; he became more and more cruelly involved, and found his honour lost at the same moment with his fortune. About this period, Northmour had been courting his daughter with great assiduity, though with small encouragement; and to him, knowing him thus disposed in his favour, Bernard Huddlestone turned for help in his extremity. It was not merely ruin and dishonour, nor merely a legal condemnation, that the unhappy man had brought upon his head. It seems he could have gone to prison with a light heart. What he feared, what kept him awake at night or recalled him from slumber into frenzy, was some secret, sudden, and unlawful attempt upon his life. Hence, he desired to bury his existence and escape to one of the islands in the South Pacific, and it was in Northmour's yacht, the *Red Earl*, that he designed to go. The yacht picked them up clandestinely upon the coast of Wales, and had once more deposited them at Graden, till she could be refitted and provisioned for the longer voyage. Nor could Clara doubt that her hand had been stipulated as the price of passage. For, although Northmour was neither unkind nor even discourteous, he had shown himself in several instances somewhat overbold in speech and manner.

I listened, I need not say, with fixed attention, and put many questions as to the more mysterious part. It was in vain. She had no clear idea of what the blow was, nor of how it was expected to fall. Her father's alarm was unfeigned and physically prostrating, and he had thought more than once of making an unconditional surrender to the police. But the scheme was finally abandoned, for he was convinced that not even the strength of our English prisons could shelter him from his pursuers. He had had many affairs with Italy, and with Italians resident in London, in the later years of his business; and these last, as Clara fancied, were somewhat connected with the doom that threatened him. He had shown great terror at the presence of an Italian seaman on board the *Red Earl*, and had bitterly and repeatedly accused Northmour in consequence. The latter had protested that Beppo (that was the seaman's name) was a capital fellow, and could be trusted to the death; but Mr Huddlestone had continued ever since to declare that all was lost, that it was only a question of days, and that Beppo would be the ruin of him yet.

I regarded the whole story as the hallucination of a mind shaken by calamity. He had suffered heavy loss by his Italian transactions; and hence the sight of an Italian was hateful to him, and the principal part in his nightmare would naturally enough be played by one of that nation.

'What your father wants,' I said, 'is a good doctor and some calming medicine.'

'But Mr Northmour?' objected your mother. 'He is untroubled by losses, and yet he shares in this terror.'

I could not help laughing at what I considered her simplicity.

'My dear,' said I, 'you have told me yourself what reward he has to look for. All is fair in love, you must remember; and if Northmour foments your father's terrors, it is not at all because he is afraid of any Italian man, but simply because he is infatuated with a charming English woman.'

She reminded me of his attack upon myself on the night of the disembarkation, and this I was unable to explain. In short, and from one thing to another, it was agreed between us, that I should set out at once for the fisher village, Graden Wester, as it was called, look up all the newspapers I could find, and see for myself if there seemed any basis of fact for these continued alarms. The next morning, at the same hour and place, I was to make my report to Clara. She said no more on that occasion about my departure; nor, indeed, did she make it a secret that she clung to the thought of my proximity as something helpful and pleasant; and, for my part, I could not have left her, if she had gone upon her knees to ask it.

I reached Graden Wester before ten in the forenoon; for in those days I was an excellent pedestrian, and the distance, as I think I have said, was little over seven miles; fine walking all the way upon the springy turf. The village is one of the bleakest on that coast, which is saying much: there is a church in a hollow; a miserable haven in the rocks, where many boats have been lost as they returned from fishing; two or three score of stone houses arranged along the beach and in two streets, one leading from the harbour, and another striking out from it at right angles; and, at the corner of these two, a very dark and cheerless tavern, by way of principal hotel.

I had dressed myself somewhat more suitably to my station in life, and at once called upon the minister in his little manse beside the graveyard. He knew me, although it was more than nine years since we had met; and when I told him that I had been long upon a walking tour, and was behind with the news, readily lent me an armful of newspapers, dating from a month back to the day before. With these I sought the tavern, and, ordering some breakfast, sat down to study the 'Huddlestone Failure.'

It had been, it appeared, a very flagrant case. Thousands of persons were reduced to poverty; and one in particular had blown out his brains as soon as payment was suspended. It was strange to myself that, while I read these details, I continued rather to sympathise with Mr Huddlestone than with his victims; so complete already was the empire of my love for my wife. A price was naturally set upon the banker's head; and, as the case was inexcusable and the public indignation thoroughly aroused, the unusual figure of £750 was offered for his capture. He was reported to have large sums of money in his possession. One day, he had been heard of in Spain; the next, there was sure intelligence that he was still lurking between Manchester and Liverpool, or along the border of Wales; and the day after, a telegram would announce his arrival in Cuba or Yucatan. But in all this there was no word of an Italian, nor any sign of mystery.

In the very last paper, however, there was one item not so clear. The accountants who were charged to verify the failure had, it seemed, come upon the traces of a very large number of thousands, which figured for some time in the transactions of the house of Huddlestone; but which came from nowhere, and disappeared in the same mysterious fashion. It was only once referred to by name, and then under the initials 'X.X.'; but it had plainly been floated for the first time into the business at a period of great

depression some six years ago. The name of a distinguished
Royal personage had been mentioned by rumour in connection with this sum. 'The cowardly desperado' – such,
I remember, was the editorial expression – was supposed
to have escaped with a large part of this mysterious fund
still in his possession.

I was still brooding over the fact, and trying to torture
it into some connection with Mr Huddlestone's danger,
when a man entered the tavern and asked for some bread
and cheese with a decided foreign accent.

'*Siete Italiano?*' said I.

'*Si, signor,*' was his reply.

I said it was unusually far north to find one of his
compatriots; at which he shrugged his shoulders, and
replied that a man would go anywhere to find work.
What work he could hope to find at Graden Wester, I
was totally unable to conceive; and the incident struck so
unpleasantly upon my mind, that I asked the landlord,
while he was counting me some change, whether he had
ever before seen an Italian in the village. He said he had
once seen some Norwegians, who had been shipwrecked
on the other side of Graden Ness and rescued by the
lifeboat from Cauldhaven.

'No!' said I; 'but an Italian like the man who has just
had bread and cheese.'

'What?' cried he, 'yon black-avised fellow wi' the teeth?
Was he an I-talian? Weel, yon's the first that ever I saw,
an' I dare say he's like to be the last.'

Even as he was speaking, I raised my eyes, and, casting
a glance into the street, beheld three men in earnest
conversation together, and not thirty yards away. One
of them was my recent companion in the tavern parlour;
the other two, by their handsome, sallow features and soft
hats, should evidently belong to the same race. A crowd
of village children stood around them, gesticulating and
talking gibberish in imitation. The trio looked singularly
foreign to the bleak dirty street in which they were standing, and the dark grey heaven that overspread them; and
I confess my incredulity received at that moment a shock
from which it never recovered. I might reason with myself

as I pleased, but I could not argue down the effect of what I had seen, and I began to share in the Italian terror.

It was already drawing towards the close of the day before I had returned the newspapers at the manse, and got well forward on to the links on my way home. I shall never forget that walk. It grew very cold and boisterous; the wind sang in the short grass about my feet; thin rain showers came running on the gusts; and an immense mountain range of clouds began to arise out of the bosom of the sea. It would be hard to imagine a more dismal evening; and whether it was from these external influences, or because my nerves were already affected by what I had heard and seen, my thoughts were as gloomy as the weather.

The upper windows of the pavilion commanded a considerable spread of links in the direction of Graden Wester. To avoid observation it was necessary to hug the beach until I had gained cover from the higher sand-hills on the little headland, when I might strike across, through the hollows, for the margin of the wood. The sun was about setting; the tide was low, and all the quicksands uncovered; and I was moving along, lost in unpleasant thought, when I was suddenly thunderstruck to perceive the prints of human feet. They ran parallel to my own course, but low down upon the beach instead of along the border of the turf; and, when I examined them, I saw at once, by the size and coarseness of the impression, that it was a stranger to me and to those in the pavilion who had recently passed that way. Not only so; but from the recklessness of the course which he had followed, steering near to the most formidable portions of the sand, he was as evidently a stranger to the country and to the ill-repute of Graden beach.

Step by step I followed the prints; until, a quarter of a mile farther, I beheld them die away into the south-eastern boundary of Graden Floe. There, whoever he was, the miserable man had perished. One or two gulls, who had, perhaps, seen him disappear, wheeled over his sepulchre with their usual melancholy piping. The sun had broken through the clouds by a last effort, and coloured the wide level of quicksands with a dusky purple. I stood for some time gazing at the spot, chilled and disheartened by my own reflections, and with a strong and commanding consciousness of death. I remember wondering how long the tragedy had taken, and whether his screams had been audible at the pavilion. And then, making a strong resolution, I was about to tear myself away, when a gust fiercer than usual fell upon this quarter of the beach, and I saw now, whirling high in air, now skimming lightly across the surface of the sands, a soft, black, felt hat, somewhat conical in shape, such as I had remarked already on the heads of the Italians.

I believe, but I am not sure, that I uttered a cry. The wind was driving the hat shoreward, and I ran round the border of the floe to be ready against its arrival. The gust fell, dropping the hat for a while upon the quicksand, and then, once more freshening, landed it a few yards from where I stood. I seized it with the interest you may imagine. It had seen some service; indeed, it was rustier than either of those I had seen that day upon the street. The lining was red, stamped with the name of the maker, which I have forgotten, and that of the place of manufacture, *Venedig*. This (it is not yet forgotten) was the name given by the Austrians to the beautiful city of Venice, then, and for long after, a part of their dominions.

The shock was complete. I saw imaginary Italians upon every side; and for the first, and, I may say, for the last time in my experience, became overpowered by what is called a panic terror. I knew nothing, that is, to be afraid of, and yet I admit that I was heartily afraid; and it was with a sensible reluctance that I returned to my exposed and solitary camp in the Sea-Wood.

There I ate some cold porridge which had been left over from the night before, for I was disinclined to make a fire; and, feeling strengthened and reassured, dismissed all these fanciful terrors from my mind, and lay down to sleep with composure.

How long I may have slept it is impossible for me to guess; but I was awakened at last by a sudden, blinding flash of light into my face. It woke me like a blow. In an instant I was upon my knees. But the light had gone as suddenly as it came. The darkness was intense. And, as it was blowing great guns from the sea and pouring with rain, the noises of the storm effectually concealed all others.

It was, I dare say, half a minute before I regained my self-possession. But for two circumstances, I should have thought I had been awakened by some new and vivid form of nightmare. First, the flap of my tent which I had shut carefully when I retired, was now unfastened; and, second, I could still perceive, with a sharpness that excluded any theory of hallucination, the smell of hot metal and of burning oil. The conclusion was obvious. I had been wakened by someone flashing a bull's-eye lantern in my face. It had been but a flash, and away. He had seen my face, and then gone. I asked myself the object of so strange a proceeding, and the answer came pat. The man, whoever he was, had thought to recognise me, and he had not. There was yet another question unresolved; and to this, I may say, I feared to give an answer; if he had recognised me, what would he have done?

My fears were immediately diverted from myself, for I saw that I had been visited in a mistake; and I became persuaded that some dreadful danger threatened the pavilion. It required some nerve to issue forth into the black and intricate thicket which surrounded and overhung the den; but I groped my way to the links, drenched with rain, beaten upon and deafened by the gusts, and fearing at every step to lay my hand upon some lurking adversary. The darkness was so complete that I might have been surrounded by an army and yet none the wiser, and the uproar of the gale so loud that my hearing was as useless as my sight.

For the rest of that night, which seemed interminably long, I patrolled the vicinity of the pavilion, without seeing a living creature or hearing any noise but the concert of the wind, the sea, and the rain. A light in the upper storey filtered through a cranny of the shutter, and kept me company till the approach of dawn.

FIVE

Tells of an interview between Northmour, Clara, and myself

With the first peep of day, I retired from the open to my old lair among the sand-hills, there to wait the coming of my wife. The morning was grey, wild, and melancholy; the wind moderated before sunrise, and then went about, and blew in puffs from the shore; the sea began to go down, but the rain still fell without mercy. Over all the wilderness of links there was not a creature to be seen. Yet I felt sure the neighbourhood was alive with skulking foes. The light that had been so suddenly and surprisingly flashed upon my face as I lay sleeping, and the hat that had been blown ashore by the wind from over Graden Floe, were two speaking signals of the peril that environed Clara and the party in the pavilion.

It was, perhaps, half-past seven, or nearer eight, before I saw the door open, and that dear figure come towards me in the rain. I was waiting for her on the beach before she had crossed the sand-hills.

'I have had such trouble to come!' she cried. 'They did not wish me to go walking in the rain.'

'Clara,' I said, 'you are not frightened!'

'No,' said she, with a simplicity that filled my heart with confidence. For my wife was the bravest as well as the best of women; in my experience, I have not found the two go always together, but with her they did; and she combined the extreme of fortitude with the most endearing and beautiful virtues.

I told her what had happened; and, though her cheek grew visibly paler, she retained perfect control over her senses.

'You see now that I am safe,' said I, in conclusion. 'They do not mean to harm me; for, had they chosen, I was a dead man last night.'

She laid her hand upon my arm.

'And I had no presentiment!' she cried.

Her accent thrilled me with delight. I put my arm about her, and strained her to my side; and, before either of us was aware, her hands were on my shoulders and my lips upon her mouth. Yet up to that moment no word of love had passed between us. To this day I remember the touch of her cheek, which was wet and cold with the rain; and many a time since, when she has been washing her face, I have kissed it again for the sake of that morning on the beach. Now that she is taken from me, and I finish my pilgrimage alone, I recall our old loving-kindnesses and the deep honesty and affection which united us, and my present loss seems but a trifle in comparison.

We may have thus stood for some seconds – for time passes quickly with lovers – before we were startled by a peal of laughter close at hand. It was not natural mirth, but seemed to be affected in order to conceal an angrier feeling. We both turned, though I still kept my left arm about Clara's waist; nor did she seek to withdraw herself; and there, a few paces off upon the beach, stood Northmour, his head lowered, his hands behind his back, his nostrils white with passion.

'Ah! Cassilis!' he said, as I disclosed my face.

'That same,' said I; for I was not at all put about.

'And so, Miss Huddlestone,' he continued slowly but savagely, 'this is how you keep your faith to your father and to me? This is the value you set upon your father's life? And you are so infatuated with this young gentleman that you must brave ruin, and decency, and common human caution –'

'Miss Huddlestone –' I was beginning to interrupt him, when he, in his turn, cut in brutally –

'You hold your tongue,' said he; 'I am speaking to that girl.'

'That girl, as you call her, is my wife,' said I; and my wife only leaned a little nearer, so that I knew she had affirmed my words.

'Your what?' he cried. 'You lie!'

'Northmour,' I said, 'we all know you have a bad temper, and I am the last man to be irritated by words. For all that,

I propose that you speak lower for I am convinced that we are not alone.'

He looked round him, and it was plain my remark had in some degree sobered his passion. 'What do you mean?' he asked.

I only said one word: 'Italians.'

He swore a round oath, and looked at us, from one to the other.

'Mr Cassilis knows all that I know,' said my wife.

'What I want to know,' he broke out, 'is where the devil Mr Cassilis comes from, and what the devil Mr Cassilis is doing here. You say that you are married; that I do not believe. If you were, Graden Floe would soon divorce you; four minutes and a half, Cassilis. I keep my private cemetery for my friends.'

'It took somewhat longer,' said I, 'for that Italian.'

He looked at me for a moment half daunted, and then, almost civilly, asked me to tell my story. 'You have too much the advantage of me, Cassilis,' he added. I complied of course; and he listened, with several ejaculations, while I told him how I had come to Graden: that it was I whom he had tried to murder on the night of landing; and what I had subsequently seen and heard of the Italians.

'Well,' said he, when I had done, 'it is here at last; there is no mistake about that. And what, may I ask, do you propose to do?'

'I propose to stay with you and lend a hand,' said I.

'You are a brave man,' he returned, with a peculiar intonation.

'I am not afraid,' said I.

'And so,' he continued, 'I am to understand that you two are married? And you stand up to it before my face, Miss Huddlestone?'

'We are not yet married,' said Clara; 'but we shall be as soon as we can.'

'Bravo!' cried Northmour. 'And the bargain? D—n it, you're not a fool, young woman; I may call a spade a spade with you. How about the bargain? You know as well as I do what your father's life depends upon. I have only to put my hands under my coat-tails and walk away, and his throat would be cut before the evening.'

'Yes, Mr Northmour,' returned Clara, with great spirit; 'but that is what you will never do. You made a bargain that was unworthy of a gentleman; but you are a gentleman for all that, and you will never desert a man whom you have begun to help.'

'Aha!' said he. 'You think I will give my yacht for nothing? You think I will risk my life and liberty for love of the old gentleman; and then, I suppose, be best man at the wedding, to wind up? Well,' he added, with an odd smile, 'perhaps you are not altogether wrong. But ask Cassilis here. *He* knows me. Am I a man to trust? Am I safe and scrupulous? Am I kind?'

'I know you talk a great deal, and sometimes, I think very foolishly,' replied Clara, 'but I know you are a gentleman, and I am not the least afraid.'

He looked at her with a peculiar approval and admiration; then, turning to me, 'Do you think I would give her up without a struggle, Frank?' said he, 'I tell you plainly, you look out. The next time we come to blows –'

'Will make the third,' I interrupted, smiling.

'Aye, true; so it will,' he said. 'I had forgotten. Well, the third time's lucky.'

'The third time, you mean, you will have the crew of the *Red Earl* to help,' I said.

'Do you hear him?' he asked, turning to my wife.

'I hear two men speaking like cowards,' said she. 'I should despise myself either to think or speak like that. And neither of you believe one word that you are saying, which makes it the more wicked and silly.'

'She's a trump!' cried Northmour. 'But she's not yet Mrs Cassilis. I say no more. The present is not for me.'

Then my wife surprised me.

'I leave you here,' she said suddenly. 'My father has been too long alone. But remember this: you are to be friends, for you are both good friends to me.'

She has since told me her reason for this step. As long as she remained, she declares that we two would have continued to quarrel; and I suppose that she was right, for when she was gone we fell at once into a sort of confidentiality.

Northmour stared after her as she went away over the sand-hill.

'She is the only woman in the world!' he exclaimed with an oath. 'Look at her action.'

I, for my part, leaped at this opportunity for a little further light. 'See here, Northmour,' said I; 'we are all in a tight place, are we not?'

'I believe you, my boy,' he answered, looking me in the eyes, and with great emphasis. 'We have all hell upon us, that's the truth. You may believe me or not, but I'm afraid of my life.'

'Tell me one thing,' said I, 'What are they after, these Italians? What do they want with Mr Huddlestone?'

'Don't you know?' he cried. 'The black old scamp had *carbonaro* funds on a deposit – two hundred and eighty thousand; and of course he gambled it away on stocks. There was to have been a revolution in the Tridentino, or Parma; but the revolution is off, and the whole wasp's nest is after Huddlestone. We shall all be lucky if we can save our skins.'

'The *carbonari!*' I exclaimed: 'God help him indeed!'

'Amen!' said Northmour. 'And now, look here: I have said that we are in a fix; and, frankly, I shall be glad of your help. If I can't save Huddlestone, I want at least to save the girl. Come and stay in the pavilion; and, there's my hand on it, I shall act as your friend until the old man is either clear or dead. But,' he added, 'once that is settled, you become my rival once again and I warn you – mind yourself.'

'Done!' said I; and we shook hands.

'And now let us go directly to the fort,' said Northmour; and he began to lead the way through the rain.

SIX

Tells of my introduction to the tall man

We were admitted to the pavilion by Clara, and I was surprised by the completeness and security of the defences.

A barricade of great strength, and yet easy to displace, supported the door against any violence from without; and the shutters of the dining-room, into which I was led directly, and which was feebly illuminated by a lamp, were even more elaborately fortified. The panels were strengthened by bars and cross-bars; and these, in their turn, were kept in position by a system of braces and struts, some abutting on the floor, some on the roof, and others, in fine, against the opposite wall of the apartment. It was at once a solid and well-designed piece of carpentry; and I did not seek to conceal my admiration.

'I am the engineer,' said Northmour. 'You remember the planks in the garden? Behold them!'

'I did not know you had so many talents,' said I.

'Are you armed?' he continued, pointing to an array of guns and pistols, all in admirable order, which stood in line against the wall or were displayed upon the sideboard.

'Thank you,' I returned; 'I have gone armed since our last encounter. But, to tell you the truth, I have had nothing to eat since early yesterday evening.'

Northmour produced some cold meat, to which I eagerly set myself, and a bottle of good Burgundy, by which, wet as I was, I did not scruple to profit. I have always been an extreme temperance man on principle; but it is useless to push principle to excess, and on this occasion I believe that I finished three-quarters of the bottle. As I ate, I still continued to admire the preparations for defence.

'We could stand a siege,' I said at length.

'Ye—es,' drawled Northmour; 'a very little one, perhaps. It is not so much the strength of the pavilion I misdoubt; it is the double danger that kills me. If we get to shooting, wild as the country is some one is sure to hear it, and then – why then it's the same thing, only different, as they say: caged by law, or killed by *carbonari*. There's the choice. It is a devilish bad thing to have the law against you in the world, and so I tell the old gentleman upstairs. He is quite of my way of thinking.'

'Speaking of that,' said I, 'what kind of person is he?'

'Oh, he!' cried the other; 'he's a rancid fellow, as far as

he goes. I should like to have his neck wrung tomorrow by all the devils in Italy. I am not in this affair for him. You take me? I made a bargain for Missy's hand, and I mean to have it too.'

'That by the way,' said I. 'I understand. But how will Mr Huddlestone take my intrusion?'

'Leave that to Clara,' returned Northmour.

I could have struck him in the face for this coarse familiarity; but I respected the truce, as, I am bound to say, did Northmour, and so long as the danger continued not a cloud arose in our relation. I bear him this testimony with the most unfeigned satisfaction; nor am I without pride when I look back upon my own behaviour. For surely no two men were ever left in a position so invidious and irritating.

As soon as I had done eating, we proceeded to inspect the lower floor. Window by window we tried the different supports, now and then making an inconsiderable change; and the strokes of the hammer sounded with startling loudness through the house. I proposed, I remember, to make loopholes; but he told me they were already made in the windows of the upper storey. It was an anxious business this inspection, and left me down-hearted. There were two doors and five windows to protect, and, counting Clara, only four of us to defend them against an unknown number of foes. I communicated my doubts to Northmour, who assured me, with unmoved composure, that he entirely shared them.

'Before morning,' said he, 'we shall all be butchered and buried in Graden Floe. For me, that is written.'

I could not help shuddering at the mention of the quick-sand, but reminded Northmour that our enemies had spared me in the wood.

'Do not flatter yourself,' said he. 'Then you were not in the same boat with the old gentleman; now you are. It's the floe for all of us, mark my words.'

I trembled for Clara; and just then her dear voice was heard calling us to come upstairs. Northmour showed me the way, and, when he had reached the landing, knocked at the door of what used to be called *My Uncle's Bedroom*, as the founder of the pavilion had designed it especially for himself.

'Come in, Northmour; come in, dear Mr Cassilis,' said a voice from within.

Pushing open the door, Northmour admitted me before him into the apartment. As I came in I could see the daughter slipping out by the side door into the study, which had been prepared as her bedroom. In the bed, which was drawn back against the wall, instead of standing, as I had last seen it, boldly across the window, sat Bernard Huddlestone, the defaulting banker. Little as I had seen of him by the shifting of the lantern on the links, I had no difficulty in recognising him for the same. He had a long and sallow countenance, surrounded by a long red beard and side whiskers. His broken nose and high cheekbones gave him somewhat the air of a Kalmuck, and his light eyes shone with the excitement of a high fever. He wore a skull-cap of black silk; a huge Bible lay open before him on the bed, with a pair of gold spectacles in the place, and a pile of other books lay in the stand by his side. The green curtains lent a cadaverous shade to his cheek; and, as he sat propped on pillows, his great stature was plainly hunched, and his head protruded till it overhung his knees. I believe if he had not died otherwise, he must have fallen a victim to consumption in the course of but a very few weeks.

He held out to me a hand, long, thin, and disagreeably hairy.

'Come in, come in, Mr Cassilis,' said he. 'Another protector – ahem! – another protector. Always welcome as a friend of my daughter's, Mr Cassilis. How they have rallied about me, my daughter's friends! May God in heaven bless and reward them for it!'

I gave him my hand, of course, because I could not help it; but the sympathy I had been prepared to feel for Clara's father was immediately soured by his appearance, and the wheedling, unreal tones in which he spoke.

'Cassilis is a good man,' said Northmour; 'worth ten.'

'So I hear,' cried Mr Huddlestone eagerly, 'so my girl tells me. Ah, Mr Cassilis, my sin has found me out, you see! I am very low, very low; but I hope equally penitent. We must all come to the throne of grace at last, Mr Cassilis. For my part, I come late indeed; but with unfeigned humility, I trust.'

'Fiddle-de-dee!' said Northmour roughly.

'No, no, dear Northmour!' cried the banker. 'You must not say that; you must not try to shake me. You forget, my dear, good boy, you forget I may be called this very night before my Maker.'

His excitement was pitiful to behold; and I felt myself grow indignant with Northmour, whose infidel opinions I well knew, and heartily derided, as he continued to taunt the poor sinner out of his humour of repentance.

'Pooh, my dear Huddlestone!' said he. 'You do yourself injustice. You are a man of the world inside and out, and were up to all kinds of mischief before I was born. Your conscience is tanned like South American leather – only you forgot to tan your liver, and that, if you will believe me, is the seat of the annoyance.'

'Rogue, rogue! bad boy!' said Mr Huddlestone, shaking his finger. 'I am no precisian, if you come to that; I always hated a precisian; but I never lost hold of something better through it all. I have been a bad boy, Mr Cassilis; I do not seek to deny that; but it was after my wife's death, and you know, with a widower, it's a different thing: sinful – I won't say no; but there is a gradation, we shall hope. And talking of that – Hark!' he broke out suddenly, his hand raised, his fingers spread, his face racked with interest and terror. 'Only the rain, bless God!' he added, after a pause, and with indescribable relief.

For some seconds he lay back among the pillows like a man near to fainting; then he gathered himself together, and, in somewhat tremulous tones, began once more to thank me for the share I was prepared to take in his defence.

'One question, sir,' said I, when he had paused. 'Is it true that you have money with you?'

He seemed annoyed by the question, but admitted with reluctance that he had a little.

'Well,' I continued, 'it is their money they are after, is it not? Why not give it to them?'

'Ah!' replied he, shaking his head, 'I have tried that already, Mr Cassilis; and alas that it should be so! but it is blood they want.'

'Huddlestone, that's a little less than fair,' said North-mour. 'You should mention that what you offered them was upwards of two hundred thousand short. The deficit is worth a reference; it is for what they call a cool sum, Frank. Then, you see, the fellows reason in their clear Italian way; and it seems to them, as indeed it seems to me, that they may just as well have both while they're about it – money and blood together, by George, and no more trouble for the extra pleasure.'

'Is it in the pavilion?' I asked.

'It is; and I wish it were in the bottom of the sea instead,' said Northmour; and then suddenly – 'What are you making faces at me for?' he cried to Mr Huddlestone, on whom I had unconsciously turned my back. 'Do you think Cassilis would sell you?'

Mr Huddlestone protested that nothing had been further from his mind.

'It is a good thing,' retorted Northmour in his ugliest manner. 'You might end by wearying us. What were you going to say?' he added, turning to me.

'I was going to propose an occupation for the afternoon,' said I. 'Let us carry that money out, piece by piece, and lay it down before the pavilion door. If the *carbonari* come, why, it's theirs at any rate.'

'No, no,' cried Mr Huddlestone; 'it does not, it cannot belong to them! It should be distributed *pro rata* among all my creditors.'

'Come now, Huddlestone,' said Northmour, 'none of that.'

'Well, but my daughter,' moaned the wretched man.

'Your daughter will do well enough. Here are two suitors, Cassilis and I, neither of us beggars, between whom she has to choose. And as for yourself, to make an end of arguments, you have no right to a farthing, and, unless I'm much mistaken, you are going to die.'

It was certainly very cruelly said; but Mr Huddlestone was a man who attracted little sympathy; and, although

I saw him wince and shudder, I mentally endorsed the rebuke; nay, I added a contribution of my own.

'Northmour and I,' I said, 'are willing enough to help you to save your life, but not to escape with stolen property.'

He struggled for awhile with himself, as though he were on the point of giving way to anger, but prudence had the best of the controversy.

'My dear boys,' he said, 'do with me or my money what you will. I leave all in your hands. Let me compose myself.'

And so we left him, gladly enough I am sure. The last that I saw, he had once more taken up his great Bible, and with tremulous hands was adjusting his spectacles to read.

SEVEN

Tells how a word was cried through the pavilion window

The recollection of that afternoon will always be graven on my mind. Northmour and I were persuaded that an attack was imminent; and if it had been in our power to alter in any way the order of events, that power would have been used to precipitate rather than delay the critical moment. The worst was to be anticipated; yet we could conceive no extremity so miserable as the suspense we were now suffering. I have never been an eager, though always a great, reader; but I never knew books so insipid as those which I took up and cast aside that afternoon in the pavilion. Even talk became impossible, as the hours went on. One or other was always listening for some sound, or peering from an upstairs window over the links. And yet not a sign indicated the presence of our foes.

We debated over and again my proposal with regard to the money; and had we been in complete possession of our faculties, I am sure we should have condemned it as unwise; but we were flustered with alarm, grasped at a straw, and determined, although it was as much as advertising Mr Huddlestone's presence in the pavilion, to carry my proposal into effect.

The sum was part in specie, part in bank paper, and part in circular notes payable to the name of James Gregory. We took it out, counted it, enclosed it once more in a despatch-box belonging to Northmour, and prepared a letter in Italian which he tied to the handle. It was signed by both of us under oath, and declared that this was all the money which had escaped the failure of the house of Huddlestone. This was, perhaps, the maddest action ever perpetrated by two persons professing to be sane. Had the despatch-box fallen into other hands than those for which it was intended, we stood criminally convicted on our own written testimony; but, as I have said, we were neither of us in a condition to judge soberly, and had a thirst for action that drove us to do something, right or wrong, rather than endure the agony of waiting. Moreover, as we were both convinced that the hollows of the links were alive with hidden spies upon our movements, we hoped that our appearance with the box might lead to a parley, and, perhaps, a compromise.

It was nearly three when we issued from the pavilion. The rain had taken off; the sun shone quite cheerfully. I have never seen the gulls fly so close about the house or approach so fearlessly to human beings. On the very doorstep one flapped heavily past our heads, and uttered its wild cry in my very ear.

'There is an omen for you,' said Northmour, who like all freethinkers was much under the influence of superstition. 'They think we are already dead.'

I made some light rejoinder, but it was with half my heart; for the circumstance had impressed me.

A yard or two before the gate, on a patch of smooth turf, we set down the despatch-box; and Northmour waved a white handkerchief over his head. Nothing replied. We raised our voices, and cried aloud in Italian that we were there as ambassadors to arrange the quarrel; but the stillness remained unbroken save by the sea-gulls and the surf. I had a weight at my heart when we desisted; and I saw that even Northmour was unusually pale. He looked

over his shoulder nervously, as though he feared that some
one had crept between him and the pavilion door.

'By God,' he said in a whisper, 'this is too much
for me!'

I replied in the same key: 'Suppose there should be none,
after all!'

'Look there,' he returned, nodding with his head, as
though he had been afraid to point.

I glanced in the direction indicated; and there, from the
northern quarter of the Sea-Wood, beheld a thin column
of smoke rising steadily against the now cloudless sky.

'Northmour', I said (we still continued to talk in whis-
pers), 'it is not possible to endure this suspense. I prefer
death fifty times over. Stay you here to watch the pavilion;
I will go forward and make sure, if I have to walk right into
their camp.'

He looked once again all round him with puckered eyes,
and then nodded assentingly to my proposal.

My heart beat like a sledge-hammer as I set out walking
rapidly in the direction of the smoke; and, though up to
that moment I had felt chill and shivering, I was suddenly
conscious of a glow of heat over all my body. The ground
in this direction was very uneven; a hundred men might
have lain hidden in as many square yards about my path.
But I had not practised the business in vain, chose such
routes as cut at the very root of concealment, and, by
keeping along the most convenient ridges, commanded
several hollows at a time. It was not long before I was
rewarded for my caution. Coming suddenly on to a mound
somewhat more elevated than the surrounding hummocks,
I saw, not thirty yards away, a man bent almost double, and
running as fast as his attitude permitted, along the bottom
of a gully. I had dislodged one of the spies from his ambush.
As soon as I sighted him, I called loudly both in English and
Italian; and he, seeing concealment was no longer possible,
straightened himself out, leaped from the gully, and made
off as straight as an arrow for the borders of the wood.

It was none of my business to pursue; I had learned what
I wanted – that we were beleaguered and watched in the
pavilion; and I returned at once, and walking as nearly as

possible in my old footsteps, to where Northmour awaited me beside the despatch-box. He was even paler than when I had left him, and his voice shook a little.

'Could you see what he was like?' he asked.

'He kept his back turned,' I replied.

'Let us get into the house, Frank. I don't think I'm a coward, but I can stand no more of this,' he whispered.

All was still and sunshiny about the pavilion as we turned to re-enter it; even the gulls had flown in a wider circuit, and were seen flickering along the beach and sand-hills; and this loneliness terrified me more than a regiment under arms. It was not until the door was barricaded that I could draw a full inspiration and relieve the weight that lay upon my bosom. Northmour and I exchanged a steady glance; and I suppose each made his own reflections on the white and startled aspect of the other.

'You were right,' I said. 'All is over. Shake hands, old man, for the last time.'

'Yes,' replied he, 'I will shake hands; for, as sure as I am here, I bear no malice. But, remember, if, by some impossible accident, we should give the slip to these blackguards, I'll take the upper hand of you by fair or foul.'

'Oh,' said I, 'you weary me!'

He seemed hurt, and walked away in silence to the foot of the stairs, where he paused.

'You do not understand,' said he. 'I am not a swindler, and I guard myself; that is all. It may weary you or not, Mr Cassilis, I do not care a rush; I speak for my own satisfaction, and not for your amusement. You had better go upstairs and court the girl; for my part, I stay here.'

'And I stay with you,' I returned. 'Do you think I would steal a march, even with your permission?'

'Frank,' he said, smiling, 'it's a pity you are an ass, for you have the makings of a man. I think I must be *fey* to-day; you cannot irritate me even when you try. Do you know,' he continued softly, 'I think we are the two most miserable men in England, you and I? we have got on to thirty without wife or child, or so much as a shop to look after – poor, pitiful, lost devils, both! And now we clash about a girl! As if there were not several millions in the United Kingdom! Ah, Frank, Frank, the one who loses this throw, be it you or me, he has my pity! It were better for him – how does the Bible say? – that a millstone were hanged about his neck and he were cast into the depth of the sea. Let us take a drink,' he concluded suddenly, but without any levity of tone.

I was touched by his words, and consented. He sat down on the table in the dining-room, and held up the glass of sherry to his eye.

'If you beat me, Frank,' he said, 'I shall take to drink. What will you do, if it goes the other way?'

'God knows,' I returned.

'Well,' said he, 'here is a toast in the meantime: "*Italia irredenta!*"'

The remainder of the day was passed in the same dreadful tedium and suspense. I laid the table for dinner, while Northmour and Clara prepared the meal together in the kitchen. I could hear their talk as I went to and fro, and was surprised to find it ran all the time upon myself. Northmour again bracketed us together, and rallied Clara on a choice of husbands; but he continued to speak of me with some feeling, and uttered nothing to my prejudice unless he included himself in the condemnation. This awakened a sense of gratitude in my heart, which combined with the immediateness of our peril to fill my eyes with tears. After all, I thought – and perhaps the thought was laughably vain – we were here three very noble human beings to perish in defence of a thieving banker.

Before we sat down to table, I looked forth from an upstairs window. The day was beginning to decline; the links were utterly deserted; the despatch-box still lay untouched where we had left it hours before.

Mr Huddlestone, in a long yellow dressing-gown, took one end of the table, Clara the other; while Northmour and I faced each other from the sides. The lamp was brightly trimmed; the wine was good; the viands, although mostly cold, excellent of their sort. We seemed to have agreed tacitly; all reference to the impending catastrophe was carefully avoided; and, considering our tragic circumstances, we made a merrier party than could have been expected.

From time to time, it is true, Northmour or I would rise from table and make a round of the defences; and, on each of these occasions, Mr Huddlestone was recalled to a sense of his tragic predicament, glanced up with ghastly eyes, and bore for an instant on his countenance the stamp of terror. But he hastened to empty his glass, wiped his forehead with his handkerchief, and joined again in the conversation.

I was astonished at the wit and information he displayed. Mr Huddlestone's was certainly no ordinary character; he had read and observed for himself; his gifts were sound; and, though I could never have learned to love the man, I began to understand his success in business, and the great respect in which he had been held before his failure. He had, above all, the talent of society; and though I never heard him speak but on this one and most unfavourable occasion, I set him down among the most brilliant conversationalists I ever met.

He was relating with great gusto, and seemingly no feeling of shame, the manoeuvres of a scoundrelly commission merchant whom he had known and studied in his youth, and we were all listening with an odd mixture of mirth and embarrassment, when our little party was brought abruptly to an end in the most startling manner.

A noise like that of a wet finger on the window-pane interrupted Mr Huddlestone's tale; and in an instant we were all four as white as paper, and sat tongue-tied and motionless round the table.

'A snail,' I said at last; for I had heard that these animals make a noise somewhat similar in character.

'Snail be d—d!' said Northmour. 'Hush!'

The same sound was repeated twice at regular intervals; and then a formidable voice shouted through the shutters the Italian word '*Traditore!*'

Mr Huddlestone threw his head in the air; his eyelids quivered; next moment he fell insensible below the table. Northmour and I had each run to the armoury and seized a gun. Clara was on her feet with her hand at her throat.

So we stood waiting, for we thought the hour of attack was certainly come; but second passed after second, and all but the surf remained silent in the neighbourhood of the pavilion.

'Quick,' said Northmour; 'upstairs with him before they come.'

EIGHT

Tells the last of the tall man

Somehow or other, by hook and crook, and between the three of us, we got Bernard Huddlestone bundled upstairs and laid upon the bed in *My Uncle's Room*. During the whole process, which was rough enough, he gave no sign of consciousness, and he remained, as we had thrown him, without changing the position of a finger. His daughter opened his shirt and began to wet his head and bosom; while Northmour and I ran to the window. The weather continued clear; the moon, which was now about full, had risen and shed a very clear light upon the links; yet, strain our eyes as we might, we could distinguish nothing moving. A few dark spots, more or less, on the uneven expanse were not to be identified; they might be crouching men, they might be shadows; it was impossible to be sure.

'Thank God,' said Northmour, 'Aggie is not coming tonight.'

Aggie was the name of the old nurse; he had not thought of her till now; but that he should think of her at all, was a trait that surprised me in the man.

We were again reduced to waiting. Northmour went to the fireplace and spread his hands before the red embers, as if he were cold. I followed him mechanically with my eyes, and in so doing turned my back upon the window. At that moment a very faint report was audible from without, and a ball shivered a pane of glass, and buried itself in the shutter two inches from my head. I heard Clara scream; and though I whipped instantly out of range and into a corner, she was there, so to speak, before me, beseeching to know if I were hurt. I felt that I could stand to be shot at every day and all day long, with such marks of solicitude for a reward; and I continued to reassure her, with the tenderest caresses and in complete forgetfulness of our situation, till the voice of Northmour recalled me to myself.

'An air-gun,' he said. 'They wish to make no noise.'

I put Clara aside, and looked at him. He was standing with his back to the fire and his hands clasped behind him; and I knew by the black look on his face, that passion was boiling within. I had seen just such a look before he attacked me, that March night, in the adjoining chamber; and, though I could make every allowance for his anger, I confess I trembled for the consequences. He gazed straight before him; but he could see us with the tail of his eye, and his temper kept rising like a gale of wind. With regular battle awaiting us outside, this prospect of an internecine strife within the walls began to daunt me.

Suddenly, as I was thus closely watching his expression and prepared against the worst, I saw a change, a flash, a look of relief upon his face. He took up the lamp which stood beside him on the table, and turned to us with an air of some excitement.

'There is one point that we must know,' said he. 'Are they going to butcher the lot of us, or only Huddlestone? Did they take you for him, or fire at you for your own *beaux yeux?*'

'They took me for him, for certain,' I replied. 'I am near as tall, and my head is fair.'

'I am going to make sure,' returned Northmour; and he stepped up to the window, holding the lamp above his head, and stood there, quietly affronting death, for half a minute.

Clara sought to rush forward and pull him from the place of danger; but I had the pardonable selfishness to hold her back by force.

'Yes,' said Northmour, turning coolly from the window; 'it's only Huddlestone they want.'

'Oh, Mr Northmour!' cried Clara; but found no more to add; the temerity she had just witnessed seeming beyond the reach of words.

He, on his part, looked at me, cocking his head, with a

fire of triumph in his eyes; and I understood at once that he
had thus hazarded his life, merely to attract Clara's notice,
and depose me from my position as the hero of the hour.
He snapped his fingers.

'The fire is only beginning,' said he. 'When they warm
up to their work, they won't be so particular.'

A voice was now heard hailing us from the entrance.
From the window we could see the figure of a man in
the moonlight; he stood motionless, his face uplifted to
ours, and a rag of something white on his extended arm;
and as we looked right down upon him, though he was a
good many yards distant on the links, we could see the
moonlight glitter on his eyes.

He opened his lips again, and spoke for some minutes
on end, in a key so loud that he might have been heard in
every corner of the pavilion, and as far away as the borders
of the wood. It was the same voice that had already shouted
'*Traditore!*' through the shutters of the dining-room; this
time it made a complete and clear statement. If the traitor
'Oddlestone' were given up, all others should be spared; if
not, no one should escape to tell the tale.

'Well, Huddlestone, what do you say to that?' asked
Northmour, turning to the bed.

Up to that moment the banker had given no sign of
life, and I, at least, had supposed him to be still lying
in a faint; but he replied at once, and in such tones as I
have never heard elsewhere, save from a delirious patient,
adjured and besought us not to desert him. It was the most
hideous and abject performance that my imagination can
conceive.

'Enough,' cried Northmour; and then he threw open
the window, leaned out into the night, and in a tone of
exultation, and with a total forgetfulness of what was due
to the presence of a lady, poured out upon the ambassador
a string of the most abominable raillery both in English
and Italian, and bade him be gone where he had come
from. I believe that nothing so delighted Northmour at
that moment as the thought that we must all infallibly
perish before the night was out.

Meantime the Italian put his flag of truce into his

pocket, and disappeared, at a leisurely pace, among the sand-hills.

'They make honourable war,' said Northmour. 'They are all gentlemen and soldiers. For the credit of the thing, I wish we could change sides – you and I, Frank, and you too, Missy, my darling – and leave that being on the bed to some one else. Tut! Don't look shocked! We are all going post to what they call eternity, and may as well be above-board while there's time. As far as I'm concerned, if I could first strangle Huddlestone and then get Clara in my arms, I could die with some pride and satisfaction. And as it is, by God, I'll have a kiss!'

Before I could do anything to interfere, he had rudely embraced and repeatedly kissed the resisting girl. Next moment I had pulled him away with a fury, and flung him heavily against the wall. He laughed long and loud, and I feared his wits had given way under the strain; for even in the best of days he had been a sparing and a quiet laugher.

'Now, Frank,' said he, when his mirth was somewhat appeased, 'it's your turn. Here's my hand. Good-bye; farewell!' Then seeing me stand rigid and indignant and holding Clara to my side – 'Man!' he broke out, 'are you angry? Did you think we were going to die with all airs and graces of society? I took a kiss; I'm glad I had it; and now you can take another if you like, and square accounts.'

I turned from him with a feeling of contempt which I did not seek to dissemble.

'As you please,' said he. 'You've been a prig in life; a prig you'll die.'

And with that he sat down in a chair, a rifle over his knee, and amused himself with snapping the lock; but I could see that his ebullition of light spirits (the only one I ever knew him to display) had already come to an end, and was succeeded by a sullen, scowling humour.

All this time our assailants might have been entering the house, and we been none the wiser; we had in truth almost forgotten the danger that so imminently overhung our days. But just then Mr Huddlestone uttered a cry, and leaped from the bed.

I asked him what was wrong.

'Fire!' he cried. 'They have set the house on fire!'

Northmour was on his feet in an instant, and he and I ran through the door of communication with the study. The room was illuminated by a red and angry light. Almost at the moment of our entrance, a tower of flame arose in front of the window, and, with a tingling report, a pane fell inwards on the carpet. They had set fire to the lean-to outhouse, where Northmour used to nurse his negatives.

'Hot work,' said Northmour. 'Let us try in your old room.'

We ran thither in a breath, threw up the casement, and looked forth. Along the whole back wall of the pavilion piles of fuel had been arranged and kindled; and it is probable they had been drenched with mineral oil, for, in spite of the morning's rain, they all burned bravely. The fire had taken a firm hold already on the outhouse, which blazed higher and higher every moment; the back door was in the centre of a red-hot bonfire; the eaves we could see, as we looked upward, were already smouldering, for the roof overhung, and was supported by considerable beams of wood. At the same time, hot, pungent, and choking volumes of smoke began to fill the house. There was not a human being to be seen to right or left.

'Ah, well!' said Northmour, 'here's the end, thank God.'

And we returned to *My Uncle's Room*. Mr Huddlestone was putting on his boots, still violently trembling, but with an air of determination such as I had not hitherto observed. Clara stood close by him, with her cloak in both hands ready to throw about her shoulders, and a strange look in her eyes, as if she were half hopeful, half doubtful of her father.

'Well, boys and girls,' said Northmour, 'how about a sally? The oven is heating; it is not good to stay here and be baked; and, for my part, I want to come to my hands with them, and be done.'

'There is nothing else left,' I replied.

And both Clara and Mr Huddlestone, though with a very different intonation, added, 'Nothing.'

As we went downstairs the heat was excessive, and the roaring of the fire filled our ears; and we had scarce reached the passage before the stairs window fell in, a branch of flame shot brandishing through the aperture, and the interior of the pavilion became lit up with that dreadful and fluctuating glare. At the same moment we heard the fall of something heavy and inelastic in the upper storey. The whole pavilion, it was plain, had gone alight like a box of matches, and now not only flamed sky-high to land and sea, but threatened with every moment to crumble and fall in about our ears.

Northmour and I cocked our revolvers. Mr Huddlestone, who had already refused a firearm, put us behind him with a manner of command.

'Let Clara open the door,' said he. 'So, if they fire a volley, she will be protected. And in the meantime stand behind me. I am the scapegoat; my sins have found me out.'

I heard him, as I stood breathless by his shoulder, with my pistol ready, pattering off prayers in a tremulous, rapid whisper; and I confess, horrid as the thought may seem, I despised him for thinking of supplications in a moment so critical and thrilling. In the meantime, Clara, who was dead white but still possessed her faculties, had displaced the barricade from the front door. Another moment, and she had pulled it open. Firelight and moonlight illuminated the links with confused and changeful lustre, and far away against the sky we could see a long trail of glowing smoke.

Mr Huddlestone, filled for the moment with a strength greater than his own, struck Northmour and myself a back-hander in the chest; and while we were thus for the moment incapacitated from action, lifting his arms above his head like one about to dive, he ran straight forward out of the pavilion.

'Here am I!' he cried – 'Huddlestone! Kill me, and spare the others!'

His sudden appearance daunted, I suppose, our hidden enemies; for Northmour and I had time to recover, to seize Clara between us, one by each arm, and to rush forth to his assistance, ere anything further had taken place. But scarce had we passed the threshold when there came near a dozen reports and flashes from every direction among the hollows of the links. Mr Huddlestone staggered, uttered a weird and freezing cry, threw up his arms over his head, and fell backward on the turf.

'*Traditore! Traditore!*' cried the invisible avengers.

And just then, a part of the roof of the pavilion fell in, so rapid was the progress of the fire. A loud, vague, and horrible noise accompanied the collapse, and a vast volume of flame went soaring up to heaven. It must have been visible at that moment from twenty miles out at sea, from the shore at Graden Wester, and far inland from the peak of Graystiel, the most eastern summit of the Caulder Hills. Bernard Huddlestone, although God knows what were his obsequies, had a fine pyre at the moment of his death.

NINE

Tells how Northmour carried out his threat

I should have the greatest difficulty to tell you what followed next after this tragic circumstance. It is all to me, as I look back upon it, mixed, strenuous, and ineffectual, like the struggles of a sleeper in a nightmare. Clara, I remember, uttered a broken sigh and would have fallen forward to earth, had not Northmour and I supported her insensible body. I do not think we were attacked; I do not remember even to have seen an assailant; and I believe we deserted Mr Huddlestone without a glance. I only remember running like a man in a panic, now carrying Clara altogether in my own arms, now sharing her weight with Northmour, now scuffling confusedly for the possession of that dear burden. Why we should have made for my camp in the Hemlock Den, or how we reached it, are points lost for ever to my recollection. The first moment at which I became definitely sure, Clara had been suffered to fall against the outside of my little tent, Northmour and I were tumbling together on the ground, and he, with contained ferocity, was striking for my head with the butt of his revolver. He had already twice wounded me on the scalp; and it is to the consequent loss of blood that I am tempted to attribute the sudden clearness of my mind.

I caught him by the wrist.

'Northmour,' I remember saying, 'you can kill me afterwards. Let us first attend to Clara.'

He was at that moment uppermost. Scarcely had the words passed my lips, when he had leaped to his feet and ran towards the tent; and the next moment, he was straining Clara to his heart and covering her unconscious hands and face with his caresses.

'Shame!' I cried. 'Shame to you, Northmour!'

And, giddy though I still was, I struck him repeatedly upon the head and shoulders.

He relinquished his grasp, and faced me in the broken moonlight.

'I had you under, and I let you go,' said he; 'and now you strike me! Coward!'

'You are the coward,' I retorted. 'Did she wish your kisses while she was still sensible of what she wanted? Not she! And now she may be dying; and you waste this precious time, and abuse her helplessness. Stand aside, and let me help her.'

He confronted me for a moment, white and menacing; then suddenly he stepped aside.

'Help her then,' said he.

I threw myself on my knees beside her, and loosened, as well as I was able, her dress and corset; but while I was thus engaged, a grasp descended on my shoulder.

'Keep your hands off her,' said Northmour fiercely. 'Do you think I have no blood in my veins?'

'Northmour,' I cried, 'if you will neither help her yourself nor let me do so, do you know that I shall have to kill you?'

'That is better!' he cried. 'Let her die also, where's the harm? Step aside from that girl! and stand up to fight.'

'You will observe,' said I, half rising, 'that I have not kissed her yet.'

'I dare you to,' he cried.

I do not know what possessed me; it was one of the things I am most ashamed of in my life, though, as my wife used to say, I knew that my kisses would be always welcome were she dead or living; down I fell again upon my knees, parted the hair from her forehead, and, with the dearest respect, laid my lips for a moment on that cold brow. It was such a caress as a father might have given; it was such a one as was not unbecoming from a man soon to die to a woman already dead.

'And now,' said I, 'I am at your service, Mr Northmour.'

But I saw, to my surprise, that he had turned his back upon me.

'Do you hear?' I asked.

'Yes,' said he, 'I do. If you wish to fight, I am ready. If not, go on and save Clara. All is one to me.'

I did not wait to be twice bidden; but, stooping again over Clara, continued my efforts to revive her. She still lay white and lifeless; I began to fear that her sweet spirit had indeed fled beyond recall, and horror and a sense of utter desolation seized upon my heart. I called her by name with the most endearing inflections; I chafed and beat her hands; now I laid her head low, now supported it against my knee; but all seemed to be in vain, and the lids still lay heavy on her eyes.

'Northmour,' I said, 'there is my hat. For God's sake bring some water from the spring.'

Almost in a moment he was by my side with the water.

'I have brought it in my own,' he said. 'You do not grudge me the privilege?'

'Northmour,' I was beginning to say as I laved her head and breast; but he interrupted me savagely.

'Oh, you hush up!' he said. 'The best thing you can do is to say nothing.'

I had certainly no desire to talk, my mind being swallowed up in concern for my dear love and her condition; so I continued in silence to do my best towards her recovery, and, when the hat was empty, returned it to him, with one word – 'More.' He had, perhaps, gone several times upon this errand, when Clara reopened her eyes.

'Now,' said he, 'since she is better, you can spare me, can you not? I wish you a good night, Mr Cassilis.'

And with that he was gone among the thicket. I made a fire, for I had now no fear of the Italians, who had even spared all the little possessions left in my encampment; and, broken as she was by the excitement and the hideous catastrophe of the evening, I managed, in one way or another – by persuasion, encouragement, warmth, and such simple remedies as I could lay my hand on – to bring her back to some composure of mind and strength of body.

Day had already come, when a sharp 'Hist!' sounded from the thicket. I started from the ground; but the voice of Northmour was heard adding, in the most tranquil tones: 'Come here, Cassilis, and alone; I want to show you something.'

I consulted Clara with my eyes, and, receiving her tacit permission, left her alone, and clambered out of the den. At some distance off I saw Northmour leaning against an elder; and, as soon as he perceived me, he began walking seaward. I had almost overtaken him as he reached the outskirts of the wood.

'Look,' said he, pausing.

A couple of steps more brought me out of the foliage. The light of the morning lay cold and clear over that well-known scene. The pavilion was but a blackened wreck; the roof had fallen in, one of the gables had fallen out; and, far and near, the face of the links was cicatrised with little patches of burnt furze. Thick smoke still went straight upwards in the windless air of the morning, and a great pile of ardent cinders filled the bare walls of the house, like coals in an open grate. Close by the islet a schooner yacht lay to, and a well-manned boat was pulling vigorously for the shore.

'The *Red Earl!*' I cried. 'The *Red Earl* twelve hours too late!'

'Feel in your pocket, Frank. Are you armed?' asked Northmour.

I obeyed him, and I think I must have become deadly pale. My revolver had been taken from me.

'You see I have you in my power,' he continued. 'I

disarmed you last night while you were nursing Clara; but this morning – here – take your pistol. No thanks!' he cried, holding up his hand. 'I do not like them; that is the only way you can annoy me now.'

He began to walk forward across the links to meet the boat, and I followed a step or two behind. In front of the pavilion I paused to see where Mr Huddlestone had fallen; but there was no sign of him, nor so much as a trace of blood.

'Graden Floe,' said Northmour.

He continued to advance till we had come to the head of the beach.

'No farther, please,' said he. 'Would you like to take her to Graden House?'

'Thank you,' replied I; 'I shall try to get her to the minister's at Graden Wester.'

The prow of the boat here grated on the beach, and a sailor jumped ashore with a line in his hand.

'Wait a minute, lads!' cried Northmour; and then lower and to my private ear: 'You had better say nothing of all this to her,' he added.

'On the contrary!' I broke out, 'she shall know everything that I can tell.'

'You do not understand,' he returned, with an air of great dignity. 'It will be nothing to her; she expects it of me. Good-bye!' he added, with a nod.

I offered him my hand.

'Excuse me,' said he. 'It's small, I know; but I can't push things quite so far as that. I don't wish any sentimental business, to sit by your hearth a white-haired wanderer, and all that. Quite the contrary: I hope to God I shall never again clap eyes on either one of you.'

'Well, God bless you, Northmour!' I said heartily.

'Oh, yes,' he returned.

He walked down the beach; and the man who was ashore gave him an arm on board, and then shoved off and leaped into the bows himself. Northmour took the tiller; the boat rose to the waves, and the oars between the thole-pins sounded crisp and measured in the morning air.

They were not yet half-way to the *Red Earl*, and I was

still watching their progress, when the sun rose out of the sea.

One word more, and my story is done. Years after, Northmour was killed fighting under the colours of Garibaldi for the liberation of the Tyrol.

The Merry Men

Eilean Aros

IT WAS a beautiful morning in the late July when I set forth on foot for the last time for Aros. A boat had put me ashore the night before at Grisapol; I had such breakfast as the little inn afforded, and, leaving all my baggage till I had an occasion to come round for it by sea, struck right across the promontory with a cheerful heart.

I was far from being a native of these parts, springing, as I did, from an unmixed Lowland stock. But an uncle of mine, Gordon Darnaway, after a poor, rough youth, and some years at sea, had married a young wife in the islands; Mary Maclean she was called, the last of her family; and when she died in giving birth to a daughter, Aros, the sea-girt farm, had remained in his possession. It brought him in nothing but the means of life, as I was well aware; but he was a man whom ill-fortune had pursued; he feared, cumbered as he was with the young child, to make a fresh adventure upon life; and remained in Aros, biting his nails at destiny. Years passed over his head in that isolation, and brought neither help nor contentment. Meantime our family was dying out in the Lowlands; there is little luck for any of that race; and perhaps my father was the luckiest of all, for not only was he one of the last to die, but he left a son to his name and a little money to support it. I was a student of Edinburgh University, living well enough at my own charges, but without kith or kin; when some news of me found its way to Uncle Gordon on the Ross of Grisapol; and he, as he was a man who held blood thicker than water, wrote to me the day he heard of my existence, and taught me to count Aros as my home. Thus it was that I came to spend my vacations in that part of the country, so far from all society and comfort, between the codfish and the moorcocks; and thus it was that now, when I had done with my classes, I was returning thither with so light a heart that July day.

The Ross, as we call it, is a promontory neither wide nor high, but as rough as God made it to this day; the deep sea on either hand of it, full of rugged isles and reefs most perilous to seamen – all overlooked from the eastward by some very high cliffs and the great peak of Ben Kyaw. *The Mountain of the Mist*, they say the words signify in the Gaelic tongue; and it is well named. For that hilltop, which is more than three thousand feet in height, catches all the clouds that come blowing from the seaward; and, indeed, I used often to think that it must make them for itself; since when all heaven was clear to the sea-level, there would ever be a streamer on Ben Kyaw. It brought water, too, and was mossy to the top in consequence. I have seen us sitting in broad sunshine on the Ross, and the rain falling black like crape upon the mountain. But the wetness of it made it often appear more beautiful to my eyes; for when the sun struck upon the hillsides, there were many wet rocks and watercourses that shone like jewels even as far as Aros, fifteen miles away.

The road that I followed was a cattle-track. It twisted so as nearly to double the length of my journey; it went over rough boulders so that a man had to leap from one to another, and through soft bottoms where the moss came nearly to the knee. There was no cultivation anywhere and not one house in the ten miles from Grisapol to Aros. Houses of course there were – three at least; but they lay so far on the one side or the other that no stranger could have found them from the track. A large part of the Ross is covered with big granite rocks, some of them larger than a two-roomed house, one beside another, with fern and deep heather in between them where the vipers breed. Any way the wind was, it was always sea-air, as salt as on a ship; the gulls were as free as moorfowl over all the Ross; and whenever the way rose a little, your eye would kindle with the brightness of the sea. From the very midst of the land, on a day of wind and high spring, I have heard the Roost roaring like a battle where it runs by Aros, and the great and fearful voices of the breakers that we call the Merry Men.

Aros itself – Aros Jay, I have heard the natives call it, and they say it means *the House of God* – Aros itself was not properly a piece of the Ross, nor was it quite an islet. It formed the south-west corner of the land, fitted close to it, and was in one place only separated from the coast by a little gut of the sea, not forty feet across the narrowest. When the tide was full, this was clear and still, like a pool on a land river; only there was a difference in the weeds and fishes and the water itself was green instead of brown; but when the tide went out, in the bottom of the ebb, there was a day or two in every month when you could pass dryshod from Aros to the mainland. There was some good pasture, where my uncle fed the sheep he lived on; perhaps the feed was better because the ground rose higher on the islet than the main level of the Ross, but this I am not skilled enough to settle. The house was a good one for that country, two stories high. It looked westward over a bay, with a pier hard by for a boat, and from the door you could watch the vapours blowing on Ben Kyaw.

On all this part of the coast, and especially near Aros, these great granite rocks that I have spoken of go down together in troops into the sea, like cattle on a summer's day. There they stand, for all the world like their neighbours ashore; only the salt water sobbing between them instead of the quiet earth, and clots of sea-pink blooming on their sides instead of heather; and the great sea-conger to wreathe about the base of them instead of the poisonous viper of the land. On calm days you can go wandering between them in a boat for hours, echoes following you about the labyrinth; but when the sea is up, Heaven help the man that hears that caldron boiling.

Off the south-west end of Aros these blocks are very many, and much greater in size. Indeed, they must grow monstrously bigger out to sea, for there must be ten sea-miles of open water sown with them as thick as a country place with houses, some standing thirty feet above the tides, some covered, but all perilous to ships; so that on a clear, westerly blowing day, I have counted, from the top of Aros, the great rollers breaking white and heavy over as many as six-and-forty buried reefs. But it is nearer in shore that the danger is worst; for the tide, here running like a mill-race, makes a long belt of broken water – a *Roost* we call it – at the tail of the land. I have often been out there in a dead calm at the slack of the tide; and a strange place it is, with the sea swirling and combing up and boiling like the caldrons of a linn, and now and again a little dancing mutter of sound as though the *Roost* were talking to itself. But when the tide begins to run again, and above all in heavy weather, there is no man could take a boat within half a mile of it, nor a ship afloat that could either steer or live in such a place. You can hear the roaring of it six miles away. At the seaward end there comes the strongest of the bubble; and it's here that these big breakers dance together – the dance of death, it may be called – that have got the name, in these parts, of the Merry Men. I have heard it said that they run fifty feet high; but that must be the green water only, for the spray runs twice as high as that. Whether they got the name from their movements, which are swift and antic, or from the shouting they make about the turn of the tide, so that all Aros shakes with it, is more than I can tell.

The truth is, that in a south-westerly wind, that part of our archipelago is no better than a trap. If a ship got through the reefs, and weathered the Merry Men, it would be to come ashore on the south coast of Aros, in Sandag Bay, where so many dismal things befell our family, as I propose to tell. The thought of all these dangers, in the place I knew so long, makes me particularly welcome the works now going forward to set lights upon the headlands and buoys along the channels of our iron-bound, inhospitable islands.

The country people had many a story about Aros, as I used to hear from my uncle's man, Rorie, an old servant of the Macleans, who had transferred his services without afterthought on the occasion of the marriage. There was some tale of an unlucky creature, a sea-kelpie, that dwelt and did business in some fearful manner of his own among the boiling breakers of the Roost. A mermaid had once met a piper on Sandag beach, and there sang to him a long, bright midsummer's night, so that in the morning he was found stricken crazy, and from thenceforward, till the day he died, said only one form of words; what they were in the original Gaelic I cannot tell, but they were thus translated: 'Ah, the sweet singing out of the sea.' Seals that haunted on that coast have been known to speak to man in his own tongue, presaging great disasters. It was here that a certain saint first landed on his voyage out of Ireland to convert the Hebrideans. And, indeed, I think he had some claim to be called a saint; for, with the boats of that past age, to make so rough a passage, and land on such a ticklish coast, was surely not far short of the miraculous. It was to him, or to some of his monkish underlings who had a cell there, that the islet owes its holy and beautiful name, the House of God.

Among these old wives' stories there was one which I was inclined to hear with more credulity. As I was told, in that tempest which scattered the ships of the Invincible Armada over all the north and west of Scotland, one great vessel came ashore on Aros, and before the eyes of some solitary people on a hilltop, went down in a moment with all hands, her colours flying even as she sank. There was some likelihood in this tale; for another of that fleet lay sunk on the north side, twenty miles from Grisapol. It was told, I thought, with more detail and gravity than its companion stories, and there was one particularity which went far to convince me of its truth: the name, that is, of the ship was still remembered, and sounded, in my ears, Spanishly. The *Espirito Santo* they called it, a great ship of many decks of guns, laden with treasure and grandees of Spain, and fierce soldadoes, that now lay fathom deep to all eternity, done with her wars and voyages, in Sandag Bay, upon the west of Aros. No more salvos of ordnance for that tall ship, the 'Holy Spirit,' no more fair winds or happy ventures; only to rot there deep in the sea-tangle and hear the shoutings of the Merry Men as the tide ran high about the island. It was a strange thought to me first and last, and only grew stranger as I learned the more of the way in which she had set sail with so proud a company, and King Philip, the wealthy king, that sent her on that voyage.

And now I must tell you, as I walked from Grisapol that day, the *Espirito Santo* was very much in my reflections. I had been favourably remarked by our then Principal in Edinburgh College, the famous writer, Dr Robertson, and by him had been set to work on some papers of an ancient date to rearrange and sift of what was worthless; and in one of these, to my great wonder, I found a note of this very ship, the *Espirito Santo*, with her captain's name, and how she carried a great part of the Spaniard's treasure, and had been lost upon the Ross of Grisapol; but in what particular spot, the wild tribes of that place and period would give no information to the King's inquiries. Putting one thing with another, and taking our island tradition together with this note of old King Jamie's perquisitions after wealth, it had come strongly on my mind that the spot for which he sought in vain could be no other than the small bay of Sandag on my uncle's land; and being a fellow of a mechanical turn, I had ever since been plotting how to weigh that good ship up again with all her ingots, ounces, and doubloons, and bring back our house of Darnaway to its long-forgotten dignity and wealth.

This was a design of which I soon had reason to repent. My mind was sharply turned on different reflections; and since I became the witness of a strange judgment of God's, the thought of dead men's treasures has been intolerable to my conscience. But even at that time I must acquit myself of sordid greed; for if I desired riches, it was not for their own sake, but for the sake of a person who was dear to my heart – my uncle's daughter, Mary Ellen. She had been educated well, and had been a time to school upon the mainland; which, poor girl, she would have been happier without. For Aros was no place for her with old Rorie the servant, and her father, who was one of the unhappiest men in Scotland, plainly bred up in a country place among

Cameronians, long a skipper sailing out of the Clyde about the islands, and now, with infinite discontent, managing his sheep and a little 'long-shore fishing for the necessary bread. If it was sometimes wearful to me, who was there but a month or two, you may fancy what it was to her who dwelt in that same desert all the year round, with the sheep and flying seagulls, and the Merry Men singing and dancing in the Roost!

TWO

What the wreck had brought to Aros

It was half-flood when I got the length of Aros; and there was nothing for it but to stand on the far shore and whistle for Rorie with the boat. I had no need to repeat the signal. At the first sound, Mary was at the door flying a handkerchief by way of answer, and the old long-legged serving-man was shambling down the gravel to the pier. For all his hurry, it took him a long while to pull across the bay; and I observed him several times to pause, go into the stern, and look over curiously into the wake. As he came nearer, he seemed to me aged and haggard, and I thought he avoided my eye. The coble had been repaired, with two new thwarts and several patches of some rare and beautiful foreign wood, the name of it unknown to me.

'Why, Rorie,' said I, as we began the return voyage, 'this is fine wood. How came you by that?'

'It will be hard to cheesel,' Rorie opined reluctantly; and just then, dropping the oars, he made another of those dives into the stern which I had remarked as he came across to fetch me, and, leaning his hand on my shoulder, stared with an awful look into the waters of the bay.

'What is wrong?' I asked, a good deal startled.

'It will be a great feesh,' said the old man, returning to his oars; and nothing more could I get out of him, but strange glances and an ominous nodding of the head. In spite of myself, I was infected with a measure of uneasiness;

I turned also, and studied the wake. The water was still and transparent, but, out here in the middle of the bay, exceeding deep. For some time I could see naught; but at last it did seem to me as if something dark – a great fish, or perhaps only a shadow – followed studiously in the track of the moving coble. And then I remembered one of Rorie's superstitions: how in a ferry in Morven, in some great, exterminating feud among the clans, a fish, the like of it unknown in all our waters, followed for some years the passage of the ferry-boat, until no man dared to make the crossing.

'He will be waiting for the right man,' said Rorie.

Mary met me on the beach, and led me up the brae and into the house of Aros. Outside and inside there were many changes. The garden was fenced with the same wood that I had noted in the boat; there were chairs in the kitchen covered with strange brocade; curtains of brocade hung from the window; a clock stood silent on the dresser; a lamp of brass was swinging from the roof; the table was set for dinner with the finest of linen and silver; and all these new riches were displayed in the plain old kitchen that I knew so well, with the highbacked settle, and the stools, and the closet-bed for Rorie; with the wide chimney the sun shone into, and the clear-smouldering peats; with the pipes on the mantelshelf and the three-cornered spittoons, filled with seashells instead of sand, on the floor; with the bare stone walls and the bare wooden floor, and the three patchwork rugs that were of yore its sole adornment – poor man's patchwork, the like of it unknown in cities, woven with homespun, and Sunday black, and seacloth polished on the bench of rowing. The room, like the house, had been a sort of wonder in that countryside, it was so neat and habitable; and to see it now, shamed by these incongruous additions, filled me with indignation and a kind of anger. In view of the errand I had come upon to Aros, the feeling was baseless and unjust; but it burned high, at the first moment, in my heart.

'Mary, girl', said I, 'this is the place I had learned to call my home, and I do not know it.'

'It is my home by nature, not by the learning,' she

replied; 'the place I was born and the place I'm like to die in; and I neither like these changes, nor the way they came, nor that which came with them. I would have liked better, under God's pleasure, they had gone down into the sea, and the Merry Men were dancing on them now.'

Mary was always serious; it was perhaps the only trait that she shared with her father; but the tone with which she uttered these words was even graver than of custom.

'Ay,' said I, 'I feared it came by wreck, and that's by death; yet when my father died, I took his goods without remorse.'

'Your father died a clean-strae death, as the folk say,' said Mary.

'True,' I returned; 'and a wreck is like a judgment. What was she called?'

'They ca'd her the *Christ-Anna*,' said a voice behind me; and, turning round, I saw my uncle standing in the doorway.

He was a sour, small, bilious man, with a long face and very dark eyes; fifty-six years old, sound and active in body, and with an air somewhat between that of a shepherd and that of a man following the sea. He never laughed, that I heard; read long at the Bible; prayed much, like the Cameronians he had been brought up among; and indeed, in many ways, used to remind me of one of the hill-preachers in the killing times before the Revolution. But he never got much comfort, nor even, as I used to think, much guidance, by his piety. He had his black fits when he was afraid of hell; but he had led a rough life, to which he would look back with envy, and was still a rough, cold, gloomy man.

As he came in at the door out of the sunlight, with his bonnet on his head and a pipe hanging in his buttonhole, he seemed, like Rorie, to have grown older and paler, the lines were deeplier ploughed upon his face, and the whites of his eyes were yellow, like old stained ivory, or the bones of the dead.

'Ay,' he repeated, dwelling upon the first part of the word, 'the *Christ-Anna*. It's an awfu' name.'

I made him my salutations, and complimented him

upon his look of health; for I feared he had perhaps been ill.

'I'm in the body,' he replied, ungraciously enough; 'aye in the body and the sins of the body, like yoursel'. Denner,' he said abruptly to Mary, and then ran on to me: 'They're grand braws, thir that we hae gotten, are they no'? Yon's a bonny knock, but it'll no gang; and the napery's by ordnar. Bonny, bairnly braws; it's for the like o' them folk sells the peace of God that passeth understanding; it's for the like o' them, an' maybe no' even sae muckle worth, folk daunton God to His face and burn in muckle hell; and it's for that reason the Scripture ca's them, as I read the passage, the accursed thing. Mary, ye girzie,' he interrupted himself to cry with some asperity, 'what for hae ye no' put out the twa candlesticks?'

'Why should we need them at high noon?' she asked. But my uncle was not to be turned from his idea. 'We'll bruik them while we may,' he said; and so two massive candlesticks of wrought silver were added to the table equipage, already so unsuited to that rough seaside farm.

'She cam' ashore Februar' 10, about ten at nicht,' he went on to me. 'There was nae wind, and a sair run o' sea; and she was in the sook o' the Roost, as I jaloose. We had seen her a' day, Rorie and me, beating to the wind. She wasna a handy craft, I'm thinking, that *Christ-Anna*; for she would neither steer nor stey wi' them. A sair day they had of it; their hands was never aff the sheets, and it perishin' cauld – ower cauld to snaw; and aye they would get a bit nip o' wind, and awa' again, to pit the emp'y hope into them. Eh, man! but they had a sair day for the last o't! He would have had a prood, prood heart that won ashore upon the back o' that.'

'And were all lost?' I cried. 'God help them!'

'Wheesht!' he said sternly. 'Nane shall pray for the deid on my hearth-stane.'

I disclaimed a Popish sense for my ejaculation; and he seemed to accept my disclaimer with unusual facility, and ran on once more upon what had evidently become a favourite subject.

'We fand her in Sandag Bay, Rorie an' me, and a' thae braws in the inside of her. There's a kittle bit, ye see, about Sandag; whiles the sook rins strong for the Merry Men; an' whiles again, when the tide's makin' hard an' ye can hear the Roost blawin' at the far-end of Aros, there comes a back-spang of current straucht into Sandag Bay. Weel, there's the thing that got the grip on the *Christ-Anna*. She but to have come in ram-stam an' stern forrit; for the bows of her are aften under, and the back-side of her is clear at hie-water o' neaps. But, man! the dunt that she cam doon wi' when she struck! Lord save us a'! but it's an unco life to be a sailor – a cauld, wanchancy life. Mony's the gliff I got mysel' in the great deep; and why the Lord should hae made yon unco water is mair than ever I could win to understand. He made the vales and the pastures, the bonny green yaird, the halesome, canty land –
>   And now they shout and sing to Thee,
>   For Thou hast made them glad,

as the Psalms say in the metrical version. No' that I would preen my faith to that clink neither; but it's bonny, and easier to mind. 'Who go to sea in ships,' they hae't again –
>   and in
>   Great waters trading be,
>   Within the deep these men God's works
>   And His great wonders see.

Weel, it's easy sayin' sae. Maybe Dauvit wasna very weel acquaint wi' the sea. But troth, if it wasna prentit in the Bible, I wad whiles be temp'it to think it wasna the Lord, but the muckle, black deil that made the sea. There's naething good comes oot o't but the fish; an' the spentacle o' God riding on the tempest, to be shüre, whilk would be what Dauvit was likely ettling at. But, man, they were sair wonders that God showed to the *Christ-Anna* – wonders, do I ca' them? Judgments, rather: judgments in the mirk nicht among the draygons o' the deep. And their souls – to think o' that – their souls, man, maybe no prepared! The sea – a muckle yett to hell!'

I observed, as my uncle spoke, that his voice was unnaturally moved and his manner unwontedly demonstrative. He leaned forward at these last words, for example, and touched me on the knee with his spread fingers, looking up into my face with a certain pallor, and I could see that his eyes shone with a deep-seated fire, and that the lines about his mouth were drawn and tremulous.

Even the entrance of Rorie, and the beginning of our meal, did not detach him from his train of thought beyond a moment. He condescended, indeed, to ask me some questions as to my success at college, but I thought it was with half his mind; and even in his extempore grace, which was, as usual, long and wandering, I could find the trace of his preoccupation, praying, as he did, that God would 'remember in mercy fower puir, feckless, fiddling sinful creatures here by their lee-lane beside the great and dowie waters.'

Soon there came an interchange of speeches between him and Rorie.

'Was it there?' asked my uncle.

'Ou, ay!' said Rorie.

I observed that they both spoke in a manner of aside, and with some show of embarrassment, and that Mary herself appeared to colour, and looked down on her plate. Partly to show my knowledge, and so relieve the party from an awkward strain, partly because I was curious, I pursued the subject.

'You mean the fish?' I asked.

'Whatten fish?' cried my uncle. 'Fish, quo' he! Fish! Your een are fu' o' fatness, man; your heid dozened wi' carnal leir. Fish! it's a bogle!'

He spoke with great vehemence, as though angry; and perhaps I was not very willing to be put down so shortly, for young men are disputatious. At least I remember I retorted hotly, crying out upon childish superstitions.

'And ye come frae the College!' sneered Uncle Gordon. 'Gude kens what they learn folk there; it's no muckle service onyway. Do ye think, man, that there's naething in a' yon saut wilderness o' a world oot wast there, wi' the sea-grasses growin', an' the sea-beasts fechtin', an' the sun glintin' down into it, day by day? Na; the sea's like the land, but fearsomer. If there's folk ashore, there's folk in the sea – deid they may be, but they're folk whatever; and as for deils, there's nane that's like the sea-deils. There's no sae muckle harm in the land-deils, when a's said and done. Lang syne, when I was a callant in the south country, I mind there was an auld, bald bogle in the Peewie Moss. I got a glisk o' him mysel', sittin' on his hunkers in a hag, as grey 's a tombstane. An', troth, he was a fearsome-like taed. But he steered naebody. Nae doobt, if ane that was a reprobate, ane the Lord hated, had gane by there wi' his sin still upon his stamach, nae doobt the creature would hae lowped upo' the likes o' him. But there's deils in the deep sea would yoke on a communicant! Eh, sirs, if ye had gane doon wi' the puir lads in the *Christ-Anna*, ye would ken by now the mercy o' the seas. If ye had sailed it for as lang as me, ye would hate the thocht of it as I do. If ye had but used the een God gave ye, ye would hae learned the wickedness o' that fause, saut, cauld, bullering creature, and of a' that's in it by the Lord's permission: labsters an' partans, an' sic-like, howking in the deid; muckle, gutsy, blawing whales; an' fish – the hale clan o' them – cauld-wamed, blind-ee'd uncanny ferlies. Oh, sirs,' he cried, 'the horror – the horror o' the sea!'

We were all somewhat staggered by this outburst; and the speaker himself, after that last hoarse apostrophe, appeared to sink gloomily into his own thoughts. But Rorie, who was greedy of superstitious lore, recalled him to the subject by a question.

'You will not ever have seen a teevil of the sea?' he asked.

'No' clearly,' replied the other, 'I misdoobt if a mere man could see ane clearly and conteenue in the body. I hae sailed wi' a lad – they ca'd him Sandy Gabart; he saw ane, shüre eneuch, an' shüre eneuch it was the end of him. We were seeven days oot frae the Clyde – a sair wark we had had – gaun north wi' seeds an' braws an' things for Macleod. We had got in ower near under the Cutchull'ns, an' had just gane about by Soa, an' were off on a lang tack, we thocht would maybe hauld as far 's Copnahow. I mind the nicht weel; a mune smoored wi' mist; a fine gaun breeze upon the water, but no' steedy; an' – what nane o' us likit to hear – anither wund gurlin' owerheid, amang thae fearsome, auld stane craigs o' the Cutchull'ns. Weel, Sandy was forrit wi' the jib sheet; we couldna see him for the mains'l, that had just begude to draw, when a' at ance he gied a skirl. I luffed for my life, for I thocht we were ower near Soa; but na, it wasna that, it was puir Sandy Gabart's deid skreigh, or near-hand, for he was deid in half an hour. A 't he could tell was that a sea-deil, or sea-bogle, or sea-spenster, or sic-like, had clum up by the bowsprit, an' gi'en him ae cauld, uncanny look. An', or the life was oot o' Sandy's body, we kent weel what the thing betokened, and why the wund gurled in the taps o' the Cutchull'ns; for doon it cam' – a wund do I ca' it! it was the wund o' the Lord's anger – an' a' that nicht we foucht like men dementit, and the neist that we kenned we were ashore in Loch Uskevagh, an' the cocks were crawing in Benbecula.'

'It will have been a merman,' Rorie said.

'A merman!' screamed my uncle, with immeasurable scorn. 'Auld wives' clavers! There's nae sic things as mermen.'

'But what was the creature like?' I asked.

'What like was it? Gude forbid that we suld ken what like it was! It had a kind of a heid upon it – man could say nae mair.'

Then Rorie, smarting under the affront, told several tales of mermen, mermaids, and sea-horses that had come ashore upon the islands and attacked the crews of boats upon the sea; and my uncle, in spite of incredulity, listened with uneasy interest.

'Aweel, aweel,' he said, 'it may be sae; I may be wrang; but I find nae word o' mermen in the Scriptures.'

'And you will find nae word of Aros Roost, maybe,' objected Rorie, and his argument appeared to carry weight.

When dinner was over, my uncle carried me forth with him to a bank behind the house. It was a very hot and quiet afternoon; scarce a ripple anywhere upon the sea, nor any voice but the familiar voice of sheep and gulls; and perhaps in consequence of this repose in nature, my kinsman showed himself more rational and tranquil than before. He spoke evenly and almost cheerfully of my career, with every now and then a reference to the lost ship or the treasures it had brought to Aros. For my part, I listened to him in a sort of trance, gazing with all my heart on that remembered scene, and drinking gladly the sea-air and the smoke of peats that had been lit by Mary.

Perhaps an hour had passed when my uncle, who had all the while been covertly gazing on the surface of the little bay, rose to his feet and bade me follow his example. Now I should say that the great run of tide at the south-west end of Aros exercises a perturbing influence round all the coast. In Sandag Bay, to the south, a strong current runs at certain periods of the flood and ebb respectively; but in this northern bay – Aros Bay, as it is called – where the house stands and on which my uncle was now gazing, the only sign of disturbance is towards the end of the ebb, and even then it is too slight to be remarkable. When there is any swell, nothing can be seen at all; but when it is calm, as it often is, there appear certain strange, undecipherable marks – sea runes, as we may name them – on the glassy surface of the bay. The like is common in a thousand places on the coast; and many a boy must have amused himself as I did, seeking to read in them some reference to himself or those he loved. It was to these marks that my uncle now directed my attention, struggling, as he did so, with an evident reluctance.

'Do ye see you scart upo' the water?' he inquired; 'yon ane wast the grey stane? Ay? Weel, it'll no' be like a letter, wull it?'

'Certainly it is,' I replied. 'I have often remarked it. It is like a C.'

He heaved a sigh as if heavily disappointed with my answer, and then added below his breath: 'Ay, for the *Christ-Anna.*'

'I used to suppose, sir, it was for myself,' said I; 'for my name is Charles.'

'And so ye saw 't afore?' he ran on, not heeding my remark. 'Weel, weel, but that's unco strange. Maybe, it's been there waitin', as a man wad say, through a' the weary ages. Man, but that's awfu'.' And then, breaking off: 'Ye'll no' see anither, will ye?' he asked.

'Yes,' said I. 'I see another very plainly, near the Ross side, where the road comes down – an M.'

'An M,' he repeated very low; and then, again after another pause: 'An' what wad ye make o' that?' he inquired.

'I had always thought it to mean Mary, sir,' I answered, growing somewhat red, convinced as I was in my own mind that I was on the threshold of a decisive explanation.

But we were each following his own train of thought to the exclusion of the other's. My uncle once more paid no attention to my words: only hung his head and held his peace; and I might have been led to fancy that he had not heard me, if his next speech had not contained a kind of echo from my own.

'I would say naething o' thae clavers to Mary,' he observed, and began to walk forward.

There is a belt of turf along the side of Aros Bay where walking is easy; and it was along this that I silently followed my silent kinsman. I was perhaps a little disappointed at having lost so good an opportunity to declare my love; but I was at the same time far more deeply exercised at the change that had befallen my uncle. He was never an ordinary, never, in the strict sense, an amiable, man; but there was nothing in even the worst that I had known of him before, to prepare me for so strange a transformation. It was impossible to close the eyes against one fact; that he had, as the saying goes, something on his mind; and as I mentally ran over the different words which might be represented by the letter M – misery, mercy, marriage, money, and the like – I was arrested with a sort of start by the word murder. I was still considering the ugly sound and fatal meaning of the word, when the direction of our walk brought us to a point from which a view was to be had to either side, back towards Aros Bay and homestead, and forward on the ocean, dotted to the north with isles, and lying to the southward blue and open to the sky. There my guide came to a halt, and stood staring for a while on that expanse. Then he turned to me and laid a hand on my arm.

'Ye think there's naething there?' he said, pointing

with his pipe; and then cried out aloud, with a kind of exultation: 'I'll tell ye, man! The deid are down there – thick like rattons!'

He turned at once, and, without another word, we retraced our steps to the house of Aros.

I was eager to be alone with Mary; yet it was not till after supper, and then but for a short while, that I could have a word with her. I lost no time beating about the bush, but spoke out plainly what was on my mind.

'Mary,' I said, 'I have not come to Aros without a hope. If that should prove well founded, we may all leave and go somewhere else, secure of daily bread and comfort; secure, perhaps, of something far beyond that, which it would seem extravagant in me to promise. But there's a hope that lies nearer to my heart than money.' And at that I paused. 'You can guess fine what that is, Mary,' I said. She looked away from me in silence, and that was small encouragement but I was not to be put off. 'All my days I have thought the world of you,' I continued; 'the time goes on and I think always the more of you; I could not think to be happy or hearty in my life without you: you are the apple of my eye.' Still she looked away, and said never a word; but I thought I saw that her hands shook. 'Mary,' I cried in fear, 'do ye no' like me?'

'Oh, Charlie man,' she said, 'is this a time to speak of it? Let me be a while; let me be the way I am; it'll not be you that loses by the waiting!'

I made out by her voice that she was nearly weeping, and this put me out of any thought but to compose her. 'Mary Ellen,' I said, 'say no more; I did not come to trouble you: your way shall be mine, and your time too; and you have told me all I wanted. Only just this one thing more: what ails you?'

She owned it was her father, but would enter into no particulars, only shook her head, and said he was not well and not like himself, and it was a great pity. She knew nothing of the wreck. 'I havena been near it,' said she. 'What for would I go near it, Charlie lad? The poor souls are gone to their account long syne; and I would just have wished they had ta'en their gear with them – poor souls!'

This was scarcely any great encouragement for me to tell her of the *Espirito Santo*; yet I did so, and at the very first word she cried out in surprise. 'There was a man at Grisapol,' she said, 'in the month of May – a little, yellow, black-avised body, they tell me, with gold rings upon his fingers, and a beard; and he was speiring high and low for that same ship.'

It was towards the end of April that I had been given these papers to sort out by Dr Robertson: and it came suddenly back upon my mind that they were thus prepared for a Spanish historian, or a man calling himself such, who had come with high recommendations to the Principal, on a mission of inquiry as to the dispersion of the great Armada. Putting one thing with another, I fancied that the visitor 'with the gold rings upon his fingers' might be the same with Dr Robertson's historian from Madrid. If that were so, he would be more likely after treasure for himself than information for a learned society. I made up my mind, I should lose no time over my undertaking; and if the ship lay sunk in Sandag Bay, as perhaps both he and I supposed, it should not be for the advantage of this ringed adventurer, but for Mary and myself, and for the good, old, honest, kindly family of the Darnaways.

THREE

Land and Sea in Sandag Bay

I was early afoot next morning; and as soon as I had a bite to eat, set forth upon a tour of exploration. Something in my heart distinctly told me that I should find the ship of the Armada; and although I did not give way entirely to such hopeful thoughts, I was still very light in spirits and walked upon air. Aros is a very rough islet, its surface strewn with great rocks and shaggy with fern and heather; and my way lay almost north and south across the highest knoll; and though the whole distance was inside of two miles, it took more time and exertion than four upon a level road. Upon the summit, I paused. Although not very high – not three hundred feet, as I think – it yet out-tops all the neighbouring lowlands of the Ross, and commands a great view of sea and islands. The sun, which had been up some time, was already hot upon my neck; the air was listless and thundery, although purely clear; away over the north-west, where the isles lie thickliest congregated, some half-a-dozen small and ragged clouds hung together in a covey; and the head of Ben Kyaw wore, not merely a few streamers, but a solid hood of vapour. There was a threat in the weather. The sea, it is true, was smooth like glass: even the Roost was but a seam in that wide mirror, and the Merry Men no more than caps of foam; but to my eye and ear, so long familiar with these places, the sea also seemed to lie uneasily; a sound of it, like a long sigh, mounted to me where I stood; and, quiet as it was, the Roost itself appeared to be revolving mischief. For I ought to say that all we dwellers in these parts attributed, if not prescience, at least a quality of warning, to that strange and dangerous creature of the tides.

I hurried on, then, with the greater speed, and had soon descended the slope of Aros to the part that we call Sandag Bay. It is a pretty large piece of water compared with the size of the isle; well sheltered from all but the prevailing wind; sandy and shoal and bounded by low sand-hills to the west, but to the eastward lying several fathoms deep along a ledge of rocks. It is upon that side that, at a certain time each flood, the current mentioned by my uncle sets so strong into the bay; a little later, when the Roost begins to work higher, an undertow runs still more strongly in the reverse direction; and it is the action of this last, as I suppose, that has scoured that part so deep. Nothing is to be seen out of Sandag Bay but one small segment of the horizon and, in heavy weather, the breakers flying high over a deep sea-reef.

From half-way down the hill, I had perceived the wreck of February last, a brig of considerable tonnage, lying, with her back broken, high and dry on the east corner of the sands; and I was making directly towards it, and already almost on the margin of the turf, when my eyes

were suddenly arrested by a spot, cleared of fern and
heather, and marked by one of those long, low, and
almost human-looking mounds that we see so commonly
in grave-yards. I stopped like a man shot. Nothing had
been said to me of any dead man or interment on the
island; Rorie, Mary, and my uncle had all equally held
their peace; of her at least, I was certain that she must
be ignorant; and yet here, before my eyes, was proof
indubitable of the fact. Here was a grave; and I had
to ask myself, with a chill, what manner of man lay
there in his last sleep, awaiting the signal of the Lord
in that solitary, sea-beat resting-place? My mind supplied
no answer but what I feared to entertain. Shipwrecked, at
least, he must have been; perhaps, like the old Armada
mariners, from some far and rich land over-sea; or perhaps
one of my own race, perishing within eyesight of the smoke
of home. I stood a while uncovered by his side, and I could
have desired that it had lain in our religion to put up some
prayer for that unhappy stranger or, in the old classic way,
outwardly to honour his misfortune. I knew, although his
bones lay there, a part of Aros, till the trumpet sounded,
his imperishable soul was forth and far away, among the
raptures of the everlasting Sabbath or the pangs of hell;
and yet my mind misgave me even with a fear, that perhaps
he was near me where I stood, guarding his sepulchre and
lingering on the scene of his unhappy fate.

Certainly it was with a spirit somewhat overshadowed
that I turned away from the grave to the hardly less
melancholy spectacle of the wreck. Her stem was above
the first arc of the flood; she was broken in two a little
abaft the foremast – though indeed she had none, both
masts having broken short in her disaster; and as the pitch
of the beach was very sharp and sudden, and the bows lay
many feet below the stern, the fracture gaped widely open,
and you could see right through her poor hull upon the
farther side. Her name was much defaced, and I could not
make out clearly whether she was called *Christiania*, after
the Norwegian city, or *Christiana*, after the good woman,
Christian's wife, in that old book the *Pilgrim's Progress*. By
her build she was a foreign ship, but I was not certain of her

nationality. She had been painted green, but the colour was faded and weathered, and the paint peeling off in strips. The wreck of the mainmast lay alongside, half-buried in sand. She was a forlorn sight, indeed, and I could not look without emotion at the bits of rope that still hung about her, so often handled of yore by shouting seamen; or the little scuttle where they had passed up and down to their affairs; or that poor noseless angel of a figure-head that had dipped into so many running billows.

I do not know whether it came most from the ship or from the grave, but I fell into some melancholy scruples, as I stood there, leaning with one hand against the battered timbers. The homelessness of men, and even of inanimate vessels, cast away upon strange shores, came strongly in upon my mind. To make a profit of such pitiful misadventures seemed an unmanly and a sordid act; and I began to think of my then quest as of something sacrilegious in its nature. But when I remembered Mary, I took heart again. My uncle would never consent to an imprudent marriage, nor would she, as I was persuaded, wed without his full approval. It behoved me, then, to be up and doing for my wife; and I thought with a laugh how long it was since that great sea-castle, the *Espirito Santo*, had left her bones in Sandag Bay, and how weak it would be to consider rights so long extinguished and misfortunes so long forgotten in the process of time.

I had my theory of where to seek for her remains. The set of the current and the soundings both pointed to the east side of the bay under the ledge of rocks. If she had been lost in Sandag Bay, and if, after these centuries, any portion of her held together, it was there that I should find it. The water deepens, as I have said, with great rapidity, and even close alongside the rocks several fathoms may be found. As I walked upon the edge I could see far and wide over the sandy bottom of the bay; the sun shone clear and green and steady in the deeps; the bay seemed rather like a great transparent crystal, as one sees them in a lapidary's shop; there was naught to show that it was water but an internal trembling, a hovering within of sun-glints and netted shadows, and now and then a faint lap and a dying bubble round the edge. The shadows of the rocks lay out for some distance at their feet, so that my own shadow, moving, pausing, and stopping on the top of that, reached sometimes half across the bay. It was above all in this belt of shadows that I hunted for the *Espirito Santo*; since it was there the undertow ran strongest, whether in or out. Cool as the whole water seemed this broiling day, it looked, in that part, yet cooler, and had a mysterious invitation for the eyes. Peer as I pleased, however, I could see nothing but a few fishes or a bush of sea-tangle, and here and there a lump of rock that had fallen from above and now lay separate on the sandy floor. Twice did I pass from one end to the other of the rocks, and in the whole distance I could see nothing of the wreck, nor any place but one where it was possible for it to be. This was a large terrace in five fathoms of water, raised off the surface of the sand to a considerable height, and looking from above like a mere outgrowth of the rocks on which I walked. It was one mass of great sea-tangles like a grove, which prevented me judging of its nature, but in shape and size it bore some likeness to a vessel's hull. At least it was my best chance. If the *Espirito Santo* lay not there under the tangles, it lay nowhere at all in Sandag Bay; and I prepared to put the question to the proof, once and for all, and either go back to Aros a rich man or cured for ever of my dreams of wealth.

I stripped to the skin, and stood on the extreme margin with my hands clasped, irresolute. The bay at that time was utterly quiet; there was no sound but from a school of porpoises somewhere out of sight behind the point; yet a certain fear withheld me on the threshold of my venture. Sad sea-feelings, scraps of my uncle's superstitions, thoughts of the dead, of the grave, of the old broken ships, drifted through my mind. But the strong sun upon my shoulders warmed me to the heart, and I stooped forward and plunged into the sea.

It was all that I could do to catch a trail of the sea-tangle that grew so thickly on the terrace; but once so far anchored I secured myself by grasping a whole armful of these thick and slimy stalks, and, planting my feet against the edge,

I looked around me. On all sides the clear sand stretched forth unbroken; it came to the foot of the rocks, scoured into the likeness of an alley in a garden by the action of the tides; and before me, for as far as I could see, nothing was visible but the same many-folded sand upon the sun-bright bottom of the bay. Yet the terrace to which I was then holding was as thick with strong sea-growths as a tuft of heather, and the cliff from which it bulged hung draped below the water-line with brown lianas. In this complexity of forms, all swaying together in the current, things were hard to be distinguished; and I was still uncertain whether my feet were pressed upon the natural rock or upon the timbers of the Armada treasureship, when the whole tuft of tangle came away in my hand, and in an instant I was on the surface, and the shores of the bay and the bright water swam before my eyes in a glory of crimson.

I clambered back upon the rocks, and threw the plant of tangle at my feet. Something at the same moment rang sharply, like a falling coin. I stooped, and there, sure enough, crusted with the red rust, there lay an iron shoe-buckle. The sight of this poor human relic thrilled me to the heart, but not with hope nor fear, only with a desolate melancholy. I held it in my hand, and the thought of its owner appeared before me like the presence of an actual man. His weather-beaten face, his sailor's hands, his sea-voice hoarse with singing at the capstan, the very foot that had once worn that buckle and trod so much along the swerving decks – the whole human fact of him, as a creature like myself, with hair and blood and seeing eyes, haunted me in that sunny, solitary place, not like a spectre, but like some friend whom I had basely injured. Was the great treasure-ship indeed below there, with her guns and chain and treasure, as she had sailed from Spain; her decks a garden for the sea-weed, her cabin a breeding-place for fish, soundless but for the dredging water, motionless but for the waving of the tangle upon her battlements – that old, populous, sea-riding castle, now a reef in Sandag Bay? Or, as I thought it likelier, was this a waif from the disaster of the foreign brig – was this shoe-buckle bought but the other day and worn by a man of my own period in the world's history, hearing the same news from day to day, thinking the same thoughts, praying, perhaps, in the same temple with myself? However it was, I was assailed with dreary thoughts; my uncle's words, 'the dead are down there,' echoed in my ears; and though I determined to dive once more, it was with a strong repugnance that I stepped forward to the margin of the rocks.

A great change passed at that moment over the appearance of the bay. It was no more that clear, visible interior, like a house roofed with glass, where the green submarine sunshine slept so stilly. A breeze, I suppose, had flawed the surface, and a sort of trouble and blackness filled its bosom, where flashes of light and clouds of shadow tossed confusedly together. Even the terrace below obscurely rocked and quivered. It seemed a graver thing to venture on this place of ambushes; and when I leaped into the sea the second time it was with a quaking in my soul.

I secured myself as at first, and groped among the waving tangle. All that met my touch was cold and soft and gluey. The thicket was alive with crabs and lobsters, trundling to and fro lop-sidedly, and I had to harden my heart against the horror of their carrion neighbourhood. On all sides I could feel the grain and the clefts of hard, living stone; no planks, no iron, not a sign of any wreck; the *Espirito Santo* was not there. I remember I had almost a sense of relief in my disappointment, and I was about ready to leave go, when something happened that sent me to the surface with my heart in my mouth. I had already stayed somewhat late over my explorations; the current was freshening with the change of the tide, and Sandag Bay was no longer a safe place for a single swimmer. Well, just at the last moment there came a sudden flush of current, dredging through the tangles like a wave. I lost one hold, was flung sprawling on my side, and, instinctively grasping for a fresh support, my fingers closed on something hard and cold. I think I knew at that moment what it was. At least I instantly left hold of the tangle, leaped for the surface, and clambered out next moment on the friendly rocks with the bone of a man's leg in my grasp.

Mankind is a material creature, slow to think and dull to

perceive connections. The grave, the wreck of the brig, and the rusty shoe-buckle were surely plain advertisements. A child might have read their dismal story, and yet it was not until I touched that actual piece of mankind that the full horror of the charnel ocean burst upon my spirit. I laid the bone beside the buckle, picked up my clothes, and ran as I was along the rocks towards the human shore. I could not be far enough from the spot; no fortune was vast enough to tempt me back again. The bones of the drowned dead should henceforth roll undisturbed by me, whether on tangle or minted gold. But as soon as I trod the good earth again and had covered my nakedness against the sun, I knelt down over against the ruins of the brig, and out of the fulness of my heart prayed long and passionately for all poor souls upon the sea. A generous prayer is never presented in vain; the petition may be refused, but the petitioner is always, I believe, rewarded by some gracious visitation. The horror, at least, was lifted from my mind; I could look with calm of spirit on that great bright creature, God's ocean; and as I set off homeward up the rough sides of Aros, nothing remained of any concern beyond a deep determination to meddle no more with the spoils of wrecked vessels or the treasures of the dead.

I was already some way up the hill before I paused to breathe and look behind me. The sight that met my eyes was doubly strange.

For, first, the storm that I had foreseen was now advancing with almost tropical rapidity. The whole surface of the sea had been dulled from its conspicuous brightness to an ugly hue of corrugated lead; already in the distance the white waves, the 'skipper's daughters,' had begun to flee before a breeze that was still insensible on Aros; and already along the curve of Sandag Bay there was a splashing run of sea that I could hear from where I stood. The change upon the sky was even more remarkable. There had begun to arise out of the south-west a huge and solid continent of scowling cloud; here and there, through rents in its contexture, the sun still poured a sheaf of spreading rays; and here and there, from all its edges, vast inky streamers lay forth along the yet unclouded sky. The menace was express and imminent. Even as I gazed, the sun was blotted out. At any moment the tempest might fall upon Aros in its might.

The suddenness of this change of weather so fixed my eyes on heaven that it was some seconds before they alighted on the bay, mapped out below my feet, and robbed a moment later of the sun. The knoll which I had just surmounted overflanked a little amphitheatre of lower hillocks sloping towards the sea, and beyond that the yellow arc of beach and the whole extent of Sandag Bay. It was a scene on which I had often looked down, but where I had never before beheld a human figure. I had but just turned my back upon it and left it empty, and my wonder may be fancied when I saw a boat and several men in that deserted spot. The boat was lying by the rocks. A pair of fellows, bareheaded, with their sleeves rolled up, and one with a boat-hook, kept her with difficulty to her moorings, for the current was growing brisker every moment. A little way off upon the ledge two men in black clothes, whom I judged to be superior in rank, laid their heads together over some task which at first I did not understand, but a second after I had made it out – they were taking bearings with the compass; and just then I saw one of them unroll a sheet of paper and lay his finger down, as though identifying features in a map. Meanwhile a third was walking to and fro, poking among the rocks and peering over the edge into the water. While I was still watching them with the stupefaction of surprise, my mind hardly yet able to work on what my eyes reported, this third person suddenly stooped and summoned his companions with a cry so loud that it reached my ears upon the hill. The others ran to him, even dropping the compass in their hurry, and I could see the bone and the shoe-buckle going from hand to hand, causing the most unusual gesticulations of surprise and interest. Just then I could hear the seamen crying from the boat, and saw them point westward to that cloud continent which was ever the more rapidly unfurling its blackness over heaven. The others seemed to consult; but the danger was too pressing to be braved, and they bundled into the boat carrying my relics with them, and set forth out of the bay with all speed of oars.

I made no more ado about the matter, but turned and ran for the house. Whoever these men were, it was fit my uncle should be instantly informed. It was not then altogether too late in the day for a descent of the Jacobites; and maybe Prince Charlie, whom I knew my uncle to detest, was one of the three superiors whom I had seen upon the rock. Yet as I ran, leaping from rock to rock, and turned the matter loosely in my mind, this theory grew ever the longer the less welcome to my reason. The compass, the map, the interest awakened by the buckle, and the conduct of that one among the strangers who had looked so often below him in the water, all seemed to point to a different explanation of their presence on that outlying, obscure islet of the western sea. The Madrid historian, the search instituted by Dr Robertson, the bearded stranger with the rings, my own fruitless search that very morning in the deep water of Sandag Bay, ran together, piece by piece, in my memory, and I made sure that these strangers must be Spaniards in quest of ancient treasure and the lost ship of the Armada. But the people living in outlying islands, such as Aros, are answerable for their own security; there is none near by to protect or even to help them; and the presence in such a spot of a crew of foreign adventurers – poor, greedy, and most likely lawless – filled me with apprehensions for my uncle's money, and even for the safety of his daughter. I was still wondering how we were to get rid of them when I came, all breathless, to the top of Aros. The whole world was shadowed over; only in the extreme east, on a hill of the mainland, one last gleam of sunshine lingered like a jewel; rain had begun to fall, not heavily, but in great drops; the sea was rising with each moment, and already a band of white encircled Aros and the nearer coasts of Grisapol. The boat was still pulling seaward, but I now became aware of what had been hidden from me lower down – a large, heavily sparred, handsome schooner, lying-to at the south end of Aros. Since I had not seen her in the morning when I had looked around so closely at the signs of the weather, and upon these lone waters where a sail was rarely visible, it was clear she must have lain last night behind the uninhabited Eilean Gour, and this proved conclusively that she was manned by strangers to our coast, for that anchorage, though good enough to look at, is little better than a trap for ships. With such ignorant sailors upon so wild a coast, the coming gale was not unlikely to bring death upon its wings.

FOUR

The Gale

I found my uncle at the gable-end, watching the signs of the weather, with a pipe in his fingers.

'Uncle,' said I, 'there were men ashore at Sandag Bay –'

I had no time to go further; indeed, I not only forgot my words, but even my weariness, so strange was the effect on Uncle Gordon. He dropped his pipe and fell back against the end of the house with his jaw fallen, his eyes staring, and his long face as white as paper. We must have looked at one another silently for a quarter of a minute, before he made answer in this extraordinary fashion: 'Had he a hair kep on?'

I knew as well as if I had been there that the man who now lay buried at Sandag had worn a hair cap, and that he had come ashore alive. For the first and only time I lost toleration for the man who was my benefactor and the father of the woman I hoped to call my wife.

'These were living men,' said I, 'perhaps Jacobites, perhaps the French, perhaps pirates, perhaps adventurers come here to seek the Spanish treasure-ship; but, whatever they may be, dangerous at least to your daughter and my cousin. As for your own guilty terrors, man, the dead sleeps well where you have laid him. I stood this morning by his grave; he will not wake before the trump of doom.'

My kinsman looked upon me, blinking, while I spoke; then he fixed his eyes for a little on the ground and pulled his fingers foolishly; but it was plain that he was past the power of speech.

'Come,' said I. 'You must think for others. You must come up the hill with me, and see this ship.'

He obeyed without a word or a look, following slowly after my impatient strides. The spring seemed to have gone out of his body, and he scrambled heavily up and down the rocks, instead of leaping, as he was wont, from one to another. Nor could I, for all my cries, induce him to make better haste. Only once he replied to me complainingly, and like one in bodily pain: 'Ay, ay, man, I'm coming.' Long before we had reached the top, I had no other thought for him but pity. If the crime had been monstrous, the punishment was in proportion.

At last we emerged above the sky-line of the hill, and could see around us. All was black and stormy to the eye; the last gleam of sun had vanished; a wind had sprung up, not yet high, but gusty and unsteady to the point; the rain, on the other hand, had ceased. Short as was the interval, the sea already ran vastly higher than when I had stood there last; already it had begun to break over some of the outward reefs, and already it moaned aloud in the sea-caves of Aros. I looked, at first in vain, for the schooner.

'There she is,' I said at last. But her new position, and the course she was now lying, puzzled me. 'They cannot mean to beat to sea,' I cried.

'That's what they mean,' said my uncle, with something like joy; and just then the schooner went about and stood upon another tack which put the question beyond the reach of doubt. These strangers, seeing a gale on hand, had thought first of sea-room. With the wind that threatened, in these reef-sown waters and contending against so violent a stream of tide, their course was certain death.

'Good God!' said I, 'they are all lost.'

'Ay,' returned my uncle, 'a'—a' lost. They hadna a chance but to rin for Kyle Dona. The gate they're gaun the noo, they couldna win through an the muckle deil were there to pilot them. Eh, man,' he continued, touching me on the sleeve, 'it's a braw nicht for a shipwreck!

Twa in ae twalmonth! Eh, but the Merry Men'll dance bonny!'

I looked at him, and it was then that I began to fancy him no longer in his right mind. He was peering up to me, as if for sympathy, a timid joy in his eyes. All that had passed between us was already forgotten in the prospect of this fresh disaster.

'If it were not too late,' I cried with indignation, 'I would take the coble and go out to warn them.'

'Na, na,' he protested, 'ye maunna interfere; ye maunna meddle wi' the like o' that. It's His' – doffing his bonnet – 'His wull. And, eh, man! but it's braw nicht for 't!'

Something like fear began to creep into my soul; and, reminding him that I had not yet dined, I proposed we should return to the house. But no; nothing would tear him from his place of outlook.

'I maun see the hail thing, man Charlie,' he explained; and then as the schooner went about a second time, 'Eh, but they han'le her bonny!' he cried. 'The *Christ-Anna* was naething to this.'

Already the men on board the schooner must have begun to realise some part, but not yet the twentieth, of the dangers that environed their doomed ship. At every lull of the capricious wind they must have seen how fast the current swept them back. Each tack was made shorter, as they saw how little it prevailed. Every moment the rising swell began to boom and foam upon another sunken reef; and ever and again a breaker would fall in sounding ruin under the very bows of her, and the brown reef and streaming tangle appear in the hollow of the wave. I tell you, they had to stand to their tackle; there was no idle man aboard that ship, God knows. It was upon the progress of a scene so horrible to any human-hearted man that my misguided uncle now pored and gloated like a connoisseur. As I turned to go down the hill, he was lying on his belly on the summit, with his hands stretched forth and clutching in the heather. He seemed rejuvenated, mind and body.

When I got back to the house already dismally affected, I was still more sadly downcast at the sight of Mary. She had her sleeves rolled up over her strong arms, and was quietly making bread. I got a bannock from the dresser and sat down to eat it in silence.

'Are ye wearied, lad?' she asked after a while.

'I am not so much wearied, Mary,' I replied, getting on my feet, 'as I am weary of delay, and perhaps of Aros too. You know me well enough to judge me fairly, say what I like. Well, Mary, you may be sure of this: you had better be anywhere but here.'

'I'll be sure of one thing,' she returned: 'I'll be where my duty is.'

'You forget, you have a duty to yourself,' I said.

'Ay, man,' she replied, pounding at the dough; 'will you have found that in the Bible, now?'

'Mary,' I said solemnly, 'you must not laugh at me just now. God knows I am in no heart for laughing. If we could get your father with us, it would be best; but with him or without him, I want you far away from here, my girl; for your own sake, and for mine, ay, and for your father's too, I want you far – far away from here. I came with other thoughts; I came here as a man comes home; now it is all changed, and I have no desire nor hope but to flee – for that's the word – flee, like a bird out of the fowler's snare, from this accursed island.'

She had stopped her work by this time.

'And do you think, now,' said she, 'do ye think, now, I have neither eyes nor ears? Do ye think I havena broken my heart to have these braws (as he calls them, God forgive him!) thrown into the sea? Do ye think I have lived with him, day in, day out, and not seen what you saw in an hour or two? No,' she said, 'I know there's wrong in it; what wrong, I neither know nor want to know. There was never an ill thing made better by meddling, that I could hear of. But, my lad, you must never ask me to leave my father. While the breath is in his body, I'll be with him. And he's not long for here, either: that I can tell you, Charlie – he's not long for here. The mark is on his brow; and better so – maybe better so.'

I was a while silent, not knowing what to say; and when I roused my head at last to speak, she got before me.

'Charlie,' she said, 'what's right for me, needna be right for you. There's sin upon this house and trouble; you are a stranger; take your things upon your back and go your ways to better places and to better folk, and if you were ever minded to come back, though it were twenty years syne, you would find me aye waiting.'

'Mary Ellen,' I said, 'I asked you to be my wife, and you said as good as yes. That's done for good. Wherever you are, I am; as I shall answer to my God.'

As I said the words, the winds suddenly burst out raving, and then seemed to stand still and shudder round the house of Aros. It was the first squall, or prologue, of the coming tempest, and as we started and looked about us, we found that a gloom like the approach of evening, had settled round the house.

'God pity all poor folks at sea!' she said. 'We'll see no more of my father till the morrow's morning.'

And then she told me, as we sat by the fire and hearkened to the rising gusts, of how this change had fallen upon my uncle. All last winter he had been dark and fitful in his mind. Whenever the Roost ran high, or, as Mary said, whenever the Merry Men were dancing, he would lie out for hours together on the Head, if it were at night, or on the top of Aros by day, watching the tumult of the sea, and sweeping the horizon for a sail. After February the tenth, when the wealth-bringing wreck was cast ashore at Sandag, he had been at first unnaturally gay, and his excitement had never fallen in degree, but only changed in kind from dark to darker. He neglected his work, and kept Rorie idle. They two would speak together by the hour at the gable-end, in guarded tones and with an air of secrecy and almost of guilt; and if she questioned either, as at first she sometimes did, her inquiries were put aside with confusion. Since Rorie had first remarked the fish that hung about the ferry, his master had never set foot but once upon the mainland of the Ross. That once – it was in the height of the springs – he had passed dry-shod while the tide was out; but, having lingered over-long on the far side, found himself cut off from Aros by the returning waters. It was with a shriek of agony that he had leaped across the gut, and he had reached home thereafter in a fever-fit of fear. A fear of the sea, a constant haunting thought of the sea, appeared in his talk and devotions, and even in his looks when he was silent.

Rorie alone came in to supper; but a little later my uncle appeared, took a bottle under his arm, put some bread in his pocket, and set forth again to his outlook, followed this time by Rorie. I heard that the schooner was losing ground, but the crew were still fighting every inch with hopeless ingenuity and courage; and the news filled my mind with blackness.

A little after sundown the full fury of the gale broke forth, such a gale as I have never seen in summer, nor, seeing how swiftly it had come, even in winter. Mary and I sat in silence, the house quaking overhead, the tempest howling without, the fire between us sputtering with raindrops. Our thoughts were far away with the poor fellows on the schooner, or my not less unhappy uncle, houseless on the promontory; and yet ever and again we were startled back to ourselves, when the wind would rise and strike the gable like a solid body, or suddenly fall and draw away, so that the fire leaped into flame and our hearts bounded in our sides. Now the storm in its might would seize and shake the four corners of the roof, roaring like Leviathan in anger. Anon, in a lull, cold eddies of tempest moved shudderingly in the room, lifting the hair upon our heads and passing between us as we sat. And again the wind would break forth in a chorus of melancholy sounds, hooting low in the chimney, wailing with flutelike softness round the house.

It was perhaps eight o'clock when Rorie came in and pulled me mysteriously to the door. My uncle, it appeared, had frightened even his constant comrade; and Rorie, uneasy at his extravagance, prayed me to come out and share the watch. I hastened to do as I was asked; the more readily as, what with fear and horror, and the electrical tension of the night, I was myself restless and disposed for action. I told Mary to be under no alarm, for I should be a safeguard on her father; and wrapping myself warmly in a plaid, I followed Rorie into the open air.

The night, though we were so little past midsummer, was as dark as January. Intervals of a groping twilight alternated with spells of utter blackness; and it was impossible to trace the reason of these changes in the flying horror of the sky. The wind blew the breath out of a man's nostrils; all heaven seemed to thunder overhead like one huge sail; and when there fell a momentary lull on Aros, we could hear the gusts dismally sweeping in the distance. Over all the lowlands of the Ross, the wind must have blown as fierce as on the open sea; and God only knows the uproar that was raging around the head of Ben Kyaw. Sheets of mingled spray and rain were driven in our faces. All round the isle of Aros the surf, with an incessant, hammering thunder, beat upon the reefs and beaches. Now louder in one place, now lower in another, like the combinations of orchestral music, the constant mass of sound was hardly varied for a moment. And loud above all this hurly-burly I could hear the changeful voices of the Roost and the intermittent roaring of the Merry Men. At that hour, there flashed into my mind the reason of the name that they were called. For the noise of them seemed almost mirthful, as it out-topped the other noises of the night; or if not mirthful, yet instinct with a portentous joviality. Nay, and it seemed even human. As when savage men have drunk away their reason, and, discarding speech, bawl together in their madness by the hour; so, to my ears, these deadly breakers shouted by Aros in the night.

Arm in arm, and staggering against the wind, Rorie and I won every yard of ground with conscious effort. We slipped on the wet sod, we fell together sprawling on the rocks. Bruised, drenched, beaten, and breathless, it must have taken us near half an hour to get from the house down to the Head that overlooks the Roost. There, it seemed, was my uncle's favourite observatory. Right in the face of it, where the cliff is highest and most sheer, a hump of earth, like a parapet, makes a place of shelter from the common winds, where a man may sit in quiet and see the tide and the mad billows contending at his feet. As he might look down from the window of a house upon some street disturbance, so, from this post, he looks down upon the tumbling of the Merry Men. On such a night, of course, he peers upon a world of blackness, where the waters wheel and boil, where the waves joust together with the noise of an explosion, and the foam towers and vanishes in the twinkling of an eye. Never before had I seen the Merry Men thus violent. The fury, height, and transiency of their spoutings was a thing to be seen and not recounted. High over our heads on the cliff rose their white columns in the darkness; and the same instant, like phantoms, they were gone. Sometimes a gust took them, and the spray would fall about us, heavy as a wave. And yet the spectacle was rather maddening in its levity than impressive by its force. Thought was beaten down by the confounding uproar; a gleeful vacancy possessed the brains of men, a state akin to madness; and I found myself at times following the dance of the Merry Men as it were a tune upon a jigging instrument.

I first caught sight of my uncle when we were still some yards away in one of the flying glimpses of twilight that chequered the pitch darkness of the night. He was standing up behind the parapet, his head thrown back and the bottle to his mouth. As he put it down, he saw and recognised us with a toss of one hand fleeringly above his head.

'Has he been drinking?' shouted I to Rorie.

'He will aye be drunk when the wind blaws,' returned Rorie in the same high key, and it was all that I could do to hear him.

'Then – was he so – in February?' I inquired.

Rorie's 'Ay' was a cause of joy to me. The murder, then, had not sprung in cold blood from calculation; it was an act of madness no more to be condemned than to be pardoned. My uncle was a dangerous madman, if you will, but he was not cruel and base as I had feared. Yet what a scene for a carouse, what an incredible vice was this that the poor man had chosen! I have always thought drunkenness a wild and almost fearful pleasure, rather demoniacal than human; but drunkenness, out here in the roaring blackness, on the edge of a cliff above that hell of waters, the man's head spinning like the Roost, his foot tottering on the edge of death, his ear watching for the signs of shipwreck, surely that, if it were credible in any one, was morally impossible in a man like my uncle, whose mind was set upon a damnatory creed and haunted by the darkest superstitions. Yet so it was; and, as we reached the bight of shelter and could breathe again, I saw the man's eye shining in the night with an unholy glimmer.

'Eh, Charlie man, it's grand!' he cried. 'See to them!' he continued, dragging me to the edge of the abyss from whence arose that deafening clamour and those clouds of spray; 'see to them dancin', man! Is that no' wicked?'

He pronounced the word with gusto, and I thought it suited the scene.

'They're yowlin' for thon schooner,' he went on, his thin, insane voice clearly audible in the shelter of the bank, 'an' she's comin' aye nearer, aye nearer, aye nearer an' nearer an' nearer; an' they ken't, the folk kens it, they ken weel it's by wi' them. Charlie, lad, they're a' drunk in yon schooner, a' dozened wi' drink. They were a' drunk in the *Christ-Anna*, at the hinder end. There's nane could droon at sea wantin' the brandy. Hoot awa, what do you ken?' with a sudden blast of anger. 'I tell ye, it canna be; they daurna droon withoot it. Ha'e,' holding out the bottle, 'tak' a sowp.'

I was about to refuse, but Rorie touched me as if in warning; and indeed I had already thought better of the movement. I took the bottle, therefore, and not only drank freely myself, but contrived to spill even more as I was doing so. It was pure spirit, and almost strangled me to swallow. My kinsman did not observe the loss, but, once more throwing back his head, drained the remainder to the dregs. Then, with a loud laugh, he cast the bottle forth among the Merry Men, who seemed to leap up, shouting, to receive it.

'Ha'e, bairns!' he cried, 'there's your han'sel. Ye'll get bonnier nor that, or morning.'

Suddenly, out in the black night before us, and not two hundred yards away, we heard, at a moment when the wind was silent, the clear note of a human voice. Instantly the wind swept howling down upon the Head, and the Roost bellowed, and churned, and danced with a new fury. But we had heard the sound, and we knew, with agony, that this was the doomed ship now close on ruin, and that what we had heard was the voice of her master issuing his last command. Crouching together on the edge, we waited, straining every sense, for the inevitable end. It was long, however, and to us it seemed like ages, ere the schooner suddenly appeared for one brief instant, relieved against a tower of glimmering foam. I still see her reefed mainsail flapping loose, as the boom fell heavily across the deck; I still see the black outline of the hull, and still think I can distinguish the figure of a man stretched upon the tiller. Yet the whole sight we had of her passed swifter than lightning; the very wave that disclosed her fell burying her for ever; the mingled cry of many voices at the point of death rose and was quenched in the roaring of the Merry Men. And with that the tragedy was at an end. The strong ship, with all her gear, and the lamp perhaps still burning in the cabin, the lives of so many men, precious surely to others, dear, at least, as heaven to themselves, had all, in that one moment, gone down into the surging waters. They were gone like a dream. And the wind still ran and shouted, and the senseless waters in the Roost still leaped and tumbled as before.

How long we lay there together, we three, speechless and motionless, is more than I can tell, but it must have been for long. At length, one by one, and almost mechanically, we crawled back into the shelter of the bank. As I lay against the parapet, wholly wretched and not entirely master of my mind, I could hear my kinsman maundering to himself in an altered and melancholy mood. Now he would repeat to himself with maudlin iteration, 'Sic a fecht as they had – sic a sair fecht as they had, puir lads, puir lads!' and anon he would bewail that 'a' the gear was as gude 's tint,' because the ship had gone down among the Merry Men instead of stranding on the shore; and throughout, the name – the *Christ-Anna* – would come and go in his divagations, pronounced with shuddering awe. The storm all this time was rapidly abating. In half an hour the wind had fallen to a breeze, and the change was accompanied or caused by a heavy, cold, and plumping rain. I must then have fallen asleep, and when I came to myself, drenched, stiff, and unrefreshed, day had already broken, grey, wet, discomfortable day; the wind blew in faint and shifting capfuls, the tide was out, the Roost was at its lowest, and only the strong beating surf round all the coasts of Aros remained to witness of the furies of the night.

FIVE

A man out of the sea

Rorie set out for the house in search of warmth and breakfast; but my uncle was bent upon examining the shores of Aros, and I felt it a part of duty to accompany him throughout. He was now docile and quiet, but tremulous and weak in mind and body; and it was with the eagerness of a child that he pursued his exploration. He climbed far down upon the rocks; on the beaches, he pursued the retreating breakers. The merest broken plank or rag of cordage was a treasure in his eyes to be secured at the peril of his life. To see him, with weak and stumbling footsteps, expose himself to the pursuit of the surf, or the snares and pitfalls of the weedy rock, kept me in a perpetual terror. My arm was ready to support him, my hand clutched him by the skirt, I helped him to draw his pitiful discoveries beyond the reach of the returning wave; a nurse accompanying a child of seven would have had no different experience.

Yet, weakened as he was by the reaction from his madness of the night before, the passions that smouldered in his nature were those of a strong man. His terror of the sea, although conquered for the moment, was still undiminished; had the sea been a lake of living flames, he could not have shrunk more panically from its touch; and once, when his foot slipped and he plunged to the mid-leg into a pool of water, the shriek that came up out of his soul was like the cry of death. He sat still for a while, panting like a dog, after that; but his desire for the spoils of shipwreck triumphed once more over his fears; once more he tottered among the curded foam; once more he crawled upon the rocks among the bursting bubbles; once more his whole heart seemed to be set on drift-wood, fit, if it was fit for anything, to throw upon the fire. Pleased as he was with what he found, he still incessantly grumbled at his ill-fortune.

'Aros,' he said, 'is no' a place for wrecks ava' – no' ava'. A' the years I've dwalt here, this ane make the second; and the best o' the gear clean tint!'

'Uncle,' said I, for we were now on a stretch of open sand, where there was nothing to divert his mind, 'I saw you last night as I never thought to see you – you were drunk.'

'Na, na,' he said, 'no' as bad as that. I had been drinking, though. And to tell ye the God's truth, it's a thing I canna mend. There's nae soberer man than me in my ordnar; but when I hear the wind blaw in my lug, it's my belief that I gang gyte.'

'You are a religious man,' I replied, 'and this is sin.'

'Ou,' he returned, 'if it wasna sin, I dinna ken that I would care for 't. Ye see, man, it's defiance. There's a sair spang o' the auld sin o' the warld in yon sea; it's an unchristian business at the best o't; an' whiles when it gets up, an' the wind skreighs – the wind an' her are a kind of sib, I'm thinking – an' thae Merry Men, the daft callants, blawin' and lauchin', and puir souls in the deid thraws warstlin' the leelang nicht wi' their bit ships – weel, it comes ower me like a glamour. I'm a deil, I ken 't. But I think naething o' the puir sailor lads; I'm wi' the sea, I'm just like ane o' her ain Merry Men.'

I thought I should touch him in a joint of his harness. I turned me towards the sea; the surf was running gaily, wave after wave, with their manes blowing behind them, riding one after another up the beach, towering, curving, falling one upon another on the trampled sand. Without, the salt air, the scared gulls, the widespread army of the sea-chargers, neighing to each other, as they gathered together to the assault of Aros; and close before us, that line on the flat sands that, with all their number and their fury, they might never pass.

'Thus far shalt thou go,' said I, 'and no farther.' And then I quoted as solemnly as I was able a verse that I had often before fitted to the chorus of the breakers:

> 'But yet the Lord that is on high,
> Is more of might by far,
> Than noise of many waters is,
> Or great sea-billows are.'

'Ay,' said my kinsman, 'at the hinder end, the Lord will triumph; I dinna misdoobt that. But here on earth, even silly men-folk daur Him to His face. It is no' wise; I am no' sayin' that it's wise; but it's the pride of the eye, and it's the lust o' life, an' it's the wale o' pleesures.'

I said no more, for we had now begun to cross a neck of land that lay between us and Sandag; and I withheld my last appeal to the man's better reason till we should stand upon the spot associated with his crime. Nor did he pursue the subject; but he walked beside me with a firmer step. The call that I had made upon his mind acted like a stimulant, and I could see that he had forgotten his search for worthless jetsam, in a profound, gloomy, and yet stirring train of thought. In three or four minutes we had topped the brae and begun to go down upon Sandag. The wreck had been roughly handled by the sea; the stem had been spun round and dragged a little lower down; and perhaps the stern had been forced a little higher, for the two parts now lay entirely separate on the beach. When we came to the grave I stopped, uncovered my head in the thick rain, and, looking my kinsman in the face, addressed him.

'A man,' said I, 'was in God's providence suffered to escape from mortal dangers; he was poor, he was naked, he was wet, he was weary, he was a stranger; he had every claim upon the bowels of your compassion; it may be that he was the salt of the earth, holy, helpful, and kind; it may be he was a man laden with iniquities to whom death was the beginning of torment. I ask you in the sight of Heaven: Gordon Darnaway, where is the man for whom Christ died?'

He started visibly at the last words; but there came no answer, and his face expressed no feeling but a vague alarm.

'You were my father's brother,' I continued: 'you have taught me to count your house as if it were my father's house; and we are both sinful men walking before the Lord among the sins and dangers of this life. It is by our evil that God leads us into good; we sin, I dare not say by His temptation, but I must say with His consent; and to any but the brutish man his sins are the beginning of wisdom. God has warned you by this crime; He warns you still by the bloody grave between our feet; and if there shall follow no repentance, no improvement, no return to Him, what can we look for but the following of some memorable judgment?'

Even as I spoke the words, the eyes of my uncle wandered from my face. A change fell upon his looks that cannot be described; his features seemed to dwindle in size, the colour faded from his cheeks, one hand rose waveringly and pointed over my shoulder into the distance, and the oft-repeated name fell once more from his lips: 'The *Christ-Anna!*'

I turned; and if I was not appalled to the same degree, as I return thanks to Heaven that I had not the cause, I was still startled by the sight that met my eyes. The form of a man stood upright on the cabin-hutch of the wrecked ship; his back was towards us; he appeared to be scanning the offing with shaded eyes, and his figure was relieved to its full height, which was plainly very great, against the sea and sky. I have said a thousand times that I am not superstitious; but at that moment, with my mind running upon death and sin, the unexplained appearance of a stranger on that sea-girt, solitary island filled me with a surprise that bordered close on terror. It seemed scarce possible that any human soul should have come ashore alive in such a sea as had raged last night along the coasts of Aros; and the only vessel within miles had gone down

before our eyes among the Merry Men. I was assailed with
doubts that made suspense unbearable, and, to put the
matter to the touch at once, stepped forward and hailed
the figure like a ship.

He turned about, and I thought he started to behold
us. At this my courage instantly revived and I called and
signed to him to draw near, and he, on his part, dropped
immediately to the sands and began slowly to approach,
with many stops and hesitations. At each repeated mark
of the man's uneasiness I grew the more confident myself;
and I advanced another step, encouraging him as I did so
with my head and hand. It was plain the castaway had
heard indifferent accounts of our island hospitality; and
indeed, about this time, the people farther north had a
sorry reputation.

'Why,' I said, 'the man is black!'

And just at that moment, in a voice that I could scarce
have recognised, my kinsman began swearing and praying
in a mingled stream. I looked at him; he had fallen on his
knees, his face was agonised; at each step of the castaway's
the pitch of his voice rose, the volubility of his utterance
and the fervour of his language redoubled. I call it prayer,
for it was addressed to God; but surely no such ranting
incongruities were ever before addressed to the Creator
by a creature: surely if prayer can be a sin, this mad
harangue was sinful. I ran to my kinsman, I seized him
by the shoulders, I dragged him to his feet.

'Silence, man,' said I, 'respect your God in words, if not
in action. Here, on the very scene of your transgressions,
He sends you an occasion of atonement. Forward and
embrace it; welcome like a father yon creature who comes
trembling to your mercy.'

With that, I tried to force him towards the black; but
he felled me to the ground, burst from my grasp, leaving
the shoulder of his jacket, and fled up the hillside towards
the top of Aros like a deer. I staggered to my feet again,
bruised and somewhat stunned; the negro had paused in
surprise, perhaps in terror, some half-way between me and
the wreck; my uncle was already far away, bounding from
rock to rock; and I thus found myself torn for a time

between two duties. But I judged, and I pray Heaven that I
judged rightly, in favour of the poor wretch upon the sands;
his misfortune was at least not plainly of his own creation;
it was one, besides, that I could certainly relieve; and I had
begun by that time to regard my uncle as an incurable and
dismal lunatic. I advanced accordingly towards the black,
who now awaited my approach with folded arms, like one
prepared for either destiny. As I came nearer, he reached
forth his hand with a great gesture, such as I had seen
from the pulpit, and spoke to me in something of a pulpit
voice, but not a word was comprehensible. I tried him
first in English, then in Gaelic, both in vain; so that it was
clear we must rely upon the tongue of looks and gestures.
Thereupon I signed to him to follow me, which he did
readily and with a grave obeisance like a fallen king; all
the while there had come no shade of alteration in his
face, neither of anxiety while he was still waiting, nor of
relief now that he was reassured; if he were a slave, as I
supposed, I could not but judge he must have fallen from
some high place in his own country, and fallen as he was,
I could not but admire his bearing. As we passed the grave,
I paused and raised my hands and eyes to heaven in token
of respect and sorrow for the dead; and he, as if in answer,
bowed low and spread his hands abroad; it was a strange
motion, but done like a thing of common custom; and
I supposed it was ceremonial in the land from which he
came. At the same time he pointed to my uncle, whom
he could just see perched upon a knoll, and touched his
head to indicate that he was mad.

We took the long way round the shore, for I feared
to excite my uncle if we struck across the island; and
as we walked, I had time enough to mature the little
dramatic exhibition by which I hoped to satisfy my
doubts. Accordingly, pausing on a rock, I proceeded to
imitate before the negro the action of the man whom I
had seen the day before taking bearings with the compass
at Sandag. He understood me at once, and, taking the
imitation out of my hands, showed me where the boat
was, pointed out seaward as if to indicate the position of
the schooner, and then down along the edge of the rock

with the words, 'Espirito Santo,' strangely pronounced, but clear enough for recognition. I had thus been right in my conjecture; the pretended historical inquiry had been but a cloak for treasure-hunting; the man who had played Dr Robertson was the same as the foreigner who visited Grisapol in spring, and now, with many others, lay dead under the Roost of Aros; there had their greed brought them, there should their bones be tossed for evermore. In the meantime the black continued his imitation of the scene, now looking up skyward as though watching the approach of the storm; now, in the character of a seaman, waving the rest to come aboard; now as an officer, running along the rock and entering the boat; and anon bending over imaginary oars with the air of a hurried boatsman; but all with the same solemnity of manner, so that I was never even moved to smile. Lastly, he indicated to me, by a pantomime not to be described in words, how he himself had gone up to examine the stranded wreck, and, to his grief and indignation, had been deserted by his comrades; and thereupon folded his arms once more, and stooped his head, like one accepting fate.

The mystery of his presence being thus solved for me, I explained to him by means of a sketch the fate of the vessel and of all aboard her. He showed no surprise nor sorrow, and, with a sudden lifting of his open hand, seemed to dismiss his former friends or masters (whichever they had been) into God's pleasure. Respect came upon me and grew stronger, the more I observed him; I saw he had a powerful mind and a sober and severe character, such as I loved to commune with; and before we reached the house of Aros I had almost forgotten, and wholly forgiven him, his uncanny colour.

To Mary I told all that had passed without suppression, though I own my heart failed me; but I did wrong to doubt her sense of justice.

'You did the right,' she said. 'God's will be done.' And she set out meat for us at once.

As soon as I was satisfied, I bade Rorie keep an eye upon the castaway, who was still eating, and set forth again myself to find my uncle. I had not gone far before I saw him sitting in the same place, upon the very topmost knoll, and seemingly in the same attitude as when I had last observed him. From that point, as I have said, the most of Aros and the neighbouring Ross would be spread below him like a map; and it was plain that he kept a bright look-out in all directions, for my head had scarcely risen above the summit of the first ascent before he had leaped to his feet and turned as if to face me. I hailed him at once, as well as I was able, in the same tones and words as I had often used before, when I had come to summon him to dinner. He made not so much as a movement in reply. I passed on a little farther, and again tried parley, with the same result. But when I began a second time to advance, his insane fears blazed up again, and still in dead silence, but with incredible speed, he began to flee from before me along the rocky summit of the hill. An hour before, he had been dead weary, and I had been comparatively active. But now his strength was recruited by the fervour of insanity, and it would have been vain for me to dream of pursuit. Nay, the very attempt, I thought, might have inflamed his terrors, and thus increased the miseries of our position. And I had nothing left but to turn homeward and make my sad report to Mary.

She heard it, as she had heard the first, with a concerned composure, and, bidding me lie down and take that rest of which I stood so much in need, set forth herself in quest of her misguided father. At that age it would have been a strange thing that put me from either meat or sleep; I slept long and deep; and it was already long past noon before I awoke and came down-stairs into the kitchen. Mary, Rorie, and the black castaway were seated about the fire in silence; and I could see that Mary had been weeping. There was cause enough, as I soon learned, for tears. First she, and then Rorie, had been forth to seek my uncle; each in turn had found him perched upon the hill-top, and from each in turn he had silently and swiftly fled. Rorie had tried to chase him, but in vain; madness lent a new vigour to his bounds; he sprang from rock to rock over the widest gullies; he scoured like the wind along the hill-tops; he doubled and twisted like a hare before the dogs; and Rorie at length gave in; and the last that he saw, my uncle was seated as before upon the crest of Aros. Even during the hottest excitement of the chase, even when the fleet-footed servant had come, for a moment, very near to capture him, the poor lunatic had uttered not a sound. He fled, and he was silent, like a beast; and this silence had terrified his pursuer.

There was something heart-breaking in the situation. How to capture the madman, how to feed him in the meanwhile, and what to do with him when he was captured, were the three difficulties that we had to solve.

'The black,' said I, 'is the cause of this attack. It may even be his presence in the house that keeps my uncle on the hill. We have done the fair thing; he has been fed and warmed under this roof; now I propose that Rorie put him across the bay in the coble, and take him through the Ross as far as Grisapol.'

In this proposal Mary heartily concurred; and bidding the black follow us, we all three descended to the pier. Certainly, Heaven's will was declared against Gordon Darnaway; a thing had happened, never paralleled before in Aros; during the storm, the coble had broken loose, and striking on the rough splinters of the pier, now lay in four feet of water with one side stove in. Three days of work at least would be required to make her float. But I was not to be beaten. I led the whole party round to where the gut was narrowest, swam to the other side, and called to the black to follow me. He signed, with the same clearness and quiet as before, that he knew not the art; and there was truth apparent in his signals, it would have occurred to none of us to doubt his truth; and that hope being over, we must all go back even as we came to the house of Aros, the negro walking in our midst without embarrassment.

All we could do that day was to make one more attempt to communicate with the unhappy madman. Again he was visible on his perch; again he fled in silence. But food and a great cloak were at least left for his comfort; the rain, besides, had cleared away, and the night promised to be even warm. We might compose ourselves, we thought, until the morrow; rest was the chief requisite, that we might be strengthened for unusual exertions; and as none cared to talk, we separated at an early hour.

I lay long awake, planning a campaign for the morrow. I was to place the black on the side of Sandag, whence he should head my uncle towards the house; Rorie in the west, I on the east, were to complete the cordon, as best we might. It seemed to me, the more I recalled the configuration of the island, that it should be possible, though hard, to force him down upon the low ground along Aros Bay; and once there, even with the strength of his madness, ultimate escape was hardly to be feared. It was on his terror of the black that I relied; for I made sure, however he might run, it would not be in the direction of the man whom he supposed to have returned from the dead, and thus one point of the compass at least would be secure.

When at length I fell asleep, it was to be awakened shortly after by a dream of wrecks, black men, and submarine adventures; and I found myself so shaken and fevered that I arose, descended the stair, and stepped out before the house. Within, Rorie and the black were asleep together in the kitchen; outside was a wonderful clear night of stars, with here and there a cloud still hanging, last stragglers of the tempest. It was near the top of the flood, and the Merry Men were roaring in the windless quiet of the night. Never, not even in the height of the tempest, had I heard their song with greater awe. Now, when the winds were gathered home, when the deep was dandling itself back into its summer slumber, and when the stars rained their gentle light over land and sea, the voice of these tide-breakers was still raised for havoc. They seemed, indeed, to be a part of the world's evil and the tragic side of life. Nor were their meaningless vociferations the only sounds that broke the silence of the night. For I could hear, now shrill and thrilling and now almost drowned, the note of a human voice that accompanied the uproar of the Roost. I knew it for my kinsman's; and a great fear fell upon me of God's judgments, and the evil in the world. I went back again into the darkness of the house as into a place of shelter, and lay long upon my bed, pondering these mysteries.

It was late when I again awoke, and I leaped into my clothes and hurried to the kitchen. No one was there; Rorie and the black had both stealthily departed long before; and my heart stood still at the discovery. I could rely on Rorie's heart, but I placed no trust in his discretion. If he had thus set out without a word, he was plainly bent upon some service to my uncle. But what service could he hope to render even alone, far less in the company of the man in whom my uncle found his fears incarnated? Even if I were not already too late to prevent some deadly mischief, it was plain I must delay no longer. With the thought I was out of the house; and often as I have run on the rough sides of Aros, I never ran as I did that fatal morning. I do not believe I put twelve minutes to the whole ascent.

My uncle was gone from his perch. The basket had indeed been torn open and the meat scattered on the turf; but, as we found afterwards, no mouthful had been tasted; and there was not another trace of human existence in that wide field of view. Day had already filled the clear heavens; the sun already lighted in a rosy bloom upon the crest of Ben Kyaw; but all below me the rude knolls of Aros and the shield of the sea lay steeped in the clear darkling twilight of the dawn.

'Rorie!' I cried; and again 'Rorie!' My voice died in the silence, but there came no answer back. If there were indeed an enterprise afoot to catch my uncle, it was plainly not in fleetness of foot, but in dexterity of stalking, that the hunters placed their trust. I ran on farther, keeping the higher spurs, and looking right and left, nor did I pause again till I was on the mount above Sandag. I could see the wreck, the uncovered belt of sand, the waves idly beating the long ledge of rocks, and on either hand the tumbled knolls, boulders, and gullies of the island. But still no human thing.

At a stride the sunshine fell on Aros, and the shadows and colours leaped into being. Not half a moment later, below me to the west, sheep began to scatter as in a panic. There came a cry. I saw my uncle running. I saw the black jump up in hot pursuit; and before I had time to understand, Rorie also had appeared, calling directions in Gaelic as to a dog herding sheep.

I took to my heels to interfere, and perhaps I had done better to have waited where I was, for I was the means of cutting off the madman's last escape. There was nothing before him from that moment but the grave, the wreck, and the sea in Sandag Bay. And yet Heaven knows that what I did was for the best.

My uncle Gordon saw in what direction, horrible to him, the chase was driving him. He doubled, darting to the right and left; but high as the fever ran in his veins, the black was still the swifter. Turn where he would, he was still forestalled, still driven toward the scene of his crime. Suddenly he began to shriek aloud, so that the coast re-echoed; and now both I and Rorie were calling on the black to stop. But all was vain, for it was written otherwise. The pursuer still ran, the chase still sped before him screaming; they avoided the grave, and skimmed close past the timbers of the wreck; in a breath they had cleared the sand; and still my kinsman did not pause, but dashed straight into the surf; and the black, now almost within reach, still followed swiftly behind him. Rorie and I both stopped, for the thing was now beyond the hands of men, and these were the decrees of God that came to pass before our eyes. There was never a sharper ending. On that steep beach they were beyond their depth at a bound; neither could swim; the black rose once for a moment with a throttling cry; but the current had them, racing seaward; and if ever they came up again, which God alone can tell, it would be ten minutes after, at the far end of Aros Roost, where the sea-birds hover fishing.

Markheim

'YES,' SAID the dealer, 'our windfalls are of various kinds. Some customers are ignorant, and then I touch a dividend on my superior knowledge. Some are dishonest,' and here he held up the candle, so that the light fell strongly on his visitor, 'and in that case,' he continued, 'I profit by my virtue.'

Markheim had but just entered from the daylight streets, and his eyes had not yet grown familiar with the mingled shine and darkness in the shop. At these pointed words, and before the near presence of the flame, he blinked painfully and looked aside.

The dealer chuckled. 'You come to me on Christmas Day,' he resumed, 'when you know that I am alone in my house, put up my shutters, and make a point of refusing business. Well, you will have to pay for that; you will have to pay for my loss of time, when I should be balancing my books; you will have to pay, besides, for a kind of manner that I remark in you to-day very strongly. I am the essence of discretion, and ask no awkward questions; but when a customer cannot look me in the eye, he has to pay for it.' The dealer once more chuckled; and then, changing to his usual business voice, though still with a note of irony, 'You can give, as usual, a clear account of how you came into the possession of the object?' he continued. 'Still your uncle's cabinet? A remarkable collector, sir!'

And the little pale, round-shouldered dealer stood almost on tip-toe, looking over the top of his gold spectacles, and nodding his head with every mark of disbelief. Markheim returned his gaze with one of infinite pity, and a touch of horror.

'This time,' said he, 'you are in error. I have not come to sell, but to buy. I have no curios to dispose of; my uncle's

cabinet is bare to the wainscot; even were it still intact, I
have done well on the Stock Exchange, and should more
likely add to it than otherwise, and my errand to-day is
simplicity itself. I seek a Christmas present for a lady,'
he continued, waxing more fluent as he struck into the
speech he had prepared; 'and certainly I owe you every
excuse for thus disturbing you upon so small a matter.
But the thing was neglected yesterday; I must produce my
little compliment at dinner; and, as you very well know, a
rich marriage is not a thing to be neglected.'

There followed a pause, during which the dealer seemed
to weigh this statement incredulously. The ticking of many
clocks among the curious lumber of the shop, and the faint
rushing of the cabs in a near thoroughfare, filled up the
interval of silence.

'Well, sir,' said the dealer, 'be it so. You are an old
customer after all; and if, as you say, you have the chance
of a good marriage, far be it from me to be an obstacle.
– Here is a nice thing for a lady now,' he went on, 'this
hand-glass – fifteenth-century, warranted; comes from a
good collection, too; but I reserve the name, in the interests
of my customer, who was just like yourself, my dear sir, the
nephew and sole heir of a remarkable collector.'

The dealer, while he thus ran on in his dry and biting
voice, had stooped to take the object from its place; and,
as he had done so, a shock had passed through Markheim,
a start both of hand and foot, a sudden leap of many
tumultuous passions to the face. It passed as swiftly as
it came, and left no trace beyond a certain trembling of
the hand that now received the glass.

'A glass,' he said hoarsely, and then paused, and
repeated it more clearly. 'A glass? For Christmas? Surely
not?'

'And why not?' cried the dealer. 'Why not a glass?'

Markheim was looking upon him with an indefinable
expression. 'You ask me why not?' he said. 'Why, look
here – look in it – look at yourself! Do you like to see it?
No! nor I – nor any man.'

The little man had jumped back when Markheim
had so suddenly confronted him with the mirror; but

now, perceiving there was nothing worse on hand, he chuckled.

'Your future lady, sir, must be pretty hard favoured,' said he.

'I ask you,' said Markheim, 'for a Christmas present, and you give me this – this damned reminder of years, and sins and follies – this hand-conscience. Did you mean it? Had you a thought in your mind? Tell me. It will be better for you if you do. Come, tell me about yourself. I hazard a guess now, that you are in secret a very charitable man?'

The dealer looked closely at his companion. It was very odd, Markheim did not appear to be laughing; there was something in his face like an eager sparkle of hope, but nothing of mirth.

'What are you driving at?' the dealer asked.

'Not charitable?' returned the other gloomily. 'Not charitable? not pious; not scrupulous; unloving, unbeloved; a hand to get money, a safe to keep it. Is that all? Dear God, man, is that all?'

'I will tell you what it is,' began the dealer, with some sharpness, and then broke off again into a chuckle. 'But I see this is a love-match of yours, and you have been drinking the lady's health.'

'Ah!' cried Markheim, with a strange curiosity. 'Ah, have you been in love? Tell me about that.'

'I,' cried the dealer. 'I in love! I never had the time, nor have I the time to-day for all this nonsense. – Will you take the glass?'

'Where is the hurry?' returned Markheim. 'It is very pleasant to stand here talking; and life is so short and insecure that I would not hurry away from any pleasure – no, not even from so mild a one as this. We should rather cling, cling to what little we can get, like a man at a cliff's edge. Every second is a cliff, if you think upon it – a cliff a mile high – high enough, if we fall, to dash us out of every feature of humanity. Hence it is best to talk pleasantly. Let us talk of each other: why should we wear this mask? Let us be confidential. Who knows? – we might become friends.'

'I have just one word to say to you,' said the dealer. 'Either make your purchase, or walk out of my shop!'

'True, true,' said Markheim. 'Enough fooling. To business. Show me something else.'

The dealer stooped once more, this time to replace the glass upon the shelf, his thin blond hair falling over his eyes as he did so. Markheim moved a little nearer, with one hand in the pocket of his greatcoat: he drew himself up and filled his lungs; at the same time many different emotions were depicted together on his face – terror, horror, and resolve, fascination and a physical repulsion; and through a haggard lift of his upper lip his teeth looked out.

'This, perhaps, may suit,' observed the dealer: and then, as he began to re-arise, Markheim bounded from behind upon his victim. The long, skewer-like dagger flashed and fell. The dealer struggled like a hen, striking his temple on the shelf, and then tumbled on the floor in a heap.

Time had some score of small voices in that shop, some stately and slow, as was becoming to their great age; others garrulous and hurried. All these told out the seconds in an intricate chorus of tickings. Then the passage of a lad's feet, heavily running on the pavement, broke in upon these smaller voices and startled Markheim into the consciousness of his surroundings. He looked about him awfully. The candle stood on the counter, its flame solemnly wagging in a draught; and by that inconsiderable movement the whole room was filled with noiseless bustle and kept heaving like a sea; the tall shadows nodding, the gross blots of darkness swelling and dwindling as with respiration, the faces of the portraits and the china gods changing and wavering like images in water. The inner door stood ajar, and peered into that leaguer of shadows with a long slit of daylight like a pointing finger.

From these fear-stricken rovings Markheim's eyes returned to the body of his victim, where it lay both humped and sprawling, incredibly small and strangely meaner than in life. In these poor, miserly clothes, in that ungainly attitude, the dealer lay like so much sawdust. Markheim had feared to see it, and, lo! it was nothing. And yet, as he gazed, this bundle of old clothes and pool of blood began to find eloquent voices. There it must lie; there was none to work the cunning hinges or direct the miracle of locomotion – there it must lie till it was found. Found! ay, and then? Then would this dead flesh lift up a cry that would ring over England, and fill the world with the echoes of pursuit. Ay, dead or not, this was still the enemy. 'Time was that when the brains were out,' he thought; and the first word struck into his mind. Time, now that the deed was accomplished – time, which had closed for the victim, had become instant and momentous for the slayer.

The thought was yet in his mind when, first one and then another, with every variety of pace and voice – one deep as the bell from a cathedral turret, another ringing on its treble notes the prelude of a waltz – the clocks began to strike the hour of three in the afternoon.

The sudden outbreak of so many tongues in that dumb chamber staggered him. He began to bestir himself, going to and fro with the candle, beleaguered by moving shadows, and startled to the soul by chance reflections. In many rich mirrors, some of home design, some from Venice or Amsterdam, he saw his face repeated and repeated, as it were an army of spies; his own eyes met and detected him; and the sound of his own steps, lightly as they fell, vexed the surrounding quiet. And still, as he continued to fill his pockets, his mind accused him, with a sickening iteration, of the thousand faults of his design. He should have chosen a more quiet hour; he should have prepared an alibi; he should not have used a knife; he should have been more cautious, and only bound and gagged the dealer, and not killed him; he should have been more bold, and killed the servant also; he should have done all things otherwise: poignant regrets, weary, incessant toiling of the mind to change what was unchangeable, to plan what was now useless, to be the architect of the irrevocable past. Meanwhile, and behind all this activity, brute terrors, like the scurrying of rats in a deserted attic, filled the more remote chambers of his brain with riot; the hand of the constable would fall heavy on his shoulder, and his nerves would jerk like a hooked fish; or he beheld, in galloping defile, the dock, the prison, the gallows, and the black coffin.

Terror of the people in the street sat down before his

mind like a besieging army. It was impossible, he thought,
but that some rumour of the struggle must have reached
their ears and set on edge their curiosity; and now, in all the
neighbouring houses, he divined them sitting motionless
and with uplifted ear – solitary people, condemned to
spend Christmas dwelling alone on memories of the past,
and now startlingly recalled from that tender exercise;
happy family parties, struck into silence round the table,
the mother still with raised finger: every degree and age
and humour, but all, by their own hearths, prying and
hearkening and weaving the rope that was to hang him.
Sometimes it seemed to him he could not move too softly;
the clink of the tall Bohemian goblets rang out loudly
like a bell; and alarmed by the bigness of the ticking, he
was tempted to stop the clocks. And then, again, with a
swift transition of his terrors, the very silence of the place
appeared a source of peril, and a thing to strike and freeze
the passer-by; and he would step more boldly, and bustle
aloud among the contents of the shop, and imitate, with
elaborate bravado, the movements of a busy man at ease
in his own house.

But he was now so pulled about by different alarms,
that, while one portion of his mind was still alert and
cunning, another trembled on the brink of lunacy. One
hallucination in particular took a strong hold on his credulity. The neighbour hearkening with white face beside
his window, the passer-by arrested by a horrible surmise
on the pavement – these could at worst suspect, they
could not know; through the brick walls and shuttered
windows only sounds could penetrate. But here, within
the house, was he alone? He knew he was; he had watched
the servant set forth sweethearting, in her poor best, 'out
for the day' written on every ribbon and smile. Yes, he
was alone, of course; and yet, in the bulk of empty
house above him, he could surely hear a stir of delicate
footing – he was surely conscious, inexplicably conscious,
of some presence. Ay, surely; to every room and corner
of the house his imagination followed it; and now it was
a faceless thing, and yet had eyes to see with; and again
it was a shadow of himself; and yet again beheld the

image of the dead dealer, reinspired with cunning and hatred.

At times, with a strong effort, he would glance at the open door which still seemed to repel his eyes. The house was tall, the skylight small and dirty, the day blind with fog; and the light that filtered down to the ground story was exceedingly faint, and showed dimly on the threshold of the shop. And yet, in that strip of doubtful brightness, did there not hang wavering a shadow?

Suddenly, from the street outside, a very jovial gentleman began to beat with a staff on the shop-door, accompanying his blows with shouts and railleries in which the dealer was continually called upon by name. Markheim, smitten into ice, glanced at the dead man. But no! he lay quite still; he was fled away far beyond ear-shot of these blows and shoutings; he was sunk beneath seas of silence; and his name, which would once have caught his notice above the howling of a storm, had become an empty sound. And presently the jovial gentleman desisted from his knocking and departed.

Here was a broad hint to hurry what remained to be done, to get forth from this accusing neighbourhood, to plunge into a bath of London multitudes, and to reach, on the other side of day, that haven of safety and apparent innocence – his bed. One visitor had come: at any moment another might follow and be more obstinate. To have done the deed, and yet not to reap the profit, would be too abhorrent a failure. The money, that was now Markheim's concern; and as a means to that, the keys.

He glanced over his shoulder at the open door; where the shadow was still lingering and shivering; and with no conscious repugnance of the mind, yet with a tremor of the belly, he drew near the body of his victim. The human character had quite departed. Like a suit half-stuffed with bran, the limbs lay scattered, the trunk doubled, on the floor; and yet the thing repelled him. Although so dingy and inconsiderable to the eye, he feared it might have more significance to the touch. He took the body by the shoulders and turned it on its back. It was strangely light and supple, and the limbs, as if they had been broken,

fell into the oddest postures. The face was robbed of all
expression; but it was as pale as wax, and shockingly
smeared with blood about one temple. That was, for
Markheim, the one displeasing circumstance. It carried
him back, upon the instant, to a certain fair-day in a
fishers' village: a grey day, a piping wind, a crowd upon
the street, a blare of brasses, the booming of drums, the
nasal voice of a ballad-singer; and a boy going to and
fro, buried over-head in the crowd and divided between
interest and fear, until, coming out upon the chief place
of concourse, he beheld a booth and a great screen with
pictures, dismally designed, garishly coloured: Brownrigg
with her apprentice; the Mannings with their murdered
guest; Weare in the death-grip of Thurtell; and a score
besides of famous crimes. The thing was as clear as an
illusion; he was once again that little boy; he was looking
once again, and with the same sense of physical revolt, at
these vile pictures; he was still stunned by the thumping
of the drums. A bar of that day's music returned upon his
memory; and at that, for the first time, a qualm came over
him, a breath of nausea, a sudden weakness of the joints,
which he must instantly resist and conquer.

He judged it more prudent to confront than to flee from
these considerations; looking the more hardily in the dead
face, bending his mind to realise the nature and greatness
of his crime. So little a while ago that face had moved with
every change of sentiment, that pale mouth had spoken,
that body had been all on fire with governable energies; and
now, and by his act, that piece of life had been arrested, as
the horologist, with interjected finger, arrests the beating
of the clock. So he reasoned in vain; he could rise to no
more remorseful consciousness; the same heart which had
shuddered before the painted effigies of crime looked on
its reality unmoved. At best, he felt a gleam of pity for one
who had been endowed in vain with all those faculties that
can make the world a garden of enchantment, one who
had never lived and who was now dead. But of penitence,
no, not a tremor.

With that, shaking himself clear of these considerations,
he found the keys and advanced towards the open door of

the shop. Outside, it had begun to rain smartly; and the sound of the shower upon the roof had banished silence. Like some dripping cavern, the chambers of the house were haunted by an incessant echoing, which filled the ear and mingled with the ticking of the clocks. And, as Markheim approached the door, he seemed to hear, in answer to his own cautious tread, the steps of another foot withdrawing up the stair. The shadow still palpitated loosely on the threshold. He threw a ton's weight of resolve upon his muscles, and drew back the door.

The faint, foggy daylight glimmered dimly on the bare floor and stairs; on the bright suit of armour posted, halbert in hand, upon the landing: and on the dark wood-carvings, and framed pictures that hung against the yellow panels of the wainscot. So loud was the beating of the rain through all the house that, in Markheim's ears, it began to be distinguished into many different sounds. Footsteps and sighs, the tread of regiments marching in the distance, the chink of money in the counting, and the creaking of doors held stealthily ajar, appeared to mingle with the patter of the drops upon the cupola and the gushing of the water in the pipes. The sense that he was not alone grew upon him to the verge of madness. On every side he was haunted and begirt by presences. He heard them moving in the upper chambers; from the shop he heard the dead man getting to his legs; and as he began with a great effort to mount the stairs, feet fled quietly before him and followed stealthily behind. If he were but deaf, he thought, how tranquilly he would possess his soul! And then again, and hearkening with ever fresh attention, he blessed himself for that unresting sense which held the outposts and stood a trusty sentinel upon his life. His head turned continually on his neck; his eyes, which seemed starting from their orbits, scouted on every side, and on every side were half-rewarded as with the tail of something nameless vanishing. The four-and-twenty steps to the first floor were four-and-twenty agonies.

On that first story, the doors stood ajar, three of them like three ambushes, shaking his nerves like the throats of cannon. He could never again, he felt, be sufficiently

immured and fortified from men's observing eyes; he
longed to be home, girt in by walls, buried among bed-
clothes, and invisible to all but God. And at that thought he
wondered a little, recollecting tales of other murderers and
the fear they were said to entertain of heavenly avengers. It
was not so, at least, with him. He feared the laws of nature,
lest, in their callous and immutable procedure, they should
preserve some damning evidence of his crime. He feared
tenfold more, with a slavish, superstitious terror, some
scission in the continuity of man's experience, some wilful
illegality of nature. He played a game of skill, depending on
the rules, calculating consequence from cause; and what if
nature, as the defeated tyrant overthrew the chess-board,
should break the mould of their succession? The like
had befallen Napoleon (so writers said) when the winter
changed the time of its appearance. The like might befall
Markheim: the solid walls might become transparent and
reveal his doings like those of bees in a glass hive; the
stout planks might yield under his foot like quicksands
and detain him in their clutch; ay, and there were soberer
accidents that might destroy him: if, for instance, the house
should fall and imprison him beside the body of his victim;
or the house next door should fly on fire, and the firemen
invade him from all sides. These things he feared; and,
in a sense, these things might be called the hands of God
reached forth against sin. But about God Himself he was
at ease: his act was doubtless exceptional, but so were his
excuses, which God knew; it was there, and not among
men, that he felt sure of justice.

When he had got safe into the drawing-room, and
shut the door behind him, he was aware of a respite
from alarms. The room was quite dismantled, uncarpeted
besides, and strewn with packing-cases and incongruous
furniture; several great pier-glasses, in which he beheld
himself at various angles, like an actor on a stage; many
pictures, framed and unframed, standing with their faces to
the wall; a fine Sheraton sideboard, a cabinet of marquetry,
and a great old bed, with tapestry hangings. The windows
opened to the floor; but by great good fortune the lower
part of the shutters had been closed, and this concealed

him from the neighbours. Here, then, Markheim drew in a packing-case before the cabinet, and began to search among the keys. It was a long business, for there were many; and it was irksome besides; for, after all, there might be nothing in the cabinet, and time was on the wing. But the closeness of the occupation sobered him. With the tail of his eye he saw the door – even glanced at it from time to time directly, like a besieged commander, pleased to verify the good estate of his defences. But in truth he was at peace. The rain falling in the street sounded natural and pleasant. Presently, on the other side, the notes of a piano were wakened to the music of a hymn, and the voices of many children took up the air and words. How stately, how comfortable was the melody! How fresh the youthful voices! Markheim gave ear to it smilingly, as he sorted out the keys; and his mind was thronged with answerable ideas and images; church-going children and the pealing of the high organ; children afield, bathers by the brookside, ramblers on the brambly common, kite-flyers in the windy and cloud-navigated sky: and then, at another cadence of the hymn, back again to church, and the somnolence of summer Sundays, and the high genteel voice of the parson (which he smiled a little to recall) and the painted Jacobean tombs, and the dim lettering of the Ten Commandments in the chancel.

And as he sat thus, at once busy and absent, he was startled to his feet. A flash of ice, a flash of fire, a bursting gush of blood went over him, and then he stood transfixed and thrilling. A step mounted the stair slowly and steadily, and presently a hand was laid upon the knob, and the lock clicked, and the door opened.

Fear held Markheim in a vice. What to expect he knew not, whether the dead man walking, or the official ministers of human justice, or some chance witness blindly stumbling in to consign him to the gallows. But when a face was thrust into the aperture, glanced round the room, looked at him, nodded and smiled as if in friendly recognition, and then withdrew again, and the door closed behind it, his fear broke loose from his control in a hoarse cry. At the sound of this the visitant returned.

'Did you call me?' he asked pleasantly, and with that he entered the room and closed the door behind him.

Markheim stood and gazed at him with all his eyes. Perhaps there was a film upon his sight, but the outlines of the new-comer seemed to change and waver like those of the idols in the wavering candlelight of the shop; and at times he thought he knew him; and at times he thought he bore a likeness to himself; and always, like a lump of living terror, there lay in his bosom the conviction that this thing was not of the earth and not of God.

And yet the creature had a strange air of the commonplace, as he stood looking on Markheim with a smile; and when he added: 'You are looking for the money, I believe?' it was in the tones of everyday politeness.

Markheim made no answer.

'I should warn you,' resumed the other, 'that the maid has left her sweetheart earlier than usual and will soon be here. If Mr Markheim be found in this house, I need not describe to him the consequences.'

'You know me?' cried the murderer.

The visitor smiled. 'You have long been a favourite of mine,' he said; 'and I have long observed and often sought to help you.'

'What are you?' cried Markheim, 'the devil?'

'What I may be,' returned the other, 'cannot affect the service I propose to render you.'

'It can,' cried Markheim; 'it does! Be helped by you? No, never; not by you! You do not know me yet; thank God, you do not know me!'

'I know you,' replied the visitant, with a sort of kind severity, or rather firmness. 'I know you to the soul.'

'Know me!' cried Markheim. 'Who can do so? My life is but a travesty and slander on myself. I have lived to belie my nature. All men do; all men are better than this disguise, that grows about and stifles them. You see each dragged away by life, like one whom bravos have seized and muffled in a cloak. If they had their own control – if you could see their faces, they would be altogether different, they would shine out for heroes and saints! I am worse than most; myself is more overlaid; my excuse is known to me and God. But, had I the time, I could disclose myself.'

'To me?' inquired the visitant.

'To you before all,' returned the murderer. 'I supposed you were intelligent. I thought – since you exist – you would prove a reader of the heart. And yet you would propose to judge me by my acts! Think of it; my acts! I was born and I have lived in a land of giants; giants have dragged me by the wrists since I was born out of my mother – the giants of circumstance. And you would judge me by my acts! But can you not look within? Can you not understand that evil is hateful to me? Can you not see within me the clear writing of conscience, never blurred by any wilful sophistry, although too often disregarded? Can you not read me for a thing that surely must be common as humanity – the unwilling sinner?'

'All this is very feelingly expressed,' was the reply, 'but it regards me not. These points of consistency are beyond my province, and I care not in the least by what compulsion you may have been dragged away, so as you are but carried in the right direction. But time flies; the servant delays, looking in the faces of the crowd and at the pictures on the hoardings, but still she keeps moving nearer; and remember, it is as if the gallows itself was striding towards you through the Christmas streets! Shall I help you; I, who know all? Shall I tell you where to find the money?'

'For what price?' asked Markheim.

'I offer you the service for a Christmas gift,' returned the other.

Markheim could not refrain from smiling with a kind of bitter triumph. 'No,' said he, 'I will take nothing at your hands; if I were dying of thrist, and it was your hand that put the pitcher to my lips, I should find the courage to refuse. It may be credulous, but I will do nothing to commit myself to evil.'

'I have no objection to a death-bed repentance,' observed the visitant.

'Because you disbelieve their efficacy!' Markheim cried.

'I do not say so,' returned the other; 'but I look on

these things from a different side, and when the life is
done my interest falls. The man has lived to serve me,
to spread black looks under colour of religion, or to sow
tares in the wheat-field, as you do, in a course of weak
compliance with desire. Now that he draws so near to
his deliverance, he can add but one act of service – to
repent, to die smiling, and thus to build up in confidence
and hope the more timorous of my surviving followers. I
am not so hard a master. Try me. Accept my help. Please
yourself in life as you have done hitherto; please yourself
more amply, spread your elbows at the board; and when
the night begins to fall and the curtains to be drawn, I tell
you, for your greater comfort, that you will find it even
easy to compound your quarrel with your conscience,
and to make a truckling peace with God. I came but
now from such a death-bed, and the room was full of
sincere mourners, listening to the man's last words: and
when I looked into that face, which had been set as a flint
against mercy, I found it smiling with hope.'

'And do you, then, suppose me such a creature?' asked
Markheim. 'Do you think I have no more generous
aspirations than to sin, and sin, and sin, and, at the
last, sneak into heaven? My heart rises at the thought. Is
this, then, your experience of mankind? or is it because you
find me with red hands that you presume such baseness?
and is this crime of murder indeed so impious as to dry
up the very springs of good?'

'Murder is to me no special category,' replied the other.
'All sins are murder, even as all life is war. I behold your
race, like starving mariners on a raft, plucking crusts out
of the hands of famine and feeding on each other's lives.
I follow sins beyond the moment of their acting; I find
in all that the last consequence is death; and to my eyes,
the pretty maid who thwarts her mother with such taking
graces on a question of a ball, drips no less visibly with
human gore than such a murderer as yourself. Do I say
that I follow sins? I follow virtues also; they differ not
by the thickness of a nail, they are both scythes for the
reaping angel of Death. Evil, for which I live, consists not
in action but in character. The bad man is dear to me;

not the bad act, whose fruits, if we could follow them far enough down the hurtling cataract of the ages, might yet be found more blessed than those of the rarest virtues. And it is not because you have killed a dealer, but because you are Markheim, that I offer to forward your escape.'

'I will lay my heart open to you,' answered Markheim. 'This crime on which you find me is my last. On my way to it I have learned many lessons; itself is a lesson, a momentous lesson. Hitherto I have been driven with revolt to what I would not; I was a bond-slave to poverty, driven and scourged. There are robust virtues that can stand in these temptations; mine was not so: I had a thirst of pleasure. But to-day, and out of this deed, I pluck both warning and riches – both the power and a fresh resolve to be myself. I become in all things a free actor in the world; I begin to see myself all changed, these hands the agents of good, this heart at peace. Something comes over me out of the past; something of what I have dreamed on Sabbath evenings to the sound of the church organ, of what I forecast when I shed tears over noble books, or talked, an innocent child, with my mother. There lies my life; I have wandered a few years, but now I see once more my city of destination.'

'You are to use this money on the Stock Exchange, I think?' remarked the visitor; 'and there, if I mistake not, you have already lost some thousands.'

'Ah,' said Markheim, 'but this time I have a sure thing.'

'This time, again, you will lose,' replied the visitor quietly.

'Ah, but I will keep back the half!' cried Markheim.

'That also you will lose,' said the other.

The sweat started upon Markheim's brow. 'Well, then, what matter?' he exclaimed. 'Say it be lost, say I am plunged again in poverty, shall one part of me, and that the worse, continue until the end to override the better? Evil and good run strong in me, haling me both ways. I do not love the one thing, I love all. I can conceive great deeds, renunciations, martyrdoms; and though I be fallen to such a crime as murder, pity is no stranger to my thoughts. I

pity the poor; who knows their trials better than myself?
I pity and help them; I prize love, I love honest laughter;
there is no good thing nor true thing on earth but I love it
from my heart. And are my vices only to direct my life, and
my virtues to lie without effect, like some passive lumber
of the mind? Not so; good, also, is the spring of acts.'

But the visitant raised his finger. 'For six-and-thirty
years that you have been in this world,' said he, 'through
many changes of fortune and varieties of humour, I have
watched you steadily fall. Fifteen years ago you would
have started at a theft. Three years back you would have
blenched at the name of murder. Is there any crime, is there
any cruelty or meanness, from which you still recoil? – five
years from now I shall detect you in the fact! Downward,
downward lies your way; nor can anything but death avail
to stop you.'

'It is true,' Markheim said huskily, 'I have in some
degree complied with evil. But it is so with all: the very
saints, in the mere exercise of living, grow less dainty, and
take on the tone of their surroundings.'

'I will propound to you one simple question,' said the
other; 'and as you answer, I shall read to you your moral
horoscope. You have grown in many things more lax;
possibly you do right to be so; and at any account, it is
the same with all men. But granting that, are you in any
one particular, however trifling, more difficult to please
with your own conduct, or do you go in all things with
a looser rein?'

'In any one?' repeated Markheim, with an anguish of
consideration. 'No,' he added, with despair, 'in none! I
have gone down in all.'

'Then,' said the visitor, 'content yourself with what you
are, for you will never change; and the words of your part
on this stage are irrevocably written down.'

Markheim stood for a long while silent, and indeed it
was the visitor who first broke the silence. 'That being
so,' he said, 'shall I show you the money?'

'And grace?' cried Markheim.

'Have you not tried it?' returned the other. 'Two or
three years ago, did I not see you on the platform of

revival meetings, and was not your voice the loudest in the hymn?'

'It is true,' said Markheim; 'and I see clearly what remains for me by way of duty. I thank you for these lessons from my soul; my eyes are opened, and I behold myself at last for what I am.'

At this moment, the sharp note of the door-bell rang through the house; and the visitant, as though this were some concerted signal for which he had been waiting, changed at once in his demeanour.

'The maid!' he cried. 'She has returned, as I forewarned you, and there is now before you one more difficult passage. Her master, you must say, is ill; you must let her in, with an assured but rather serious countenance – no smiles, no overacting, and I promise you success! Once the girl within, and the door closed, the same dexterity that has already rid you of the dealer will relieve you of this last danger in your path. Thenceforward you have the whole evening – the whole night, if needful – to ransack the treasures of the house and to make good your safety. This is help that comes to you with the mask of danger. Up!' he cried; 'up, friend; your life hangs trembling in the scales: up, and act!'

Markheim steadily regarded his counsellor. 'If I be condemned to evil acts,' he said, 'there is still one door of freedom open – I can cease from action. If my life be an ill thing, I can lay it down. Though I be, as you say truly, at the beck of every small temptation, I can yet, by one decisive gesture, place myself beyond the reach of all. My love of good is damned to barrenness; it may, and let it be! But I have still my hatred of evil; and from that, to your galling dissapointment, you shall see that I can draw both energy and courage.'

The features of the visitor began to undergo a wonderful and lovely change: they brightened and softened with a tender triumph, and, even as they brightened, faded and dislimned. But Markheim did not pause to watch or understand the transformation. He opened the door and went downstairs very slowly, thinking to himself. His past went soberly before him; he beheld it as it was, ugly

and strenuous like a dream, random as chance-medley –
a scene of defeat. Life, as he thus reviewed it, tempted
him no longer; but on the farther side he perceived a
quiet haven for his bark. He paused in the passage, and
looked into the shop, where the candle still burned by the
dead body. It was strangely silent. Thoughts of the dealer
swarmed into his mind, as he stood gazing. And then the
bell once more broke out into impatient clamour.

He confronted the maid upon the threshold with something like a smile.

'You had better go for the police,' said he: 'I have killed
your master.'

THE STRANGE CASE OF

Dr Jekyll

AND

Mr Hyde

To
Katharine De Mattos

*It's ill to loose the bands that God decreed to bind;
Still will we be the children of the heather and the wind.
Far away from home, O it's still for you and me
That the broom is blowing bonnie in the north countrie.*

Strange Case
of Dr Jekyll and Mr Hyde

STORY OF THE DOOR

MR UTTERSON the lawyer was a man of a rugged countenance, that was never lighted by a smile; cold, scanty and embarrassed in discourse; backward in sentiment; lean, long, dusty, dreary and yet somehow lovable. At friendly meetings, and when the wine was to his taste, something eminently human beaconed from his eye; something indeed which never found its way into his talk, but which spoke not only in these silent symbols of the after-dinner face, but more often and loudly in the acts of his life. He was austere with himself; drank gin when he was alone, to mortify a taste for vintages; and though he enjoyed the theatre, had not crossed the doors of one for twenty years. But he had an approved tolerance for others; sometimes wondering, almost with envy, at the high pressure of spirits involved in their misdeeds; and in any extremity inclined to help rather than to reprove. 'I incline to Cain's heresy,' he used to say quaintly: 'I let my brother go to the devil in his own way.' In this character, it was frequently his fortune to be the last reputable acquaintance and the last good influence in the lives of down-going men. And to such as these, so long as they came about his chambers, he never marked a shade of change in his demeanour.

No doubt the feat was easy to Mr Utterson; for he was undemonstrative at the best, and even his friendships seemed to be founded in a similar catholicity of good-nature. It is the mark of a modest man to accept his friendly circle ready-made from the hands of opportunity; and that was the lawyer's way. His friends were those of his

own blood or those whom he had known the longest; his
affections, like ivy, were the growth of time, they implied
no aptness in the object. Hence, no doubt, the bond that
united him to Mr Richard Enfield, his distant kinsman,
the well-known man about town. It was a nut to crack
for many, what these two could see in each other or what
subject they could find in common. It was reported by
those who encountered them in their Sunday walks, that
they said nothing, looked singularly dull, and would hail
with obvious relief the appearance of a friend. For all that,
the two men put the greatest store by these excursions,
counted them the chief jewel of each week, and not only
set aside occasions of pleasure, but even resisted the calls
of business, that they might enjoy them uninterrupted.

It chanced on one of these rambles that their way led
them down a by-street in a busy quarter of London. The
street was small and what is called quiet, but it drove
a thriving trade on the week-days. The inhabitants were
all doing well, it seemed, and all emulously hoping to
do better still, and laying out the surplus of their gains
in coquetry; so that the shop fronts stood along that
thoroughfare with an air of invitation, like rows of smiling
saleswomen. Even on Sunday, when it veiled its more
florid charms and lay comparatively empty of passage, the
street shone out in contrast to its dingy neighbourhood, like
a fire in a forest; and with its freshly painted shutters, well-
polished brasses and general cleanliness and gaiety of note,
instantly caught and pleased the eye of the passenger.

Two doors from one corner, on the left hand going east,
the line was broken by the entry of a court; and just at that
point, a certain sinister block of building thrust forward
its gable on the street. It was two storeys high; showed
no window, nothing but a door on the lower storey and
a blind forehead of discoloured wall on the upper; and
bore in every feature, the marks of prolonged and sordid
negligence. The door, which was equipped with neither
bell nor knocker, was blistered and distained. Tramps
slouched into the recess and struck matches on the panels;
children kept shop upon the steps; the schoolboy had tried
his knife on the mouldings; and for close on a generation,

no one had appeared to drive away these random visitors or to repair their ravages.

Mr Enfield and the lawyer were on the other side of the by-street; but when they came abreast of the entry, the former lifted up his cane and pointed.

'Did you ever remark that door?' he asked; and when his companion had replied in the affirmative, 'It is connected in my mind,' added he, 'with a very odd story.'

'Indeed?' said Mr Utterson, with a slight change of voice, 'and what was that?'

'Well, it was this way,' returned Mr Enfield: 'I was coming home from some place at the end of the world, about three o'clock of a black winter morning, and my way lay through a part of town where there was literally nothing to be seen but lamps. Street after street, and all the folks asleep   street after street, all lighted up as if for a procession and all as empty as a church – till at last I got into that state of mind when a man listens and listens and begins to long for the sight of a policeman. All at once, I saw two figures: one a little man who was stumping along eastward at a good walk, and the other a girl of maybe eight or ten who was running as hard as she was able down a cross street. Well, sir, the two ran into one another naturally enough at the corner; and then came the horrible part of the thing; for the man trampled calmly over the child's body and left her screaming on the ground. It sounds nothing to hear, but it was hellish to see. It wasn't like a man; it was like some damned Juggernaut. I gave a view halloa, took to my heels, collared my gentleman, and brought him back to where there was already quite a group about the screaming child. He was perfectly cool and made no resistance, but gave me one look, so ugly that it brought out the sweat on me like running. The people who had turned out were the girl's own family; and pretty soon, the doctor, for whom she had been sent, put in his appearance. Well, the child was not much the worse, more frightened, according to the Sawbones; and there you might have supposed would be an end to it. But there was one curious circumstance. I had taken a loathing to my gentleman at first sight. So had the child's family,

which was only natural. But the doctor's case was what
struck me. He was the usual cut and dry apothecary, of no
particular age and colour, with a strong Edinburgh accent,
and about as emotional as a bagpipe. Well, sir, he was like
the rest of us; every time he looked at my prisoner, I saw
that Sawbones turn sick and white with the desire to kill
him. I knew what was in his mind, just as he knew what was
in mine; and killing being out of the question, we did the
next best. We told the man we could and would make such
a scandal out of this, as should make his name stink from
one end of London to the other. If he had any friends or any
credit, we undertook that he should lose them. And all the
time, as we were pitching it in red hot, we were keeping the
women off him as best we could, for they were as wild as
harpies. I never saw a circle of such hateful faces; and there
was the man in the middle, with a kind of black, sneering
coolness – frightened too, I could see that – but carrying
it off, sir, really like Satan. 'If you choose to make capital
out of this accident,' said he, 'I am naturally helpless. No
gentleman but wishes to avoid a scene,' says he. 'Name
your figure.' Well, we screwed him up to a hundred pounds
for the child's family; he would have clearly liked to stick
out; but there was something about the lot of us that meant
mischief, and at last he struck. The next thing was to get
the money; and where do you think he carried us but to
that place with the door? – whipped out a key, went in, and
presently came back with the matter of ten pounds in gold
and a cheque for the balance on Coutts's, drawn payable to
bearer and signed with a name that I can't mention, though
it's one of the points of my story, but it was a name at least
very well known and often printed. The figure was stiff; but
the signature was good for more than that, if it was only
genuine. I took the liberty of pointing out to my gentleman
that the whole business looked apocryphal, and that a man
does not, in real life, walk into a cellar door at four in the
morning and come out of it with another man's cheque
for close upon a hundred pounds. But he was quite easy
and sneering. 'Set your mind at rest,' says he, 'I will stay
with you till the banks open and cash the cheque myself.'
So we all set off, the doctor, and the child's father, and our

friend and myself, and passed the rest of the night in my chambers; and next day, when we had breakfasted, went in a body to the bank. I gave in the cheque myself, and said I had every reason to believe it was a forgery. Not a bit of it. The cheque was genuine.'

'Tut-tut,' said Mr Utterson.

'I see you feel as I do,' said Mr Enfield. 'Yes, it's a bad story. For my man was a fellow that nobody could have to do with, a really damnable man; and the person that drew the cheque is the very pink of the proprieties, celebrated too, and (what makes it worse) one of your fellows who do what they call good. Black mail, I suppose; an honest man paying through the nose for some of the capers of his youth. Black Mail House is what I call that place with the door, in consequence. Though even that, you know, is far from explaining all,' he added, and with the words fell into a vein of musing.

From this he was recalled by Mr Utterson asking rather suddenly: 'And you don't know if the drawer of the cheque lives there?'

'A likely place isn't it?' returned Mr Enfield. 'But I happen to have noticed his address; he lives in some square or other.'

'And you never asked about – the place with the door?' said Mr Utterson.

'No, sir: I had a delicacy,' was the reply. 'I feel very strongly about putting questions; it partakes too much of the style of the day of judgment. You start a question, and it's like starting a stone. You sit quietly on the top of a hill; and away the stone goes, starting others; and presently some bland old bird (the last you would have thought of) is knocked on the head in his own back garden and the family have to change their name. No, sir, I make it a rule of mine: the more it looks like Queer Street, the less I ask.'

'A very good rule, too,' said the lawyer.

'But I have studied the place for myself,' continued Mr Enfield. 'It seems scarcely a house. There is no other door, and nobody goes in or out of that one but, once in a great while, the gentleman of my adventure. There are three windows looking on the court on the first floor; none below; the windows are always shut but they're clean. And then there is a chimney which is generally smoking; so somebody must live there. And yet it's not so sure; for the buildings are so packed together about that court, that it's hard to say where one ends and another begins.'

The pair walked on again for a while in silence; and then 'Enfield,' said Mr Utterson, 'that's a good rule of yours.'

'Yes, I think it is,' returned Enfield.

'But for all that,' continued the lawyer, 'there's one point I want to ask: I want to ask the name of that man who walked over the child.'

'Well,' said Mr Enfield, 'I can't see what harm it would do. It was a man of the name of Hyde.'

'Hm,' said Mr Utterson. 'What sort of a man is he to see?'

'He is not easy to describe. There is something wrong with his appearance; something displeasing, something downright detestable. I never saw a man I so disliked, and yet I scarce know why. He must be deformed somewhere; he gives a strong feeling of deformity, although I couldn't specify the point. He's an extraordinary looking man, and yet I really can name nothing out of the way. No, sir; I can make no hand of it; I can't describe him. And it's not want of memory; for I declare I can see him this moment.'

Mr Utterson again walked some way in silence and obviously under a weight of consideration. 'You are sure he used a key?' he inquired at last.

'My dear sir . . .' began Enfield, surprised out of himself.

'Yes, I know,' said Utterson; 'I know it must seem strange. The fact is, if I do not ask you the name of the other party, it is because I know it already. You see, Richard, your tale has gone home. If you have been inexact in any point, you had better correct it.'

'I think you might have warned me,' returned the other with a touch of sullenness. 'But I have been pedantically exact, as you call it. The fellow had a key; and what's more, he has it still. I saw him use it, not a week ago.'

Mr Utterson sighed deeply but said never a word; and the young man presently resumed. 'Here is another lesson to say nothing,' said he. 'I am ashamed of my long tongue. Let us make a bargain never to refer to this again.'

'With all my heart,' said the lawyer. 'I shake hands on that, Richard.'

SEARCH FOR MR HYDE

That evening, Mr Utterson came home to his bachelor house in sombre spirits and sat down to dinner without relish. It was his custom of a Sunday, when this meal was over, to sit close by the fire, a volume of some dry divinity on his reading desk, until the clock of the neighbouring church rang out the hour of twelve, when he would go soberly and gratefully to bed. On this night, however, as soon as the cloth was taken away, he took up a candle and went into his business room. There he opened his safe, took from the most private part of it a document endorsed on the envelope as Dr Jekyll's Will, and sat down with a clouded brow to study its contents. The will was holograph, for Mr Utterson, though he took charge of it now that it was made, had refused to lend the least assistance in the making of it; it provided not only that, in case of the decease of Henry Jekyll, M.D., D.C.L., LL.D., F.R.S., &C., all his possessions were to pass into the hands of his 'friend and benefactor Edward Hyde,' but that in case of Dr Jekyll's 'disappearance or unexplained absence for any period exceeding three calendar months,' the said Edward Hyde should step into the said Henry Jekyll's shoes without further delay and free from any burthen or obligation, beyond the payment of a few small sums to the members of the doctor's household. This document had long been the lawyer's eyesore. It offended him both as a lawyer and as a lover of the sane and customary sides of life, to whom the fanciful was the immodest. And hitherto it was his ignorance of Mr Hyde that had swelled his indignation; now, by a sudden turn, it was his knowledge. It was already bad enough when the name was but a name of which he could learn no more. It was worse when it began to be clothed upon with detestable attributes; and out of the shifting, insubstantial mist that had so long baffled his eye, there leaped up the sudden, definite presentment of a fiend.

'I thought it was madness,' he said, as he replaced the obnoxious paper in the safe, 'and now I begin to fear it is disgrace.'

With that he blew out his candle, put on a great coat and set forth in the direction of Cavendish Square, that citadel of medicine, where his friend, the great Dr Lanyon, had his house and received his crowding patients. 'If anyone knows, it will be Lanyon,' he had thought.

The solemn butler knew and welcomed him; he was subjected to no stage of delay, but ushered direct from the door to the dining-room where Dr Lanyon sat alone over his wine. This was a hearty, healthy, dapper, red-faced gentleman, with a shock of hair prematurely white, and a boisterous and decided manner. At sight of Mr Utterson, he sprang up from his chair and welcomed him with both hands. The geniality, as was the way of the man, was somewhat theatrical to the eye; but it reposed on genuine feeling. For these two were old friends, old mates both at school and college, both thorough respecters of themselves and of each other, and, what does not always follow, men who thoroughly enjoyed each other's company.

After a little rambling talk, the lawyer led up to the subject which so disagreeably preoccupied his mind.

'I suppose, Lanyon,' said he, 'you and I must be the two oldest friends that Henry Jekyll has?'

'I wish the friends were younger,' chuckled Dr Lanyon. 'But I suppose we are. And what of that? I see little of him now.'

'Indeed?' said Utterson. 'I thought you had a bond of common interest.'

'We had,' was the reply. 'But it is more than ten years since Henry Jekyll became too fanciful for me. He began to go wrong, wrong in mind; and though of course I continue to take an interest in him for old sake's sake as they say, I see and I have seen devilish little of the man. Such unscientific balderdash,' added the doctor, flushing suddenly purple, 'would have estranged Damon and Pythias.'

This little spirt of temper was somewhat of a relief to Mr Utterson. 'They have only differed on some point of science,' he thought; and being a man of no scientific passions (except in the matter of conveyancing) he even added: 'It is nothing worse than that!' He gave his friend a few seconds to recover his composure, and then approached the question he had come to put. 'Did you ever come across a protégé of his – one Hyde?' he asked.

'Hyde?' repeated Lanyon. 'No. Never heard of him. Since my time.'

That was the amount of information that the lawyer carried back with him to the great, dark bed on which he tossed to and fro, until the small hours of the morning began to grow large. It was a night of little ease to his toiling mind, toiling in mere darkness and besieged by questions.

Six o'clock struck on the bells of the church that was so conveniently near to Mr Utterson's dwelling, and still he was digging at the problem. Hitherto it had touched him on the intellectual side alone; but now his imagination also was engaged or rather enslaved; and as he lay and tossed in the gross darkness of the night and the curtained room, Mr Enfield's tale went by before his mind in a scroll of lighted pictures. He would be aware of the great field of lamps of a nocturnal city; then of the figure of a man walking swiftly; then of a child running from the doctor's; and then these met, and that human Juggernaut trod the child down and passed on regardless of her screams. Or else he would see a room in a rich house, where his friend lay asleep, dreaming and smiling at his dreams; and then the door of that room would be opened, the curtains of the bed plucked apart, the sleeper recalled, and lo! there would stand by his side a figure to whom power was given, and even at that dead hour, he must rise and do its bidding. The figure in these two phases haunted the lawyer all night; and if at any time he dozed over, it was but to see it glide more stealthily through sleeping houses, or move the more swiftly and still the more swiftly, even to dizziness, through wider labyrinths of lamplighted city, and at every street corner crush a child and leave her screaming. And still the figure had no face by which he might know it; even in his dreams, it had no face, or one that baffled him and melted before his eyes; and thus it was that there sprang up and grew apace in the lawyer's mind a singularly strong, almost an inordinate, curiosity to behold the features of the real Mr Hyde. If he could but once set eyes on him, he thought the mystery would lighten and perhaps roll altogether away, as was the habit of mysterious things when well examined. He might see a reason for his friend's strange preference or bondage (call it which you please) and even for the startling clauses of the will. And at least it would be a face worth seeing: the face of a man who was without bowels of mercy: a face which had but to show itself to raise up, in the mind of the unimpressionable Enfield, a spirit of enduring hatred.

From that time forward, Mr Utterson began to haunt the door in the by-street of shops. In the morning before office hours, at noon when business was plenty and time scarce, at night under the face of the fogged city moon, by all lights and at all hours of solitude or concourse, the lawyer was to be found on his chosen post.

'If he be Mr Hyde,' he had thought, 'I shall be Mr Seek.'

And at last his patience was rewarded. It was a fine dry night; frost in the air; the streets as clean as a ballroom floor; the lamps, unshaken by any wind, drawing a regular pattern of light and shadow. By ten o'clock, when the shops were closed, the by-street was very solitary and, in spite of the low growl of London from all round, very silent. Small sounds carried far; domestic sounds out of the houses were clearly audible on either side of the roadway; and the rumour of the approach of any passenger preceeded him by a long time. Mr Utterson had been some minutes at his post, when he was aware of an odd, light footstep drawing near. In the course of his nightly patrols, he had long grown accustomed to the quaint effect with which the footfalls of a single person, while he is still a great way off, suddenly spring out distinct from the vast hum and clatter of the city. Yet his attention had never before been so sharply and decisively arrested; and it was with a strong, superstitious prevision of success that he withdrew into the entry of the court.

The steps drew swiftly nearer, and swelled out suddenly louder as they turned the end of the street. The lawyer, looking forth from the entry, could soon see what manner of man he had to deal with. He was small and very plainly dressed, and the look of him, even at that distance, went somehow strongly against the watcher's inclination. But he made straight for the door, crossing the roadway to save time; and as he came, he drew a key from his pocket like one approaching home.

Mr Utterson stepped out and touched him on the shoulder as he passed. 'Mr Hyde, I think?'

Mr Hyde shrank back with a hissing intake of the breath. But his fear was only momentary; and though he did not look the lawyer in the face, he answered coolly enough: 'That is my name. What do you want?'

'I see you are going in,' returned the lawyer. 'I am an old friend of Dr Jekyll's – Mr Utterson of Gaunt Street – you must have heard my name; and meeting you so conveniently, I thought you might admit me.'

'You will not find Dr Jekyll; he is from home,' replied Mr Hyde, blowing in the key. And then suddenly, but still without looking up, 'How did you know me?' he asked.

'On your side,' said Mr Utterson, 'will you do me a favour?'

'With pleasure,' replied the other. 'What shall it be?'

'Will you let me see your face?' asked the lawyer.

Mr Hyde appeared to hesitate, and then, as if upon some sudden reflection, fronted about with an air of defiance; and the pair stared at each other pretty fixedly for a few seconds. 'Now I shall know you again,' said Mr Utterson. 'It may be useful.'

'Yes,' returned Mr Hyde, 'it is as well we have met; and *à propos*, you should have my address.' And he gave a number of a street in Soho.

'Good God!' thought Mr Utterson, 'can he too have been thinking of the will?' But he kept his feelings to himself and only grunted in acknowledgement of the address.

'And now,' said the other, 'how did you know me?'

'By description,' was the reply.

'Whose description?'

'We have common friends,' said Mr Utterson.

'Common friends?' echoed Mr Hyde, a little hoarsely.
'Who are they?'

'Jekyll, for instance,' said the lawyer.

'He never told you,' cried Mr Hyde, with a flush of anger.
'I did not think you would have lied.'

'Come,' said Mr Utterson, 'that is not fitting language.'

The other snarled aloud into a savage laugh; and the next
moment, with extraordinary quickness, he had unlocked
the door and disappeared into the house.

The lawyer stood awhile when Mr Hyde had left him,
the picture of disquietude. Then he began slowly to mount
the street, pausing every step or two and putting his hand
to his brow like a man in mental perplexity. The problem
he was thus debating as he walked, was one of a class
that is rarely solved. Mr Hyde was pale and dwarfish, he
gave an impression of deformity without any nameable
malformation, he had a displeasing smile, he had borne
himself to the lawyer with a sort of murderous mixture
of timidity and boldness, and he spoke with a husky,
whispering and somewhat broken voice; all these were
points against him, but not all of these together could
explain the hitherto unknown disgust, loathing and fear
with which Mr Utterson regarded him. 'There must be
something else,' said the perplexed gentleman. 'There *is*
something more, if I could find a name for it. God bless
me, the man seems hardly human! Something troglodytic,
shall we say? or can it be the old story of Dr Fell? or is it the
mere radiance of a foul soul that thus transpires through,
and transfigures, its clay continent? The last, I think; for O
my poor old Harry Jekyll, if ever I read Satan's signature
upon a face, it is on that of your new friend.'

Round the corner from the by-street, there was a square
of ancient, handsome houses, now for the most part
decayed from their high estate and let in flats and chambers
to all sorts and conditions of men: map-engravers, archi-
tects, shady lawyers and the agents of obscure enterprises.

One house, however, second from the corner, was still occupied entire; and at the door of this, which wore a great air of wealth and comfort, though it was now plunged in darkness except for the fan-light, Mr Utterson stopped and knocked. A well-dressed, elderly servant opened the door.

'Is Dr Jekyll at home, Poole?' asked the lawyer.

'I will see, Mr Utterson,' said Poole, admitting the visitor, as he spoke, into a large, low-roofed, comfortable hall, paved with flags, warmed (after the fashion of a country house) by a bright, open fire, and furnished with costly cabinets of oak. 'Will you wait here by the fire, sir? or shall I give you a light in the dining-room?'

'Here, thank you,' said the lawyer, and he drew near and leaned on the tall fender. This hall, in which he was now left alone, was a pet fancy of his friend the doctor's; and Utterson himself was wont to speak of it as the pleasantest room in London. But to-night there was a shudder in his blood; the face of Hyde sat heavy on his memory; he felt (what was rare with him) a nausea and distaste of life; and in the gloom of his spirits, he seemed to read a menace in the flickering of the firelight on the polished cabinets and the uneasy starting of the shadow on the roof. He was ashamed of his relief, when Poole presently returned to announce that Dr Jekyll was gone out.

'I saw Mr Hyde go in by the old dissecting room door, Poole,' he said. 'Is that right, when Dr Jekyll is from home?'

'Quite right, Mr Utterson, sir,' replied the servant. 'Mr Hyde has a key.'

'Your master seems to repose a great deal of trust in that young man, Poole,' resumed the other musingly.

'Yes, sir, he do indeed,' said Poole. 'We have all orders to obey him.'

'I do not think I ever met Mr Hyde?' asked Utterson.

'O, dear no, sir. He never *dines* here,' replied the butler. 'Indeed we see very little of him on this side of the house; he mostly comes and goes by the laboratory.'

'Well, good night, Poole.'

'Good night, Mr Utterson.'

And the lawyer set out homeward with a very heavy heart.

'Poor Harry Jekyll,' he thought, 'my mind misgives me he is in deep waters! He was wild when he was young; a long while ago to be sure; but in the law of God, there is no statute of limitations. Ay, it must be that; the ghost of some old sin, the cancer of some concealed disgrace; punishment coming, *pede claudo*, years after memory has forgotten and self-love condoned the fault.' And the lawyer, scared by the thought, brooded awhile on his own past, groping in all the corners of memory, lest by chance some Jack-in-the-Box of an old iniquity should leap to light there. His past was fairly blameless; few men could read the rolls of their life with less apprehension; yet he was humbled to the dust by the many ill things he had done, and raised up again into a sober and fearful gratitude by the many that he had come so near to doing, yet avoided. And then by a return on his former subject, he conceived a spark of hope. 'This Master Hyde, if he were studied,' thought he, 'must have secrets of his own: black secrets, by the look of him; secrets compared to which poor Jekyll's worst would be like sunshine. Things cannot continue as they are. It turns me cold to think of this creature stealing like a thief to Harry's bedside; poor Harry, what a wakening! And the danger of it; for if this Hyde suspects the existence of the will, he may grow impatient to inherit. Ay, I must put my shoulder to the wheel – if Jekyll will but let me,' he added, 'if Jekyll will only let me.' For once more he saw before his mind's eye, as clear as a transparency, the strange clauses of the will.

DR JEKYLL WAS QUITE AT EASE

A fortnight later, by excellent good fortune, the doctor gave one of his pleasant dinners to some five or six old cronies, all intelligent, reputable men and all judges of good wine; and Mr Utterson so contrived that he remained behind after the others had departed. This was no new arrangement, but a thing that had befallen many scores of times. Where Utterson was liked, he was liked well. Hosts loved to detain the dry lawyer, when the light-hearted and the loose-tongued had already their foot on the threshold; they liked to sit awhile in his unobtrusive company, practising for solitude, sobering their minds in the man's rich silence after the expense and strain of gaiety. To this rule, Dr Jekyll was no exception; and as he now sat on the opposite side of the fire – a large, well-made, smooth-faced man of fifty, with something of a slyish cast perhaps, but every mark of capacity and kindness – you could see by his looks that he cherished for Mr Utterson a sincere and warm affection.

'I have been wanting to speak to you, Jekyll,' began the latter. 'You know that will of yours?'

A close observer might have gathered that the topic was distasteful; but the doctor carried it off gaily. 'My poor Utterson,' said he, 'you are unfortunate in such a client. I never saw a man so distressed as you were by my will; unless it were that hide-bound pedant, Lanyon, at what he called my scientific heresies. O, I know he's a good fellow – you needn't frown – an excellent fellow, and I always mean to see more of him; but a hide-bound pedant for all that; an ignorant, blatant pedant. I was never more disappointed in any man than Lanyon.'

'You know I never approved of it,' pursued Utterson, ruthlessly disregarding the fresh topic.

'My will? Yes, certainly, I know that,' said the doctor, a trifle sharply. 'You have told me so.'

'Well, I tell you so again,' continued the lawyer. 'I have been learning something of young Hyde.'

The large handsome face of Dr Jekyll grew pale to the very lips, and there came a blackness about his eyes. 'I do not care to hear more,' said he. 'This is a matter I thought we had agreed to drop.'

'What I heard was abominable,' said Utterson.

'It can make no change. You do not understand my position,' returned the doctor, with a certain incoherency of manner. 'I am painfully situated, Utterson; my position is a very strange – a very strange one. It is one of those affairs that cannot be mended by talking.'

'Jekyll,' said Utterson, 'you know me: I am a man to be trusted. Make a clean breast of this in confidence; and I make no doubt I can get you out of it.'

'My good Utterson,' said the doctor, 'this is very good of you, this is downright good of you, and I cannot find words to thank you in. I believe you fully; I would trust you before any man alive, ay, before myself, if I could make the choice; but indeed it isn't what you fancy; it is not so bad as that; and just to put your good heart at rest, I will tell you one thing: the moment I choose, I can be rid of Mr Hyde. I give you my hand upon that; and I thank you again and again; and I will just add one little word, Utterson, that I'm sure you'll take in good part: this is a private matter, and I beg of you to let it sleep.'

Utterson reflected a little looking in the fire.

'I have no doubt you are perfectly right,' he said at last, getting to his feet.

'Well, but since we have touched upon this business, and for the last time I hope,' continued the doctor, 'there is one point I should like you to understand. I have really a very great interest in poor Hyde. I know you have seen him; he told me so; and I fear he was rude. But I do sincerely take a great, a very great interest in that young man; and if I am taken away, Utterson, I wish you to promise me that you will bear with him and get his rights for him. I think you would, if you knew all; and it would be a weight off my mind if you would promise.'

'I can't pretend that I shall ever like him,' said the lawyer.

'I don't ask that,' pleaded Jekyll, laying his hand upon the other's arm; 'I only ask for justice; I only ask you to help him for my sake, when I am no longer here.'

Utterson heaved an irrepressible sigh. 'Well,' said he. 'I promise.'

THE CAREW MURDER CASE

Nearly a year later, in the month of October 18—, London was startled by a crime of singular ferocity and rendered all the more notable by the high position of the victim. The details were few and startling. A maid servant living alone in a house not far from the river, had gone upstairs to bed about eleven. Although a fog rolled over the city in the small hours, the early part of the night was cloudless, and the lane, which the maid's window overlooked, was brilliantly lit by the full moon. It seems she was romantically given, for she sat down upon her box, which stood immediately under the window, and fell into a dream of musing. Never (she used to say, with streaming tears, when she narrated that experience) never had she felt more at peace with all men or thought more kindly of the world. And as she so sat she became aware of an aged and beautiful gentleman with white hair, drawing near along the lane; and advancing to meet him, another and very small gentleman, to whom at first she paid less attention. When they had come within speech (which was just under the maid's eyes) the older man bowed and accosted the other with a very pretty manner of politeness. It did not seem as if the subject of his address were of great importance; indeed, from his pointing, it sometimes appeared as if he were only inquiring his way; but the moon shone on his face as he spoke, and the girl was pleased to watch it, it seemed to breathe such an innocent and old-world kindness of disposition, yet with something high too, as of a well-founded self-content. Presently her eye wandered to the other, and she was surprised to recognise in him a certain Mr Hyde, who had once visited her master and for whom she had conceived a dislike. He had in his hand a heavy cane, with which he was trifling; but he answered never a word, and seemed to listen with an ill-contained impatience. And then all of a sudden he broke out in a great flame of anger, stamping with his foot, brandishing the cane, and carrying on (as the maid described it) like a madman. The old gentleman took a step back, with the air of one very much surprised and a trifle hurt; and at that Mr Hyde broke out of all bounds and clubbed him to the earth. And next moment, with ape-like fury, he was trampling his victim under foot, and hailing down a storm of blows, under which the bones were audibly shattered and the body jumped upon the roadway. At the horror of these sights and sounds, the maid fainted.

It was two o'clock when she came to herself and called

for the police. The murderer was gone long ago; but there lay his victim in the middle of the lane, incredibly mangled. The stick with which the deed had been done, although it was of some rare and very tough and heavy wood, had broken in the middle under the stress of this insensate cruelty; and one splintered half had rolled in the neighbouring gutter – the other, without doubt, had been carried away by the murderer. A purse and a gold watch were found upon the victim; but no cards or papers, except a sealed and stamped envelope, which he had been probably carrying to the post, and which bore the name and address of Mr Utterson.

This was brought to the lawyer the next morning, before he was out of bed; and he had no sooner seen it, and been told the circumstances, than he shot out a solemn lip. 'I shall say nothing till I have seen the body,' said he; 'this may be very serious. Have the kindness to wait while I dress.' And with the same grave countenance he hurried through his breakfast and drove to the police station, whither the body had been carried. As soon as he came into the cell, he nodded.

'Yes,' said he, 'I recognise him. I am sorry to say that this is Sir Danvers Carew.'

'Good God, sir,' exclaimed the officer, 'is it possible?' And the next moment his eye lighted up with professional ambition. 'This will make a deal of noise,' he said. 'And perhaps you can help us to the man.' And he briefly narrated what the maid had seen, and showed the broken stick.

Mr Utterson had already quailed at the name of Hyde; but when the stick was laid before him, he could doubt no longer: broken and battered as it was, he recognised it for one that he had himself presented many years before to Henry Jekyll.

'Is this Mr Hyde a person of small stature?' he inquired.

'Particularly small and particularly wicked-looking, is what the maid calls him,' said the officer.

Mr Utterson reflected; and then, raising his head, 'If you will come with me in my cab,' he said, 'I think I can take you to his house.'

It was by this time about nine in the morning, and the first fog of the season. A great chocolate-coloured pall lowered over heaven, but the wind was continually charging and routing these embattled vapours; so that as the cab crawled from street to street, Mr Utterson beheld a marvellous number of degrees and hues of twilight; for here it would be dark like the backend of evening; and there would be a glow of a rich, lurid brown, like the light of some strange conflagration; and here, for a moment, the fog would be quite broken up, and a haggard shaft of daylight would glance in between the swirling wreaths. The dismal quarter of Soho seen under these changing glimpses, with its muddy ways, and slatternly passengers, and its lamps, which had never been extinguished or had been kindled afresh to combat this mournful reïnvasion of darkness, seemed, in the lawyer's eyes, like a district of some city in a nightmare. The thoughts of his mind, besides, were of the gloomiest dye; and when he glanced at the companion of his drive, he was conscious of some touch of that terror of the law and the law's officers, which may at times assail the most honest.

As the cab drew up before the address indicated, the fog lifted a little and showed him a dingy street, a gin palace, a low French eating house, a shop for the retail of penny numbers and twopenny salads, many ragged children huddled in the doorways, and many women of many different nationalities passing out, key in hand, to have a morning glass; and the next moment the fog settled down again upon that part, as brown as umber, and cut him off from his blackguardly surroundings. This was the home of Henry Jekyll's favourite; of a man who was heir to a quarter of a million sterling.

An ivory-faced and silvery-haired old woman opened the door. She had an evil face, smoothed by hypocrisy; but her manners were excellent. Yes, she said, this was Mr Hyde's, but he was not at home; he had been in that night very late, but had gone away again in less than an hour; there was nothing strange in that; his habits were very irregular, and he was often absent; for instance, it was nearly two months since she had seen him till yesterday.

'Very well then, we wish to see his rooms,' said the lawyer; and when the woman began to declare it was impossible, 'I had better tell you who this person is,' he added. 'This is Inspector Newcomen of Scotland Yard.'

A flash of odious joy appeared upon the woman's face. 'Ah!' said she, 'he is in trouble! What has he done?'

Mr Utterson and the inspector exchanged glances. 'He don't seem a very popular character,' observed the latter. 'And now, my good woman, just let me and this gentleman have a look about us.'

In the whole extent of the house, which but for the old woman remained otherwise empty, Mr Hyde had only used a couple of rooms; but these were furnished with luxury and good taste. A closet was filled with wine; the plate was of silver, the napery elegant; a good picture hung upon the walls, a gift (as Utterson supposed) from Henry Jekyll, who was much of a connoisseur; and the carpets were of many piles and agreeable in colour. At this moment, however, the rooms bore every mark of having been recently and hurriedly ransacked; clothes lay about the floor, with their pockets inside out; lockfast drawers stood open; and on the hearth there lay a pile of gray ashes, as though many papers had been burned. From these embers the inspector disinterred the butt end of a green cheque book, which had resisted the action of the fire; the other half of the stick was found behind the door; and as this clinched his suspicions, the officer declared himself delighted. A visit to the bank, where several thousand pounds were found to be lying to the murderer's credit, completed his gratification.

'You may depend upon it, sir,' he told Mr Utterson: 'I have him in my hand. He must have lost his head, or he never would have left the stick or, above all, burned the cheque book. Why, money's life to the man. We have nothing to do but wait for him at the bank, and get out the handbills.'

This last, however, was not so easy of accomplishment; for Mr Hyde had numbered few familiars – even the master of the servant maid had only seen him twice; his family could nowhere be traced; he had never been photographed; and the few who could describe him differed widely, as common observers will. Only on one point, were they agreed; and that was the haunting sense of unexpressed deformity with which the fugitive impressed his beholders.

INCIDENT OF THE LETTER

It was late in the afternoon, when Mr Utterson found his way to Dr Jekyll's door, where he was at once admitted by Poole, and carried down by the kitchen offices and across a yard which had once been a garden, to the building which was indifferently known as the laboratory or the dissecting rooms. The doctor had bought the house from the heirs of a celebrated surgeon; and his own tastes being rather chemical than anatomical, had changed the destination of the block at the bottom of the garden. It was the first time that the lawyer had been received in that part of his friend's quarters; and he eyed the dingy windowless structure with curiosity, and gazed round with a distasteful sense of strangeness as he crossed the theatre, once crowded with eager students now lying gaunt and silent, the tables laden with chemical apparatus, the floor strewn with crates and littered with packing straw, and the light falling dimly through the foggy cupola. At the further end, a flight of stairs mounted to a door covered with red baize; and through this Mr Utterson was at last received into the doctor's cabinet. It was a large room, fitted round with glass presses, furnished, among other things, with a cheval-glass and a business table, and looking out upon the court by three dusty windows barred with iron. The fire burned in the grate; a lamp was set lighted on the chimney shelf, for even in the houses the fog began to lie thickly; and there, close up to the warmth, sat Dr Jekyll, looking deadly sick. He did not rise to meet his visitor, but held out a cold hand and bade him welcome in a changed voice.

'And now,' said Mr Utterson, as soon as Poole had left them, 'you have heard the news?'

The doctor shuddered. 'They were crying it in the square,' he said. 'I heard them in my dining room.'

'One word,' said the lawyer. 'Carew was my client, but so are you, and I want to know what I am doing. You have not been mad enough to hide this fellow?'

'Utterson, I swear to God,' cried the doctor. 'I swear to God I will never set eyes on him again. I bind my honour to you that I am done with him in this world. It is all at an end. And indeed he does not want my help; you do not know him as I do; he is safe, he is quite safe; mark my words, he will never more be heard of.'

The lawyer listened gloomily; he did not like his friend's feverish manner. 'You seem pretty sure of him,' said he; 'and for your sake, I hope you may be right. If it came to a trial, your name might appear.'

'I am quite sure of him,' replied Jekyll; 'I have grounds for certainty that I cannot share with anyone. But there is one thing on which you may advise me. I have – I have received a letter; and I am at a loss whether I should show it to the police. I should like to leave it in your hands, Utterson; you would judge wisely I am sure; I have so great a trust in you.'

'You fear, I suppose, that it might lead to his detection?' asked the lawyer.

'No,' said the other. 'I cannot say that I care what becomes of Hyde; I am quite done with him. I was thinking of my own character, which this hateful business has rather exposed.'

Utterson ruminated awhile; he was surprised at his friend's selfishness, and yet relieved by it. 'Well,' said he, at last, 'let me see the letter.'

The letter was written in an odd, upright hand and signed 'Edward Hyde': and it signified, briefly enough, that the writer's benefactor, Dr Jekyll, whom he had long so unworthily repaid for a thousand generosities, need labour under no alarm for his safety as he had means of escape on which he placed a sure dependence. The lawyer liked this letter well enough; it put a better colour on the intimacy than he had looked for; and he blamed himself for some of his past suspicions.

'Have you the envelope?' he asked.

'I burned it,' replied Jekyll, 'before I thought what I was about. But it bore no postmark. The note was handed in.'

'Shall I keep this and sleep upon it?' asked Utterson.

'I wish you to judge for me entirely,' was the reply. 'I have lost confidence in myself.'

'Well, I shall consider,' returned the lawyer. 'And now one word more: it was Hyde who dictated the terms in your will about that disappearance?'

The doctor seemed seized with a qualm of faintness; he shut his mouth tight and nodded.

'I knew it,' said Utterson. 'He meant to murder you. You have had a fine escape.'

'I have had what is far more to the purpose,' returned the doctor solemnly: 'I have had a lesson – O God, Utterson, what a lesson I have had!' And he covered his face for a moment with his hands.

On his way out, the lawyer stopped and had a word or two with Poole. 'By the by,' said he, 'there was a letter handed in to-day: what was the messenger like?' But Poole was positive nothing had come except by post; 'and only circulars by that,' he added.

This news sent off the visitor with his fears renewed. Plainly the letter had come by the laboratory door; possibly, indeed, it had been written in the cabinet; and if that were so, it must be differently judged, and handled with the more caution. The newsboys, as he went, were crying themselves hoarse along the footways: 'Special edition. Shocking murder of an M.P.' That was the funeral oration of one friend and client; and he could not help a certain apprehension lest the good name of another should be sucked down in the eddy of the scandal. It was, at least, a ticklish decision that he had to make; and self-reliant as he was by habit, he began to cherish a longing for advice. It was not to be had directly; but perhaps, he thought, it might be fished for.

Presently after, he sat on one side of his own hearth, with Mr Guest, his head clerk, upon the other, and midway between, at a nicely calculated distance from

the fire, a bottle of a particular old wine that had long
dwelt unsunned in the foundations of his house. The fog
still slept on the wing above the drowned city, where the
lamps glimmered like carbuncles; and through the muffle
and smother of these fallen clouds, the procession of the
town's life was still rolling in through the great arteries
with a sound as of a mighty wind. But the room was
gay with firelight. In the bottle the acids were long ago
resolved; the imperial dye had softened with time, as the
colour grows richer in stained windows; and the glow of
hot autumn afternoons on hillside vineyards, was ready to
be set free and to disperse the fogs of London. Insensibly
the lawyer melted. There was no man from whom he kept
fewer secrets than Mr Guest; and he was not always sure
that he kept as many as he meant. Guest had often been
on business to the doctor's; he knew Poole; he could
scarce have failed to hear of Mr Hyde's familiarity about
the house; he might draw conclusions: was it not as well,
then, that he should see a letter which put that mystery
to rights? and above all since Guest, being a great student
and critic of handwriting, would consider the step natural
and obliging? The clerk, besides, was a man of counsel; he
would scarce read so strange document without dropping
a remark; and by that remark Mr Utterson might shape his
future course.

'This is a sad business about Sir Danvers,' he said.

'Yes, sir, indeed. It has elicited a great deal of public
feeling,' returned Guest. 'The man, of course, was mad.'

'I should like to hear your views on that,' replied
Utterson. 'I have a document here in his handwriting; it
is between ourselves, for I scarce know what to do about
it; it is an ugly business at the best. But there it is; quite
in your way: a murderer's autograph.'

Guest's eyes brightened, and he sat down at once and
studied it with passion. 'No, sir,' he said; 'not mad; but it
is an odd hand.'

'And by all accounts a very odd writer,' added the
lawyer.

Just then the servant entered with a note.

'Is that from Doctor Jekyll, sir?' inquired the clerk.

'I thought I knew the writing. Anything private, Mr Utterson?'

'Only an invitation to dinner. Why? do you want to see it?'

'One moment. I thank you, sir;' and the clerk laid the two sheets of paper alongside and sedulously compared their contents. 'Thank you, sir,' he said at last, returning both; 'it's a very interesting autograph.'

There was a pause, during which Mr Utterson struggled with himself. 'Why did you compare them, Guest?' he inquired suddenly.

'Well, sir,' returned the clerk, 'there's a rather singular resemblance; the two hands are in many points identical: only differently sloped.'

'Rather quaint,' said Utterson.

'It is, as you say, rather quaint,' returned Guest.

'I wouldn't speak of this note, you know,' said the master.

'No, sir,' said the clerk. 'I understand.'

But no sooner was Mr Utterson alone that night, than he locked the note into his safe where it reposed from that time forward. 'What!' he thought. 'Henry Jekyll forge for a murderer!' And his blood ran cold in his veins.

REMARKABLE INCIDENT OF DOCTOR LANYON

Time ran on; thousands of pounds were offered in reward, for the death of Sir Danvers was resented as a public injury; but Mr Hyde had disappeared out of the ken of the police as though he had never existed. Much of his past was unearthed, indeed, and all disreputable: tales came out of the man's cruelty, at once so callous and violent, of his vile life, of his strange associates, of the hatred that seemed to have surrounded his career; but of his present whereabouts, not a whisper. From the time he had left the house in Soho on the morning of the murder, he was simply blotted out; and gradually, as time drew on, Mr Utterson began to recover from the hotness of his alarm, and to grow more at quiet with himself. The death of Sir Danvers was, to his way of thinking, more than paid for by the disappearance of Mr Hyde. Now that that evil influence had been withdrawn, a new life began for Dr Jekyll. He came out of his seclusion, renewed relations with his friends, became once more their familiar guest and entertainer; and whilst he had always been known for charities, he was now no less distinguished for religion. He was busy, he was much in the open air, he did good; his face seemed to open and brighten, as if with an inward consciousness of service; and for more than two months, the doctor was at peace.

On the 8th of January Utterson had dined at the doctor's with a small party; Lanyon had been there; and the face of the host had looked from one to the other as in the old days when the trio were inseparable friends. On the 12th, and again on the 14th, the door was shut against the lawyer. 'The doctor was confined to the house,' Poole said, 'and saw no one.' On the 15th, he tried again, and was again refused; and having now been used for the last two months to see his friend almost daily, he found this return of solitude to weigh upon his spirits. The fifth night, he had in Guest to dine with him; and the sixth he betook himself to Doctor Lanyon's.

There at least he was not denied admittance; but when he came in, he was shocked at the change which had taken place in the doctor's appearance. He had his death-warrant written legibly upon his face. The rosy man had grown pale; his flesh had fallen away; he was visibly balder and older; and yet it was not so much these tokens of a swift physical decay that arrested the lawyer's notice, as a look in the eye and quality of manner that seemed to testify to some deep-seated terror of the mind. It was unlikely that the doctor should fear death; and yet that was what Utterson was tempted to suspect. 'Yes,' he thought; 'he is a doctor, he must know his own state and that his days are counted; and the knowledge is more than he can bear.' And yet when Utterson remarked on his ill-looks, it was with an air of great firmness that Lanyon declared himself a doomed man.

'I have had a shock,' he said, 'and I shall never recover.

It is a question of weeks. Well, life has been pleasant; I liked it; yes, sir, I used to like it. I sometimes think if we knew all, we should be more glad to get away.'

'Jekyll is ill, too,' observed Utterson. 'Have you seen him?'

But Lanyon's face changed, and he held up a trembling hand. 'I wish to see or hear no more of Doctor Jekyll,' he said in a loud, unsteady voice. 'I am quite done with that person; and I beg that you will spare me any allusion to one whom I regard as dead.'

'Tut-tut,' said Mr Utterson; and then after a considerable pause, 'Can't I do anything?' he inquired. 'We are three very old friends, Lanyon; we shall not live to make others.'

'Nothing can be done,' returned Lanyon; 'ask himself.'

'He will not see me,' said the lawyer.

'I am not surprised at that,' was the reply. 'Some day, Utterson, after I am dead, you may perhaps come to learn the right and wrong of this. I cannot tell you. And in the meantime, if you can sit and talk with me of other things, for God's sake, stay and do so; but if you cannot keep clear of this accursed topic, then, in God's name, go, for I cannot bear it.'

As soon as he got home, Utterson sat down and wrote to Jekyll, complaining of his exclusion from the house, and asking the cause of this unhappy break with Lanyon; and the next day brought him a long answer, often very pathetically worded, and sometimes darkly mysterious in drift. The quarrel with Lanyon was incurable. 'I do not blame our old friend,' Jekyll wrote, 'but I share his view that we must never meet. I mean from henceforth to lead a life of extreme seclusion; you must not be surprised, nor must you doubt my friendship, if my door is often shut even to you. You must suffer me to go my own dark way. I have brought on myself a punishment and a danger that I cannot name. If I am the chief of sinners, I am the chief of sufferers also. I could not think that this earth contained a place for sufferings and terrors so unmanning; and you can do but one thing, Utterson, to lighten this destiny, and that is to respect my silence.' Utterson was amazed; the dark influence of Hyde had been withdrawn, the doctor had returned to his old tasks and amities; a week ago, the prospect had smiled with every promise of a cheerful and an honoured age; and now in a moment, friendship, and peace of mind and the whole tenor of his life were wrecked. So great and unprepared a change pointed to madness; but in view of Lanyon's manner and words, there must lie for it some deeper ground.

A week afterwards Dr Lanyon took to his bed, and in something less than a fortnight he was dead. The night after the funeral, at which he had been sadly affected, Utterson locked the door of his business room, and sitting there by the light of a melancholy candle, drew out and set before him an envelope addressed by the hand and sealed with the seal of his dead friend. 'PRIVATE: for the hands of J. G. Utterson ALONE and in case of his predecease *to be destroyed unread*,' so it was emphatically superscribed; and the lawyer dreaded to behold the contents. 'I have buried one friend to-day,' he thought: 'what if this should cost me another?' And then he condemned the fear as a disloyalty, and broke the seal. Within there was another enclosure, likewise sealed, and marked upon the cover as 'not to be opened till the death or disappearance of Dr Henry Jekyll.' Utterson could not trust his eyes. Yes, it was disappearance; here again, as in the mad will which he had long ago restored to its author, here again were the idea of a disappearance and the name of Henry Jekyll bracketed. But in the will, that idea had sprung from the sinister suggestion of the man Hyde; it was set there with a purpose all too plain and horrible. Written by the hand of Lanyon, what should it mean? A great curiosity came on the trustee, to disregard the prohibition and dive at once to the bottom of these mysteries; but professional honour and faith to his dead friend were stringent obligations; and the packet slept in the inmost corner of his private safe.

It is one thing to mortify curiosity, another to conquer it; and it may be doubted if, from that day forth, Utterson desired the society of his surviving friend with the same eagerness. He thought of him kindly; but his thoughts were disquieted and fearful. He went to call indeed; but he was perhaps relieved to be denied admittance; perhaps, in his heart, he preferred to speak with Poole upon the doorstep and surrounded by the air and sounds of the open city, rather than to be admitted into that house of voluntary bondage, and to sit and speak with its inscrutable recluse. Poole had, indeed, no very pleasant news to communicate. The doctor, it appeared, now more than ever confined himself to the cabinet over the laboratory, where he would sometimes even sleep; he was out of spirits, he had grown very silent, he did not read; it seemed as if he had something on his mind. Utterson became so used to the unvarying character of these reports, that he fell off little by little in the frequency of his visits.

INCIDENT AT THE WINDOW

It chanced on Sunday, when Mr Utterson was on his usual walk with Mr Enfield, that their way lay once again through the bystreet; and that when they came in front of the door, both stopped to gaze on it.

'Well,' said Enfield, 'that story's at an end at least. We shall never see more of Mr Hyde.'

'I hope not,' said Utterson. 'Did I ever tell you that I once saw him, and shared your feeling of repulsion?'

'It was impossible to do the one without the other,' returned Enfield. 'And by the way what an ass you must have thought me, not to know that this was a back way to Dr Jekyll's! It was partly your own fault that I found it out, even when I did.'

'So you found it out, did you?' said Utterson. 'But if that be so, we may step into the court and take a look at the windows. To tell you the truth, I am uneasy about poor Jekyll; and even outside, I feel as if the presence of a friend might do him good.'

The court was very cool and a little damp, and full of premature twilight, although the sky, high up overhead, was still bright with sunset. The middle one of the three windows was half way open; and sitting close beside it, taking the air with an infinite sadness of mien, like some disconsolate prisoner, Utterson saw Dr Jekyll.

'What! Jekyll!' he cried. 'I trust you are better.'

'I am very low, Utterson,' replied the doctor drearily, 'very low. It will not last long, thank God.'

'You stay too much indoors,' said the lawyer. 'You should be out, whipping up the circulation like Mr Enfield and me. (This is my cousin – Mr Enfield – Dr Jekyll.) Come now; get your hat and take a quick turn with us.'

'You are very good,' sighed the other. 'I should like to very much; but no, no, no, it is quite impossible; I dare not. But indeed, Utterson, I am very glad to see you; this is really a great pleasure; I would ask you and Mr Enfield up, but the place is really not fit.'

'Why then,' said the lawyer, good-naturedly, 'the best thing we can do is to stay down here and speak with you from where we are.'

'That is just what I was about to venture to propose,' returned the doctor with a smile. But the words were hardly uttered, before the smile was struck out of his face and succeeded by an expression of such abject terror and despair, as froze the very blood of the two gentlemen below. They saw it but for a glimpse, for the window was instantly thrust down; but that glimpse had been sufficient and they turned and left the court without a word. In silence, too, they traversed the bystreet; and it was not until they had come into a neighbouring thoroughfare, where even upon a Sunday there were still some stirrings of life, that Mr Utterson at last turned and looked at his companion. They were both pale; and there was an answering horror in their eyes.

'God forgive us, God forgive us,' said Mr Utterson.

But Mr Enfield only nodded his head very seriously, and walked on once more in silence.

THE LAST NIGHT

Mr Utterson was sitting by his fireside one evening after dinner, when he was surprised to receive a visit from Poole.

'Bless me, Poole, what brings you here?' he cried; and then taking a second look at him, 'What ails you?' he added, 'is the doctor ill?'

'Mr Utterson,' said the man, 'there is something wrong.'

'Take a seat, and here is a glass of wine for you,' said the lawyer. 'Now, take your time, and tell me plainly what you want.'

'You know the doctor's ways, sir,' replied Poole, 'and how he shuts himself up. Well, he's shut up again in the cabinet; and I don't like it, sir – I wish I may die if I like it. Mr Utterson, sir, I'm afraid.'

'Now, my good man,' said the lawyer, 'be explicit. What are you afraid of?'

'I've been afraid for about a week,' returned Poole, doggedly disregarding the question; 'and I can bear it no more.'

The man's appearance amply bore out his words; his manner was altered for the worse; and except for the moment when he had first announced his terror, he had not once looked the lawyer in the face. Even now, he sat with the glass of wine untasted on his knee, and his eyes directed to a corner of the floor. 'I can bear it no more,' he repeated.

'Come,' said the lawyer, 'I see you have some good reason, Poole; I see there is something seriously amiss. Try to tell me what it is.'

'I think there's been foul play,' said Poole, hoarsely.

'Foul play!' cried the lawyer, a good deal frightened and rather inclined to be irritated in consequence. 'What foul play? What does the man mean?'

'I daren't say, sir,' was the answer; 'but will you come along with me and see for yourself?'

'Mr Utterson's only answer was to rise and get his hat and great coat; but he observed with wonder the greatness of the relief that appeared upon the butler's face, and perhaps with no less, that the wine was still untasted when he set it down to follow.

It was a wild, cold, seasonable night of March, with a pale moon, lying on her back as though the wind had tilted her, and a flying wrack of the most diaphanous

and lawny texture. The wind made talking difficult, and
flecked the blood into the face. It seemed to have swept
the streets unusually bare of passengers, besides; for Mr
Utterson thought he had never seen that part of London
so deserted. He could have wished it otherwise; never in
his life had he been conscious of so sharp a wish to see
and touch his fellow-creatures; for struggle as he might,
there was borne in upon his mind a crushing anticipation
of calamity. The square, when they got there, was all full of
wind and dust, and the thin trees in the garden were lashing
themselves along the railing. Poole, who had kept all the
way a pace or two ahead, now pulled up in the middle of
the pavement, and in spite of the biting weather, took off his
hat and mopped his brow with a red pocket-handkerchief.
But for all the hurry of his coming, these were not the dews
of exertion that he wiped away, but the moisture of some
strangling anguish; for his face was white and his voice,
when he spoke, harsh and broken.

'Well, sir,' he said, 'here we are, and God grant there be
nothing wrong.'

'Amen, Poole,' said the lawyer.

Thereupon the servant knocked in a very guarded manner; the door was opened on the chain; and a voice asked
from within, 'Is that you, Poole?'

'It's all right,' said Poole. 'Open the door.'

The hall, when they entered it, was brightly lighted up;
the fire was built high; and about the hearth the whole of
the servants, men and women, stood huddled together like
a flock of sheep. At the sight of Mr Utterson, the housemaid
broke into hysterical whimpering; and the cook, crying out
'Bless God! it's Mr Utterson,' ran forward as if to take him
in her arms.

'What, what? Are you all here?' said the lawyer peevishly.
'Very irregular, very unseemly; your master would be far
from pleased.'

'They're all afraid,' said Poole.

Blank silence followed, no one protesting; only the maid
lifted up her voice and now wept loudly.

'Hold your tongue!' Poole said to her, with a ferocity of
accent that testified to his own jangled nerves; and indeed,

when the girl had so suddenly raised the note of her lamentation, they had all started and turned towards the inner door with faces of dreadful expectation. 'And now,' continued the butler, addressing the knife-boy, 'reach me a candle, and we'll get this through hands at once.' And then he begged Mr Utterson to follow him, and led the way to the back garden.

'Now, sir,' said he, 'you come as gently as you can. I want you to hear, and I don't want you to be heard. And see here, sir, if by any chance he was to ask you in, don't go.'

Mr Utterson's nerves, at this unlooked-for termination, gave a jerk that nearly threw him from his balance; but he recollected his courage and followed the butler into the laboratory building and through the surgical theatre, with its lumber of crates and bottles, to the foot of the stair. Here Poole motioned him to stand on one side and listen; while he himself, setting down the candle and making a great and obvious call on his resolution, mounted the steps and knocked with a somewhat uncertain hand on the red baize of the cabinet door.

'Mr Utterson, sir, asking to see you,' he called; and even as he did so, once more violently signed to the lawyer to give ear.

A voice answered from within: 'Tell him I cannot see anyone,' it said complainingly.

'Thank you, sir,' said Poole, with a note of something like triumph in his voice; and taking up his candle, he led Mr Utterson back across the yard and into the great kitchen, where the fire was out and the beetles were leaping on the floor.

'Sir,' he said, looking Mr Utterson in the eyes, 'was that my master's voice?'

'It seems much changed,' replied the lawyer, very pale, but giving look for look.

'Changed? Well, yes, I think so,' said the butler. 'Have I been twenty years in this man's house, to be deceived about his voice? No, sir; master's made away with; he was made away with, eight days ago, when we heard him cry out upon the name of God: and *who's* in there instead of him, and *why* it stays there, is a thing that cries to Heaven, Mr Utterson!'

'This is a very strange tale, Poole; this is rather a wild tale, my man,' said Mr Utterson, biting his finger. 'Suppose it were as you suppose, supposing Dr Jekyll to have been – well, murdered, what could induce the murderer to stay? That won't hold water; it doesn't commend itself to reason.'

'Well, Mr Utterson, you are a hard man to satisfy, but I'll do it yet,' said Poole. 'All this last week (you must know) him, or it, or whatever it is that lives in that cabinet, has been crying night and day for some sort of medicine and cannot get it to his mind. It was sometimes his way – the master's, that is – to write his orders on a sheet of paper and throw it on the stair. We've had nothing else this week back; nothing but papers, and a closed door, and the very meals left there to be smuggled in when nobody was looking. Well, sir, every day, ay, and twice and thrice in the same day, there have been orders and complaints, and I have been sent flying to all the wholesale chemists in town. Every time I brought the stuff back, there would be another paper telling me to return it, because it was not pure, and another order to a different firm. This drug is wanted bitter bad, sir, whatever for.'

'Have you any of these papers?' asked Mr Utterson.

Poole felt in his pocket and handed out a crumpled note, which the lawyer, bending nearer to the candle, carefully examined. Its contents ran thus: 'Dr Jekyll presents his compliments to Messrs. Maw. He assures them that their last sample is impure and quite useless for his present purpose. In the year 18—, Dr J. purchased a somewhat large quantity from Messrs. M. He now begs them to search with the most sedulous care, and should any of the same quality be left, to forward it to him at once. Expense is no consideration. The importance of this to Dr J. can hardly be exaggerated.' So far the letter had run composedly enough, but here with a sudden splutter of the pen, the writer's emotion had broken loose. 'For God's sake,' he had added, 'find me some of the old.'

'This is a strange note,' said Mr Utterson; and then sharply, 'How do you come to have it open?'

'The man at Maw's was main angry, sir, and he threw it back to me like so much dirt,' returned Poole.

'This is unquestionably the doctor's hand, do you know?' resumed the lawyer.

'I thought it looked like it,' said the servant rather sulkily; and then, with another voice, 'But what matters hand of write,' he said. 'I've seen him!'

'Seen him?' repeated Mr Utterson. 'Well?'

'That's it!' said Poole. 'It was this way. I came suddenly into the theatre from the garden. It seems he had slipped out to look for this drug or whatever it is; for the cabinet door was open, and there he was at the far end of the room digging among the crates. He looked up when I came in, gave a kind of cry, and whipped upstairs into the cabinet. It was but for one minute that I saw him, but the hair stood upon my head like quills. Sir, if that was my master, why had he a mask upon his face? If it was my master, why did he cry out like a rat, and run from me? I have served him long enough. And then . . .' the man paused and passed his hand over his face.

'These are all very strange circumstances,' said Mr Utterson, 'but I think I begin to see daylight. Your master, Poole, is plainly seized with one of those maladies that both torture and deform the sufferer; hence, for aught I know, the alteration of his voice; hence the mask and his avoidance of his friends; hence his eagerness to find this drug, by means of which the poor soul retains some hope of ultimate recovery – God grant that he be not deceived! There is my explanation; it is sad enough, Poole, ay, and appalling to consider; but it is plain and natural, hangs well together and delivers us from all exorbitant alarms.'

'Sir,' said the butler, turning to a sort of mottled pallor, 'that thing was not my master, and there's the truth. My master' – here he looked round him and began to whisper – 'is a tall fine build of a man, and this was more of a dwarf.' Utterson attempted to protest. 'O, sir,' cried Poole, 'do you think I do not know my master after twenty years? do you think I do not know where his head comes to in the cabinet door, where I saw him every morning of my life? No, sir, that thing in the mask was never Doctor Jekyll – God knows what it was, but it was never Doctor Jekyll; and it is the belief of my heart that there was murder done.'

'Poole,' replied the lawyer, 'if you say that, it will become my duty to make certain. Much as I desire to spare your master's feelings, much as I am puzzled by this note which seems to prove him to be still alive, I shall consider it my duty to break in that door.'

'Ah, Mr Utterson, that's talking!' cried the butler.

'And now comes the second question,' resumed Utterson: 'Who is going to do it?'

'Why, you and me, sir,' was the undaunted reply.

'That is very well said,' returned the lawyer; 'and whatever comes of it, I shall make it my business to see you are no loser.'

'There is an axe in the theatre,' continued Poole; 'and you might take the kitchen poker for yourself.'

The lawyer took that rude but weighty instrument into his hand, and balanced it. 'Do you know, Poole,' he said, looking up, 'that you and I are about to place ourselves in a position of some peril?'

'You may say so, sir, indeed,' returned the butler.

'It is well, then, that we should be frank,' said the other. 'We both think more than we have said; let us make a clean breast. This masked figure that you saw, did you recognise it?'

'Well, sir, it went so quick, and the creature was so doubled up, that I could hardly swear to that,' was the answer. 'But if you mean, was it Mr Hyde? – why, yes, I think it was! You see, it was much of the same bigness; and it had the same quick light way with it; and then who else could have got in by the laboratory door? You have not forgot, sir, that at the time of the murder he had still the key with him? But that's not all. I don't know, Mr Utterson, if ever you met this Mr Hyde?'

'Yes,' said the lawyer, 'I once spoke with him.'

'Then you must know as well as the rest of us that there was something queer about that gentleman – something that gave a man a turn – I don't know rightly how to say it, sir, beyond this: that you felt it in your marrow kind of cold and thin.'

'I own I felt something of what you describe,' said Mr Utterson.

'Quite so, sir,' returned Poole. 'Well, when that masked thing like a monkey jumped from among the chemicals and whipped into the cabinet, it went down my spine like ice. O, I know it's not evidence, Mr Utterson; I'm book-learned enough for that; but a man has his feelings, and I give you my bible-word it was Mr Hyde!'

'Ay, ay,' said the lawyer. 'My fears incline to the same point. Evil, I fear, founded – evil was sure to come – of that connection. Ay, truly, I believe you; I believe poor Harry is killed; and I believe his murderer (for what purpose, God alone can tell) is still lurking in his victim's room. Well, let our name be vengeance. Call Bradshaw.'

The footman came at the summons, very white and nervous.

'Pull yourself together, Bradshaw,' said the lawyer. 'This suspense, I know, is telling upon all of you; but it is now our intention to make an end of it. Poole, here, and I are going to force our way into the cabinet. If all is well, my shoulders are broad enough to bear the blame. Meanwhile, lest anything should really be amiss, or any malefactor seek to escape by the back, you and the boy must go round the corner with a pair of good sticks, and take your post at the laboratory door. We give you ten minutes, to get to your stations.'

As Bradshaw left, the lawyer looked at his watch. 'And now, Poole, let us get to ours,' he said; and taking the poker under his arm, he led the way into the yard. The scud had banked over the moon, and it was now quite dark. The wind, which only broke in puffs and draughts into that deep well of building, tossed the light of the candle to and fro about their steps, until they came into the shelter of the theatre, where they sat down silently to wait. London hummed solemnly all around; but nearer at hand, the stillness was only broken by the sound of a footfall moving to and fro along the cabinet floor.

'So it will walk all day, sir,' whispered Poole; 'ay, and

the better part of the night. Only when a new sample comes from the chemist there's a bit of a break. Ah, it's an ill-conscience that's such an enemy to rest! Ah, sir, there's blood foully shed in every step of it! But hark again, a little closer – put your heart in your ears, Mr Utterson, and tell me, is that the doctor's foot?'

The steps fell lightly and oddly, with a certain swing, for all they went so slowly; it was different indeed from the heavy creaking tread of Henry Jekyll. Utterson sighed. 'Is there never anything else?' he asked.

Poole nodded. 'Once,' he said. 'Once I heard it weeping!'

'Weeping? how that?' said the lawyer, conscious of a sudden chill of horror.

'Weeping like a woman or a lost soul,' said the butler. 'I came away with that upon my heart, that I could have wept too.'

But now the ten minutes drew to an end. Poole disinterred the axe from under a stack of packing straw; the candle was set upon the nearest table to light them to the attack; and they drew near with bated breath to where that patient foot was still going up and down, up and down, in the quiet of the night.

'Jekyll,' cried Utterson, with a loud voice, 'I demand to see you.' He paused a moment, but there came no reply. 'I give you fair warning, our suspicions are aroused, and I must and shall see you,' he resumed; 'if not by fair means then by foul – if not of your consent, then by brute force!'

'Utterson,' said the voice, 'for God's sake, have mercy!'

'Ah, that's not Jekyll's voice – it's Hyde's!' cried Utterson. 'Down with the door, Poole.'

Poole swung the axe over his shoulder; the blow shook the building, and the red baize door leaped against the lock and hinges. A dismal screech, as of mere animal terror, rang from the cabinet. Up went the axe again, and again the panels crashed and the frame bounded; four times the blow fell; but the wood was tough and the fittings were of excellent workmanship; and it was not until the fifth, that the lock burst in sunder and the wreck of the door fell inwards on the carpet.

The besiegers, appalled by their own riot and the stillness that had succeeded, stood back a little and peered in. There lay the cabinet before their eyes in the quiet lamplight, a good fire glowing and chattering on the hearth, the kettle singing its thin strain, a drawer or two open, papers neatly set forth on the business table, and nearer the fire, the things laid out for tea; the quietest room, you would have said and, but for the glazed presses full of chemicals, the most commonplace that night in London.

Right in the midst there lay the body of a man sorely contorted and still twitching. They drew near on tiptoe, turned it on its back and beheld the face of Edward Hyde. He was dressed in clothes far too large for him, clothes of the doctor's bigness; the cords of his face still moved with a semblance of life, but life was quite gone; and by the crushed phial in the hand and the strong smell of kernels that hung upon the air, Utterson knew that he was looking on the body of a self-destroyer.

'We have come too late,' he said sternly, 'whether to save or punish. Hyde is gone to his account; and it only remains for us to find the body of your master.'

The far greater proportion of the building was occupied by the theatre, which filled almost the whole ground story and was lighted from above, and by the cabinet, which formed an upper story at one end and looked upon the court. A corridor joined the theatre to the door on the bystreet; and with this, the cabinet communicated separately by a second flight of stairs. There were besides a few dark closets and a spacious cellar. All these they now thoroughly examined. Each closet needed but a glance, for all were empty and all, by the dust that fell from their doors, had stood long unopened. The cellar, indeed, was filled with crazy lumber, mostly dating from the times of the surgeon who was Jekyll's predecessor; but even as they opened the door, they were advertised of the uselessness of further search, by the fall of a perfect mat of cobweb which had for years sealed up the entrance. Nowhere was there any trace of Henry Jekyll, dead or alive.

Poole stamped on the flags of the corridor. 'He must be buried here,' he said, hearkening to the sound.

'Or he may have fled,' said Utterson, and he turned to examine the door in the bystreet. It was locked; and lying near by on the flags, they found the key, already stained with rust.

'This does not look like use,' observed the lawyer.

'Use!' echoed Poole. 'Do you not see, sir, it is broken? much as if a man had stamped on it.'

'Ay,' continued Utterson, 'and the fractures, too, are rusty.' The two men looked at each other with a scare. 'This is beyond me, Poole,' said the lawyer. 'Let us go back to the cabinet.'

They mounted the stair in silence, and still with an occasional awestruck glance at the dead body, proceeded more thoroughly to examine the contents of the cabinet. At one table, there were traces of chemical work, various measured heaps of some white salt being laid on glass saucers, as though for an experiment in which the unhappy man had been prevented.

'That is the same drug that I was always bringing him,' said Poole; and even as he spoke, the kettle with a startling noise boiled over.

This brought them to the fireside, where the easy chair was drawn cosily up, and the tea things stood ready to the sitter's elbow, the very sugar in the cup. There were several books on a shelf; one lay beside the tea things open, and Utterson was amazed to find it a copy of a pious work, for which Jekyll had several times expressed a great esteem, annotated, in his own hand, with startling blasphemies.

Next, in the course of their review of the chamber, the searchers came to the cheval glass, into whose depths they looked with an involuntary horror. But it was so turned as to show them nothing but the rosy glow playing on the roof, the fire sparkling in a hundred repetitions along the glazed front of the presses, and their own pale and fearful countenances stooping to look in.

'This glass have seen some strange things, sir,' whispered Poole.

'And surely none stranger than itself,' echoed the lawyer in the same tones. 'For what did Jekyll' – he caught himself up at the word with a start, and then conquering the weakness: 'what could Jekyll want with it?' he said.

'You may say that!' said Poole.

Next they turned to the business table. On the desk among the neat array of papers, a large envelope was uppermost, and bore, in the doctor's hand, the name of Mr Utterson. The lawyer unsealed it, and several enclosures fell to the floor. The first was a will, drawn in the same eccentric terms as the one which he had returned six months before, to serve as a testament in case of death and as a deed of gift in case of disappearance; but in place of the name of Edward Hyde, the lawyer, with indescribable amazement, read the name of Gabriel John Utterson. He looked at Poole, and then back at the paper, and last of all at the dead malefactor stretched upon the carpet.

'My head goes round,' he said. 'He has been all these days in possession; he had no cause to like me; he must have raged to see himself displaced; and he has not destroyed this document.'

He caught up the next paper; it was a brief note in the doctor's hand and dated at the top. 'O Poole!' the lawyer cried, 'he was alive and here this day. He cannot have been disposed of in so short a space, he must be still alive, he must have fled! And then, why fled? and how? and in that case, can we venture to declare this suicide? O, we must be careful. I foresee that we may yet involve your master in some dire catastrophe.'

'Why don't you read it, sir?' asked Poole.

'Because I fear,' replied the lawyer solemnly. 'God grant I have no cause for it!' And with that he brought the paper to his eyes and read as follows.

'My dear Utterson, – When this shall fall into your hands, I shall have disappeared, under what circumstances I have not the penetration to foresee, but my instinct and all the circumstances of my nameless situation tell me that the end is sure and must be early. Go then, and first read the narrative which Lanyon warned me he was to place in your hands; and if you care to hear more, turn to the confession of

'Your unworthy and unhappy friend,
'HENRY JEKYLL.'

'There was a third enclosure?' asked Utterson.

'Here, sir,' said Poole, and gave into his hands a considerable packet sealed in several places.

The lawyer put it in his pocket. 'I would say nothing of this paper. If your master has fled or is dead, we may at least save his credit. It is now ten; I must go home and read these documents in quiet; but I shall be back before midnight, when we shall send for the police.'

They went out, locking the door of the theatre behind them; and Utterson, once more leaving the servants gathered about the fire in the hall, trudged back to his office to read the two narratives in which this mystery was now to be explained.

DOCTOR LANYON'S NARRATIVE

On the ninth of January, now four days ago, I received by the evening delivery a registered envelope, addressed in the hand of my colleague and old school-companion, Henry Jekyll. I was a good deal surprised by this; for we were by no means in the habit of correspondence; I had seen the man, dined with him, indeed, the night before; and I could imagine nothing in our intercourse that should justify the formality of registration. The contents increased my wonder; for this is how the letter ran:

'10th December, 18—

'Dear Lanyon, – You are one of my oldest friends; and although we may have differed at times on scientific questions, I cannot remember, at least on my side, any break in our affection. There was never a day when, if you had said to me, 'Jekyll, my life, my honour, my reason, depend upon you,' I would not have sacrificed my fortune or my left hand to help you. Lanyon, my life, my honour, my reason, are all at your mercy; if you fail me to-night, I am lost. You might suppose, after this preface, that I am going to ask you for something dishonourable to grant. Judge for yourself.

'I want you to postpone all other engagements for to-night – ay, even if you were summoned to the bedside of an emperor; to take a cab, unless your carriage should be actually at the door; and with this letter in your hand for consultation, to drive straight to my house. Poole, my butler, has his orders; you will find him waiting your arrival with a locksmith. The door of my cabinet is then to be forced; and you are to go in alone; to open the glazed press (letter E) on the left hand, breaking the lock if it be shut; and to draw out, *with all its contents as they stand*, the fourth drawer from the top or (which is the same thing) the third from the bottom. In my extreme distress of mind, I have a morbid fear of misdirecting you; but even if I am in error, you may know the right drawer by its contents: some powders, a phial and a paper book. This drawer I beg of you to carry back with you to Cavendish Square exactly as it stands.

'That is the first part of the service: now for the second. You should be back, if you set out at once on the receipt of this, long before midnight; but I will leave you that amount of margin, not only in the fear of one of those obstacles that can neither be prevented nor foreseen, but because an hour when your servants are in bed is to be preferred for what will then remain to do. At midnight, then, I have to ask you to be alone in your consulting room, to admit with your own hand into the house a man who will present himself in my name, and to place in his hands the drawer that you will have brought with you from my cabinet. Then you will have played your part and earned my gratitude completely. Five minutes, afterwards, if you insist upon an explanation, you will have understood that these arrangements are of capital importance; and that by the neglect of one of them, fantastic as they must appear, you might have charged your conscience with my death or the shipwreck of my reason.

'Confident as I am that you will not trifle with this appeal, my heart sinks and my hand trembles at the bare thought of such a possibility. Think of me at this hour, in a strange place, labouring under a blackness of distress that no fancy can exaggerate, and yet well aware that, if you will but punctually serve me, my troubles will roll away like a story that is told. Serve me, my dear Lanyon, and save

'Your friend,
'H.J.'

'P.S. I had already sealed this up when a fresh terror struck upon my soul. It is possible that the post office may fail me, and this letter not come into your hands until tomorrow morning. In that case, dear Lanyon, do my errand when it shall be most convenient for you in the course of the day; and once more expect my messenger at midnight. It may then already be too late; and if that passes without event, you will know that you have seen the last of Henry Jekyll.'

Upon the reading of this letter, I made sure my colleague was insane; but till that was proved beyond the possibility of doubt, I felt bound to do as he requested. The less I understood of this farrago, the less I was in a position to judge of its importance; and an appeal so worded could not be set aside without a grave responsibility. I rose accordingly from table, got into a hansom, and drove straight to Jekyll's house. The butler was awaiting my arrival; he had received by the same post as mine a registered letter of instruction and had sent at once for a locksmith and a carpenter. The tradesmen came while we were yet speaking; and we moved in a body to old Dr Denman's surgical theatre from which (as you are doubtless aware) Jekyll's private cabinet is most conveniently entered. The door was very strong, the lock excellent; the carpenter avowed he would have great trouble and have to do much damage, if force were to be used; and the locksmith was near despair. But this last was a handy fellow, and after two hours' work, the door stood open. The press marked E was unlocked; and I took out the drawer, had it filled up with straw and tied in a sheet, and returned with it to Cavendish Square.

Here I proceeded to examine its contents. The powders were neatly enough made up, but not with the nicety of the dispensing chemist; so that it was plain they were of Jekyll's private manufacture; and when I opened one of the wrappers, I found what seemed to me a simple, crystalline salt of a white colour. The phial, to which I next turned my attention, might have been about half-full of a blood-red liquor, which was highly pungent to the sense of smell and seemed to me to contain phosphorus and some volatile ether. At the other ingredients, I could make no guess. The book was an ordinary version book and contained little but a series of dates. These covered a period of many years, but I observed that the entries ceased nearly a year ago and quite abruptly. Here and there a brief remark was appended to a date, usually no more than a single word: 'double' occurring perhaps six times in a total of several hundred entries; and once very early in the list and followed by several marks of exclamation, 'total failure!!!' All this, though it whetted my curiosity, told me little that was definite. Here were a phial of some tincture, a paper of some salt, and the record of a series of experiments that had led (like too many of Jekyll's investigations) to no end of practical usefulness. How could the presence of these articles in my house affect either the honour, the sanity, or the life of my flighty colleague? If his messenger could go to one place, why could he not go to another? And even granting some impediment, why was this gentleman to be received by me in secret? The more I reflected, the more convinced I grew that I was dealing with a case of cerebral disease; and though I dismissed my servants to bed, I loaded an old revolver that I might be found in some posture of self-defence.

Twelve o'clock had scarce rung out over London, ere the knocker sounded very gently on the door. I went myself at the summons, and found a small man crouching against the pillars of the portico.

'Are you come from Dr Jekyll?' I asked.

He told me 'yes' by a constrained gesture; and when

I had bidden him enter, he did not obey me without a searching backward glance into the darkness of the square. There was a policeman not far off, advancing with his bull's eye open; and at the sight, I thought my visitor started and made greater haste.

These particulars struck me, I confess, disagreeably; and as I followed him into the bright light of the consulting room, I kept my hand ready on my weapon. Here, at last, I had a chance of clearly seeing him. I had never set eyes on him before, so much was certain. He was small, as I have said; I was struck besides with the shocking expression of his face, with his remarkable combination of great muscular activity and great apparent debility of constitution, and – last but not least – with the odd, subjective disturbance caused by his neighbourhood. This bore some resemblance to incipient rigor, and was accompanied by a marked sinking of the pulse. At the time, I set it down to some idiosyncratic, personal distaste, and merely wondered at the acuteness of the symptoms; but I have since had reason to believe the cause to lie much deeper in the nature of man, and to turn on some nobler hinge than the principle of hatred.

This person (who had thus, from the first moment of his entrance, struck in me what I can only describe as a disgustful curiosity) was dressed in a fashion that would have made an ordinary person laughable: his clothes, that is to say, although they were of rich and sober fabric, were enormously too large for him in every measurement – the trousers hanging on his legs and rolled up to keep them from the ground, the waist of the coat below his haunches, and the collar sprawling wide upon his shoulders. Strange to relate, this ludicrous accoutrement was far from moving me to laughter. Rather, as there was something abnormal and misbegotten in the very essence of the creature that now faced me – something seizing, surprising and revolting – this fresh disparity seemed but to fit in with and to reinforce it; so that to my interest in the man's nature and character, there was added a curiosity as to his origin, his life, his fortune and status in the world.

These observations, though they have taken so great a

space to be set down in, were yet the work of a few seconds. My visitor was, indeed, on fire with sombre excitement.

'Have you got it?' he cried. 'Have you got it?' And so lively was his impatience that he even laid his hand upon my arm and sought to shake me.

I put him back, conscious at his touch of a certain icy pang along my blood. 'Come, sir,' said I. 'You forget that I have not yet the pleasure of your acquaintance. Be seated, if you please.' And I showed him an example, and sat down myself in my customary seat and with as fair an imitation of my ordinary manner to a patient, as the lateness of the hour, the nature of my preoccupations, and the horror I had of my visitor, would suffer me to muster.

'I beg your pardon, Dr Lanyon,' he replied civilly enough. 'What you say is very well founded; and my impatience has shown its heels to my politeness. I come here at the instance of your colleague, Dr Henry Jekyll, on a piece of business of some moment; and I understood . . .' he paused and put his hand to his throat, and I could see, in spite of his collected manner, that he was wrestling against the approaches of the hysteria – 'I understood, a drawer . . .'

But here I took pity on my visitor's suspense, and some perhaps on my own growing curiosity.

'There it is, sir,' said I, pointing to the drawer, where it lay on the floor behind a table and still covered with the sheet.

He sprang to it, and then paused, and laid his hand upon his heart; I could hear his teeth grate with the convulsive action of his jaws; and his face was so ghastly to see that I grew alarmed both for his life and reason.

'Compose yourself,' said I.

He turned a dreadful smile to me, and as if with the decision of despair, plucked away the sheet. At sight of the contents, he uttered one loud sob of such immense relief that I sat petrified. And the next moment, in a voice that was already fairly well under control, 'Have you a graduated glass?' he asked.

I rose from my place with something of an effort and gave him what he asked.

He thanked me with a smiling nod, measured out a few minims of the red tincture and added one of the powders. The mixture, which was at first of a reddish hue, began, in proportion as the crystals melted, to brighten in colour, to effervesce audibly, and to throw off small fumes of vapour. Suddenly and at the same moment, the ebullition ceased and the compound changed to a dark purple, which faded again more slowly to a watery green. My visitor, who had watched these metamorphoses with a keen eye, smiled, set down the glass upon the table, and then turned and looked upon me with an air of scrutiny.

'And now,' said he, 'to settle what remains. Will you be wise? will you be guided? will you suffer me to take this glass in my hand and to go forth from your house without further parley? or has the greed of curiosity too much command of you? Think before you answer, for it shall be done as you decide. As you decide, you shall be left as you were before, and neither richer nor wiser, unless the sense of service rendered to a man in mortal distress may be counted as a kind of riches of the soul. Or, if you shall so prefer to choose, a new province of knowledge and new avenues to fame and power shall be laid open to you, here, in this room, upon the instant; and your sight shall be blasted by a prodigy to stagger the unbelief of Satan.'

'Sir,' said I, affecting a coolness that I was far from truly possessing, 'you speak enigmas, and you will perhaps not wonder that I hear you with no very strong impression of belief. But I have gone too far in the way of inexplicable services to pause before I see the end.'

'It is well,' replied my visitor. 'Lanyon, you remember your vows: what follows is under the seal of our profession. And now, you who have so long been bound to the most narrow and material views, you who have denied the virtue of transcendental medicine, you who have derided your superiors – behold!'

He put the glass to his lips and drank at one gulp. A cry followed; he reeled, staggered, clutched at the table and held on, staring with injected eyes, gasping with open mouth; and as I looked there came, I thought, a change – he seemed to swell – his face became suddenly black and the features seemed to melt and alter – and the next moment, I had sprung to my feet and leaped back against the wall, my arm raised to shield me from that prodigy, my mind submerged in terror.

'O God!' I screamed, and 'O God!' again and again; for there before my eyes – pale and shaken, and half fainting, and groping before him with his hands, like a man restored from death – there stood Henry Jekyll!

What he told me in the next hour, I cannot bring my mind to set on paper. I saw what I saw, I heard what I heard, and my soul sickened at it; and yet now when that sight has faded from my eyes, I ask myself if I believe it, and I cannot answer. My life is shaken to its roots; sleep has left me; the deadliest terror sits by me at all hours of the day and night; I feel that my days are numbered, and that I must die; and yet I shall die incredulous. As for the moral turpitude that man unveiled to me, even with tears of penitence, I cannot, even in memory, dwell on it without a start of horror. I will say but one thing, Utterson, and that (if you can bring your mind to credit it) will be more than enough. The creature who crept into my house that night was, on Jekyll's own confession, known by the name of Hyde and hunted for in every corner of the land as the murderer of Carew.

HASTIE LANYON.

HENRY JEKYLL'S FULL STATEMENT OF THE CASE

I was born in the year 18— to a large fortune, endowed besides with excellent parts, inclined by nature to industry, fond of the respect of the wise and good among my fellow-men, and thus, as might have been supposed, with every guarantee of an honourable and distinguished future. And indeed the worst of my fault was a certain impatient gaiety of disposition, such as has made the happiness of many, but such as I found it hard to reconcile with my imperious desire to carry my head high, and wear a more than commonly grave countenance before the public.

Hence it came about that I concealed my pleasures; and that when I reached years of reflection, and began to look round me and take stock of my progress and position in the world, I stood already committed to a profound duplicity of life. Many a man would have even blazoned such irregularities as I was guilty of; but from the high views that I had set before me, I regarded and hid them with an almost morbid sense of shame. It was thus rather the exacting nature of my aspirations than any particular degradation in my faults, that made me what I was and, with even a deeper trench than in the majority of men, severed in me those provinces of good and ill which divide and compound man's dual nature. In this case, I was driven to reflect deeply and inveterately on that hard law of life, which lies at the root of religion and is one of the most plentiful springs of distress. Though so profound a double-dealer, I was in no sense a hypocrite; both sides of me were in dead earnest; I was no more myself when I laid aside restraint and plunged in shame, than when I laboured, in the eye of day, at the furtherance of knowledge or the relief of sorrow and suffering. And it chanced that the direction of my scientific studies, which led wholly towards the mystic and the transcendental, reacted and shed a strong light on this consciousness of the perennial war among my members. With every day, and from both sides of my intelligence, the moral and the intellectual, I thus drew steadily nearer to that truth, by whose partial discovery I have been doomed to such a dreadful shipwreck: that man is not truly one, but truly two. I say two, because the state of my own knowledge does not pass beyond that point. Others will follow, others will outstrip me on the same lines; and I hazard the guess that man will be ultimately known for a mere polity of multifarious, incongruous and independent denizens. I for my part, from the nature of my life, advanced infallibly in one direction and in one direction only. It was on the moral side, and in my own person, that I learned to recognise the thorough and primitive duality of man; I saw that, of the two natures that contended in the field of my consciousness, even if I could rightly be said to be either, it was only because I was radically both; and from an early date, even before the course of my scientific discoveries had begun to suggest the most naked possibility of such a miracle, I had learned to dwell with pleasure, as a beloved daydream, on the thought of the separation of these elements. If each, I told myself, could but be housed in separate identities, life would be relieved of all that was unbearable; the unjust might go his way, delivered from the aspirations and remorse of his more upright twin; and the just could walk steadfastly and securely on his upward path, doing the good things in which he found his pleasure, and no longer exposed to disgrace and penitence by the hands of this extraneous evil. It was the curse of mankind that these incongruous faggots were thus bound together – that in the agonised womb of consciousness, these polar twins should be continuously struggling. How, then, were they dissociated?

I was so far in my reflections when, as I have said, a side light began to shine upon the subject from the laboratory table. I began to perceive more deeply than it has ever yet been stated, the trembling immateriality, the mist-like transience, of this seemingly so solid body in which we walk attired. Certain agents I found to have the power to shake and to pluck back that fleshly vestment, even as a wind might toss the curtains of a pavilion. For two good reasons, I will not enter deeply into this scientific branch of my confession. First, because I have been made to learn that the doom and burthen of our life is bound forever on man's shoulders, and when the attempt is made to cast it off, it but returns upon us with more unfamiliar and more awful pressure. Second, because as my narrative will make alas! too evident, my discoveries were incomplete. Enough, then, that I not only recognised my natural body for the mere aura and effulgence of certain of the powers that made up my spirit, but managed to compound a drug by which these powers should be dethroned from their supremacy, and a second form and countenance substituted, none the less natural to me because they were the expression, and bore the stamp, of lower elements in my soul.

I hesitated long before I put this theory to the test of practice. I knew well that I risked death; for any drug that so potently controlled and shook the very fortress of identity, might by the least scruple of an overdose or at the least inopportunity in the moment of exhibition, utterly blot out that immaterial tabernacle which I looked to it to change. But the temptation of a discovery so singular and profound, at last overcame the suggestions of alarm. I had long since prepared my tincture; I purchased at once, from a firm of wholesale chemists, a large quantity of a particular salt which I knew, from my experiments, to be the last ingredient required; and late one accursed night, I compounded the elements, watched them boil and smoke together in the glass, and when the ebullition had subsided, with a strong glow of courage, drank off the potion.

The most racking pangs succeeded: a grinding in the bones, deadly nausea, and a horror of the spirit that cannot be exceeded at the hour of birth or death. Then these agonies began swiftly to subside, and I came to myself as if out of a great sickness. There was something strange in my sensations, something indescribably new and, from its very novelty, incredibly sweet. I felt younger, lighter, happier in body; within I was conscious of a heady recklessness, a current of disordered sensual images running like a mill race in my fancy, a solution of the bonds of obligation, an unknown but not an innocent freedom of the soul. I knew myself, at the first breath of this new life, to be more wicked, tenfold more wicked, sold a slave to my original evil; and the thought, in that moment, braced and delighted me like wine. I stretched out my hands, exulting in the freshness of these sensations; and in the act, I was suddenly aware that I had lost in stature.

There was no mirror, at that date, in my room; that which stands beside me as I write, was brought there later on and for the very purpose of these transformations. The night, however, was far gone into the morning – the morning, black as it was, was nearly ripe for the conception of the day – the inmates of my house were locked in the most rigorous hours of slumber; and I determined, flushed as I was with hope and triumph, to venture in my new shape as far as to my bedroom. I crossed the yard, wherein the constellations looked down upon me, I could have thought, with wonder, the first creature of that sort that their unsleeping vigilance had yet disclosed to them; I stole through the corridors, a stranger in my own house; and coming to my room, I saw for the first time the appearance of Edward Hyde.

I must here speak by theory alone, saying not that which I know, but that which I suppose to be most probable. The evil side of my nature, to which I had now transferred the stamping efficacy, was less robust and less developed than the good which I had just deposed. Again, in the course of my life, which had been, after all, nine tenths a life of effort, virtue and control, it had been much less exercised and much less exhausted. And hence, as I think, it came about that Edward Hyde was so much smaller, slighter and younger than Henry Jekyll. Even as good shone upon the countenance of the one, evil was written broadly and plainly on the face of the other. Evil besides (which I must still believe to be the lethal side of man) had left on that body an imprint of deformity and decay. And yet when I looked upon that ugly idol in the glass, I was conscious of no repugnance, rather of a leap of welcome. This, too, was myself. It seemed natural and human. In my eyes it bore a livelier image of the spirit, it seemed more express and single, than the imperfect and divided countenance, I had been hitherto accustomed to call mine. And in so far I was doubtless right. I have observed that when I wore the semblance of Edward Hyde, none could come near to me at first without a visible misgiving of the flesh. This, as I take it, was because all human beings, as we meet them, are commingled out of good and evil: and Edward Hyde, alone in the ranks of mankind, was pure evil.

I lingered but a moment at the mirror: the second and conclusive experiment had yet to be attempted; it yet remained to be seen if I had lost my identity beyond redemption and must flee before daylight from a house that was no longer mine; and hurrying back to my cabinet, I once more prepared and drank the cup, once more suffered the pangs of dissolution, and came to myself once more with the character, the stature and the face of Henry Jekyll.

That night I had come to the fatal cross roads. Had I approached my discovery in a more noble spirit, had I risked the experiment while under the empire of generous or pious aspirations, all must have been otherwise, and from these agonies of death and birth, I had come forth an angel instead of a fiend. The drug had no discriminating action; it was neither diabolical nor divine; it but shook the doors of the prisonhouse of my disposition; and like the captives of Philippi, that which stood within ran forth. At that time my virtue slumbered; my evil, kept awake by ambition, was alert and swift to seize the occasion; and the thing that was projected was Edward Hyde. Hence, although I had now two characters as well as two appearances, one was wholly evil, and the other was still the old Henry Jekyll, that incongruous compound of whose reformation and improvement I had already learned to despair. The movement was thus wholly toward the worse.

Even at that time, I had not yet conquered my aversion to the dryness of a life of study. I would still be merrily disposed at times; and as my pleasures were (to say the least) undignified, and I was not only well known and highly considered, but growing towards the elderly man, this incoherency of my life was daily growing more unwelcome. It was on this side that my new power tempted me until I fell in slavery. I had but to drink the cup, to doff at once the body of the noted professor, and to assume, like a thick cloak, that of Edward Hyde. I smiled at the notion; it seemed to me at the time to be humorous; and I made my preparations with the most studious care. I took and furnished that house in Soho, to which Hyde was tracked by the police; and engaged as housekeeper a creature whom I well knew to be silent and unscrupulous. On the other side, I announced to my servants that a Mr Hyde (whom I described) was to have full liberty and power about my house in the square; and to parry mishaps, I even called and made myself a familiar object, in my second character. I next drew up that will to which you so much objected; so that if anything befell me in the person of Doctor Jekyll, I could enter on that of Edward Hyde without pecuniary loss. And thus fortified, as I supposed, on every side, I began to profit by the strange immunities of my position.

Men have before hired bravos to transact their crimes, while their own person and reputation sat under shelter. I was the first that ever did so for his pleasures. I was the first that could thus plod in the public eye with a load of genial respectability, and in a moment, like a schoolboy, strip off these lendings and spring headlong into the sea of liberty. But for me, in my impenetrable mantle, the safety was complete. Think of it – I did not even exist! Let me but escape into my laboratory door, give me but a second or two to mix and swallow the draught that I had always standing ready; and whatever he had done, Edward Hyde would pass away like the stain of breath upon a mirror; and there in his stead, quietly at home, trimming the midnight lamp in his study, a man who could afford to laugh at suspicion, would be Henry Jekyll.

The pleasures which I made haste to seek in my disguise were, as I have said, undignified; I would scarce use a harder term. But in the hands of Edward Hyde, they soon began to turn towards the monstrous. When I would come back from these excursions, I was often plunged into a kind of wonder at my vicarious depravity. This familiar that I called out of my own soul, and sent forth alone to do his good pleasure, was a being inherently malign and villainous; his every act and thought centered on self; drinking pleasure with bestial avidity from any degree of torture to another; relentless like a man of stone. Henry Jekyll stood at times aghast before the acts of Edward Hyde; but the situation was apart from ordinary laws, and insidiously relaxed the grasp of conscience. It was Hyde, after all, and Hyde alone, that was guilty. Jekyll was no worse; he woke again to his good qualities seemingly unimpaired; he would even make haste, where it was possible, to undo the evil done by Hyde. And thus his conscience slumbered.

Into the details of the infamy at which I thus connived (for even now I can scarce grant that I committed it) I have no design of entering; I mean but to point out the warnings and the successive steps with which my chastisement approached. I met with one accident which, as it brought on no consequence, I shall no more than mention. An act of cruelty to a child aroused against me the anger of a passer by, whom I recognised the other day in the person of your kinsman; the doctor and the child's family joined him; there were moments when I feared for my life; and at last, in order to pacify their too just resentment, Edward Hyde had to bring them to the door, and pay them in a cheque drawn in the name of Henry Jekyll. But this danger was easily eliminated from the future, by opening an account at another bank in the name of Edward Hyde himself; and when, by sloping my own hand backward, I had supplied my double with a signature, I thought I sat beyond the reach of fate.

Some two months before the murder of Sir Danvers, I had been out for one of my adventures, had returned at a late hour, and woke the next day in bed with somewhat odd sensations. It was in vain I looked about me; in vain I saw the decent furniture and tall proportions of my room in the square; in vain that I recognised the pattern of the bed curtains and the design of the mahogany frame; something still kept insisting that I was not where I was, that I had not wakened where I seemed to be, but in the little room in Soho where I was accustomed to sleep in the body of Edward Hyde. I smiled to myself, and, in my psychological way, began lazily to inquire into the elements of this illusion, occasionally, even as I did so, dropping back into a comfortable morning doze. I was still so engaged when, in one of my more wakeful moments, my eye fell upon my hand. Now the hand of Henry Jekyll (as you have often remarked) was professional in shape and size: it was large, firm, white and comely. But the hand which I now saw, clearly enough, in the yellow light of a mid-London morning, lying half shut on the bed clothes, was lean, corded, knuckly, of a dusky pallor and thickly shaded with a swart growth of hair. It was the hand of Edward Hyde.

I must have stared upon it for near half a minute, sunk as I was in the mere stupidity of wonder, before terror woke up in my breast as sudden and startling as the crash of cymbals; and bounding from my bed, I rushed to the mirror. At the sight that met my eyes, my blood was changed into something exquisitely thin and icy. Yes, I had gone to bed Henry Jekyll, I had awakened Edward Hyde. How was this to be explained? I asked myself; and then, with another bound of terror – how was it to be remedied? It was well on in the morning; the servants were up; all my drugs were in the cabinet – a long journey, down two pair of stairs, through the back passage, across the open court and through the anatomical theatre, from where I was then standing horror-struck. It might indeed be possible to cover my face; but of what use was that, when I was unable to conceal the alteration in my stature? And then with an overpowering sweetness of relief, it came back upon my mind that the servants were already used to the coming and going of my second self. I had soon dressed, as well as I was able, in clothes of my own size: had soon passed through the house, where Bradshaw stared and drew back at seeing Mr Hyde at such an hour and in such a strange array; and ten minutes later, Dr Jekyll had returned to his own shape and was sitting down, with a darkened brow, to make a feint of breakfasting.

Small indeed was my appetite. This inexplicable incident, this reversal of my previous experience, seemed, like the Babylonian finger on the wall, to be spelling out the letters of my judgment; and I began to reflect more seriously than ever before on the issues and possibilities of my double existence. That part of me which I had the power of projecting, had lately been much exercised and nourished; it had seemed to me of late as though the body of Edward Hyde had grown in stature, as though (when I wore that form) I were conscious of a more generous tide of blood; and I began to spy a danger that, if this were much prolonged, the balance of my nature might be permanently overthrown, the power of voluntary change be forfeited, and the character of Edward Hyde become irrevocably mine. The power of the drug had not been always equally displayed. Once, very early in my career, it had totally failed me; since then I had been obliged on more than one occasion to double, and once, with infinite risk of death, to treble the amount; and these rare uncertainties had cast hitherto the sole shadow on my contentment. Now, however, and in the light of that morning's accident, I was led to remark that whereas, in the beginning, the difficulty had been to throw off the body of Jekyll, it had of late, gradually but decidedly transferred itself to the other side. All things therefore seemed to point to this: that I was slowly losing hold of my original and better self, and becoming slowly incorporated with my second and worse.

Between these two, I now felt I had to choose. My two natures had memory in common, but all other faculties were most unequally shared between them. Jekyll (who was composite) now with the most sensitive apprehensions, now with a greedy gusto, projected and shared in the pleasures and adventure of Hyde; but Hyde was indifferent to Jekyll, or but remembered him as the mountain bandit remembers the cavern in which he conceals himself from pursuit. Jekyll had more than a father's interest; Hyde had more than a son's indifference. To cast in my lot with Jekyll, was to die to those appetites which I had long secretly indulged and had of late begun to pamper. To cast it in with Hyde, was to die to a thousand interests and aspirations, and to become, at a blow and forever, despised and friendless. The bargain might appear unequal; but there was still another consideration in the scales; for while Jekyll would suffer smartingly in the fires of abstinence, Hyde would be not even conscious of all that he had lost. Strange as my circumstances were, the terms of this debate are as old and commonplace as man; much the same inducements and alarms cast the die for any tempted and trembling sinner; and it fell out with me, as it falls with so vast a majority of my fellows, that I chose the better part and was found wanting in the strength to keep to it.

Yes, I preferred the elderly and discontented doctor, surrounded by friends and cherishing honest hopes; and bade a resolute farewell to the liberty, the comparative youth, the light step, leaping pulses and secret pleasures, that I had enjoyed in the disguise of Hyde. I made this choice perhaps with some unconscious reservation, for I neither gave up the house in Soho, nor destroyed the clothes of Edward Hyde, which still lay ready in my cabinet. For two months, however, I was true to my determination; for two months, I led a life of such severity as I had never before attained to, and enjoyed the compensations of an approving conscience. But time began at last to obliterate the freshness of my alarm; the praises of conscience began to grow into a thing of course; I began to be tortured with throes and longings, as of Hyde struggling after freedom; and at last, in an hour of moral weakness, I once again compounded and swallowed the transforming draught.

I do not suppose that, when a drunkard reasons with himself upon his vice, he is once out of five hundred times affected by the dangers that he runs through his brutish, physical insensibility; neither had I, long as I had considered my position, made enough allowance for the complete moral insensibility and insensate readiness to evil, which were the leading characters of Edward Hyde. Yet it was by these that I was punished. My devil had been long caged, he came out roaring. I was conscious, even when I took the draught, of a more unbridled, a more furious propensity to ill. It must have been this, I suppose, that stirred in my soul that tempest of impatience with which I listened to the civilities of my unhappy victim; I declare at least, before God, no man morally sane could have been guilty of that crime upon so pitiful a provocation; and that I struck in no more reasonable spirit than that in which a sick child may break a plaything. But I had voluntarily stripped myself of all those balancing instincts, by which even the worst of us continues to walk with some degree of steadiness among temptations; and in my case, to be tempted, however slightly, was to fall.

Instantly the spirit of hell awoke in me and raged. With a transport of glee, I mauled the unresisting body, tasting delight from every blow; and it was not till weariness had begun to succeed, that I was suddenly, in the top fit of my delirium, struck through the heart by a cold thrill of terror. A mist dispersed; I saw my life to be forfeit; and fled from the scene of these excesses, at once glorying and trembling, my lust of evil gratified and stimulated, my love of life screwed to the topmost peg. I ran to the house in Soho, and (to make assurance doubly sure) destroyed my papers; thence I set out through the lamplit streets, in the same divided ecstasy of mind, gloating on

my crime, light-headedly devising others in the future, and
yet still hastening and still hearkening in my wake for the
steps of the avenger. Hyde had a song upon his lips as
he compounded the draught, and as he drank it, pledged
the dead man. The pangs of transformation had not done
tearing him, before Henry Jekyll, with streaming tears of
gratitude and remorse, had fallen upon his knees and lifted
his clasped hands to God. The veil of self-indulgence was
rent from head to foot, I saw my life as a whole: I followed
it up from the days of childhood, when I had walked with
my father's hand, and through the self-denying toils of my
professional life, to arrive again and again, with the same
sense of unreality, at the damned horrors of the evening. I
could have screamed aloud; I sought with tears and prayers
to smother down the crowd of hideous images and sounds
with which my memory swarmed against me; and still,
between the petitions, the ugly face of my iniquity stared
into my soul. As the acuteness of this remorse began to die
away, it was succeeded by a sense of joy. The problem of
my conduct was solved. Hyde was thenceforth impossible;
whether I would or not, I was now confined to the better
part of my existence; and O, how I rejoiced to think it! with
what willing humility, I embraced anew the restrictions of
natural life! with what sincere renunciation, I locked the
door by which I had so often gone and come, and ground
the key under my heel!

The next day, came the news that the murder had been
overlooked, that the guilt of Hyde was patent to the world,
and that the victim was a man high in public estimation.
It was not only a crime, it had been a tragic folly. I think
I was glad to know it; I think I was glad to have my better
impulses thus buttressed and guarded by the terrors of the
scaffold. Jekyll was now my city of refuge; let but Hyde peep
out an instant, and the hands of all men would be raised to
take and slay him.

I resolved in my future conduct to redeem the past; and
I can say with honesty that my resolve was fruitful of some
good. You know yourself how earnestly in the last months
of last year, I laboured to relieve suffering; you know that
much was done for others, and that the days passed quietly,

almost happily for myself. Nor can I truly say that I wearied of this beneficent and innocent life; I think instead that I daily enjoyed it more completely; but I was still cursed with my duality of purpose; and as the first edge of my penitence wore off, the lower side of me, so long indulged, so recently chained down, began to growl for license. Not that I dreamed of resuscitating Hyde; the bare idea of that would startle me to frenzy: no, it was in my own person, that I was once more tempted to trifle with my conscience; and it was as an ordinary secret sinner, that I at last fell before the assaults of temptation.

There comes an end to all things; the most capacious measure is filled at last; and this brief condescension to my evil finally destroyed the balance of my soul. And yet I was not alarmed; the fall seemed natural, like a return to the old days before I had made my discovery. It was a fine, clear, January day, wet under foot where the frost had melted, but cloudless overhead; and the Regent's park was full of winter chirruppings and sweet with Spring odours. I sat in the sun on a bench; the animal within me licking the chops of memory; the spiritual side a little drowsed, promising subsequent penitence, but not yet moved to begin. After all, I reflected I was like my neighbours; and then I smiled, comparing myself with other men, comparing my active goodwill with the lazy cruelty of their neglect. And at the very moment of that vainglorious thought, a qualm came over me, a horrid nausea and the most deadly shuddering. These passed away, and left me faint; and then as in its turn the faintness subsided, I began to be aware of a change in the temper of my thoughts, a greater boldness, a contempt of danger, a solution of the bonds of obligation. I looked down; my clothes hung formlessly on my shrunken limbs; the hand that lay on my knee was corded and hairy. I was once more Edward Hyde. A moment before I had been safe of all men's respect, wealthy, beloved – the cloth laying for me in the dining room at home; and now I was the common quarry of mankind, hunted, houseless, a known murderer, thrall to the gallows.

My reason wavered, but it did not fail me utterly. I have more than once observed that, in my second character, my faculties seemed sharpened to a point and my spirits more tensely elastic; thus it came about that, where Jekyll perhaps might have succumbed, Hyde rose to the importance of the moment. My drugs were in one of the presses of my cabinet; how was I to reach them? That was the problem that (crushing my temples in my hands) I set myself to solve. The laboratory door I had closed. If I sought to enter by the house, my own servants would consign me to the gallows. I saw I must employ another hand, and thought of Lanyon. How was he to be reached? how persuaded? Supposing that I escaped capture in the streets, how was I to make my way into his presence? and how should I, an unknown and displeasing visitor, prevail on the famous physician to rifle the study of his colleague, Dr Jekyll? Then I remembered that of my original character, one part remained to me: I could write my own hand; and once I had conceived that kindling spark, the way that I must follow became lighted up from end to end.

Thereupon, I arranged my clothes as best I could, and summoning a passing hansom, drove to an hotel in Portland street, the name of which I chanced to remember. At my appearance (which was indeed comical enough, however tragic a fate these garments covered) the driver could not conceal his mirth. I gnashed my teeth upon him with a gust of devilish fury; and the smile withered from his face – happily for him – yet more happily for myself, for in another instant I had certainly dragged him from his perch. At the inn, as I entered, I looked about me with so black a countenance as made the attendants tremble; not a look did they exchange in my presence; but obsequiously took my orders, led me to a private room, and brought me wherewithal to write. Hyde in danger of his life was a creature new to me: shaken with inordinate anger, strung to the pitch of murder, lusting to inflict pain. Yet the creature was astute; mastered his fury with a great effort of the will; composed his two important letters, one to Lanyon and one to Poole; and that he might receive actual evidence of their being posted, sent them out with directions that they should be registered.

Thenceforward, he sat all day over the fire in the private

room, gnawing his nails; there he dined, sitting alone with
his fears, the waiter visibly quailing before his eye; and
thence, when the night was fully come, he set forth in
the corner of a closed cab, and was driven to and fro
about the streets of the city. He, I say – I cannot say, I.
That child of Hell had nothing human; nothing lived in
him but fear and hatred. And when at last, thinking the
driver had begun to grow suspicious, he discharged the
cab and ventured on foot, attired in his misfitting clothes,
an object marked out for observation, into the midst of
the nocturnal passengers, these two base passions raged
within him like a tempest. He walked fast, hunted by
his fears, chattering to himself, skulking through the less
frequented thoroughfares, counting the minutes that still
divided him from midnight. Once a woman spoke to him,
offering, I think, a box of lights. He smote her in the face,
and she fled.

When I came to myself at Lanyon's, the horror of my
old friend perhaps affected me somewhat: I do not know;
it was at least but a drop in the sea to the abhorrence with
which I looked back upon these hours. A change had come
over me. It was no longer the fear of the gallows, it was the
horror of being Hyde that racked me. I received Lanyon's
condemnation partly in a dream; it was partly in a dream
that I came home to my own house and got into bed.
I slept after the prostration of the day, with a stringent
and profound slumber which not even the nightmares that
wrung me could avail to break. I awoke in the morning
shaken, weakened, but refreshed. I still hated and feared
the thought of the brute that slept within me, and I had
not of course forgotten the appalling dangers of the day
before; but I was once more at home, in my own house
and close to my drugs; and gratitude for my escape shone
so strong in my soul that it almost rivalled the brightness
of hope.

I was stepping leisurely across the court after breakfast,
drinking the chill of the air with pleasure, when I was seized
again with those indescribable sensations that heralded the
change; and I had but the time to gain the shelter of my
cabinet, before I was once again raging and freezing with

the passions of Hyde. It took on this occasion a double dose to recall me to myself; and alas, six hours after, as I sat looking sadly in the fire, the pangs returned, and the drug had to be re-administered. In short, from that day forth it seemed only by a great effort as of gymnastics, and only under the immediate stimulation of the drug, that I was able to wear the countenance of Jekyll. At all hours of the day and night, I would be taken with the premonitory shudder; above all, if I slept, or even dozed for a moment in my chair, it was always as Hyde that I awakened. Under the strain of this continually impending doom and by the sleeplessness to which I now condemned myself, ay, even beyond what I had thought possible to man, I became, in my own person, a creature eaten up and emptied by fever, languidly weak both in body and mind, and solely occupied by one thought: the horror of my other self. But when I slept, or when the virtue of the medicine wore off, I would leap almost without transition (for the pangs of transformation grew daily less marked) into the possession of a fancy brimming with images of terror, a soul boiling with causeless hatreds, and a body that seemed not strong enough to contain the raging energies of life. The powers of Hyde seemed to have grown with the sickliness of Jekyll. And certainly the hate that now divided them was equal on each side. With Jekyll, it was a thing of vital instinct. He had now seen the full deformity of that creature that shared with him some of the phenomena of consciousness, and was co-heir with him to death: and beyond these links of community, which in themselves made the most poignant part of his distress, he thought of Hyde, for all his energy of life, as of something not only hellish but inorganic. This was the shocking thing; that the slime of the pit seemed to utter cries and voices; that the amorphous dust gesticulated and sinned; that what was dead, and had no shape, should usurp the offices of life. And this again, that the insurgent horror was knit to him closer than a wife, closer than an eye; lay caged in his flesh, where he heard it mutter and felt it struggle to be born; and at every hour of weakness, and in the confidence of slumber, prevailed against him, and deposed him out of life. The hatred of Hyde for Jekyll, was of a different order. His terror of the gallows drove him continually to commit temporary suicide, and return to his subordinate station of a part instead of a person; but he loathed the necessity, he loathed the despondency into which Jekyll was now fallen, and he resented the dislike with which he was himself regarded. Hence the apelike tricks that he would play me, scrawling in my own hand blasphemies on the pages of my books, burning the letters and destroying the portrait of my father; and indeed, had it not been for his fear of death, he would long ago have ruined himself in order to involve me in the ruin. But his love of life is wonderful; I go further: I, who sicken and freeze at the mere thought of him, when I recall the abjection and passion of this attachment, and when I know how he fears my power to cut him off by suicide, I find it in my heart to pity him.

It is useless, and the time awfully fails me, to prolong this description; no one has ever suffered such torments, let that suffice; and yet even to these, habit brought – no, not alleviation – but a certain callousness of soul, a certain acquiescence of despair; and my punishment might have gone on for years, but for the last calamity which has now fallen, and which has finally severed me from my own face and nature. My provision of the salt, which had never been renewed since the date of the first experiment, began to run low. I sent out for a fresh supply, and mixed the draught; the ebullition followed, and the first change of colour, not the second; I drank it and it was without efficiency. You will learn from Poole how I have had London ransacked; it was in vain; and I am now persuaded that my first supply was impure, and that it was that unknown impurity which lent efficacy to the draught.

About a week has passed, and I am now finishing this statement under the influence of the last of the old powders. This, then, is the last time, short of a miracle, that Henry Jekyll can think his own thoughts or see his own face (now how sadly altered!) in the glass. Nor must I delay too long to bring my writing to an end; for if my narrative has hitherto escaped destruction, it has been by a combination of great prudence and great good luck. Should the throes of change take me in the act of writing it, Hyde will tear it in pieces; but if some time shall have elapsed after I have laid it by, his wonderful selfishness and circumscription to the moment will probably save it once again from the action of his apelike spite. And indeed the doom that is closing on us both, has already changed and crushed him. Half an hour from now, when I shall again and forever reindue that hated personality, I know how I shall sit shuddering and weeping in my chair, or continue, with the most strained and fearstruck ecstasy of listening, to pace up and down this room (my last earthly refuge) and give ear to every sound of menace. Will Hyde die upon the scaffold? or will he find the courage to release himself at the last moment? God knows; I am careless; this is my true hour of death, and what is to follow concerns another than myself. Here then, as I lay down the pen and proceed to seal up my confession, I bring the life of that unhappy Henry Jekyll to an end.

Glossary

aik, oak
bauld, bold
begude, began
ben the house, inside the house
bestial, livestock
bield, shelter
bieldy, sheltered
birks, birch trees
birling, whirling, ringing
bit, little
black-a-vised, dark
    complexioned, grim looking
bogle, ghost
brunstane, brimstone
brunt, burned
buckled to, got down to it
bût, bode, likely to
callant, lad, youth
caller, fresh
cantrip, trick, spell
carline, old woman
causeway, road
chafts, cheeks, jaws
chappin', striking (clock)
clachan, village
clamjamfry, crowd, rabble
claught, clawed
clavers, idle chatter
collieshangie, commotion,
    turmoil
come forrit, (come forward) to
    take communion
corbie craws, carrion crows
corp, corpse
craig, neck

croonin', singing lowly
    and sadly
cuist, cast
cummers, women
daffin', playing
deave, deafen
deil a, devil a (not a trace of)
denners, dinners
dirl, ring, vibrate
door cheeks, doorposts
duds, clothes, rags
dunt, stroke, blow, knock
dwining, failing, fading
eldritch, uncanny, eerie
fa', befall
fash, bother, trouble
feared, afraid
feck, a lot
forbye, apart from
fleyed, frightened
forjaskit, exhausted
gab, talk
gang, to go
gangrel, vagabond
gart, made, caused
gate, way; *far gate*, a long way
gear, possessions
girn, grimace
glebe, land belonging to
    the manse
glisk, glimpse
gloaming, twilight
glower, scowl
grat, wept
gousty, gusty

grogram goun, dress made of wool and silk

guidmen, tenants, husbands

guidwives, wives, householders

grue, chill, shiver

hasp, latch

haud nor to bind (neither to), unstoppable, not to be controlled

hinder end (at the), in the long run, finally

hirsle, shuffle

howe, hollow

howff, haunt, hang-out, shelter

jaloosed, suspected

keekit, peeped

ken, kenned, to know, knew

kye, cattle

laigh, low

lang or, long before

leed, lead

linkin', loping

limmer, disreputable woman

lown, still, sheltered, calm

lowp, jump, leap

lug, ear

maned, moaned

mirk, dark

mistrysted, let down, crossed

moo, mouth

morn's morning, the day after tomorrow

muckle, much, big, great

mutch, cap worn by older women

neuk, corner, end

owercome, refrain

oxter, armpit

pechin', panting

pickle, a little

pitmirk, dark as the pit, pitch-dark

plenished, furnished

powney, pony

reishling, rushing, rustling

sark, shirt, shift

saughs, willows

scrieghin', screeching

scunner, thrill of disgust

shoon, shoes

sib, kin to

siccan, such like

simmer, summer

sinsyne, ever since then

skelloch, scream

skelp, slap

skirled, shrieked

slavered, drooled

slockened, moistened, refreshed

smoored, smothered

sough, noise, sound, whisper, report

soum, swim

spate, rush, flood

spunk, spark

spunkies, wills o' the wisp

steeked, shut

steer, disturbance

stravaguin', roaming

swat, sweat

syne, since

thir, those, these

thirled, bound to

thrapple, throat

thrawn, crooked, twisted; also stubborn, perverse

threep, argue

unco, strange, extraordinary; very

upshot, outcome

upsitten, unbothered, inactive

unstreakit, unlaid-out (corpse)

want, lack, be without

wars'lin, struggling

wean, child

weary fa', may ill befall

wheen, a few

whilk, which
win, reach, travel
wud, mad
yett, gate